SANDRA BROWN

WHERE THERE'S SMOKE

WARNER BOOKS

A *Warner* Book

First published in the USA in 1993 by Warner Books
First published in Great Britain in 1993
by Little, Brown and Company
This edition published by Warner Books in 1994
Reprinted 1998, 1999, 2000

A CIP catalogue record for this book is
available from the British Library.

ISBN 0 7515 0605 2

Printed in England by Clays Ltd, St Ives plc

Warner Books
A Division of
Little, Brown and Company (UK)
Brettenham House
Lancaster Place
London WC2E 7EN

Acknowledgments

During the writing of this book, I relied heavily on the assistance of experts in widely varied fields of endeavor, all of whom were cooperative in spirit and generous with their time. I wish to extend many thanks to:

Mr. Bob McNeece, who knows more about the oil business than I could ever comprehend;

Mr. Larry Collier, a "pumper" whom I stumbled upon by accident, but who proved to be such a valuable source of information;

Dr. Ernest Stroupe, M.D., an emergency room physician, who, along with the friendly and helpful people of Mother Frances Hospital, Tyler, Texas, talked me through the medical sequences of the story;

And a pilot who shared not only his knowledge of aviation, but a candid account of events he'd rather be forgotten.

SANDRA BROWN
October 26, 1992

Chapter One

*H*e'd never particularly liked cats.

His problem, however, was that the woman lying beside him purred like one. Deep satisfaction vibrated through her from her throat to her belly. She had narrow, tilted eyes and moved with sinuous, fluid motion. She didn't walk, she stalked. Her foreplay had been a choreographed program of stretching and rubbing herself against him like a tabby in heat, and when she climaxed, she had screamed and clawed his shoulders.

Cats seemed sneaky and sly and, to his way of thinking, untrustworthy. He'd always been slightly uncomfortable turning his back to one.

"How was I?" Her voice was as sultry as the night beyond the pleated window shades.

"You don't hear me complaining, do you?"

Key Tackett also had an aversion to postcoital evaluation. If it was good, chatter was superfluous. If it wasn't, well, the less said the better.

She mistook his droll response as a compliment and slithered off the wide bed. Naked, she crossed the room to her cluttered dressing table and lit a cigarette with a jeweled lighter. "Want one?"

"No, thanks."

"Drink?"

"If it's handy. A quick one." Bored now, he gazed at the crystal chandelier in the center of the ceiling. The fixture was gaudy and distinctly ugly. It was too large for the bedroom even with the light bulbs behind the glass teardrops dimmed to a mere glimmer.

The shocking pink carpet was equally garish, and the portable brass bar was filled with ornate crystal decanters. She poured him a shot of bourbon. "You don't have to rush off," she told him with a smile. "My husband's out of town, and my daughter's spending the night at a friend's house."

"Male or female?"

"Female. For chrissake, she's only sixteen."

It would be unchivalrous of him to mention that she had acquired her reputation for being an easy lay long before reaching the age of sixteen. He remained silent, mostly from indifference.

"My point is, we've got till morning." Handing Key the drink, she sat down beside him, nudging his hip with hers.

He raised his head from the silk-encased pillow and sipped the straight bourbon. "I gotta get home. Here I've been back in town for . . ." he checked his wristwatch, "three and a half hours, and have yet to darken the door of the family homestead."

"You said they weren't expecting you tonight."

"No, but I promised to get home as soon as I could manage it."

She twined a strand of his dark hair around her finger. "But you didn't count on running into me at The Palm the minute you hit town, did you?"

He drained his drink and thrust the empty tumbler at her. "Wonder why they call it The Palm. There isn't a palm tree within three hundred miles of here. You go there often?"

"Often enough."

Key returned her wicked grin. "Whenever your old man's out of town?"

"And whenever the boredom of this wide place in the road gets unbearable, which, God knows, is practically every day. I can usually find some interesting company at The Palm."

He glanced at her abundant breasts. "Yeah, I bet you can. Bet you enjoy getting every man in the place all worked up and sporting a hard-on."

"You know me so well." Laughing huskily, she bent down to brush her damp lips across his.

He turned his head away. "I don't know you at all."

"Why that's not true, Key Tackett." She sat back, looking affronted. "We went through school together."

"I went through school with a lot of kids. Doesn't mean I knew all of them beyond saying hello."

"But you kissed me."

"Liar." Chivalry aside, he added, "I didn't like standing in line, so I never even asked you out."

Her feline eyes squinted with malice that vanished in an instant. As quickly as she extended her claws, they were retracted. "We never actually went on a date, no," she purred. "But one Friday night after a victory against Gladewater, you and the rest of the football team came strutting off the field. My friends and me—with just about everybody else in Eden Pass—lined up along the sideline to cheer as you went past on your way to the field house.

"You," she emphasized, digging her fingernail into his bare chest, "were the outstanding stud among all the studs. You were the sweatiest, and your jersey was the dirtiest, and of course all the girls thought you were the handsomest. You thought so too, I think."

She paused for him to comment, but Key regarded her impassively. He was remembering dozens of Friday nights like the one she had just described. Pregame jitters and postwin exhilaration. The glare of the stadium lights. The cadence of the marching band. The smell of fresh popcorn. The pep squad. The cheering crowds.

And Jody, cheering louder than anybody. Cheering for him. That had been a long time ago.

"When you went past me," she continued, "you grabbed me around the waist, lifted me clean off the ground, hauled me up against you, and kissed me smack on the mouth. Hard. Kinda barbaric-like."

"Hmm. You sure?"

"Sure I'm sure. I creamed my panties." She leaned over him, pressing her nipples against his chest. "I waited a long time to have you finish what you started then."

"Well, I'm glad to have been of service." He swatted her fanny and sat up. "Scoot." Reaching around her, he retrieved his jeans.

"You really are leaving?" she asked, surprised.

"Yep."

Frowning, she ground out her cigarette in a nightstand ashtray. "Son of a bitch," she muttered. Then, taking a different tack, she came off the bed and swept aside his jeans before he could step into them. She bumped against his middle seductively.

"It's late, Key. Everybody out at your mama's house will be sound asleep. You'd just as well stay with me tonight." She reached between his strong thighs and fondled him, with audacity and know-how, boldly looking into his face as her fingers coaxed a response. "You haven't lived until you've partaken of one of my breakfast specialties."

Key's lips twitched with amusement. "Served in bed?"

"Damn straight. With all the trimmings. I even— " She broke off suddenly, her hands reflexively clenching hard enough to cause him to grimace.

"Hey, watch out. Them's the family jewels."

"Shh!" Releasing him, she ran on tiptoe toward the open bedroom door. As she reached it, a male voice called out. "Sugar pie, I'm home."

"*Shit!*" No longer languid and seductive, she turned toward Key. "You've got to get out of here," she hissed. "Now!"

Key had already stepped into his jeans and was bending

down to search for his boots. "How do you suggest I do that?" he whispered.

"Sugar? You upstairs?" Key heard footsteps on the marble tiles of the entry below, then on the carpet of the stairs. "I got away early and decided to come on home tonight instead of waiting for morning."

She frantically motioned Key toward the French doors on the far side of the room. Scooping up his boots and shirt, he pulled open the doors and slipped through them. He was outside on the balcony before he remembered that the master bedroom was on the second floor of the house. Peering over the wrought-iron railing, he saw no easy way down.

Swearing beneath his breath, he quickly reviewed his options. What the hell? He'd faced worse situations. Typhoons, bullets, an earthquake or two, acts of God, and man-made mayhem. A husband coming home unexpectedly wasn't a new experience for him, either. He'd just have to bluff his way through and hope for the best.

He stepped back into the bedroom but pulled up short on the threshold of the French doors. The nightstand drawer was open. His lover was now reclining in bed clutching the satin sheet to her chin with one hand. With the other, she was aiming a pistol straight at him.

"What the hell are you doing?"

Her piercing scream stunned him. A second later, a blast from her pistol shattered his eardrums. It was a few pounding heartbeats later before he realized that he'd been hit. He gazed down at the searing wound in his left side, then raised his incredulous eyes back to her.

The running footsteps had now reached the hallway. "Sugar pie!"

Again she screamed, a bloodcurdling sound. Again she aimed the gun.

Galvanized, Key spun around just as she fired. He thought she missed but couldn't afford the time to check. He tossed his boots and shirt over the railing, threw his left leg over, then his right, and balanced on an inch of support before leaping through the darkness to the ground below.

He landed hard on his right ankle. Pain shimmied up through his shin, thigh, and groin before slamming into his gut. Blinking hard, he gasped for breath, prayed he wouldn't vomit, and strove to remain conscious as he swept up his boots and shirt and ran like hell.

Lara jumped at the sound of hard knocking on her back door.

She'd been absorbed in a syrupy Bette Davis classic. Muting the television with the remote control, she listened. The knocking came again, harder and more urgent. Throwing off the afghan covering her legs, she left the comfort of her living-room sofa and hurried down the hallway, switching on lights as she went.

When she reached the back room of the clinic, she saw the silhouette of a man against the partially open miniblinds on the door. Cautiously she crept forward and peered through a crack in the blinds.

Beneath the harsh glare of the porch light his face looked waxy and set. The lower half of it was shadowed by a day-old beard. Sweat had plastered several strands of unruly dark hair to his forehead. Beneath dense, dark eyebrows, he squinted through the blinds.

"Doc?" He raised his fist and pounded on the door again. "Hey, Doc, open up! I'm making a hell of a mess on your back steps." He wiped his forehead with the back of his hand, and Lara saw blood.

Putting aside her caution, she disengaged the alarm system and unlocked the door. As soon as the latch gave way, he shouldered his way through and stumbled, barefoot, into the room.

"You took long enough," he mumbled. "But all's forgiven if you still keep a bottle of Jack Daniel's stashed in here." He moved straight to a white enamel cabinet and bent down to open the bottom drawer.

"There's no Jack Daniel's in there."

At the sound of her voice, he spun around. He gaped at her for several seconds. Lara gaped back. He had an animalistic quality that both attracted and repelled her, and although she was inured to the smell of fresh blood, she could smell his.

Instinctively she wanted to recoil, but not from fear. Her impulse was a feminine one of self-defense. She held her ground, however, subjecting herself to his disbelieving and disapproving stare.

"Who the hell are you? Where's Doc?" He was scowling darkly and holding the bloodied tail of his unbuttoned shirt against his side.

"You'd better sit down. You're hurt."

"No shit, lady. Where's Doc?"

"Probably asleep in his bed at his fishing cabin on the lake. He retired and moved out there several months ago."

He glared at her. Finally, in disgust, he said, "Great. That's just fuckin' great." He muttered curses as he shoved his fingers through his hair. Then he took a few lurching steps toward the door and careened into the examination table.

Reflexively Lara reached for him. He staved her off but remained leaning against the padded table. Breathing heavily and wincing in pain, he said, "Can I have some whiskey?"

"What happened to you?"

"What's it to you?"

"I didn't just move into Dr. Patton's house. I took over his medical practice."

His sapphire eyes snapped up to meet hers. "You're a doctor?"

She nodded and spread her arms to indicate the examination room.

"Well I'll be damned." His eyes moved over her. "You must be a real hit at the hospital wearing that getup," he said, lifting his chin to indicate her attire. "Is that the latest thing in lady doctor outfits?"

She had on a long white shirt over a pair of leggings that ended at her knees. Despite her bare feet and legs, she assumed an authoritarian tone. "I don't generally wear my lady doctor outfits past midnight. It's after hours, but I'm still licensed to practice medicine, so why don't you forget how I'm dressed and let me look at your wound. What happened?"

"A little accident."

As she slipped his shirt from his shoulders, she noticed that his belt was unbuckled and only half the buttons of his fly were fastened. She prized his bloody hand away from the wound on his left side, about waist level.

"That's a gunshot!"

"Naw. Like I told you, I had a little accident."

Clearly, he was lying, something he seemed accustomed to doing frequently and without repentance. "What kind of 'accident'?"

"I fell on a pitchfork." He motioned down at the wound. "Just clean it out, put a Band-Aid on it, and tomorrow I'll be fine."

She straightened up and unsmilingly met his grinning face. "Cut the crap, all right? I know a bullet wound when I see one," she said. "I can't take care of this here. You belong in the county hospital."

Turning her back on him, she moved to the phone and began punching out numbers. "I'll make you as comfortable as I can until the ambulance arrives. Please lie down. As soon as I've completed the call, I'll do what I can to stop the bleeding. Yes, hello," she said into the receiver when her call was answered. "This is Dr. Mallory in Eden Pass. I have an emer— "

His hand came from behind her and broke the connection. Alarmed, she looked at him over her shoulder.

"I'm not going to any damn hospital," he said succinctly. "No ambulance. This is nothing. Nothing, understand? Just stop the bleeding and slap a bandage on it. Easy as pie. Have you got any whiskey?" he asked for the third time.

Stubbornly, Lara began redialing. Before she completed the sequence of numbers, he plucked the receiver from her hand and angrily yanked it out of the phone, leaving the cord dangling from his fist.

She turned and confronted him, but, for the first time since opening the door, she was afraid. Even in this small East Texas town, drug abuse was a problem. Shortly after moving into the clinic, she had installed a burglar alarm system to prevent thefts of prescription drugs and narcotic painkillers.

He must have sensed her apprehension. With a clatter, he dropped the telephone receiver onto a cabinet and smiled grimly. "Look, Doc, if I'd come here to hurt you, I'd have already done it and gotten the hell out. I just don't want to involve a bunch of people in this. No hospital, okay? Take care of me here, and I'll be on my merry way." Even as he spoke, his lips became taut and colorless. He drew an audible breath through clenched teeth.

"Are you about to pass out?"

"Not if I can help it."

"You're in a lot of pain."

"Yeah," he conceded, slowly nodding his head. "It hurts like a son of a bitch. Are you going to let me bleed to death while we argue about it?"

She studied his resolute face for a moment longer and reached the conclusion that she either had to do it his way or he'd leave. The former was preferable to the latter, in which case she would be risking the patient's health and possibly his life. She ordered him to lie down and lower his jeans.

"I've used that same line a dozen times myself," he drawled as he eased himself onto the table.

"That doesn't surprise me." Unimpressed by his boast, she moved to a basin and washed her hands with disinfectant soap. "If you know Doc Patton well enough to know where he stashed his Jack Daniel's, you must live here."

"Born and raised."

"Then why didn't you know he'd retired?"

"I've been away for a while."

"Were you a regular patient of his?"

"All my life. He got me through chicken pox, tonsillitis, two broken ribs, a broken collarbone, a broken arm, and an altercation with a rusty tin can that was serving as second base. Still got the scar on my thigh where I landed when I slid in."

"Were you called out?"

"Hell no," he replied, as though that were beyond the realm of possibility. "More than once I've come through that back door in the middle of the night, needing Doc to patch me up for one reason or another. He wasn't as stingy with the medicinal whiskey as you are. What's that you're fixing there?"

"A sedative." She calmly depressed the plunger of a syringe and sent a spurt of medication into the air.

She then set it down and swabbed his upper arm with a cotton ball soaked in alcohol. Before she knew what he was about to do, he picked up the syringe, pushed the plunger with his thumb and squirted the fluid onto the floor.

"Do you think I'm stupid, or what?"

"Mr.— "

"If you want me anesthetized, get me a glass of whiskey. You're not pumping anything into my bloodstream that'll knock me out and give you an opportunity to call the hospital."

"And the sheriff. I'm required by law to report a gunshot wound to the authorities."

He struggled to sit up and when he did, the open wound

gushed bright red blood. He groaned. Lara hastily slipped on a pair of surgical gloves and began stanching the flow with gauze pads so that she could determine how serious the wound was.

"Afraid I'll give you AIDS?" he asked, nodding at her gloved hands.

"Professional precaution."

"No worry," he said with a slow grin. "I've been real careful all my life."

"You weren't so careful tonight. Were you caught cheating at poker? Flirting with the wrong woman? Or were you cleaning your pistol when it accidentally went off?"

"I told you, it was a— "

"Yes. A pitchfork. Which would have punctured instead of tearing off a chunk of tissue." She worked quickly and effectively. "Look, I've got to trim off the rough edges of the wound and put in some deep sutures. It's going to be painful. I must anesthetize you."

"Forget it." He hitched his hip over the side of the table as though to leave.

Lara stopped him by placing the heels of her hands on his shoulders. The fingers of her gloves were bloody. "Lidocaine? Local anesthetic," she explained. She took a vial from her cabinet and let him read the label. "Okay?"

He nodded tersely and watched as she prepared another syringe. She injected him near the wound. When the surrounding tissue was deadened, she clipped the debris from around the wound, irrigated it with a saline solution, sutured the interior, and put in a drain.

"What the hell is that?" he asked. He was pale and sweating profusely, but he had watched every swift and economic movement of her hands.

"It's called a penrose drain. It drains off blood and fluid and helps prevent infection. I'll remove it in a few days." She closed the wound with sutures and placed a sterile bandage over it.

After dropping the bloody gloves into a marked metal trash can that designated contaminated materials, Lara returned to the sink to wash her hands. She then asked him to sit up while she wrapped an Ace bandage around his trunk to keep the dressing in place.

She stepped away from him and looked critically at her handiwork. "You're lucky he wasn't a better marksman. A few inches to the right and the bullet could have penetrated several vital organs."

"Or a few inches lower, and I couldn't have penetrated anything ever again."

Lara gave him a retiring look. "How lucky for you."

She had remained professionally detached, although each time her arms had encircled him while bandaging his wound, her cheek had come close to his wide chest. He had a lean, sunbaked, hair-spattered torso. The Ace bandage bisected his hard, flat belly. She'd worked the emergency rooms of major city hospitals; she'd stitched up shady characters before—but none quite this glib, amusing, and handsome.

"Believe it, Doc. I've got the luck of the devil."

"Oh, I believe it. You appear to be a man who lives on the edge and survives by his wits. When did you last have a tetanus shot?"

"Last year." She looked at him skeptically. He raised his right hand as though taking an oath. "Swear to God."

He eased himself over the side of the examination table and stood with his hip propped against it while he rebuttoned his jeans. He left his belt unbuckled. "What do I owe you?"

"Fifty dollars for the after-hours office call, fifty for the sutures and dressing, twelve each for the injections, including the one you wasted, and forty for the medication."

"Medication?"

She removed two plastic bottles from a locked cabinet

and handed them to him. "An antibiotic and a pain pill. Once the lidocaine wears off, it'll hurt."

He withdrew a money clip from the front pocket of his snug jeans. "Let's see, fifty plus fifty, plus twenty-four, plus forty comes to— "

"One sixty-four."

He cocked an eyebrow, seeming amused by her prompt tabulation. "Right. One hundred and sixty-four." He extracted the necessary bills and laid them on the examination table. "Keep the change," he said when he put down a five-dollar bill instead of four ones.

Lara was surprised that he had that much cash on him. Even after paying her, he still had a wad of currency in high denominations. "Thank you. Take two of the antibiotic capsules tonight, then four a day until you've taken all of them."

He read the labels, opened the bottle of pain pills and shook out one. He tossed it back and swallowed it dry. "It'd go down better with a shot of whiskey." His voice rose on a hopeful, inquiring note.

She shook her head. "Take one every four hours. Two if absolutely necessary. Take them with water," she emphasized, seriously doubting that he'd stick to those instructions. "Tomorrow afternoon around four-thirty, come in and I'll change your dressing."

"For another fifty bucks, I guess."

"No, that's included."

"Much obliged."

"Don't be. As soon as you leave, I'm calling Sheriff Baxter."

Crossing his arms over his bare chest, he regarded her indulgently. "And get him out of bed at this time of night?" He shook his head remorsefully. "I've known poor old Elmo Baxter all my life. He and my daddy were buddies. They were youngsters during the oil boom, see? It was kinda like going through a war together, they said.

"They used to hang out around the drilling sites, came to be like mascots to the roughnecks and wildcatters. Ran errands for them to buy hamburgers, cigarettes, moonshine, whatever they wanted. He and my daddy probably procured some things that old Elmo would rather not recall," he said with a wink.

"Anyway, go ahead and call him. But once he gets here, he'll be nothing but glad to see me. He'll slap me on the back and say something like, 'Long time no see,' and ask what the hell I've been up to lately." He paused to gauge Lara's reaction. Her stony stare didn't faze him.

"Elmo's overworked and underpaid. Calling him out this late over this piddling accident of mine will get him all out of sorts, and he's already cantankerous by nature. If you ever have a real emergency, like some crazy dopehead breaking in here looking for something to stop the little green monsters from crawling out of his eye sockets, the sheriff'll think twice before rushing to your rescue.

"Besides," he added, lowering his voice, "folks won't take kindly to you when they hear that you can't be trusted with their secrets. People in a small town like Eden Pass put a lot of stock in privileged information."

"I doubt that many even know the definition of privileged information," Lara refuted dryly. "And contrary to what you say, in the time I've been here, I've learned just how far-reaching and accurate the grapevine is. A secret has a short life span in this town.

"But your message to me about Sheriff Baxter came through loud and clear. What you're telling me is that he enforces a good ol' boy form of justice and that even if I reported your bullet wound, that would be the end of it."

"More'n likely," he replied honestly. "Around here, if the sheriff investigated every shooting, he'd be plumb worn out in a month."

Realizing that he probably was right, Lara sighed. "Were you shot while committing a crime?"

"A few sins, maybe," he said, giving her a slow, lazy smile. His blue eyes squinted mischievously. "But I don't think they're illegal."

She finally relinquished her professional posture and laughed. He didn't appear to be a criminal, although he was almost certainly a sinner. She doubted that he was dangerous, except perhaps to a susceptible woman.

"Hey, the lady doctor's not so stuffy after all. She can smile. Got a real nice smile, too." Narrowing his eyes, he asked softly, "What else have you got that's real nice?"

Now it was her turn to fold her arms across her chest. "Do these come-on lines usually work for you?"

"I've always thought that where boys and girls are concerned, talk is practically unnecessary."

"Really?"

"Saves time and energy. Energy better spent on doing other things."

"I don't dare ask 'Like what?'"

"Go ahead, ask. I don't embarrass easily. Do you?"

It had been a long time since a man had flirted with her. Even longer since she had flirted back. It felt good. But only for a few seconds. Then she remembered why she couldn't afford to flirt, no matter how harmlessly. Her smile faltered, then faded. She drew herself up and resumed her professional demeanor. "Don't forget your shirt," she said curtly.

"You can throw it away." He took a step away from the table, but fell back against it, his face contorted in pain. "Shitfire!"

"What?"

"My goddamn ankle. I twisted it when I . . . Hell of a sprain, I think."

She knelt down and as gently as possible worked up the right leg of his jeans. "Good Lord! Why didn't you show me this sooner?" The ankle was swollen and discolored.

"Because I was bleeding like a stuck hog. First things

first. It'll be all right." He bent over, pushed aside her probing hands, and pulled down his pants leg.

"You should have it X-rayed. It could be broken."

"It isn't."

"You're not qualified to give a medical opinion."

"No, but I've had enough broken bones to know when one's broken, and this one isn't."

"I can't take responsibility if— "

"Relax, will you? I'm not going to hold you responsible for anything." Shirtless, shoeless, he hopped toward the door through which he'd entered.

"Would you like to wash your hands before you go?" she offered.

He looked down at the bloodstains and shook his head. "They've been dirtier."

Lara felt derelict in her duties as a physician treating him this way. But he was an adult, accountable for his own actions. She'd done as much as he had permitted.

"Don't forget to take your antibiotics," she cautioned as she slipped under his right arm and fit her left shoulder into his armpit. She placed her left arm around him for additional support as he hopped through the door, his right arm across her shoulders. A pickup truck was parked a few yards from the back steps. Its front tires had narrowly missed her bed of struggling petunias.

"Do you have some crutches?"

"I'll find some if I need them."

"You'll need them. Don't put any weight on your ankle for several days. When you get home, put an ice pack on it and keep it elevated whenever possible. And remember to come in at— "

"Four-thirty tomorrow. I wouldn't miss it."

She looked up at him. He tilted his head down to look at her. Their gazes came together and held. Lara felt the heat emanating from his body. He was muscular and fit, and she was certain that his vital body would heal quickly. He was a physical specimen, which she had tried, not entirely successfully, to regard through purely professional eyes.

His eyes scanned her, looking intently at her face, her hair, her mouth. In a low, rough voice he said, "You sure as hell don't look like any doctor I've ever seen." His hand slid from her shoulder to her hip. "You don't feel like one either."

"What is a doctor supposed to feel like?"

"Not like this," he rasped, gently squeezing her.

He kissed her then. Abruptly and impertinently, he stamped her lips with his.

Gasping in surprise, Lara disengaged herself. Her heart was knocking and she felt hot all over. A thousand options on how to react flashed through her mind, but she considered that the best one was to pretend the kiss hadn't happened. Taking issue with it would only give it importance. She would be forced to acknowledge it, discuss it with him, and that, she hastily reasoned, should be avoided.

So she assumed a cool, haughty tone as she asked, "Would you like me to drive you somewhere?"

He was grinning from ear to ear, as though he saw straight through her attempt to conceal her discomposure. "No, thanks," he replied cockily. "This truck's got automatic transmission. I'll manage with my left foot."

She nodded brusquely. "If I hear of any crimes that occurred tonight, I'll have to report this incident to Sheriff Baxter."

Laughing even as he grimaced in pain, he climbed into the cab of the pickup. "Don't worry. You're not obstructing justice." He drew an imaginary X over his left breast. "Cross my heart and hope to die, stick a cross-tie in my eye." The engine sputtered to life. He dropped the gear shift into reverse. "Bye-bye, Doc."

"Be careful, Mr.— "

"Tackett," he told her through the open window. "But call me Key."

Everything inside Lara went very still. It seemed her heart, which had been racing only moments earlier, ceased to beat at all. Blood drained from her head, making her dizzy. She must have gone drastically pale, but it was too dark for him to notice as he backed the pickup to the end of the driveway. He tapped his horn twice and saluted her with the tips of his fingers as the truck rumbled away into the darkness.

Lara plopped down onto the cool concrete steps, which were speckled with drying drops of blood. She covered her face with damp, trembling hands. The night was seasonably warm and balmy, but she shivered inside her loose white shirt. Goose bumps broke out along her legs. Her mouth had gone dry.

Key Tackett. Clark's younger brother. He'd finally come home. This was the day she'd been anticipating. He was essential to the daring plan she'd spent the past year developing and cultivating. Now, he was here. Somehow, some way, she must enlist his help. But how?

Dr. Lara Mallory was the last person Key Tackett wanted to know.

Chapter Two

As she did every morning of her life, Janellen Tackett left her solitary bed the instant the alarm went off. The bathtub faucets squeaked, and the hot-water pipes knocked loudly within the walls of the house, but these sounds were so commonplace she didn't even notice them.

Janellen had spent all of her thirty-three years in this house and couldn't imagine living anyplace else, or even wanting to. Her daddy had built it for his bride over forty years ago, and although it had been redecorated and modernized with the passing decades, the indelible marks Janellen and her brothers had left on its walls and the scarred hardwood floors remained. These flaws added to its character, like laugh lines in a woman's face.

Clark and Key had regarded the house as merely a dwelling. But Janellen considered it an integral member of the family, as essential to her heritage as were her parents. With a lover's attention to detail, she had explored it so many times she intimately knew it from attic to cellar. It was as familiar to her as her own body. Maybe even more so. She never focused her thoughts on her body, never contemplated her own being, never stopped to consider her life and wonder whether she was happy. She simply accepted things as they were.

Following her shower, she dressed for work in a khaki skirt and a simple cotton blouse. Her hosiery had no tint; her brown leather shoes had been designed for comfort, not fashion. She pulled her dark hair into a practical ponytail. Her only article of jewelry was a plain wristwatch. She applied very little makeup. One quick whisk of powder blusher across her cheeks, a little mascara on the tips of her eyelashes, a dab of pink lip gloss, and she was ready to greet the day.

The sun was rising as she made her way down the dim staircase, through the first-story hallway, and into the kitchen, where she switched on the overhead light fixtures, filling every nook and cranny with the blue-white light of an operating room. Janellen despised the invasive cold glare because it kept the otherwise traditional kitchen from being cozy.

But Jody liked it that way.

Mechanically, she started the coffee. She had religiously kept to this morning routine since the last live-in housekeeper had been dismissed. When Janellen was fifteen, she had declared that she no longer needed a baby-sitter, that she was capable of getting herself off to school and of cooking her mother's breakfast in the process.

Maydale, their current housekeeper, worked only five hours a day. She did the heavy cleaning and the laundry and got dinner started. But for all practical purposes, along with her responsibilities at Tackett Oil and Gas Company, Janellen managed the household.

She checked the refrigerator to make sure there was a pitcher of orange juice ready and poured half-and-half into the cream pitcher. Jody wasn't supposed to be drinking half-and-half in her coffee because of the fat content, but she insisted on it anyway. Jody always got her way.

While the coffeemaker gurgled and hissed, Janellen filled a watering can with distilled water and went out onto the screened back porch to sprinkle her ferns and begonias.

That's when she saw the pickup truck. She didn't recognize it, but it was parked as though it belonged in that particular spot near the back door. It was parked right where Key had always—She did an about-face, almost spilling the contents of the watering can before returning it to the counter. She raced from the kitchen and down the hallway, grabbed the newel post and executed a childlike spiral around it, then charged up the stairs. Reaching the second floor, she dashed to the last bedroom on the right and, without pausing to knock, barged in.

"Key!"

"*What?*"

Running his fingers through his dark, tousled hair, he lifted his head off the pillow. He blinked her into focus. Then he moaned, clutched his side, and flopped back down. "Jesus! Don't sneak up on me like that. Had a bedouin do that to me once, and I almost gutted him before realizing he was one of the few friendly to us."

Heedless of his reprimand, Janellen quickly threw herself across her brother's chest. "Key! You're home. When did you get here? Why'd you sneak in without waking us? Oh, you're home. Thank you, thank you, thank you for coming." She hugged his neck hard and pecked several kisses on his forehead and cheeks.

"Okay, okay, I get it. You're glad to see me." He grumbled and staved off her kisses, but as he struggled to a sitting position, he was smiling. "Hiya, sis." Through bloodshot eyes, he looked her over. "Let's see. No gray hairs. You've still got most of your teeth. Haven't put on more'n five or six pounds. Overall, I'd say you look no worse for wear."

"I haven't put on a single ounce, I'll have you know. And I look just like I always have. Unfortunately." Without coyness, she added, "You and Clark were the pretty ones of the family, remember? I'm the plain Jane. Or in this case, Janellen."

"Now why would you want to piss me off first thing?" he asked. "Why go and say something like that?"

"Because it's true." She gave a slight shrug as though it

was of little or no consequence. "Let's don't waste breath talking about me. I want to know about you. Where'd you come from and when did you get in?"

"Your message was channeled to me through that London phone number I gave you," he told her around a huge yawn. "It caught up with me in Saudi. Been traveling for three, maybe four days. Hard to keep track when you're crossing that many time zones. Came through Houston yesterday and dropped off the company plane. Got into Eden Pass last night sometime."

"Why didn't you wake us up? Who's truck is that? How long can you stay?"

He raked back his hair and winced as though each follicle were bruised. "One question at a time, please. I didn't wake you up because it was late and there was no point. I borrowed the truck from a buddy in Houston who has to deliver a plane to Longview in a couple of days. He'll pick it up then and drive it back. And . . . what was the last one?"

"How long can you stay?" She folded her hands beneath her chin, looking like a little girl about to say her bedtime prayers. "Don't say 'just a few days.' Don't say 'a week.' Say you're staying for a long time."

He reached for her folded hands and clasped them. "The contract I had with that oil outfit in Saudi was almost up anyway. Right now I haven't got anything cooking. I'll leave my departure date open. We'll wait and see how it goes, okay?"

"Okay. Thank you, Key." Tears glistened in her fine blue eyes. When it came to that family trait, she hadn't been passed over. "I hated to bother you with the situation here, but— "

"It was no bother."

"Well it *felt* like a bother. I wouldn't have contacted you if I didn't think that having you here might somehow make things . . . better."

"What's going on, Janellen?"

"It's Mama. She's sick, Key."

"Is her blood pressure kicking up again?"

"It's worse than that." Janellen twisted her hands. "She's started having memory blackouts. They don't last long. At first I didn't even notice them. Then Maydale mentioned several instances when Mama lost things and accused her of moving them. She introduces topics into conversations that we've already talked about."

"She's getting up there in years, Janellen. These are probably nothing more than early signs of senility."

"Maybe, but I don't believe so. I'm afraid it's more serious than just aging because there are days when I can tell she doesn't feel well, much as she tries to cover up."

"What does the doctor say?"

"She won't see one," she exclaimed with frustration. "Dr. Patton prescribed medication to control her blood pressure, but that was over a year ago. She browbeats the pharmacist into refilling the prescription and says that's sufficient. She won't listen when I urge her to see another doctor for a checkup."

He smiled wryly. "That sounds like Jody all right. Knows better than anybody about everything."

"Please, Key, don't be critical of her. Help her. Help me."

He cuffed her chin gently and said, "You've carried the responsibility alone for too long. It's time I gave you some relief." His lips narrowed. "If I can."

"You can. This time it'll be different between you and Mama."

Grunting with skepticism, he threw off the sheet and swung his feet to the floor. "Hand me my jeans, please."

Janellen was about to turn and reach for the jeans bunched up on the seat of the easy chair when she noticed the bandage around his middle. "What happened to you?" she exclaimed. "And look at your ankle!"

He nonchalantly examined his swollen ankle. "It was kind of a rowdy homecoming."

"How'd you get hurt? Is it serious?"

"No. The jeans, please."

Still sitting on the edge of the bed, he extended his hand. Janellen recognized the stubborn set of her brother's scruffy jaw and handed him his pants, then knelt to help guide his bare feet through the legs.

"Your ankle's swollen twice its size," she muttered with concern. "Can you stand on it?"

"My doctor advised me not to," he answered dryly. "Give me a hand."

She helped support him as he put all his weight on his left foot and eased the jeans up his legs and over his hips. As he buttoned his fly, he gave her the naughty smile that had wreaked havoc on a legion of virtuous reputations.

Janellen couldn't began to guess how many women her brothers had worked their magic on, especially Key. She'd always entertained a fantasy of spoiling a mixed blend of nieces and nephews, but it remained an unfulfilled dream. Key liked women, a wide assortment of them. She saw no indication that he'd soon settle down into marriage.

"You're pretty good at helping a man into his pants," he remarked teasingly. "Been helping one out of his lately? I hope," he added.

"Hush!"

"Well?"

"No!" She could feel herself blushing. Key had always been able to make her blush.

"Why not?"

"I'm not interested, that's why," she replied loftily. "Besides, no one's been swept off his feet by my dazzling face and form."

"There's nothing wrong with either," he said staunchly. "But they're hardly dazzling."

"No, because you've got it into your stubborn head

that you're plain Jane, so you dress the part. You're so . . ." disdainfully, he gestured at her prim blouse, "buttoned up."

"Buttoned up?"

"Yeah. What you need to do is unbutton. Unhook. Unstrap. Get loose, sis."

She pretended to be aghast. "As an old maid, I take exception to such trashy talk."

"Old maid! Who the hell . . .? You listen to me, Janellen." He pointed his index finger at the tip of her nose. "You're *not* old."

"I'm not exactly an ingenue either."

"You're two years younger than me. That makes you thirty-four."

"Not quite."

"Okay, thirty-three. Far from over the hill. Hell, broads these days wait until they're forty to start having kids."

"Those who do wouldn't appreciate your referring to them as 'broads.'"

"You get my drift," he insisted. "You haven't even reached your sexual peak yet."

"Key, please."

"And the only reason you're still a 'maid,' *if* you are— "

"I am."

"More's the pity . . . is because you clam up and shy away from any guy who even thinks about getting into your pants."

Janellen, stricken by his crudeness, stared at him speechlessly. She worked around men eight hours a day, five days a week, and occasionally on weekends. As a rule, their language was colorful and to the point, but they monitored it when Miss Janellen was within hearing. When her employees addressed her, they cleaned up their act.

Of course Jody would shoot on sight any man using vulgarities in either her or her daughter's presence.

Paradoxically, Jody herself had an extensive vocabulary of obscenities and blasphemies, an irony that seemed to escape her.

The fact that Janellen emanated an invisible repellent against casual and unguarded behavior didn't please her. In fact, she considered this characteristic a liability. It set her apart and proved that she didn't attract men in any way, on any level including friendship. She couldn't even be one of the boys, although she'd grown up having to contend with two older brothers.

She wasn't so much affronted by Key's salty language as she was stunned. In a way she took it as a compliment. Key, however, couldn't guess that.

"Oh, hell," he muttered remorsefully and stroked her cheek. "I'm sorry. I didn't mean to say that. It's just that you're too hard on yourself. Lighten up, for chrissake. Have some fun. Take off a year and go to Europe. Raise hell. Create a ruckus. Scare up a scandal. Broaden your scope. Life's too short to be taken so seriously. It's passing you by."

She smiled, clasped his hand, and kissed the back of it. "Apology accepted. I know you didn't mean to hurt my feelings or insult me. But you're wrong, Key. Life isn't passing me by. My life is here, and I'm content with it. I'm so busy, I don't know how I'd fit in another interest, romantic or otherwise.

"Granted, my life isn't as exciting as yours, but I don't want it to be. You're the globe-trotter. I'm a homebody, not at all suited to hell-raising and ruckuses and scandals."

She laid her hand on his forearm. "I don't want to argue with you on your first day home since Clark's . . ." She couldn't bring herself to complete the sentence. She dropped her hand from his arm. "Let's go downstairs. The coffee should be ready by now."

"Good. I could use a cup or two before facing the old lady. What time does she usually get up?"

"The old lady is up."

In the doorway stood their mother, Jody Tackett.

Bowie Cato came awake when he was nudged hard in the ribs with the toe of a boot. "Hey, you, get up."

Bowie opened his eyes and rolled onto his back. It took him several seconds to remember he was sleeping in the storeroom of The Palm, the loudest, raunchiest, and seediest tavern in a row of loud, raunchy, and seedy taverns lining both sides of the two-lane highway on the outskirts of Eden Pass.

As the recently hired janitor, Bowie did most of his work after 2:00 A.M., when the tavern closed, and that was on a slow night. In addition to the piddling salary he earned, the owner had granted him permission to sleep on the storeroom floor in a sleeping bag.

"What's goin' on?" he asked groggily. It seemed he hadn't slept for more than a few hours.

"Get up." He got the boot in the ribs again, more like a bona fide kick this time. His first impulse was to grab the offending foot and sling it aside, throwing its owner off balance and landing him flat on his ass.

But Bowie had spent the last three years in the state pen for giving vent to a violent impulse and he wasn't keen on the idea of serving another three.

Without comment or argument, he sat up and shook his muzzy head. Squinting through the sunlight coming from the window, he saw the silhouettes of two men standing over him.

"I'm sorry, Bowie." Speaking now was Hap Hollister, owner of The Palm. "I told Gus that you'd been here all night, didn't leave the premises once since seven o'clock last evenin', but he said he had to check you out anyway on account of you being an ex-con. He and the sheriff asked around last night and, best as they can tell, at the present, you're the only suspicious character in town."

"I seriously doubt that," Bowie mumbled as he slowly

came to his feet. "It's all right, Hap." He gave his new employer a grim smile, then faced bald, bloated, burly sheriff's deputy. "What's up?"

"What's up," the deputy repeated nastily, "is that Ms. Darcy Winston nearly got herself raped and murdered in her own bed last night. That's what's up." He gave them the details of the attempted break-in.

"I'm awful sorry to hear that." Bowie divided his gaze between the uniformed deputy and Hap, but they continued to stare back at him wordlessly. He raised and lowered his shoulders in a quick, quizzical motion. "Who's Ms. Darcy Winston?"

"Like you don't know," the deputy sneered.

"I *don't* know."

"You, uh, were talking to her last night, Bowie," Hap said regretfully. "She was here while you were on duty. Redheaded, big tits, had on those purple, skinny-legged britches. Lots of jewelry."

"Oh." He didn't recall the jewelry, but those tits were memorable all right, and he figured that Ms. Darcy Winston knew it better than anybody. She'd been guzzling margaritas like they were lime-flavored soda pop and giving encouragement to every man in the place, including him, the lowly sweep-up boy.

"I talked to her," he told the deputy, "but we didn't get around to swapping names."

"She was talking to everybody, Gus," Hap interjected.

"But only this 'un has a prison record. Only this 'un is out on parole."

Bowie shifted his weight and ordered his tensing muscles to relax. Dammit, he knew instinctively that trouble was just around the corner, barreling full steam ahead, ready to knock him down. He hoped to hell he could get out of its path, but the odds didn't look good.

This two-hundred-fifty-pound sheriff's deputy was a bully. Bowie had tangled with too many in his lifetime not to recognize one on sight. He'd seen them large and muscular; he'd seen them small and wiry. A man's size and strength had nothing to do with it. The common denominator was a meanness-for-meanness' sake that shone in their eyes.

Bowie had first encountered it in his stepfather soon after his desperate, widowed mother had married the drunken son of a bitch who got off by slapping him around. Later, he'd recognized it in the junior high school boys' gym teacher who daily, deliberately, humiliated the kids who weren't natural athletes.

Standing up to his abusive stepfather and defending those pitiful kids against the gym teacher had been the start of the troubles that had eventually landed Bowie in county jail as a juvenile offender. Slow to learn, years later he'd graduated to state prison.

But this wasn't his fight. He didn't know Darcy Winston and couldn't care less about the attack on her. He told himself that if he just stayed cool it would be all right. "I was here at The Palm all night, just like Hap told you."

The deputy surveyed him up one side and down the other. "Take off your clothes."

"Excuse me?"

"What, are you deaf? Take off your clothes. Strip."

"Gus," Hap said apprehensively. "You sure that's necessary? The boy here— "

"Back off, Hap," the deputy snapped. "Let me do my job, will ya? Ms. Winston shot at the intruder. We know she hit him 'cause there was blood on her balcony railing and on the pool deck. He left a trail of it as he ran off through the bushes." He hitched up his gun holster, which fit in the deep crevice beneath his overlapping beer belly. "Let's see if you've got a bullet wound anywhere. Take off your clothes, jailbird."

Bowie's temper snapped. "Go fuck yourself."

The deputy's face turned as red as a billiard ball. His

piggish eyes were almost buried in narrowing folds of florid fat.

Now there'd be hell to pay.

Making an animalistic grunt, the officer lunged for Bowie. Bowie dodged him. The deputy took a wild swing, which Bowie also deflected. Hap Hollister shouldered his way between them. "Hey, you two! I don't want any trouble here. I'm sure y'all don't either."

"I'm gonna break every bone in that little cocksucker's body."

"No, you ain't, Gus." Gus struggled against Hollister's restraining arms, but Hap had tussled with angry drunks many times and was no small man himself. He could handle the deputy. "Sheriff Baxter would have your ass if you harassed a suspect."

"I'm not a suspect!" Bowie shouted.

Still restraining Gus, Hap glared at Bowie over the deputy's meaty shoulder. "Don't go shooting off your mouth like that, kid. It's stupid. Now, apologize."

"Like hell!"

"Apologize!" Hap roared. "Don't make me sorry I stood up for you."

While the deputy seethed, Hap and Bowie exchanged challenging stares. Bowie reconsidered. If he didn't keep a job, his parole officer would be after him. It was a lousy, goin'-nowhere job, but it was gainful employment that demonstrated his desire to reintegrate into society.

He for sure as hell wouldn't go back to Huntsville. Even if he had to kiss the ass of every thick-necked meathead with a badge pinned to his shirt, he wouldn't go back to prison.

"I take it back." For good measure, he unbuttoned his shirt and showed his chest and back to the deputy. "No bullet holes. I was here all night."

"And there's probably three dozen or so witnesses who can testify to that, Gus," Hap said. "Somebody else tried to break into Ms. Darcy Winston's bedroom last night. It wasn't Bowie."

Gus wasn't ready to concede, although it was obvious that he had the wrong man. "Funny that as soon as this parolee hits town, we get the first report of a serious crime in as long as I can remember."

"Coincidence," Hap said.

"I reckon," the deputy grumbled, although he continued to glare suspiciously at Bowie.

Hap diverted him with a piece of local gossip. "By the way, guess who else blew into town last night. Key Tackett."

"No shit?"

Hap's maneuver worked. The deputy relaxed his official stance and propped his elbow on a shelf, for the time being forgetting Bowie and the purpose of his visit to the honky-tonk. Bowie just wanted to return to the sleeping bag and get some rest. He yawned.

The deputy asked, "What'd old Key look like? Gone to fat yet?" Laughing, he slapped his belly affectionately.

"Hell, no. Hasn't changed a smidgen since his senior year when he led the varsity team all the way to the state playoffs. Tall, dark, and handsome as the devil hisself. Those blue eyes of his still spear into everything they land on. Still the smartass he always was, too. First time he's been back to town since they buried his brother."

Bowie's ears perked up. He remembered the man they were talking about. Tackett was the kind of man who made a distinct impression on folks—male and female alike. Men wanted to be like him. Women wanted to be with him. He'd no more than sat down on a barstool when Ms. What's-her-name with the red hair and big tits had grafted herself to him. They'd been real friendly, too, for more than half an hour. Tackett had left within minutes of her slinking exit.

Interesting coincidence? Mentally Bowie scoffed. He didn't believe in coincidence. But they could cut out his tongue and feed it to a coyote before he'd tell the deputy what he'd seen.

"Clark's passing—that was a tough time for ol' Jody," Gus was saying.

"Yeah."

"She ain't been the same since that boy died."

"And on top of that, that woman doctor moved into town and got the gossips all stirred up again."

The deputy stared into near space for a moment, sorrowfully shaking his head. "What possessed her to come to Eden Pass after what happened between her and Clark Tackett? I tell you, Hap, folks nowadays ain't worth shit. Don't care nothin' about nobody's feelings but their own."

"You're right, Gus." Hap sighed and slapped the deputy on the shoulder. "Say, when you get off duty, come have a beer on the house." Bowie was impressed by Hap's diplomacy as he steered the deputy out of the storeroom and through the empty bar, expounding as he went on the sad state of the world.

Bowie lay back down on the sleeping bag, stacked his hands behind his head, and stared up at the ceiling. Cobwebs formed an intricate canopy across the bare beams. As Bowie watched, an industrious spider added to it.

Momentarily Hap returned. Taking a seat on a case of Beefeater's, he lit a cigarette, then offered one to Bowie, who accepted and tipped his head forward as Hap lit it for him. They smoked in companionable silence. Finally Hap said, "Might ought to think about looking for another job."

Bowie propped himself up on one elbow. He wasn't surprised, but he wasn't going to take the news lying down—literally. "You firing me, Hap?"

"Not outright, no."

"I had nothing to do with that bitch."

"I know."

"Then why am I catching the flap? Who is she anyway?

You'd think by the way y'all talked about her that she's the Queen of Sheba."

Hap chuckled. "To her husband she is. Fergus Winston is superintendent of our school system. Owns a motel on the other end of town and does pretty good with it. He's 'bout twenty years older than Darcy. Ugly as a mud fence and not too bright. Folks figure she married him for his money. Who knows?" He shrugged philosophically.

"All I know is, anytime Darcy can shake Fergus, she's out here looking for action. Hot little piece," he added without rancor. "Had her myself a time or two. Years back when we were just kids." He pointed the lighted end of his cigarette toward Bowie. "If a thief did break into her bedroom last night, she might have shot him for *not* raping her."

Bowie shared a laugh with him, but the humor was short-lived. "Why are you letting me go, Hap?"

"For your own good."

"As long as I don't personally serve liquor, my parole officer said— "

"It's not that. You do the work I hired you for." He regarded Bowie through world-weary eyes. "I run a fairly clean place, but lots of lowlifes come through the door every night. Anything can happen and sometimes does. Take my advice and find a place to work where you ain't so likely to run into trouble. Understand?"

Bowie understood. It was the story of his life. He just seemed to attract trouble no matter what he did or didn't do; and an honest, hardworking sort like Hap Hollister didn't need a natural-born troublemaker working in his bar. Resignedly he said, "Employers ain't exactly lining up to offer jobs to ex-cons. Can you give me a few days?"

Hap nodded. "Until you find something else you can bunk here. Use my pickup to get around if you need to." Hap anchored his cigarette in the corner of his lips as he stood. "Well, I got a stack of bills to pay. Don't be in a hurry to get up. You had a short night."

Left alone, Bowie lay down again but knew he wouldn't go back to sleep. From the start he'd known that there was little future in working at The Palm, but the job had also provided lodging. He had thought—hoped—that it would be a temporary respite, like a halfway house between prison and life on the outside. But no. Thanks to a broad he didn't even know, and to some son of a bitch committing a B and E, he was back to square zero.

Where he'd been stuck all his life.

Chapter Three

*J*ody Tackett and her son gazed at each other across the distance that separated them. It was a gulf that hadn't been spanned in thirty-six years, and Key doubted it ever would be.

He forced a smile. "Hi, Jody." He'd stopped using any derivative of Mother years ago.

"Key." She turned a baleful gaze on Janellen. "I guess this is your doing."

Key placed his arm across his sister's shoulders. "Don't blame Janellen. Surprising y'all was my idea."

Jody Tackett harrumphed, her way of letting Key know that she knew he was lying. "Did I hear you say the coffee was ready?"

"Yes, Mama," Janellen replied eagerly. "I'll cook you and Key a big breakfast to celebrate his homecoming."

"I'm not so sure his homecoming is cause for celebration." Having said that, Jody turned and walked away.

Key let out a deep sigh. He hadn't expected a warm embrace, not even an obligatory hug. He and his mother had never shared that kind of affection. For as far back as he could remember, Jody had been unapproachable and inaccessible to him, and he'd taken his cues from her.

For years they had coexisted under an undeclared truce. When they were together, he was polite and expected the same courtesy to be extended to him. Sometimes it was, sometimes it wasn't. This morning she had been flagrantly hostile, even though he was her only living son.

Maybe that was why.

"Be patient with her, Key," Janellen pleaded. "She doesn't feel well."

"I see what you mean," he remarked thoughtfully. "When did she start looking so old?"

"It's been over a year, but she still hasn't fully recovered from . . . you know."

"Yeah." He paused. "I'll try not to upset her while I'm here." He looked at his sister and smiled wryly. "Is there a pair of crutches in the house?"

"Right where you left them after your car wreck." She went to the closet and retrieved a pair of aluminum crutches from the rear corner.

"While you're at it, get me a shirt, too," he told her. "Mine didn't make it home last night."

He ignored her inquisitive glance and pointed at the shirts hanging in the closet. She brought him a plain white cotton one that smelled faintly of mothballs. He put it on but left it unbuttoned. Securing the padded braces of the crutches in his armpits, he indicated the door with a motion of his head. "Let's go."

"You look pale. Are you feeling up to this?"

"No. But I sure as hell don't want to hold up Jody's breakfast."

She was already seated at the kitchen table sipping coffee and smoking a cigarette when Key hobbled in. Janellen went unnoticed as she began preparing the meal. Key sat across from his mother and propped his crutches against the edge of the table. He was keenly aware of his bearded face and mussed hair.

As always, Jody was perfectly neat, although she wasn't an attractive woman. The Texas sun had left her complexion spotted and lined. Having no tolerance for vanity, her only concession to softening her appearance was a light dusting of dime-store face powder. For all her adult life she had kept a standing weekly appointment at the beauty parlor to have her hair washed and set, but only because she couldn't be bothered to do it herself. It took twenty minutes for her short, gray hair to dry under the hood dryer. During that twenty minutes a manicurist clipped and buffed her short, square nails. She never had them polished.

She wore dresses only for church on Sundays and when a social occasion absolutely demanded it. This morning she was wearing a plaid cotton shirt and a pair of slacks, both crisply starched and ironed.

As she ground out her cigarette, she addressed Key in a tone as intimidating as her stare. "What'd you do this time?"

Her words were accusatory, clearly implying that Key was responsible for his misfortune. He was, but it wouldn't have mattered if he had been a victim of whimsical fate. Accidents had *always* been his fault.

When he'd fallen from the branches of the pecan tree that he and Clark had been climbing together, Jody had said that a broken collarbone was no better than he deserved for doing such a damn fool thing. When a Little League batter hit him in the temple with a bat, giving him a concussion, he'd been lectured for not keeping his mind on the game. When a gelding stepped on his foot, Jody had accused him of spooking the horse. When a firecracker exploded in his hand and busted open his thumb on the Fourth of July, he'd been punished. Clark had gotten off scot-free, although he'd been shooting off firecrackers alongside his brother.

But there was one time when Jody's wrath had been justified. If Key hadn't been so drunk, if he hadn't been driving ninety-five on that dark country road, he might have made that curve, missed that tree, and gone on to fulfill his mother's ambitions for him to be the starting quarterback on an NFL team. She would never forgive him for messing up her plans for his life.

Based on past experience, Key knew better than to expect maternal sympathy. But her judgmental tone of voice set his teeth on edge.

His reply was succinct. "I twisted my ankle."

"What about that?" she asked, raising her coffee cup toward the wide Ace bandage swathing his middle.

"Shark bite." He threw his sister a wink and a grin.

"Don't smart-mouth me!" Jody's voice cracked like a whip.

Here we go, Key thought dismally. Hell, he didn't want this. "It's nothing, Jody. Nothing." Janellen sat a cup of steaming coffee in front of him. "Thanks, sis. This is all for me."

"Don't you want anything to eat?"

"No, thanks. I'm not hungry."

She masked her disappointment behind a tentative smile that wrenched his heart. Poor Janellen. She had to put up with the old lady's crap every day. Jody had an uncanny talent for making every inquiry an inquisition, every observation a criticism, every glance a condemnation. How did Janellen endure her intolerance day in, day out? Why did she? Why didn't she find herself a respectable fellow and get married? So what if she wasn't madly in love with him? Nobody could be as difficult to live with as Jody.

Then again, Jody wasn't as critical of Janellen as she was of him. She hadn't been that way with Clark either. He seemed to be cursed with a talent for inciting his mother's anger. He figured it was because he was the spit and image of his father, and God knows Clark Junior had provoked Jody till the day he died. She hadn't shed a single tear at his funeral.

Key had. He had never cried before, or since, but he'd bawled like a baby at Clark Junior's grave, and not because his daddy had always been an attentive parent. Most of Key's recollections of him centered around farewells that had always left him feeling bereft. But whatever rare, happy memories of childhood Key had revolved around his daddy, who was boisterous and fun, who laughed and told jokes, who always drew a crowd of admirers with his glib charm.

Key was only nine years old when his father was killed, but with the inexplicable wisdom of a child, he'd realized that his best chance to be loved was being buried in that grave.

As though reading his mind, Jody suddenly asked, "Did you come home to watch me die?" Key looked at her sharply. "Because if you did," she added, "you're in for a big disappointment. I'm not going to die anytime soon."

Her expression was combative, but Key chose to treat the riling question as a joke. "Glad to hear that, Jody, 'cause my dark suit is at the cleaners. Actually, I came home to see how y'all are getting along."

"You've never given a damn how we were getting along before. Why now?"

The last thing Key felt like doing was tangling with his mother. He wasn't exactly in top physical form this morning, and Jody always disturbed his mental state. She was lethal to a sense of humor and an optimistic outlook. He'd wanted to make this reunion easy, if for no other reason than to please his long-suffering sister. Jody, however, seemed determined to make it difficult.

"I was born here," Key said evenly. "This is my home. Or it used to be. Aren't I welcome here anymore?"

"Of course you're welcome, Key," Janellen said urgently. "Mama, do you want bacon or sausage?"

"Whatever." Jody gestured irritably, as though brushing off a housefly. As she lit another cigarette, she asked Key, "Where've you been all this time?"

"Most recently Saudi Arabia." He sipped his coffee, recounting for Jody what he'd told Janellen earlier, omitting that it had been Janellen's request that had brought him home.

"I was flying wild well-control crews to and from a burning well. Hauled supplies every now and then, had a few medical emergencies. But they were finishing up there, and I didn't have another contract pending, so I thought I'd hang around here for a spell. You might find this hard to believe, but I started missing Eden Pass. I haven't been home in more than a year, not since Clark's funeral."

He sipped his coffee again. Several seconds passed before he realized that Janellen was staring at him like a nocturnal animal caught in a pair of headlights and that Jody was scowling.

Slowly he returned his coffee cup to the saucer. "What's the matter?"

"Nothing," Janellen said hastily. "Do you need a refill on coffee?"

"Yeah, but I'll get it. I think the bacon's burning." Smoke was rising from the frying pan.

Key hopped to the counter and poured himself a coffee refill. He needed another pain pill, but he'd left them upstairs in his bathroom. In spite of the doctor's orders, he'd washed down two of the tablets with a tumbler of whiskey before going to bed. That had gotten him through the night.

Now, the pain was back. He wished he had the gumption to take the bottle of brandy that Janellen used for baking from the pantry and lace his coffee with it. But that would only give Jody another reason to harp on him. For the time being, he'd have to live with the throbbing pain in his side and the heavy discomfort in his right ankle.

As cavalier as he'd been about his injuries, he winced involuntarily as he hopped back to his seat. "Are you going to tell us how you got so banged up?" Jody asked.

"No."

"I don't like being kept in the dark."

"Believe me, you don't want to know."

"I have little doubt of that," she remarked sourly. "It's just that I don't want to hear the sordid facts from somebody else."

"Don't worry about it. It's not your concern."

"It'll be my concern once it gets around town that on your first night home you wound up in the hospital."

"I didn't go to the hospital. I went to Doc Patton's place and found a lady doctor there who's pretty as a picture," he said with a wide grin. "She treated me."

Janellen dropped a metal spatula, which clattered onto the top of the cooking range. At first Key thought that hot bacon grease had popped out of the skillet and burned her hand. Then he noticed the hard, implacable expression on Jody's face and recognized it as fury. He'd seen it often enough to know it well.

"What's going on? How come y'all are looking at me like I just pissed on a grave?"

"You have." There was a low, wrathful hum behind Jody's words. "You've just pissed on your brother's grave."

"What the hell are you talking about?"

"Key— "

"The doctor," Jody said, angrily interrupting Janellen and banging her fist on the table. "Didn't you notice her name?"

Key thought back. He hadn't been so badly hurt that certain attributes had gone unnoticed—things like her expressive hazel eyes, her attractively disheveled hair, and her long, shapely legs. He'd even made a mental note of the color of her toenail polish and the fragrance she wore. He recalled these intimate details, but he didn't know her name. What could it matter to Jody and Janellen? Unless they were prejudiced against all women in the medical profession because of one.

As he considered that thought, he began to experience a sick gnawing in his gut. Jesus, it couldn't be. "What's her name?"

Jody only glared at him. He looked to Janellen for an answer. She was nervously wringing out a dry dish towel, misery etched on each feature of her face. "Lara Mallory is the name she goes by professionally," she whispered. "Her married name is— "

"Lara Porter," Key finished in a low, lifeless voice. Janellen nodded.

"Christ." He raised his fists to his eyes and mentally pictured the woman he'd met the night before. She didn't match the bimbo featured in all the tabloid photographs. None of her deft mannerisms or candid expressions corresponded with the mental images he'd painted of Lara Porter, the woman who'd been his brother's downfall, the woman who some political analysts hypothesized had changed the course of American history.

Finally Key lowered his hands and gave a helpless, apologetic shrug. "I had no way of knowing. She never gave me her name, and I didn't ask. I didn't recognize her from the pictures I'd seen. That all happened . . . what?—five, six years ago?"

He hated himself for babbling excuses, knowing full well that the damage had been done and that Jody wasn't going to forgive him no matter what he said now. So he took another tack and asked, "What the hell is Lara Porter doing in Eden Pass?"

"Does it matter?" Jody asked brusquely. "She's here. And you're to have nothing to do with her, understand? By the time I get finished with her, she'll tuck tail and slink out of town the same way she slunk in.

"Until that time, the Tacketts and anybody who wants to stay on speaking terms with us are to treat her with nothing except the contempt she deserves. That includes you. That *especially* includes you."

She jabbed her cigarette toward him to make her point. "Have all the sluts you want, Key, as I'm sure you will. But stay away from her."

Key immediately went on the defensive and raised his voice to match his mother's. "What are you yelling at me for? I wasn't caught humping her, Clark was."

Jody rose slowly to her feet and leaned on the table,

bearing down on her younger son over bottles of catsup and Tabasco sauce. "How dare you speak that way about him. Don't you have an ounce of decency, a smidgen of respect for your brother?"

"*Clark*," Key shouted, rising and squaring off against Jody across the table. "His name was Clark, and what kind of respect do you pay him by not even speaking his name out loud?"

"It hurts to talk about him, Key."

"Why?" He rounded on Janellen, who'd timidly made the comment.

"Well, because . . . because his death was so untimely. So tragic."

"Yes, it was. But it shouldn't cancel out his life." He turned back to Jody. "Before he died, Daddy saw to it that Clark and I shared some good times. He wanted us to be close in spite of you, and we were. God knows Clark and I were poles apart in everything, but he was my brother. I loved him. I mourned him when he died. But I refuse to pretend that he didn't exist just to spare your feelings."

"You aren't fit to speak your brother's name."

It hurt. Even now it cut him to the quick when she said things like that. She left him no recourse except to lash back. "If he was so bloody perfect, we wouldn't be having this conversation, Jody. There would never have been a Lara Porter in our lives. No bad press. No scandal. No shame. Clark would have remained the Golden Boy of Capitol Hill."

"Shut up!"

"Gladly." He shoved the crutches under his arms and headed for the back door.

"Key, where are you going?" Janellen asked in a panicked voice.

"I've got a doctor's appointment."

Defiantly he glared at Jody, then let the door slam behind him.

* * *

Lara had spent a restless night. Even under the best of circumstances she wasn't a sound sleeper. Frequently her sleep was interrupted by bad dreams and long intervals of wakefulness. She listened for cries that she would never hear again. Sorrow was the basis of her habitual insomnia.

Last night, meeting Key Tackett had made sleep particularly elusive. She had awakened with a dull headache. Encircling her eyes were dark rings, which cosmetics had helped to camouflage but hadn't eliminated. Two cups of strong black coffee had relieved the headache, but she couldn't cast off the disturbing thoughts about her late-night caller.

She hadn't believed it was possible for any other man to be as attractive as Clark Tackett, but Key was. The brothers were different types, certainly. Clark had had the spit-and-polish veneer of a Marine recruit. There was never a strand of his blond hair out of place. His impeccably tailored clothes were always well pressed; his shoes shone like mirrors. He had epitomized the clean-cut guy next door, the all-American boy whom any mother would love her daughter to bring home.

Key was the type from whom mothers hid their daughters. Although just as handsome as Clark, he was as dissimilar to his brother as a street thug to an Eagle Scout.

Key was a professional pilot. According to Clark, he flew a plane by instinct and put more faith in his own judgment and motor skills than he did in aeronautical instruments. He relied on technology only when given no other choice. Clark had boasted that there wasn't an aircraft made that his brother couldn't fly, but Key had opted to freelance rather than work for a commercial airline.

"Too many rules and regulations for him," Clark had said, smiling with indulgent affection for his younger brother. "Key likes answering to no one but himself."

Having met him and experienced firsthand the compelling allure of his mischievous smile, Lara couldn't imagine Key Tackett dressed in a spiffy captain's uniform, speaking to his passengers in a melodious voice about the weather conditions in their destination city.

Sitting in cockpits a great deal of the time had left him with attractive squint lines radiating from his eyes—eyes as blue as Clark's. But Clark had been blond and fair. Key's eyes were surrounded with thick, blunt, black eyelashes. He was definitely the black sheep of the family, even in physical terms. His hair was thick and dark and as undisciplined as he. Clark had never sported a five o'clock shadow. Key hadn't shaved for days. Oddly, the stubble had contributed to, not detracted from, his appeal.

The brothers were fine specimens of the human animal. Clark had been a domesticated pet. Key was still untamed. When angered—or aroused—Lara imagined he would growl.

"Good morning."

She jumped as though she'd been caught doing something she should feel guilty for. "Oh, good morning, Nancy. I didn't hear you come in."

"I'll say. You were a million miles away." The nurse/receptionist placed her handbag in the file case and put on a pastel lab coat. "What happened to the telephone in the examination room?" She had come in through the back door before joining Lara in a small alcove where they kept supplies, beverages, and snacks. The kitchen of the attached house remained for Lara's personal use.

"It was flimsy, so I decided to replace it."

Because she hadn't yet sorted out her feelings about Key Tackett's visit to the clinic, she wasn't ready to discuss it with Nancy. "Coffee?" She held up the carafe.

"Absolutely." The nurse added two teaspoons of sugar to the steaming mug Lara handed her. "Are there any doughnuts left?"

"In the cabinet. I thought you were dieting."

Nancy Baker found the doughnuts and demolished half of one with a single bite, then licked the sugar glaze off her fingers. "I gave up dieting," she said unapologetically. "I'm too busy to count calories. And if I dieted from now till doomsday, I'd never be a centerfold. Besides, Clem likes me this way. Says there's more to love."

Smiling, Lara asked, "How was your day off?"

"Well," Nancy replied, smacking her lips, "all things considered, it was okay. The dog's in heat, and Little Clem found a pair of his sister's tap shoes, put them on, and wore them all day long on the wrong feet. When we tried to take them off, he screamed bloody murder, so it was easier just to let him wear them and look goofy. Tapping feet I can live with, screaming I can't."

Nancy's stories about her chaotic household never failed to be entertaining. She complained good-naturedly about her hectic routine, which revolved around three active children, all of whom were going through a "stage," but Lara knew her nurse loved her husband and her children and wouldn't have traded places with anyone.

Nancy had responded to an ad Lara had placed in the local newspaper, and Lara had hired her after their first interview, partially because Nancy was her sole applicant. Nancy was well qualified, although she'd taken time off from nursing to have Little Clem two years ago.

"Now that it's time to potty train him," she'd told Lara, "I'd rather go back to work and let Granny Baker do the honors."

Lara had liked her instantly and was even a little jealous of her. She'd had chaos in her life, too, but it hadn't been the crazy, happy kind that Nancy experienced daily. It had been the life-altering kind, the kind that wounded and left deep scars. Her calamities had been irrevocable.

"If it weren't for Clem," Nancy was saying as she finished her second doughnut, "I'd have killed the dog, possibly the kids, too, and then pulled my hair out. But when he came home from work, he insisted we drop the kids at his mother's house and go to dinner by ourselves. We pigged out on Beltbusters and onion rings at the Dairy Queen. It was great.

"After Little Clem went to sleep, I hid the tap shoes in the top of the closet so he wouldn't be reminded of them today. This morning Big Clem dropped the dog off at the vet, where she'll either get laid or spayed. By the way, if they've got a willing sire available, do you want dibs on a puppy?"

"No, thanks," Lara said, laughing.

"Don't blame you. I'll probably be stuck with the whole damn litter." She washed her hands in the sink. "I'd better go check the appointment book to see who's coming in today."

Both knew that the appointment book wasn't filled. There were far more empty time slots than confirmed appointments. She had been in Eden Pass for six months but was still struggling to increase her practice. If she hadn't had a savings account to fall back on, she would have had to close the clinic long before now.

Greater than the financial considerations were the professional ones. She was a good doctor. She wanted to practice medicine . . . although she wouldn't necessarily have chosen to do so in Eden Pass.

Eden Pass had been chosen for her.

This practice had been a gift handed to her when she least expected it, though it facilitated a plan she'd been formulating for some time. She had needed a viable excuse to approach Key Tackett. When the opportunity to place herself in his path had presented itself, she had seized it. But not without acknowledging that being the only GP in a small town would be a difficult transition for her.

She had also known it would be an even greater adjustment for the townsfolk who were accustomed to Doc Patton and his small cluttered office in the clinic.

She had earned the diplomas now adorning the walls. The medical books on the shelves belonged to her. But the office still bore the former occupant's masculine imprint. As soon as it was economically feasible, she intended to paint the dark paneling and replace the leather maroon furniture with something brighter and more contemporary.

These planned changes would be only cosmetic. Changing the minds of people would take much more time and effort. Before his retirement, Dr. Stewart Patton had been a general practitioner in Eden Pass for more than forty years and in that time he had never made a single enemy. Since taking over his practice, Lara was frequently asked, "Where's Doc?" with the same suspicious inflection as Key Tackett had used when he posed the question to her last night, as though she had displaced the elderly doctor for self-gain.

Dr. Lara Mallory had a long way to go before earning the same level of confidence as Doc Patton had held with the people of Eden Pass. She knew she could never cultivate the affection of her patients that Doc Patton had enjoyed, because she was, after all, the scarlet woman who'd been involved with Clark Tackett. Everyone in his hometown knew her as such. That's why her arrival had taken them by surprise. Lara had wishfully reasoned that once they recovered from the initial shock and realized that she was a qualified physician, they would forget the scandal.

Unfortunately, she had underestimated Jody Tackett's staggering influence over the community. Although they'd never met face to face, Clark's mother was crippling her attempts to succeed.

One afternoon when she was feeling particularly despondent, she'd brought it up with Nancy. "I guess it's no mystery why people in Eden Pass are willing to drive twenty miles to the next town to see a doctor."

"Course not," Nancy said. "Jody Tackett has put out

the word that anybody who comes near this office, no matter how sick, will be on her shit list."

"Because of Clark?"

"Hmm. Everyone in town knows the scintillating details of y'all's affair. It had almost been laid to rest when Clark died. Then you showed up a few months afterward. Jody got pissed and set her mind to making you an outcast."

"Then why are you willing to work for me?"

Nancy took a deep breath. "My daddy was a pumper for Tackett Oil and Gas for twenty-five years. This was years ago, when Clark Senior was still head honcho." She paused. "You know that Clark—your Clark—was a third-generation Clark Tackett, don't you? His granddaddy was Clark Senior and his daddy Clark Junior."

"Yes. He told me."

"Okay, so anyway," Nancy resumed, "there was an accident at one of the wells and my daddy was killed."

"Did the Tacketts admit culpability?"

"They did what they had to do to cover themselves legally. Mama got all the insurance money she was entitled to. But none of them came to the funeral. Nobody called. They had the flower shop deliver a big spray of chrysanthemums to the church, but none of them saw fit to visit my mama.

"I was just a kid at the time, but I thought then, and still think, that it was rotten of them to be so standoffish. True, Daddy's death didn't make a ripple in one barrel of their filthy oil, but he was a loyal, hardworking employee. Since then I've had a low opinion of all the Tacketts, but particularly of Jody."

"Why particularly of Jody?"

"Because she only married Clark Junior to get her greedy hands on Tackett Oil." Nancy inched forward in her chair. "See, Clark Senior was a wildcatter at the height of the boom. He struck oil the first time he drilled and made a shitload of money virtually overnight, then kept right on making it. Clark Junior came along.

His main ambition in life was to have a good time and spend as much of his daddy's money as he could, mostly on gambling, whiskey, and women."

She sighed reminiscently. "He was the best-looking man I ever laid eyes on. Women from all over mourned his passing. But Jody sure as hell didn't. When he died she got what she'd wanted all along."

"Tackett Oil?"

"Total control. The old man was already dead. When Clark Junior slid off that icy mountain—in the Himalayas, I think it was—and broke his neck, Jody rolled up her shirtsleeves and went to work."

Nancy needed no encouragement to talk.

"She's tough as boot leather. Came from a poor farming family. Their house got blown down by a tornado. They all got killed except her. A widow lady took her in and finished raising her.

"Jody was as smart as they come and got a scholarship to Texas Tech. Straight out of college she went to work for Clark Senior. She was a land man and acquired some of his best leases even after everybody thought all the oil in East Texas was spoken for. The old man liked her. Jody was everything that Clark Junior wasn't—responsible, ambitious, driven. I think Clark Senior was the one behind the marriage."

"What do you mean?"

"The story is that Clark Junior had knocked up a debutante from Fort Worth. Her daddy had mob connections and, for all his money and social standing, was nothing but a glorified pimp. Clark Senior wanted no part of that, so he rushed Clark Junior into marriage with Jody.

"I don't know if that's true, but it's possible. Clark Junior loved to party. He could have had his pick from hundreds of women. Why would he agree to saddle himself with Jody if not to get out of a scrape with a mobster?

"Anyhow, they got married. Clark the Third didn't come along for years. The nastier gossips said it took

Clark Junior that long to work up a hard-on for Jody, who never was a beauty. In fact, she goes out of her way to be plain. I guess she thinks that brains and beauty cancel out each other."

"Didn't she mind Clark Junior's womanizing?"

Nancy shrugged. "If she did, she didn't let on. She ignored his philandering and concentrated on running the business. I guess she didn't care about him nearly as much as she did the price of crude. Left to him, he probably would have bankrupted Tackett Oil. Not Jody. She's prospered when others have fallen by the wayside. She's a ruthless businesswoman."

"I'm getting a taste of her ruthlessness," Lara said quietly.

"Well, you have to understand where she's coming from about that." Nancy leaned forward and lowered her voice, although there was no one around to overhear them. "The only thing Jody loved better than Tackett Oil was her boy, Clark. She thought the sun rose and set in him. I guess he never crossed her. Anyway, she had his future all mapped out, including a stint in the White House. She blames you for destroying that dream."

"She and everyone else."

After a reflective moment, Nancy said, "Be careful, Dr. Mallory. Jody has money and power and an ax to grind. That makes her dangerous." She patted Lara's hand. "Personally, I'm rooting for anyone outside her favor."

Nancy was in the minority. In the months since that conversation, there'd been no discernible increase in the number of patients who came to the clinic. Only a few people in Eden Pass had risked Jody's disfavor by seeking Lara's professional services. Ironically, one of them was Jody's own son.

Surely by now Key Tackett had discovered his blunder. Her name had probably ricocheted off the walls of the Tacketts' house with the ferocity of a racquetball.

Let them curse her. She had come to Eden Pass with a specific goal in mind, and it wasn't to win the Tacketts' regard. She wanted something, but it wasn't approval.

When it came time for her to demand of them what they owed her, she didn't care if they liked her or not.

Relatively speaking, this was a busy morning. She was scheduled to see five patients before noon. Her first was an elderly woman who rattled off a litany of complaints. Upon examining her, Lara discovered she was as healthy as a horse, if a bit lonely. She prescribed some pills—which were really multivitamin tablets—and told the woman about the fun exercise classes at the Methodist Church.

Nancy ushered in the next patient, a cantankerous three-year-old boy with an earache and a fever of one hundred two. Lara was getting the specifics of his illness from his frazzled mother when she heard a commotion coming from the reception area at the front of the building. Returning the squalling three-year-old to the arms of his mother, she excused herself and stepped into the hallway.

"Nancy, what's going on?" she called out.

It wasn't her receptionist who came crashing through the connecting door, but Key Tackett. His crutches didn't slow him down as he stormed toward her. Clearly he was furious.

Even though he came to within inches of her before stopping, Lara held her ground. "Your appointment isn't until this afternoon, Mr. Tackett."

The mother had followed Lara into the hallway and was standing behind her. The child's wailing had risen to a deafening level. Nancy had come up behind Key, looking ready to do battle in Lara's defense. She and Key were between them, but only Lara felt trapped.

"Why didn't you tell me last night who you were?"

Ignoring his question, she said, "As you can see, I'm

very busy this morning. I have patients waiting. If there's something you wish to discuss with me, please make an appointment with my receptionist."

"I've got something to discuss with you, all right." A bead of sweat rolled down his temple. Most of the color had been leeched from his face. Both were manifestations of pain.

"I think you should sit down, Mr. Tackett. You're in a weakened state, certainly in no condition to— "

"Cut the medical bullshit," he shouted. "Why didn't you tell me last night that you're the whore who ruined my brother's life?"

Chapter Four

*T*he ugly words struck like blows. Feeling light-headed, Lara took a deep breath and held it. The floor and walls of the corridor seemed to tilt precariously. She reached out and braced herself against the wainscoting.

Nancy elbowed her way past Key. "Now see here, Key Tackett, you can't barge into a doctor's office and create a ruckus like this."

"I'd love to chat with you, Nancy, and reminisce about old times, but I'm here to see the doctor." He spoke the last word like an epithet.

By now Lara had regained some composure. She motioned Nancy toward the mother and crying child. "Please see to Mrs. Adams and Stevie. I'll be with them as soon as possible."

Nancy was reluctant to comply, but after giving Key a threatening look, she shooed the woman and child back into the examination room and soundly closed the door behind them.

Lara stepped around Key and addressed the curious patients who were huddled in the doorway, peering down the hall. "Please take your seats," Lara said in as calm a voice as she could muster. "We've had a slight disruption in our office procedure. As you can see, Mr. Tackett is hurt and needs immediate medical attention, but he'll be taken care of and on his way shortly."

"Don't bet on it."

The waiting patients heard him and regarded her uncertainly. "I'll be with you as soon as I can," she reassured them. Then, confronting Key, she said, "I'll see you in my office."

The moment she closed her office door behind them, she vented her anger. "How dare you speak to me like that in front of an office full of patients! I ought to have you arrested."

"That scene could have been avoided," he said, motioning toward the hallway with his head, "if you'd told me who you were last night."

"You didn't ask for my name, and I didn't learn yours until seconds before you left."

"Well, you know it now."

"Yes, I know it now, and I'm not at all surprised to discover that you're a Tackett. Arrogance is a family trait."

"This isn't about the Tacketts. This is about you. What the hell are you doing in our town?"

"*Your* town? That's a curious choice of words for someone who spends very little time residing here. Clark told me that you're rarely in Eden Pass. To what do we owe the honor of this visit?"

He came a menacing step closer. "I told you before to cut the bullshit. I didn't come here to play word games with you, Doc, so don't try to divert me from the point."

"Which is?"

"What the hell you're doing here!" he shouted.

Suddenly the door swung open and Nancy poked her head around. "Dr. Mallory? Want me to . . . do something?"

He didn't move a muscle, didn't indicate in any way that he had even heard her or noticed the interruption.

Subconsciously Lara had been preparing herself for this clash, so she wasn't that surprised at his angry appearance. Since it seemed inevitable that they have a showdown, she decided just to get it over with.

She glanced at the nurse. "No, thank you, Nancy. Try

to keep the patients pacified until I can get to them."
Then, looking up into Key's enraged face, she added,
"I'll try to keep Mr. Tackett's unreasonable temper under
control."

Nancy obviously had misgivings about Lara's decision,
but she left them alone. Lara gestured toward a chair.
"Please sit down, Mr. Tackett. You're ashen."

"I'm fine."

"Hardly. You're swaying."

"I said I'm fine," he repeated testily, raising his voice
again.

"All right, have it your way. But I don't think either
of us wants repeated what we say to each other. Will you
kindly keep your voice lowered?"

Leaning on his crutches, he bent forward until his face
was within inches of hers. "You don't want what we say
repeated because you're afraid that the few people who
don't already know will find out that your husband caught
you butt naked in the sack with my brother."

She had heard the accusation many times before, and
there seemed to be no antidote for its vicious sting. Time
hadn't diminished its effect.

Turning her back to him, she moved to the window,
which offered a view of the gravel parking lot. One of
the patients who'd been waiting in the reception area
was getting into her car. She couldn't have looked more
sheepish if she were leaving an adult bookstore with a
brown paper bag full of dirty magazines. Her retreating
car raised a cloud of dust.

Watching her had given Lara time to form a response.
"I'm trying very hard to put the incident with your brother
behind me and get on with my life."

She turned to face him again and felt much more
comfortable with space between them, although, even
from a distance, his presence was potent. He still hadn't
shaved and he looked more disreputable than he had the
night before. Most disquieting was the raw sexuality he

emanated. She sensed it. Keenly. Doing so seemed to give credence to his low opinion of her, and that bothered her tremendously.

Lowering her gaze, she said, "Don't I deserve a second chance, Mr. Tackett? It happened a long time ago."

"I know how long it's been. Five years. Everybody in the nation knows exactly when it happened, because the morning you were caught in bed with my brother marked the beginning of the end for him. His life was never the same."

"Neither was mine!"

"I guess not," he snorted sarcastically. "Not after you became the nation's most celebrated femme fatale."

"I didn't want to be."

"You should have thought of that before you sneaked into Clark's bedroom. Jesus," he said, shaking his head in bafflement. "Didn't you have any better sense than to commit adultery while your husband was sleeping in the room down the hall?"

Learning to conceal her emotions had become a matter of survival. At the height of the scandal, she had developed a means of stiffly setting the features of her face so they would reveal nothing of what she was thinking or feeling. She resorted to the technique now. To keep her voice from betraying her, she said nothing.

"Some of the details are a little hazy," he said. "Clear them up for me."

"I don't choose to discuss it with you. Besides, I've got patients."

"*I'm* a patient, remember?" He propped his crutches against the edge of her desk and, using it for support, hopped on his left foot toward her. "Give me your full treatment."

The innuendo wasn't accidental. His wicked grin reinforced it. Lara didn't respond, at least not visibly.

"Come on, Doc. Fill in the blanks. Clark had hosted a dinner party the night before, right?"

Lara remained stubbornly silent.

"I've got all day," he warned softly. "Not a damn thing to do but stay off my ankle. I can do that someplace else, or I can do it right here. Makes no difference to me."

Calling the sheriff and having him physically removed was a possibility, but he'd already told her that Sheriff Baxter was an old family friend. Involving him would only create more of an incident than this already was. What was the point of prolonging the situation except to save face? That had been sacrificed years ago. Since, she'd become a pro at swallowing pride.

"Clark had invited a group of people out from Washington to spend an evening in the country," she told him. "Randall and I were among those guests."

"It wasn't the first time you'd been to Clark's cottage in Virginia, was it?"

"No."

"You were familiar with the house."

"Yes."

"In fact, because Clark was a bachelor, you'd served as his official hostess lots of times."

"I had helped him organize several dinner parties."

"And that sort of put you two together."

"Naturally, we had to plan menus— "

"Oh, naturally."

"Clark was a public official. Even casual gatherings involved planning and preparation."

"Have I disputed anything?"

His condescension was as infuriating as his angry accusations. Lara suddenly realized that her hands had clenched into tight fists. She willed them to relax.

"Arranging all these dinner parties," he continued, "planning and preparing and such, must have taken up a lot of your time."

"I enjoyed it. It was a welcome break from my duties at the hospital."

"Uh-huh. So while you two—you and Clark—had your

heads together making all these plans, you became very, uh, close."

"Yes," she answered softly. "Your brother was a charismatic man. He had a magnetic personality. I don't believe I've ever met anyone who could match his energy, his verve. He appeared to be in motion even when standing still. He got excited about things and had such high ideals, such ambitious goals not only for himself but for the nation. It was no mystery to me why the voters of Texas elected him to Congress."

"Fresh out of law school," he told her, although she already knew that. "He served only one term in the House of Representatives before deciding to try for the Senate. Beat the incumbent by a landslide."

"Your brother was a man of vision. I could listen to him talk for hours on any subject. His enthusiasm and conviction were contagious."

"Sounds like love."

"I've admitted that we were very close."

"But you were married."

"Actually, Clark and Randall were friends before I ever met him. Randall introduced us."

"Ahh." He held up his index finger. "Enter the husband. The poor cuckold. What a cliché. Always the last to know that his wife is screwing around. And with his best friend to boot. Didn't ol' Randall become suspicious when you insisted on spending that night in Virginia instead of returning to Washington with the other guests?"

"It was Clark's idea. He and Randall were scheduled to play golf the following day. It would have been ludicrous to drive back to D.C., then return early the next morning. Randall saw the logic."

"That must have been real convenient for you, Doc. I mean, to have your husband accommodate you like that. Did you also fuck him that night just to throw him off track?"

She slapped him, hard. The slap startled her as much

as it did Key. In her entire life she'd never struck anyone.
She wouldn't have thought she was capable of it.

Learning to control herself had been a critical part of
her upbringing. Giving over to one's emotions had been
unthinkable in her parents' house. Crying jags, uproarious
laughter, any form of unbridled emotional expression was
considered unacceptable behavior. That ability to detach
herself had served her well in Washington.

She didn't know how Key had managed to breach her
conditioned restraint, but he had. If the palm of her hand
hadn't been smarting so badly, she wouldn't have believed
she'd really slapped him.

Faster than her thoughts could register this, he encircled her wrist, drew her against him, and pushed her
arm up behind her back. "Don't ever do that again."
The words were precisely enunciated through straight,
thin lips that barely moved. His eyes were as direct and
brilliant as laser beams.

"You can't talk to me like that."

"Oh yeah? Why not?"

"You haven't got the right to judge me."

"The hell I don't. In some parts of the world they still
stone women for being unfaithful to their husbands."

"Would it have evened the score for you if I'd been
stoned? Believe me, being brutalized by the media is just
as deadly." The hand within his grip was becoming numb.
She flexed her fingers. "You're hurting me."

Slowly he released her and took a step back. "Reflexes."

That was as close as she was going to get to an apology.
Strange under the circumstances, but she thought he
sincerely regretted hurting her.

He winced and pressed his hand against his side.

"Are you in pain?"

"It's nothing."

"Do you want something?"

"No."

As a physician, her instinct was to reach out and lay her

hands on him, render assistance. But she didn't. For one thing, he would shun her concern. But primarily she was apprehensive about touching him for any reason. Only now that the contact had been broken did she realize how closely he'd held her against him.

As she massaged circulation back into her hand, she tried to make a joke of it, as much to reassure herself as him. "I don't ordinarily slap my patients."

The attempted levity didn't work. He didn't even smile. Indeed, he was single-mindedly scrutinizing her face. "I didn't recognize you last night from the pictures I'd seen," he said. "You look different now."

"I've aged five years."

He shook his head. "It's more than that. Your hair's different."

She touched her hair self-consciously. "I don't lighten it anymore. Randall liked my hair lighter."

"Back to the husband. Poor Randall. Guess he felt like the rug had been yanked out from under him, huh? Wonder why he stayed with you?" His voice had regained the underpinnings of sarcasm.

"I mean there you were, Randall Porter's lawfully wed-ded wife, featured on the cover of the *National Enquirer*, being exposed as Senator Clark Tackett's married lover. The photos showed Randall hustling you away from the cottage, wrapped up in your nightie."

"You don't need to reacquaint me with the reports. I remember them well."

"And what does Randall do?" he asked as though she hadn't spoken. "He's with the State Department, right? A diplomat. He's supposed to have a way with words, a glib answer for everything. But does he deny the allegations? No. Does he step forward and defend your honor? No. Does he renounce you as a cheating slut? No. Does he proclaim that you've realized the error of your ways and become a born-again Christian? No."

He planted his hands on his knees and leaned forward.

"Randall makes like a goddamn clam. Says nothing for the record before hightailing it off to that banana republic and hauling you with him. 'No comment' was all the media ever prized out of him."

He shrugged ruefully. "But then I guess there's not much you can say when your wife is caught screwing your best friend right under your nose and their affair becomes a political incident of national importance."

"I guess not." She was determined not to lose control again, no matter how provocative he became.

"Even though Randall died a martyr's death in service to his country, if you ask me, he was a coward."

"Well, I didn't ask you, Mr. Tackett. Furthermore, I refuse to discuss my late husband and our personal life with you. But while we're on the subject of cowardice, what about your brother's? He didn't go on the record with a denial or defend my honor, either." Like her husband, Clark had failed to make a statement of apology or explanation. He'd forsaken her to confront the disgrace alone. Their combined silence was as good as an indictment and had been the most humiliating indignity she'd had to bear, both publicly and privately.

"The jig was up. What could he do?"

"Oh, he did plenty. Do you really believe that Randall was assigned to Montesangre on a whim?"

"I never thought about it."

"Well think about it now. That country is a hellhole," she said emphatically. "A cesspool. An ugly, dirty, corrupt little republic. Politically speaking, it was a powder keg of violence ready to explode.

"Randall didn't choose to go there, Mr. Tackett. He didn't ask for the assignment. Your brother saw to it that we were sent," she said disdainfully. "His way of dealing with the scandal wasn't to confront it but to sweep it under the rug."

"How'd he manage that? Thanks to you, no one wanted

to know him. His friends turned out to be the fair weather variety."

"But several people over at State owed Clark favors. He called them in, and—presto!—Randall was assigned to the most potentially dangerous area in the world at that time.

"Do you know the Bible story of David and Bathsheba?" Giving him no time to answer, she explained. "King David sent Bathsheba's husband to the front lines of battle, virtually guaranteeing that he would be killed. And he was."

"But that's where your parallel ends," he said, sliding off the edge of the desk and moving to stand directly in front of her again. "King David kept Bathsheba with him. Doesn't speak very well of you, does it?" he asked with a sneer. "Clark didn't value you enough to keep you around. You must have been a lousy mistress."

Spots of fiery indignation appeared on her cheeks. "Following the scandal, Clark and I had no future together."

"He had no future, period. You cost him his career in politics. He didn't even embarrass his political party by running again. He knew that Americans had had their fill of statesmen getting caught in compromising positions with bimbos."

"I am not a bimbo."

"Exception noted. You can probably type," he said caustically. "The point is that until you came along, my brother was Washington's golden boy. After that morning in Virginia, he became a pariah on Capitol Hill."

"Don't cry 'Poor Clark' to me! Your brother knew the potential consequences of his actions."

"And was willing to take the risks, is that it?"

"Precisely."

"Just what is it you do in bed that's so damn great it can separate a man from his better judgment?"

"I won't even honor that with a response," she shot

back angrily. "Do you think Clark was the only one to suffer consequences?" She splayed her hand over her chest. "I suffered losses too. My career, for instance, which was as important to me as Clark's was to him."

"You left the country."

"What did it matter? Even if I hadn't gone to Montesangre with Randall, I never would have had an opportunity to practice medicine in and around Washington. I'd still be struggling to practice anywhere if Clark's guilt hadn't compelled him to buy me this place."

"What?" His head snapped back.

Lara sucked in a sharp little breath. Her lips parted in amazement. She could tell that his stunned expression was authentic. "You didn't know?"

His eyebrows came together in a steep frown above the bridge of his nose.

"I can't believe it," she murmured. Carefully gauging his reaction, she said, "Clark bought this place from Dr. Patton when he retired, then deeded it over to me."

He stared at her for several ponderous moments, his gaze so intense it was difficult for her to meet it, but she did so unflinchingly. Confusion and suspicion warred within his eyes. "You're lying."

"You don't have to take my word for it. It's a matter of public record."

"I was there when Clark's will was read. There was no mention of you. I would have remembered."

"He arranged it that way. Ask your sister. Ask your mother. She's repeatedly threatened to contest the legality of my ownership, but Clark saw to it that it's ironclad." She drew herself up straight and tall. Key's ignorance of this one fact had given her a distinct edge.

"I didn't learn about it myself until after his death. His attorney notified me. I was dumbfounded and thought there had to be some mistake because Clark and I had had no contact whatsoever since the scandal."

"You expect me to believe that?"

"I don't give a damn whether you believe it or not," she snapped.

"So, out of the blue, my brother buys a piece of property worth . . . what? A couple hundred grand? And gives it to you." He made a scoffing sound. "Bullshit. You must have put him up to it."

"I tell you, I hadn't seen or spoken to him in years," she insisted. "I didn't want to. Why would I want to see the man who had let me take the fall for a public scandal, who'd exiled me to that godforsaken place, who'd been indirectly responsible for the death of my—" She broke off.

"Your husband?" Key smiled slyly. "Ah, how soon they forget."

"No, Mr. Tackett, my daughter." She turned away only long enough to lift a picture frame from her desk. Holding it at arm's length, she thrust it at him so that he was nose to nose with the face in the photograph.

"Meet Ashley. My baby. My beautiful baby girl. She was also killed in Montesangre. Or, as you so eloquently put it, she died a martyr's death in service to her country." Tears filled Lara's eyes, blurring her image of Key. Then her arms sprang back with the impetus of pistons, and she clutched the picture frame to her chest.

Key muttered an expletive. After a long moment he said, "I'm sorry about your kid. I was in France at the time and read about it in an English newspaper. I also remember reading that Clark attended the memorial service for Porter and your daughter."

"Yes, Clark attended, but I wasn't there. I was still in the hospital in Miami, recovering from my injuries." Wearily she brushed back a loose strand of hair and returned the frame to her desk. "Your brother made no effort to contact me, and I was relieved. For his part in banishing us to Montesangre, I think I could have killed him if I'd seen him then."

"You didn't resent him to the point of rejecting his bequeathal."

"No, I didn't. Because of my notoriety, I was turned down for job after job. In all the years since my recovery, I wasn't able to hold a position for very long—only until the hospital bigwigs linked Dr. Lara Mallory to Lara Porter. It didn't matter how capably I fulfilled my duties, I was invited to leave.

"Clark must have known that and obviously felt that he owed me something for all that I'd lost. He tried to secure my professional future. Otherwise, why would he buy this facility for me, completely furnished, ready to occupy if I chose to?"

Speculatively she tilted her head to one side. "It's curious that he drowned only days after adding that codicil to his will."

His reaction was fiercely defensive. She could see that even before he spoke. "What the hell are you suggesting with that remark?"

"Surely the rumors regarding Clark's drowning death reached you. There's speculation that it wasn't an accident at all, but a suicide."

"You're full of shit," he said, his lip curling. "And so is anybody who gave that rumor a second's thought. Clark took the boat into the lake to fish. Knowing him, he was too damned hardheaded to keep his life vest on. I wouldn't have been wearing one of the damned things either."

"Clark was a strong swimmer. He could have saved himself."

"Ordinarily," he said curtly. "Something must have happened."

"Like what? There was no storm that day, no evidence of trouble with the outboard motor. The boat didn't capsize. What do you think happened?"

He worked his inner cheek between his teeth but didn't come up with an answer. "All I know is that my brother wouldn't have taken his own life. And whatever reasons he had for giving you this place, he took to the grave."

"His reasons don't really matter, do they? I'm here."

"Which brings me back to my original question. Why would you want to come here? Clark was Eden Pass's favorite son. You're considered nothing but a whore who destroyed his political future. My mother will see to it that no one forgets that."

Considering the angry mood of the moment, this wasn't the time to divulge her real reason for coming to Eden Pass. That could wait until their mutual hostility eased—if that was possible. It was safer now to address his last statement.

"I'm sure she'll try."

"Is this place," he said, indicating the office with a sweep of his hand, "worth the grief? And believe me, Jody can dish it out."

"I want to practice medicine, Mr. Tackett. I'm a good doctor. All I ask is to be allowed to run my medical practice without interference."

"Well, it isn't going to be easy," he said slowly. "In fact, I think your life here in Eden Pass will make Hell pale by comparison."

"Should I take that as a threat?"

"Just stating the facts, Doc. Nobody in Eden Pass will dare offend Jody by becoming your patient. You can count on that. Too many families depend on Tackett Oil for their livelihoods. They'll drive forty miles for an aspirin before they'll darken your door."

He grinned. "It's going to be amusing to sit back and watch how long it takes you to fold up and go back where you came from. Before it's all over, there'll be fireworks. Guess you should be thanked for relieving the boredom around here." He slipped his crutches under his arms and limped toward the door.

Turning back, he gave her a slow, insulting once-over. "Clark was a damn fool to throw everything away for a woman. All I can figure is that you must be really hot in the sack. But is a roll with you worth losing all he lost? I seriously doubt it." His eyes moved down her body. "You're not even that good-looking."

He left the door open behind him, a clear indication of his contempt. Lara waited until she heard him leave through the front door, then sat down behind her desk. Her knees felt rubbery. Placing her elbows on the top of her desk, she rested her forehead on the heels of her hands. They were cold and clammy, yet her face and chest were emanating fiery heat.

Lowering her hands, she gazed at Ashley's photograph. Smiling sadly, she reached out to stroke her daughter's chubby cheek, but touched only cool, unyielding glass. From that drooling smile, those laughing eyes, Lara fed her resolve. Until she had from them what she wanted, she could and would withstand any hardship the Tacketts might impose.

Nancy came rushing in. "Dr. Mallory, are you all right?"

"I don't recommend a daily dose of him," Lara replied, forcing a smile. "But, yes, I'm fine."

The nurse disappeared and returned seconds later with a glass of ice water. "Drink this. Probably ought to be something stronger. Key has a knack for turning people inside out."

"Thank you." Lara drank greedily. "Just so you'll know, Nancy, he was here last night. He had sprained his ankle and came here expecting to find Dr. Patton." To protect Key's privacy and her own culpability, she didn't tell her nurse about the gunshot wound she had declined to report to the authorities.

Without being invited, Nancy plopped down in the chair facing Lara's desk. "Key Tackett always has been meaner than sin. I remember he once brought a live rattler to school in a toe-sack and terrorized all us girls with it. God knows how he kept from being bit himself. I guess that snake had better sense than to tangle with him.

"He's drop-dead gorgeous, but I'm sure he knows it. Those blue eyes and lazy smile have admitted him to many a set of parted thighs. I'm sure he's good at it, too. God knows he's had plenty of practice. Scores of women would line up to prove me right, but personally I've always thought he was a prize asshole."

Forcing a professional-looking smile to her lips, Lara said, "Give me a few minutes, please. I need to collect my thoughts and freshen up, then I'll resume seeing the patients."

"Dr. Mallory," Nancy said kindly, "one by one your patients suddenly remembered 'important' things they had to do." Dropping the formality, she sympathetically added, "Honey, there's not a soul waiting out there to see you."

Chapter Five

*J*anellen was seated behind her desk in the business office of Tackett Oil and Gas Company. The square brick building had been designed by men, built by men, and furnished for men back in Clark Senior's heyday. Jody hadn't given a flip about decor. Most of the men who worked for Tackett Oil had been employees for years and they were accustomed to the office, comfortable with it. So even though Janellen spent more time there than anyone else, it never occurred to her to renovate or otherwise enhance the appearance of the office merely to please herself.

The only personal touch she had added was an ivy plant that she'd potted in a clay container shaped like a bunny. It was crouched on the corner of her desk, partially hidden by correspondence, invoices, and other paperwork.

Managing the office with unstinting efficiency was a matter of pride for Janellen. She opened it every weekday morning at nine sharp, checked the answering machine for messages and the FAX machine for overnight transmissions, then consulted the large calendar on which she jotted down notes to herself ranging from "call church re: altar flowers"—to commemorate her late father's birthday—to "dentist appointment in Longview."

This morning, however, she was preoccupied with her mother's health and the pervasive antagonism between Jody and Key. They hadn't raised their voices to each other since the morning following Key's unexpected homecoming, but the atmosphere crackled with hostile static whenever they were in the same room.

Janellen did her best to act as a buffer but was largely unsuccessful. Through Eden Pass's active grapevine, Jody had heard about Key's return visit to Dr. Lara Mallory's office. She accused him of flagrantly disobeying her; he reminded her that he was no longer a kid who needed to be told what to do and what not to do. She said he'd made an ass of himself; he said he'd learned to do that by example.

And so it went.

Mealtimes were torturous. The burden of carrying on a conversation fell to Janellen, and it was an exhausting challenge. Jody never had been an avid conversationalist at the dining table and was even less so now.

To his credit, Key made an effort. He regaled them with anecdotes of his adventures. Jody didn't think his stories were funny. She shot down all his attempts at humor and consistently turned the topic back to Dr. Mallory, which never failed to inflame Key's short temper. As soon as he finished eating, he invented an excuse to leave the house. Janellen knew he went out drinking because he rarely returned until the wee hours of the morning, and his tread on the stairs was usually unsteady.

He probably was womanizing, too, but the town grapevine was stumped when it came to who might be receiving his favors.

He'd been home a week, but his return had fallen far short of Janellen's expectations. Instead of brightening Jody's outlook, Key's presence in the house had only made her more short-tempered. Which was puzzling. When he was away, Jody fretted over not hearing from him and worried for his safety. She was never demonstrative, but Janellen had seen the relief that registered in her face whenever they received a card from him letting them know that he was all right.

Now that he was home, nothing he did pleased her.

If he was taciturn, she rebuked him. If he attempted conciliation, she rebuffed him. She took issue with the slightest provocation, and, Janellen conceded, her brother could be provoking. Like oil and water, his moods never seemed to mix with Jody's.

Things had really turned nasty the evening he'd confronted her about the codicil to Clark's will. "Why wasn't I informed that he'd bought and deeded that property to Lara Mallory?"

"Because it was none of your business," Jody retorted. What Clark had done was incomprehensible, especially to his mother. Janellen knew she had agonized over it. She wished Key had never learned of it. Barring that, she wished he'd never raised the subject with Jody.

"None of my business?" he repeated incredulously. "Don't you think such a stupid decision on his part should have been brought to my attention? It affects all of us."

"I don't know Clark's reasons for doing what he did," Jody shouted. "But I won't have you, of all people, calling your brother stupid."

"I didn't. I said his decision was stupid."

"Same difference."

Their heated argument had lasted for half an hour and only left Key furious and Jody's blood pressure skyrocketing. No one would ever know what had prompted Clark to do what he'd done. Janellen thought it futile to surmise his motivations. What she knew for certain was that her older brother would have been greatly distressed by the friction he'd unwittingly caused. Their home was a gloomy, antagonistic environment that Janellen wished desperately and vainly to change.

"Ma'am?"

Janellen had been so lost in thought that she jumped at the unexpected sound of a man's voice. He was standing just inside the doorway, backlighted by the sun, his face in shadow.

Embarrassed at being caught daydreaming, she surged to her feet and ran a self-conscious hand down the placket of her blouse. "I'm sorry. Can I help you?"

"Maybe. I hope."

He removed a straw cowboy hat and ambled closer to her desk. His legs were slightly bowed. He was much shorter than Key, not even six feet would be her guess. He wasn't muscle-bound but seemed tough, strong, and wiry. His clothes were clean and appeared new.

"I'm looking for work, ma'am. Wondered if y'all had any openings."

"I'm sorry, we don't at present, Mr . . .?"

"Cato, ma'am. Bowie Cato."

"Pleased to meet you, Mr. Cato. I'm Janellen Tackett. What kind of job are you looking for? If you're new to Eden Pass, I might be able to refer you to another oil company."

"Thank you kindly for offering, but it wouldn't do any good. I've already asked around. Saved the best till last, you might say," he added with a fleeting grin. "Seems nobody's hiring."

She smiled sympathetically. "I'm afraid that's all too true, Mr. Cato. The economy in East Texas is tight, especially in the oil industry. Practically nobody's drilling. Of course, a lot of existing wells are still producing."

His woebegone brown eyes lit up. "Yes, ma'am, well that's mostly what I did before—that is, I was a pumper. Maintained several wells for another outfit."

"So you have experience? You know the business?"

"Oh yes, ma'am. Out in West Texas. Grew up in a pissant, uh, I mean a *small* town close to Odessa. Worked in the Permian Basin fields since I was twelve." He paused, as though giving her an opportunity to change her mind after hearing his qualifications. When she said nothing, he bobbed his head in conclusion. "Well, much obliged to you anyway, ma'am."

"Wait!" As soon as Janellen realized that she had reflexively extended a hand to him, she snatched it back and, flustered, clasped it with her other and held them against her waist.

He regarded her curiously. "Yes, ma'am?"

"As long as you're here, you could fill out an application. If we have an opening anytime soon . . . I'm not expecting one, you understand, but it wouldn't hurt to leave an application in our files."

He thought it over for a moment. "No, I reckon it wouldn't hurt."

Janellen sat down behind her desk and motioned him into the chair facing it. In her bottom drawer, along with other business forms, she kept a few standard employment applications. She passed one to him. "Do you need a pen?"

"Please."

"Would you like some coffee?"

"No, thanks."

Picking up the pen she had given him, he lowered his head and proceeded to print his name on the top line of the application.

Janellen judged him to be about Key's age, although his face was marked with more character lines, and there was a sprinkling of gray in his sideburns. His hair was brown. It bore the imprint of his hatband in a ring around his head.

Suddenly he looked up and caught her staring at him. Before thinking, she blurted, "W-would you care for a cup of coffee?" Then she remembered that she'd offered him one less than thirty seconds ago. "I'm sorry. I already asked you, didn't I?"

"Yes, ma'am. I still don't care for any. Thanks, though." He bent back to the application.

Janellen fidgeted with a paper clip, wishing she had left on the radio after listening to the morning news, wishing there were some form of noise to fill the yawning silence, wishing she weren't so miserably ill-equipped when it came to making small talk.

At last he completed the form and passed it and the ballpoint pen back to her. She scanned the top few lines and was astounded to find that he was much younger than Key, actually two years younger than herself. It had been a rough thirty-one years for him.

Her eyes moved down the form. "You're currently employed at The Palm? The honky-tonk?"

"That's right, ma'am." He cleared his throat and rolled his shoulders self-consciously. "I grant you, it's not much of a job. Only temporary."

"I didn't mean to put it down," she said hastily. "Somebody has to work in those places." That came out sounding insulting, too. Her teeth closed over her lower lip. "My brother goes there all the time."

"Yeah, he's been pointed out to me. I don't recall ever seeing you there."

She got the distinct impression that he was trying to suppress a smile. In a nervous gesture, she moved her hand to the placket of her blouse and began fiddling with the buttons. "No, I've . . . I've never been there."

"Yes, ma'am."

Janellen wet her lips. "Let's see," she said, referring again to the application form. "Before The Palm you were working at the state— "

She faltered over the next plainly printed word. Too appalled by her blunder even to look at him, she stared at his application until the lines and words ran together.

"That's right, ma'am," he said quietly. "I did time in Huntsville State Prison. I'm on parole. That's why I need a job real bad."

Mustering all her courage, she lifted her eyes to meet his. "I'm sorry that I don't have anything for you, Mr. Cato." To her consternation, she realized she meant it.

"Well," he said, rising, "it was a long shot anyway."

"Why do you say that?"

He shrugged. "Being I'm an ex-con and all."

She wouldn't lie and tell him that his prison record would have no bearing on his chance for employment at Tackett Oil. Jody wouldn't hear of hiring him. However, Janellen was reluctant to let him leave without some word of encouragement. "Do you have other possibilities in mind?"

"Not so's you'd notice." He replaced his hat and pulled it low over his brows. "Thank you for your time, Miss Tackett."

"Goodbye, Mr. Cato."

He backed out the office door, closing it behind him, then sauntered across the concrete porch, jogged down the steps, and climbed into a pickup truck.

Janellen shot from her chair and quickly moved to the door. Through the venetian blinds, she watched him drive away. At the highway, he turned the pickup in the direction of The Palm.

More depressed than before, she returned to her desk. The paperwork was waiting for her, but she was disinclined to approach it with her usual self-discipline. Instead she picked up the application form that Bowie Cato had filled out and carefully reread each vital statistic.

He had put an X beside "single" to designate his marital status. The space for filling in next of kin had been left blank. Suddenly, Janellen realized that she was being a snoop. It wasn't as though she were actually considering him for a job. She didn't have one to offer him, and even if she did, Jody would have a fit if she hired an ex-con.

Impatient with herself for lollygagging away half the morning, she shoved Bowie Cato's application into the bottom drawer of her desk and got down to business.

"Not that tie, Fergus. For God's sake." Darcy Winston cursed with exasperation. "Can't you see that it clashes with your shirt?"

"You know me, sugar pie," he said with an affable shrug. "I'm color-blind."

"Well, I'm not. Switch it with this one." She pulled another necktie from the rack in his closet and thrust it at him. "And hurry up. We're the main attraction tonight, and you're going to make us late."

"I've already apologized once for running late. A busload of retirees from Fayetteville made an unscheduled stop at The Green Pine. Thirty-seven of them. I had to help check them in. Nice bunch of people. They'd been down in Harlingen for two weeks, building a Baptist mission for the Mex'cans. Holding Bible schools and such. Said those Mex'can kids took to snowcones like— "

"For chrissake, Fergus, I don't care," she interrupted impatiently. "Just finish dressing, please. I'm going to hurry Heather along."

Darcy stalked along the upstairs hallway of their spacious home toward their only child's bedroom. "Heather, are you ready?"

She knocked out of habit but entered without waiting for permission. "Heather, hang up that damn phone and get dressed!"

The sixteen-year-old cupped the mouthpiece. "I'm ready, Mother. I'm just talking to Tanner until it's time to leave."

"It's time." Darcy snatched the receiver away from her, sweetly said, "Goodbye, Tanner," then dropped it back into its cradle.

"Mother!" Heather exclaimed. "How rude! I could just die! You're so mean to him! Why'd you do that?"

"Because we're expected at the schoolhouse right now."

"It's not even six-thirty yet. We're not scheduled to be there until seven."

Darcy wandered over to her daughter's dressing table and rummaged among the perfume bottles until she found a fragrance she liked, then sprayed herself with it.

Piqued, Heather asked, "What's wrong with your perfume? You have dozens to choose from. Why do you use mine?"

"You spend too much time on the phone with Tanner," Darcy said, ignoring Heather's complaint.

"I do not."

"Boys don't like girls who are too available."

"Mother, please don't meddle in my jewelry box. You leave it in a mess every time you open it." Reaching around Darcy, Heather flipped down the lid.

Darcy pushed her aside and defiantly reopened the lavender velvet box. "What have you got stashed away in here that you don't want me to see?"

"Nothing!"

"If you're smoking joints . . ."

"I'm not!"

Darcy riffled through the contents of the jewelry box but found only an assortment of earrings, bracelets, rings, pendants, and a strand of pearls that Fergus had bought for Heather the day she was born.

"See? I told you."

"Don't sass me, young lady." She slammed down the lid and scrutinized Heather with a critical eye. "And before we leave, wipe off about half of that eye shadow. You look like a tramp."

"I do not."

Darcy popped a Kleenex from the box and shoved it into Heather's hand. "You're probably behaving like one, too, every time you're out with Tanner Hoskins."

"Tanner respects me."

"And pigs fly. He wants to get in your pants, and so will every other man you ever meet."

Dismissing Heather's protests to the contrary, Darcy left the room and went downstairs. She felt pleased with herself. She believed parents should never let their kids get the upper hand and so she stayed on Heather like fleas on a hound. Every minute of Heather's day was reported to Darcy, who insisted on knowing where her daughter was, whom she was with, and for how long she was with them. According to Darcy Winston, only an informed parent could exercise the control necessary to raise teenagers.

By and large, Heather was obedient. Her active school schedule didn't allow much time during which she could get into trouble, but in the summer, when free time was easier to come by, opportunities for mischief-making were plentiful.

Darcy's vigilance wasn't based so much on maternal instinct as it was on memories of her own adolescence. She knew all the tricks a youngster could pull on gullible parents because she had pulled each one herself. Hell, she'd invented them.

If her mother had been more strict, more observant of her comings and goings, Darcy's youth might not have been so short-lived. She might not have been married at eighteen.

Her father had deserted her mother when Darcy was nine, and although she was at first sympathetic with her mother's dilemma, Darcy soon became contemptuous of her. Over the years, her contempt grew into open rebellion. By the time she was Heather's age she was running with a wild crowd that got drunk every night and frequently traded sex partners.

She graduated high school by the skin of her teeth—actually by giving a blow-job to a biology teacher with thick glasses and damp hands. During the summer following commencement, she got pregnant by a drummer in a country-western band. She tracked him to De Ridder, Louisiana, where he denied he'd ever met her. In a way, Darcy was glad he claimed no responsibility. He was a no-talent loser, a dopehead who spent his piddling portion of the band's earnings on substances he could smoke, snort, or shoot into his veins.

When she returned to Eden Pass, her future looked

dim. Fortuitously, she stopped for breakfast at The Green
Pine Motel. Flashing his horsy, toothy grin, Fergus
Winston, who was settled into middle-aged bachelorhood,
greeted her at the door of the busy coffeeshop.

Instead of perusing the menu, Darcy watched Fergus
ring up the cash register receipts. Halfway through her
first cup of coffee, she reached a life-altering decision.
Within two hours she had a job. Two weeks beyond that,
she had netted a husband.

On their wedding night, Fergus believed with all his
heart that he'd married a virgin, and several weeks later,
when Darcy announced that she was pregnant, it never
occurred to him that her child had been sired by anyone
except himself.

In all the years since, it still hadn't occurred to him,
although Heather had been almost eight weeks "prema-
ture" and had still weighed in at a healthy seven and a
half pounds.

Fergus didn't have time to dwell on these inconsisten-
cies because Darcy kept his mind on the motel. Over the
years she had convinced him that a clever businessman
spent money in order to make it. He had revamped
the food service, updated the motel's decor, and leased
billboards on the interstate.

On one point Fergus stood firm. Only he had access
to The Green Pine Motel's ledgers. No matter how
persuasively Darcy cajoled, he alone did the bookkeep-
ing. She surmised that he wasn't reporting all his profits to
the IRS, which was all right with her. What annoyed her
was that, given access to the books, she probably would
have been able to find loopholes that he'd overlooked.
But in sixteen years of marriage he hadn't budged from
his original position. It was one of the few arguments
between them that Darcy lost.

Having remained a bachelor for so long, he was totally
smitten with his young, pretty, redheaded wife and their
daughter and considered himself the luckiest man alive.

He was a generous husband. He'd built Darcy the finest house in Eden Pass. She'd had carte blanche to furnish it out of design studios in Dallas and Houston. She drove a new car every year. He was an adoring parent to Heather, who had twined him around her little finger as easily as her mother had.

He was unflappable and unsuspecting, even when Darcy took her first extramarital lover three months after Heather was born. He was a guest at the motel, a saddle salesman from El Paso on his way to Memphis. They used room 203. It had been easy to tell Fergus that she was going to visit her mother for a few hours.

In spite of her frequent infidelities, Darcy was sincerely fond of Fergus, mainly because his position in the community had considerably evated hers and because he gave her every material thing her heart desired. She smiled at him now as he came downstairs arm in arm with Heather. "You two make a handsome pair," she said. "Everybody in town is going to be at that meeting tonight, and all eyes are going to be on the Winston family."

Fergus placed his arm across her shoulders and kissed her forehead. "I'll be pleased and proud to stand at the podium with the two prettiest ladies in Eden Pass."

Heather rolled her eyes.

Fergus was too earnest to notice the gesture. "I'm just sick about the reason for this town meeting, though." He sighed as he gazed into his beloved wife's face. "I shudder when I think that a burglar could have harmed you."

"It gives me goosebumps, too." Darcy patted his cheek, then impatiently squirmed free of his embrace. "We'd better go or we'll be late. On the other hand," she added with a smug laugh, "they can't start without us, can they?"

Chapter Six

*L*ara had specific reasons for wanting to attend the town meeting.

If Eden Pass was experiencing a crime wave, she needed to be aware of it. She lived alone and needed to take precautions to protect herself and her property.

It was also important to her future in Eden Pass that she become actively involved in all facets of community life. She'd already bought a season ticket to the home football games and had contributed to the fund to buy a new traffic light for the only busy intersection downtown. If she was seen frequently in everyday settings, like the Sak'n'Save grocery store and the filling station, maybe the townsfolk would stop perceiving her as an outsider. Maybe they would even accept her, in spite of Jody Tackett.

Her third reason for wanting to attend the meeting was far more personal. She found it curious that the outbreak of crime coincided with Key Tackett's coming to her back doorstep with a bleeding bullet wound. It was highly unlikely that he'd been breaking into the Fergus Winston home with burglary in mind, but it was a jarring coincidence that, for her peace of mind, she wanted laid to rest.

The high school auditorium, the pride of the consolidated school's campus, was frequently used as a community center. Lara arrived early, but the parking lot was already jammed with cars, minivans, and pickup trucks. The meeting had been deemed "vitally important" by the local newspaper. In it Sheriff Elmo Baxter had been quoted as saying, "Everybody ought to be at this meeting. It's up to the citizens of Eden Pass to stop this rash of crime before it gets out of hand. Nip it in the bud, so to speak. We have a clean, decent little town here, and as long as I'm sheriff, that's how it's going to stay."

His urging had yielded a good turnout. Lara was just one of a crowd who flocked toward the well-lighted building. As she entered the auditorium, however, she was singled out. In her wake she left whispered conversations. They were absorbed by the din created by the crowd, but she was aware of them nevertheless.

Trying to ignore the turned heads and gawking stares, she smiled pleasantly, greeting those she recognized—Mr. Hoskins from the supermarket, the lady who clerked in the post office, and a few who'd been brave enough to cross Jody Tackett's implied picket line to seek her professional services.

Rather than taking one of the available seats in the rear of the auditorium, which would have been convenient but cowardly, Lara moved down the congested center aisle. She spotted Nancy and Clem Baker and their brood. Nancy motioned for her to join them, but she shook her head and found a chair in the third row.

Her courage in the face of so much adverse attention was a pose. It was discomforting to know that tongues were wagging and that dozens of pairs of eyes were aimed at the back of her head, most of them critically. She knew that personal aspects of her life were being reviewed in hushed voices so that the children wouldn't hear about the brazen hussy in their midst.

Lara could not control what people thought or said, but it still hurt to know that her character was being bludgeoned and there wasn't a damn thing she could do to prevent it. Her only means of self-preservation would be to remain at home, but to her that was not a viable option. She had every right to attend a community function. Why should she be cowed by gossips and people so spineless they allowed themselves to be influenced by an aging old bitch, as she had come to think of Jody Tackett.

Obviously Mrs. Tackett had a much higher opinion of herself. When she made her fashionably late entrance, she strode down the center aisle looking neither right nor left. She felt that friendliness was either a waste of time or beneath her dignity. In any case, she didn't stop to chat even with those who spoke to her.

Her bearing was militant, but she wasn't as physically imposing as Lara had expected. Clark had described his mother in such elaborate terms that Lara recognized her, but she had formed a mental picture of Jody that fit midway between Joan Crawford and Joan of Arc.

Instead, Jody was a short, stocky, gray-haired woman who was average in appearance and attired in clothing that was high in quality but low in fashion flair. Her hands were blunt and unadorned. Her features were harsh to the point of appearing masculine, and she embodied the iron will for which she was known.

A hush fell over the crowd as she moved down the aisle. Her arrival was as good as an announcement that the meeting could begin. Indubitably she was Eden Pass's number-one citizen, deferred to by all.

Lara was perhaps the only one in the auditorium who realized that Jody Tackett was seriously ill.

She had the telltale wrinkles of a heavy smoker around her mouth and eyes. Beyond that, her skin was friable. Bruises and splotches dotted her arms. As she extended her hand to the mayor, Lara noticed that her cuticles were thick. Such clubbing was symptomatic of pending arterial problems.

Following on Jody's heels was a woman who appeared to be about Lara's age. Her smiles were genuine but uncertain. She seemed uncomfortable with sharing her mother's limelight. Janellen perfectly matched Clark's description. He had once referred to his sister as "mousy," but he hadn't meant it unkindly.

"Daddy doted on her. Maybe if he hadn't died when she was so young, she would have eventually blossomed. Mother didn't have much time to cultivate her. She was too busy keeping the business together. I guess growing up around Key and Mother and me, all Type A's, made sis shy and softspoken. She rarely got a word in edgewise."

Janellen had a delicate face and a fair complexion. Her mouth was too small, and her nose was a trifle long, but, like her brothers, she had spectacular blue eyes that more than compensated for her unremarkable features.

Since Jody had obviously influenced her, her lack of style was no surprise. But even Jody's clothing made more of a fashion statement than Janellen's. She was downright dowdy. Her severe hairstyle was sorely unflattering. It was as though she worked at making herself unattractive so that she would go unnoticed and remain in the large shadow that Jody cast.

Key brought up the rear. Unlike his mother, he didn't march down the aisle undeterred. He stopped frequently along the way to swap greetings and anecdotes with people he obviously hadn't seen in a while. Lara picked up snatches of these friendly exchanges.

"As I live and breathe! It's Key Tackett!"

"Hey, Possum! You ugly son of a bitch, how's life treating you?"

While someone named Possum was expounding upon his successful feed and fertilizer business, Key happened to glimpse Lara. When he did a double take, her stomach muscles tightened. They held each other's stare until Possum, so nicknamed no doubt because he bore an unfortunate resemblance to the marsupial, asked him a direct question.

"Sorry, what?" Key pulled his stare away from Lara, but not before Possum and others sitting nearby noticed who had momentarily captured his attention.

"Uh, I said . . ." Possum was so busy shifting his beady eyes between Lara and Key that he couldn't restate his question.

Thankfully, the high school principal chose that moment to approach the lectern on the stage. He spoke into the microphone. It was dead. After fiddling with the controls, he blasted everyone's eardrums with, "Thank y'all for coming out tonight." He finally adjusted the volume and repeated his welcome.

Key promised to meet Possum the next day for a beer, then joined Jody and Janellen in the front row where the mayor had saved seats for them.

The meeting got under way, the school principal presiding. He introduced the Fergus Winston family, who emerged as a unit from behind the gold velvet curtains. Lara observed them with interest. The teenage girl, who was introduced as Heather, seemed mortified to be seen with her parents in such a public arena. Mrs. Winston didn't appear to be on the verge of collapse as the school principal's solemn tone suggested. A picture of health, she was fairly bursting with vitality. The stage lights made her red hair look like flames. She demurely slid her hand into the crook of her husband's elbow.

Lara instantly distrusted her.

Fergus was a tall man with a perpetual stoop. Thinning gray hair inadequately covered his pointed, balding head. There were deep laugh lines around his wide mouth, but he wasn't smiling as he took the high school principal's place behind the lectern and gave his account of their harrowing experience.

By angling slightly to her left, Lara could see Key Tackett in the chair next to his sister's. His elbows were propped on the armrests, and he was tapping his steepled fingers against his lips. His ankle—the one he'd sprained—was propped on the opposite knee. He was slouching in his seat, and his eyes moved restlessly about as though he was finding the proceedings exceedingly dull, as eager for them to conclude as a young boy in church.

Lara looked again toward the stage and saw that she wasn't the only one watching Key. Mrs. Winston had him locked in her sights, too. Her expression was sly, almost smug.

"Well, that's all I've got to tell y'all," Mr. Winston concluded, "except to say to be on the lookout for any suspicious characters, any strangers around town, and to report any unusual happenings to the sheriff." To applause, he relinquished the microphone to the sheriff.

Elmo Baxter was a slovenly man who moved with the speed of a slug and had the world-weary expression of a basset hound. "I 'preciate Fergus and Darcy sharing their experience." He shifted his weight. "But don't y'all get the fool notion of sleeping with a loaded gun under your pillow. If you see signs of a break-in or notice a stranger hanging around your neighborhood, report it to my office. Me or Gus'll check it out using proper police procedure.

"Don't go taking the law into your own hands, y'all hear? Now, me and the city council decided we need a Crime Watch committee like they have in big cities. This committee would organize folks in the different neighborhoods to keep a lookout on goings-on and help everybody stay informed. Naturally it'll need a chairman. I'll take nominations now."

"I volunteer myself," Darcy Winston announced in a clear, loud voice.

She received a burst of applause. Fergus squeezed her hand and looked down at her with naked adoration.

"And I'd like for Key Tackett to serve as co-chairman," Darcy added.

Key jerked to attention. His boot landed hard on the floor, and Lara saw him wince. "What the hell did she say?" Everybody laughed at his stunned reaction. "I don't even live here anymore. Besides, what do I know about committees?"

The amused sheriff tugged on his elongated earlobe. "I reckon knowing about committees isn't a requirement, but if a man ever knew about taking care of hisself, it's you. Right, Jody?"

She looked across Janellen at her son. "I think you ought to do it. Since when have you performed a community service?"

"Since he led the fighting Devils to the state championship!" Possum leaped into the center aisle and began waving his hands high over his head. "Let's hear it for the fearsome number 'leven, Key Tackett!"

Others stood and joined the cheering. Antsy children used the interruption as an opportunity to escape their parents. Rowdy teens gave one another high fives as they raced for the exits. Regaining control was out of the question, so Sheriff Baxter placed his lips close to the mike and said, "All in favor say 'aye.' Motion carries. Y'all are dismissed. Be careful driving home."

Lara was swept along into the aisle. Standing on tiptoe, she was able to see Darcy Winston imperiously motioning for Key to join her on the stage. She looked like a woman fully capable of shooting a fleeing lover in order to prevent getting caught with him. There was calculation in her perpetually pursed lips and tilted eyes.

"Excuse me."

Lara responded to the polite request coming from behind her and stepped aside, then turned to apologize for dawdling. She came eye to eye with Janellen.

Janellen was caught in a hesitant smile that quickly turned into a small, round O of dismay. Unabashedly she gaped at Lara.

"Hello, Miss Tackett," Lara said politely. "Excuse me for blocking the aisle."

"You're . . . you're . . ."

"I'm Lara Mallory."

"Yes, I . . ."

Even if Janellen could have formed an appropriate response, Jody gave her no chance to speak. "What's the holdup, Janellen?" When she too noticed Lara, her expression hardened with malice.

"At last we meet, Mrs. Tackett," Lara said, extending her right hand.

Jody acknowledged neither her outstretched hand nor the greeting. She only nudged her daughter forward. "Move along, Janellen. I suddenly feel the need for some fresh air."

For several moments, Lara was immobilized by Jody's angry stare. But the chance meeting hadn't gone unnoticed, and soon she became aware of the studious avoidance of the crowd. Self-consciously she retracted her right hand. As she moved up the aisle, she was given a wide berth. She might as well have had leprosy. No one even looked at her.

At the exit, she paused and glanced back at the stage. Key had joined Mrs. Winston there. Scornfully, Lara turned away. They deserved each other.

Since Darcy was about as subtle as a carnival barker, Key was given no choice but to join her on stage. After making such a production of flagging him up there, it would have aroused curiosity if he hadn't heeded her request.

As he had moved toward the stage, he had tried to locate Lara Mallory in the crowd, and was shocked to see her talking to his mother.

He watched as Jody spurned her handshake and brusquely herded Janellen up the aisle. To her credit, Dr. Mallory didn't quail or lose her composure. She didn't burst into tears or shout epithets at their retreating backs. Instead she held her head high as she moved gracefully toward the exit.

Key was tempted to charge after her and—do what? Ask her why she had picked on his brother when there were thousands of randy young bucks in Washington, D.C., just itching to get laid?

See if she could clarify for him the haunting circumstances surrounding his brother's death?

Demand that she leave town by dawn, or else?

He would look like a damn fool and he didn't want to give her that satisfaction. Besides, he had a matter to settle with Darcy. Best to get that out of the way before tackling another crisis.

He climbed the steps to the stage. "Just what the hell are you up to, Darcy?"

"Hi, Key!" She was all smiles, and, despite his angry scowl, she manipulated him into an introduction. "Have you met my daughter? Heather, this is Mr. Key Tackett."

"Hello, Mr. Tackett." The girl spoke politely, but she obviously had other things on her mind. "Tanner's waiting for me," she told her mother. "Can I go now?"

"Come straight home."

"But everybody's going out to the lake."

"At this time of night? No."

"Mo-*ther*! Everybody's going. Please."

The stare Darcy fixed on Heather conveyed unspoken warnings. "Be home by eleven-thirty. Not a second later."

Heather protested sulkily. "Nobody else has to come in that early."

"Take it or leave it, young lady."

She took it. After bidding Key an obligatory goodbye, she joined a handsome young man waiting for her in front of the stage.

While Darcy had been arguing with Heather over the girl's curfew, Key had been watching Lara Mallory's solitary progress up the aisle. There was something very noble about her carriage. Before she went through the exit, she turned and looked toward the stage.

"Key?"

"What?" Only after the doctor disappeared did he turn

his attention back to Darcy. Having followed the direction of his gaze, she too was focused on the exit doors at the rear of the auditorium.

"So, our scandalous new doctor put in an appearance tonight," she remarked cattily. "Have you had the honor of making her acquaintance?"

"Fact is, I have. She patched me up after you shot me." Key got a kick out of wiping off Darcy's complacent smile.

"You went to *her?*" she exclaimed. "Have you lost your freaking mind? I thought you'd have the good sense to go to the hospital, where you'd be known, but at least it's out of town."

"I was looking for Doc Patton. Nobody told me that he'd retired."

"Or that your brother set up his ex-mistress in business here?"

"No. Nobody told me that either."

He tried to keep his voice free of telltale inflection, but Darcy wouldn't have noticed anyway. He could tell the wheels of her scheming brain were in full gear.

"She could report the gunshot wound to the sheriff," she said worriedly.

"She could, but I doubt she will." He glanced toward the exit. "She's got enough to worry about. Besides, she couldn't prove anything. No bullet. It tore off a chunk of flesh on its way through." He leaned down and spoke softly so they wouldn't be overheard by those loitering about. "I ought to skin you alive for shooting at me. You could have killed me, you dumb bitch."

"Don't talk to me like that," she hissed, which was hard to do while keeping her deceptively friendly smile in place. "If I hadn't acted quickly, Fergus would have caught us mother-nekkid and screwing like rabbits. He could have killed us, and no jury in this state would have convicted him."

"Sugarplum?"

She spun around at the sound of her husband's voice. Key hitched his chin at him. "Hey, Fergus. It's been a long time."

"How're you doin', Key?"

"Can't complain."

Years ago there had been a rift between Fergus and Jody. It had something to do with the Tackett oil lease adjacent to Fergus's motel property. The details were murky, and Key had never wanted to know them badly enough to ferret them out. He figured that Jody, in her lust for oil and the power and money that went with it, had somehow cheated Fergus.

Their dispute was none of his business, except that Fergus had always looked at him like he was lower than buzzard shit, but that might have had more to do with how he had conducted himself during his youth. More than once he and Possum and their crowd had nursed their hangovers in the coffeeshop of Fergus's motel. He vaguely remembered puking up pints of sour mash in the rosebushes in front of The Green Pine after a particularly wild bacchanal.

Anyway, Fergus Winston didn't like him, but Key had never lost sleep over it.

"I'm not real excited about this committee job your wife just roped me into. By the way," he said to Darcy, "I'm resigning. Effective immediately."

"You can't resign. You haven't even started."

"All the more reason. I didn't ask to be part of any Crime Watch committee. I don't want to be. Find yourself another co-chairman."

She flashed him her most dazzling smile. "Obviously he wants to be begged, Fergus. Why don't you bring the car around to the front door? I'll meet you there. In the meantime, I'll do my best to change Key's ornery mind."

Key watched Fergus amble into the wings of the stage, calling good night to the custodian who was patiently waiting for everybody to leave so he could secure the building.

Darcy waited until her husband was out of earshot before turning back to Key. Keeping her voice low, she said, "Can't you see an opportunity when it all but bites you in the ass?"

"What do you mean, sugarplum?" he asked with mock innocence.

"I mean," she stressed, "that if we're on the same committee, people won't think anything about our being seen together." His stare remained opaque. Exasperated, she spelled it out. "We could get together anytime we wanted and wouldn't have to sneak around in order to do it."

He waited about three beats before bursting into laughter. "You think I'd sleep with you again?" As suddenly as it had started, his laughter ceased, and his face became taut with anger. "I'm royally pissed at you, Mrs. Winston. You could have killed me with that damn handgun of yours. As it is, I can barely climb into a cockpit with this bum ankle."

She gazed at him through eyes gone smoky. "Small price to pay for the fun we had, wouldn't you say?"

"Not even close, sugarplum. You act like that's the golden fleece," he said, glancing pointedly at her crotch, "but I've had better. Lots better. Anyway, if you think I'd touch it again after this stunt you've pulled, then you're as crazy as you are easy."

The smoke in her eyes cleared. He saw fire. "I wouldn't fuck *you* again, either!"

"Then from what I hear, I'm in a minority of one."

Darcy was livid. "You're a son of a bitch and always have been, Key Tackett."

"You're right on the money there," he said with a terse nod. "In the most literal sense of the words."

"Go to hell."

Since there were still people milling about and visiting

in the aisles of the auditorium, there was nothing more
she could do except conceal her wrath, turn on her heel,
and flounce away. She gave clipped replies to those who
bade her good night as she stormed up the aisle.

Key followed at a more leisurely pace, feeling amused,
pleased, and vaguely dissatisfied all at the same time.
Darcy deserved his digs, but he hadn't derived as much
pleasure from insulting her as he had anticipated.

Like a dutiful servant, Fergus was waiting for her
beside their El Dorado, holding the passenger door
open. As Darcy slid into the seat, Key overheard her
say, "Hurry up and get me home, Fergus. I've got a
splitting headache."

Key felt sorry for Fergus, but not because he'd slept
with his wife; hell, just about everybody in pants had at
one time or another. But even though his motel made
money, he would never be an entrepreneur. That required
a certain attitude that was clearly lacking in his long, thin
face, his bad posture, and in his conservative approach to
business. There were the Jody Tacketts of the world, and
there were the Fergus Winstons. The aggressors and the
vanquished. Some steamrollered their way through life
while others either moved aside for them or got rolled
over. In life and in love, Fergus fell into the latter
category.

Such passivity was beyond Key's understanding. Why
would Fergus ignore Darcy's unfaithfulness? Why was he
willing to be an object of scorn? Why did he accept and
forgive her infidelity?

Love?

Like hell, Key scoffed. Love was a word that poets
and songwriters used. They vested the emotion with
tremendous powers over the human heart and mind,
but they were wrong. It didn't transform lives like the
saccharine lyrics claimed it could. Key had never seen
any evidence of its magic, unless it was black magic.

Love had caused his young heart to break when his

father was killed, leaving him without an ally in a hostile environment. Love had kept his sister emotionally and psychologically chained to their mother. Love had cost Clark his promising career as a statesman. Had love also compelled Randall Porter to stay with his whoring wife?

Not for me, Key averred as he crossed the parking lot, his stride as long as his injured ankle would allow. Love, forgiveness, and turning the other cheek were concepts that belonged in Sunday school lessons. They didn't apply in real life. Not in his life, anyway. If, during a mental lapse, he ever got married, and if he ever found his wife in the arms of another man, he'd kill them both.

Reaching his car, he jammed the key into the lock.

"Good evening, Mr. Tackett."

He turned, stunned to find Lara Mallory standing beside him. A breeze was gently tugging at her clothing and hair. Her face was partially in shadow, the remainder bathed in moonlight. Although she was the last person he wanted to see at the moment, she looked damned gorgeous and for a moment he felt as though he'd been poleaxed.

His reaction was irritated, as was evident in his voice. "Did you follow me out here?"

"Actually I've been waiting for you."

"I'm touched. How'd you know where to find me?"

"I've seen you driving around town in this car. It's distinctive, to say the very least."

"It was my daddy's."

The Lincoln was a mile-long gas-guzzler almost two decades old, but Key had left instructions at Bo's Garage and Body Shop that it always was to be kept in showroom condition. He drove it whenever he was home and by doing so felt connected to the father he had lost.

The car had mirrored Clark Junior's flamboyant personality. Yellow inside and out, it sported gaudy gold accents on the grille and hubcaps. Key affectionately referred to it as the "pimp-mobile." Jody frowned on the car's nickname, possibly because she knew it to be fairly accurate.

"You're still limping," Lara said. "You should be using your crutches."

"Screw that. They're a pain in the ass."

"You could do your ankle irreparable damage."

"I'll take my chances."

"How's your side? You didn't come back to the clinic."

"No shit."

"That drain should be removed."

"I pulled it out myself."

"Oh, I see. A tough guy. Well, at least you've shaved . . . with a butter knife, I suppose."

He said nothing because he had the uncomfortable impression that she was mocking him.

"Are you changing the dressing regularly? If not, it could still become infected. Is the wound healing properly?"

"It's fine. Look," he said, propping his elbow on the roof of the car, "should I consider this a house call? Are you going to bill me for a consultation?"

"Not this time."

"Gee, Doc, thanks. Good night."

"Actually," she said, taking a step toward him, "I have something else to speak to you about and thought you would rather I do it here where we can't be overheard."

"Guess again. Whatever you want to talk about, I'm in no mood to hear. In fact, my mood tonight is what you might call fractious. Do yourself a favor and make yourself scarce."

He was about to duck into the driver's seat when she surprised him further by grabbing his arm. "You've got gall, Mr. Tackett. I give you credit for that. Or was it Mrs. Winston's idea to fake a break-in rather than get caught in adultery?"

Key was taken aback, but only momentarily. She was

gazing at him solemnly, so solemnly that he smiled. "Well I'll be damned. The Whiz Kid thinks she's got it all figured out."

"Mr. Winston interrupted you while you were in bed with his wife, didn't he?"

"Why ask me? You've got all the answers."

"While escaping you sprained your ankle. To cover your tracks, Mrs. Winston shot at you. It's a scene straight out of a bad movie. Did you know she was going to shoot at you?"

"What the hell do you care?"

"That means you didn't."

"Don't put words in my mouth," he said crossly. "My question stands. What do you care? Or do you just have an unnatural curiosity about the love lives of other people?"

"The only reason I care," she said heatedly, "is because you barged into my clinic and called me a whore for doing the same thing you did."

"It's not quite the same thing, is it?"

"Oh really? How is it different?"

"Because Darcy and I weren't hurting anybody."

"Not hurting anybody!" she cried. "She's married. You claimed that was my most grievous sin."

"No, your most grievous sin was getting caught."

"So as long as her husband remains in the dark, it's okay for you to have an affair with her?"

"Not okay, maybe. But not catastrophic. The only ones suffering any consequences are the sinners."

"Hardly, Mr. Tackett. You've whipped an entire town into a panic over a 'crime wave' that doesn't even exist."

"That wasn't any of my doing. Fergus freaked out when he heard Darcy screaming and firing that pistol. He got a little carried away."

"Or maybe he used the mythical intruder to conveniently allay his own suspicions."

That possibility also had occurred to Key, but he wasn't going to admit it. "I'm not responsible for what went on inside his head."

"Doesn't it bother you that you've instilled fear into a whole town?"

"Fear?" he scoffed. "Hell. Folks are loving the scare. Eating it up. They have something to keep their minds off the heat during these last dull weeks before Labor Day. Sheriff Baxter told me that attempted break-ins and window-peepers have been reported all over town."

He chuckled. "Take Miss Winnie Fern Lewis for example. She lives in a spooky old three-story house over on Cannon Street. We used to tear down her clothesline every Halloween because she was mean and stingy and handed out only penny candy.

"Anyway, just yesterday Elmo told me that Miss Winnie Fern's reported a man standing outside her bedroom window watching her undress for six nights straight. She claims she can't describe or identify him because he always hides behind her rose o' sharons where he 'manipulates himself to sexual climax,' is the way she put it to Elmo. If he kept a straight face it's better than I could do.

"There's no window-peeper jacking off behind Miss Winnie Fern's rose o' sharons any more than there's a man in the moon, but she hasn't had a thrill like that in years, so what's the harm?"

"In other words, you feel that you've provided a community service?"

"Could be. People in a small town like Eden Pass need something to generate excitement." He moved closer, close enough to catch the scent of her perfume. "What about you, Doc?" he asked in a low pitch. "What are you doing to generate some excitement, seeing as how Eden Pass doesn't have any legislators to seduce?"

She shuddered with indignation, and immediately Key realized he had lied when he told her he didn't see what had attracted his brother. Anger flattered Lara Mallory. With her head thrown back in that haughty angle, she could have been the proud bust on the prow of a sailing ship.

Except that she was softer. Much softer. He thought of softness each time the south breeze flattened her clothes against her body or lifted strands of hair away from her cheeks. She also had a very soft-looking mouth.

Not liking his train of thought, he asked, "Picked out your next victim yet?"

"Clark wasn't my victim!"

"You're the only married woman he ever got mixed up with."

"Which indicates that he was more discriminating than you."

"Or less."

Furious, she turned on her heel and would have stalked away if his hand hadn't shot out and brought her back around. "Since you started this, you're damned well going to hear me out."

She shook back her hair. "Well?"

"You said that my accusations were unfair."

"That's right. They're grossly unfair. You don't know anything about my relationship with Clark, only what you've read in the tabloids or deduced in your own dirty mind."

He grinned. She had just placed her slender foot into the snare. "Well, you don't know doodle-dee-squat about my relationship with Darcy, or with anyone else for that matter. Yet you ambush me out here and start preaching sin like a fire-breathing Bible thumper. If it was wrong for me to jump to conclusions about you, shouldn't it be just as wrong for you to hang me without a trial?"

Before she had time to reply, he released her, slid into the front seat of the yellow Lincoln, and started the motor. Through the open window he added, "You're not only a whoring wife, you're a goddamn hypocrite."

Chapter Seven

*L*ara drove aimlessly. The night was clear and warm. The breeze served only as a conveyer of the heat that emanated from the earth of this vast, hard place.

Texas.

"Texas isn't just a place," she had heard Clark say many times. "It's a state of mind. Xanadu with cowboy boots."

Lara had never set foot on Texas soil until six months ago, when she claimed the gift he had bequeathed her. She had brought with her preconceptions influenced by Hollywood—the barren, windswept landscapes interrupted only by rolling tumbleweeds like in *Giant*, and *Hud*, and *The Last Picture Show*. Those movies had accurately depicted Texas, but only the western portion of it.

East Texas was green. The verdant forests were comprised of some hardwoods but mostly pines, their trunks dark and straight and aligned so perfectly that Nature could have used a ruler to space them. In the springtime these forests were dappled with patches of pastel color from blooming dogwood and wild fruit trees. Herds of beef and dairy cattle grazed in lush pastures. Lakes brimming with fish were fed by rivers and creeks that had a history of overflowing their banks.

And everywhere there was space, large tracts of land that Texans took for granted if they had never traveled to the crowded Northeast, which most of them scorned as a breeding ground for perverts, pinkos, and pansies.

They had no use whatsoever for Yankees.

Their children pledged allegiance to the flag of the United States of America, but the native-born considered themselves Texans first, Americans second. The blood of the heroes of the Alamo flowed in their veins. Their heritage was rich with larger-than-life characters, and although their state carved a prominent notch in the Bible Belt, they were conversely boastful of bandits and ne'er-do-wells who had become folk heroes. The more notorious the character, the more popular the legends.

If Lara was having a difficult time understanding the people, she had instantly admired their land. County roads radiated from Eden Pass like the spokes of a wheel. Upon leaving the high school, she had selected one at random and had been driving without a destination for about an hour. She was well outside the city limits, and although she couldn't pinpoint exactly where she was, she didn't feel lost.

Steering her car onto the gravel shoulder, she cut the engine. As the motor noise died, she was engulfed by the sound of a discordant choir of cicadas, crickets, and bullfrogs. The wind rustled the leaves of the cottonwood saplings growing on the banks of the shallow ditches that lined the road.

She folded her hands over the steering wheel and rested her forehead on them, berating herself for letting Key Tackett get the best of her.

She had done exactly as he'd said: She'd cast stones without knowing all the facts. There were a thousand extenuating circumstances that could put a different complexion on what appeared a shabby affair. She realized that circumstances were not always what they seemed. Unknown factors often made the difference between right and wrong, good and evil, innocence and guilt. Shouldn't she know that better than anyone?

Her thoughts made her claustrophobic, so she left the car. An open meadow extended as far as she could see on either side of the road. In the near distance, beneath a sprawling pecan tree, a small herd of cattle was settled for the night. Several oil wells, pumping rhythmically, were eerily silhouetted as dark, moving shadows against the night. Rhythmically, they dipped their horse-shaped heads toward the earth, paying it homage like faithful disciples at prayer.

She supposed they were Tackett wells.

It hadn't rained in over a week, so the ditch was dry. She crossed it easily and moved to the wire fence that surrounded the pasture. Being careful of the sharp barbs, she leaned against a rough cedar post and, tilting her head back, gazed at the panoply of stars and a bright half-moon.

"What are you doing here, Lara?"

It was a question she frequently asked herself. Even before Clark's death, she had grappled with the idea of coming here and confronting him with her terms for settling their account. She'd planned to present him with a bill for repayment for all that she'd lost.

He died before she had implemented her plan. Although, tragic as his death was, it had little bearing on her achieving her goal. Clark wasn't essential to her plan. Key was.

Key. He despised her. Because of that, her task wasn't going to be easy. However, the difficulty didn't dampen her determination. Medical training had taught her that in order for things to get better, they often had to get worse. Before wounds could heal, they had to be lanced and the poison excised. She was willing to endure anything, no matter how painful, in order to lay to rest the ghosts that haunted her.

Only then would she finally have the peace that had escaped her since her daughter's death. Only then would she be able to put the tragedies of the past behind her and get on with the remainder of her life, either in Eden Pass or somewhere else.

The years following her return from Montesangre after the deaths of Randall and Ashley had been a wasteland of time. She hadn't lived; she'd existed. Full of despair and heartache and loneliness, she had moved through the days without connecting with anything around her. Work might have salved her heartache, but she'd been denied the opportunity. She was a pariah, an object of curiosity and ridicule, Clark Tackett's whore.

That's what Key had called her. A whore. Jody thought of her that way, too. Lara had seen the unmitigated contempt in her eyes. She'd expected nothing else, really.

Even her own parents had condemned her. They never had shared a warm relationship with their only child, but it had been especially strained since the scandal. They certainly couldn't understand why she would want to set up her medical practice in an out-of-the-way place like Eden Pass, Texas, particularly since that was Tackett territory.

"They need a doctor there," Lara had told them when they voiced their incredulity over her decision.

"Doctors are needed everywhere," her father had argued. "Why go there?"

"Because she always places herself in the worst possible situation, dear." Her mother spoke softly but coldly. "It's a habit she's acquired strictly to annoy us."

Her father added, "Taking the path of least resistance isn't a crime, Lara. After all that's happened, I would think you'd have learned that."

They would have been aghast if she'd told them the real purpose behind her move to Texas, so she didn't confide it. Making a futile attempt at self-defense, she'd said, "I know it won't be easy to establish a practice there, but it's the best opportunity I've been offered."

"And you have only yourself to blame for that, and for all your other misfortunes. If you had listened to your mother and me in the first place, your life wouldn't be in shambles now."

She could have reminded them that they had encouraged her to marry Randall Porter. Even before meeting him, they'd been impressed by his credentials. He was charming and urbane and cosmopolitan. He was fluent in three languages and held a promising position in the State Department, an attribute they liked to throw up to their society friends.

They still regarded Randall as a saint for remaining married to her after the spectacle she'd made of herself with Senator Tackett. Would it make any difference to them, she wondered, if they knew how unhappy she'd been with Randall long before he introduced her to Clark?

Uncomfortable with her memories, Lara retraced her steps to her car and was about to get in when she became aware of a sound coming from overhead. Looking up, she spotted an airplane. It was nothing but a blinking dot of light on the horizon, but it came closer, flying low. In fact, it was cruising at a dangerously low altitude, barely clearing the treetops of the forest bordering the pasture. The aircraft was small—a single-engine plane, she guessed, with her limited knowledge of aviation.

It swooped in low over the pasture and crossed the road about a hundred yards from Lara's parked car. She sucked in her breath as the plane approached the far woods. Only seconds before it reached the tree line, the plane's nose reared back at a drastic angle as it went into a steep climb, then banked to the left and gradually ascended to a safer altitude. Lara watched it until she could no longer see the lights.

Would someone be crop dusting at this time of night? Would chemicals be dusted over pastures where cattle were grazing? No, this had to be a stunt flyer.

"Fool," she muttered as she got into her car and turned on the ignition.

Of course, most considered her a fool for coming to Eden Pass and effectively waving a red flag at the

Tacketts. But when one has absolutely nothing to lose, one isn't so shy of taking tremendous risks. What could the Tacketts say or do to her that hadn't already been said and done?

Once they had met her demand, she would gladly leave them to their town. In the meantime, she didn't care what they thought of her. She must, however, get them past their aversion even to talk to her. But how?

Jody was unapproachable.

Key was snide and abusive, and she didn't welcome subjecting herself to more of him until absolutely necessary.

Janellen? She had sensed in Clark's sister a spark of curiosity before Jody interceded. Could that curiosity be a chink she could use to pierce the Tackett armor?

It was worth a try.

Janellen was vexed with herself. She'd designated today to pay bills and had organized her desk accordingly. But when she reached for the folder in which she filed their accounts payable, she remembered having taken it to the shop the day before, wanting to compare the invoices with the equipment they had received to make certain that everything was in order. It wasn't like her to be so absentminded, and she chastised herself for it as she drove the mile from the office to the shop, as the workers called it.

The shop was actually uglier than the headquarters. As the company grew, the original building had been added onto several times to accommodate an ever-increasing inventory of equipment, supplies, and vehicles. Since it was Saturday, the building was deserted. Janellen pulled her car around back and parked near a rear door that opened directly into a tiny cubicle of an office. Here the men had access to a telephone, refrigerator, microwave, coffeemaker, bulletin board, and individual pigeonholes labeled with their names into which Janellen placed their paychecks twice a month.

Using her key, she let herself in and, ignoring the pin-up calendars and the odor of stale tobacco smoke, she moved behind the metal desk where she remembered last having the folder. When she found it, she tucked it under her arm, and was about to leave when she heard movement beyond the door that connected the office with the garage. She opened the door and was about to call out when the unusual situation stopped her from speaking.

The oversized garage door was closed and the building, having few windows, was dim. A pickup had been squeezed between two Tackett company trucks. Into the pickup one of her men was loading small machinery, pipe, and other supplies that were the tools of their trade. He was checking the items against a list that he carried in the breast pocket of his shirt. Consulting it one last time, he climbed into the cab of the pickup.

Janellen scrambled from her hiding place and rushed forward to block his exit, placing herself between his bug-splattered grille and escape.

"Miss Janellen!" he exclaimed. "I . . . I didn't know you were here."

"What are you doing here on a Saturday morning, Muley?"

His face turned red beneath his tan, and he tugged on the bill of his cap with the blue Tackett Oil logo on it. "You know as well as I do, Miss Janellen, that I ran my route this morning."

"After which you're officially off."

"Just thought I'd get a head start on Monday morning. Came by to pick up some stuff."

"With the garage door shut and all the lights out?" She pointed at the back of the truck. "And you aren't loading that equipment into a company truck, but your own pickup, Muley. You're stealing from us, aren't you?"

"That's old equipment, Miss Janellen. Nobody's using it."

"So you decided to help yourself."

"Like I said, nobody's using it. It's going to waste."

"But it was bought and paid for by Tackett Oil. It's not yours to dispose of." Janellen drew herself up and took a deep breath. "Take the things out of the truck, please."

When he was finished, he hooked his thumbs into his belt and faced her belligerently. "You gonna dock my pay or what?"

"No, I'm not going to dock your pay. I'm firing you."

He underwent an instantaneous attitude change. His thumbs were removed from his belt loops. His hands clenched into fists at his sides. He took two hulking steps toward her. "The hell you say. Jody hired me and only she can fire me."

"Which she'd do in a heartbeat when she found out you were stealing from her. After she cut off your hand."

"You don't know what she'd do. Besides, you can't prove a goddamn thing. For all you know, I was going to offer to buy this stuff from you."

She shook her head somewhat sadly, feeling betrayed. "But you didn't, Muley. You made no such offer. You sneaked in here on a Saturday when you didn't think anyone would be around and loaded the stuff into your pickup truck. I'm sorry. My decision is final. You can pick up your last check on the fifteenth."

"You rich bitch," he said with a sneer. "I'll go, but only because I think this company is in deep shit. Everybody knows Jody is on her last leg. You think you can run this company as good as her?" He snorted. "Nobody ever takes you seriously. We laugh at you, did you know that? Yeah, us guys come in here after our shifts and talk about you. It's amusing how you're trying to take over for your mama 'cause you ain't got nothing better to do with your time. Like fuck, for instance. We've got a running bet, you know, on whether or not you've still

got your cherry. I say it's in there as solid as cement.
Even if you are heir to all that Tackett money, who'd
want to fuck a woman so brittle she'd break when you
mounted her?"

Janellen reeled from the ugly insults. Her ears rang
loudly and her skin prickled as though stung by a thousand
fire ants. Miraculously, she held her ground. "If you're
not out of here in ten seconds, I'll call Sheriff Baxter and
have you arrested."

He flicked his middle finger at her and got back into
his truck. He turned on the motor, gunned it, and shot
from the garage like a rocket.

Janellen stumbled to the switch on the wall and quickly
lowered and locked the garage door, then ran into the
office and locked that door, too.

She crumpled into the chair behind the desk and,
bending slightly from the waist, hugged her elbows. She'd
stood up to a two-hundred-thirty-pound brute, but now
that it was over, she was shaking uncontrollably and her
teeth were chattering.

In hindsight, confronting Muley had been foolish. He
could have harmed her, even killed her, and never come
under suspicion. It would have been believed that a
vagrant thief had killed her—perhaps the one who had
broken into the Winstons' home.

She rocked back and forth on the cracked vinyl
cushion. What had possessed her to challenge him?
She must have a bravery gene she didn't know about.
It had produced that spark of temerity when she'd
needed it.

It took her a half-hour to calm down. By then she had
begun to realize the ramifications of her impulsiveness.
Her spontaneous decision to fire Muley had been correct.
Now, however, she must inform Jody. She had little doubt
that Jody would back her decision, but she dreaded telling
her. Perhaps she wouldn't tell her until she had found a
replacement. But how would she go about doing that? It

wouldn't be easy to find a man as qualified. Muley was a good pumper—

Bowie Cato.

His name sprang into her mind and caused her heart to flutter. She'd thought about him a lot, more than just in passing, more than was decent, more than she liked to admit. Frequently she'd found herself daydreaming about his bowlegged gait and recalling the way his brown eyes viewed the world with a sad cynicism.

Dare she call him and ask if he was still interested in a job?

He'd probably left town.

Besides, what kind of fool would hire an ex-con after firing an employee for stealing?

Jody would have a tizzy. Her blood pressure would soar, and it would be Janellen's fault if she became seriously ill.

She enumerated a dozen solid objections but reached for the phone book and looked up the number of The Palm. Her call was answered on the first ring.

"Is . . . Yes, I'm calling for . . . Who is this please?" Her brave gene had returned to hibernation.

"Who did you want?"

"Well, this is Janellen Tackett. I'm looking for— "

"He ain't here."

"I beg your pardon?"

"Your brother's not here. He came in last night after that town meeting. Stayed 'bout half an hour. Knocked back three doubles in record time. Then he left. Said he was going flying." The man chuckled. "I sure as hell wouldn't have got into an airplane with him. Not with all that scotch sloshing behind his belt and considering the mood he was in."

"Oh dear," Janellen murmured. The pimp-mobile hadn't been in its usual place this morning. She had hoped it signified that Key was up and out early, not that he hadn't come home at all.

"This is Hap Hollister, Miss Janellen. I own The Palm. If Key comes in, can I give him a message for you? Want him to call home?"

"Yes, please. I'd like to know that he's all right."

"Aw hell, you know Key. He can take care of himself."

"Yes, but please have him call anyway."

"Will do. Bye-bye."

"Actually, Mr. Hollister," she cut in hastily, "I was calling for another reason."

"Well?" he said when she hesitated.

Janellen dried her sweating palm on her skirt. "Do you still have a young man working for you named Bowie Cato?"

Lara was weeding her petunia bed when a blue station wagon careened around the nearest corner, hopped the curb, sped up her driveway, and screeched to a halt in the loose gravel. The driver's door burst open and a young man dressed in swimming trunks clambered out, his eyes wild with fright.

"Doctor! My little girl . . . she . . . her arm . . . Jesus, God, help us!"

Lara dropped her trowel and came out of the flower bed like a sprinter off the starting blocks. She stripped off her gardening gloves as she ran to the passenger side of the car and opened the door. The woman inside was even more hysterical than the man. She was holding a child of about three in her lap. There was a lot of blood.

"What happened?" Lara leaned into the car and gently prized the woman's arms away from the girl. The blood was bright red—arterial bleeding.

"We were on our way to the lake," the man sobbed. "Letty was in the backseat, riding with her arm out the window. I didn't think I was that close to the corner when I turned. The telephone pole . . . oh, God, oh, Jesus."

The child's arm had been almost severed. The shoulder

ball joint was grotesquely exposed. Blood was spurting from the severed artery. Her skin was virtually blue, her breathing shallow and rapid. She was unresponsive.

"Hand me a towel."

The man yanked one from a folded stack of beach towels on the backseat and shoved it toward Lara. She pressed it firmly against the wound. "Hold it in place until I get back." The mother nodded though she continued to sob. "Apply as much pressure as you can." To the father she said, "Clear out the back of the car."

She raced for the door of her clinic. Even as she gathered up the paraphernalia for a glucose IV, she called the Flight for Life number at Mother Frances Hospital in Tyler.

"This is Dr. Mallory in Eden Pass. I need a helicopter. The patient is a child. She's in shock, cyanotic, unresponsive, significant loss of blood. Her right arm is almost severed. No sign of head, back, or neck injury. She can be moved."

"Can you get her to the Dabbert County landing strip?"

"Yes."

"Both choppers are currently out. We'll dispatch to you asap."

Lara hung up the phone, grabbed her emergency bag, and ran back outside. In what must have been a frenzy, the panicked father had emptied the back of his station wagon. The driveway was now littered with deflated air mattresses and inner tubes, a picnic basket, six-packs of soft drinks, two Thermoses, an ice chest, and an old quilt.

"Help me get her into the back."

Together Lara and the child's father lifted her from her mother's lap and carried her to the rear of the car. Lara climbed in and guided the child's body down as her father laid her on the carpet. The mother scrambled in and hunkered down on the other side of her daughter.

"Get me the quilt." The man brought it to her, and Lara used it to cover the child to retain her body heat. "Drive us to the county landing strip. I hope you know where it is."

He nodded.

"A helicopter will soon be there to take her to Tyler." He slammed the tailgate and ran to the driver's side. Within two minutes of their arrival, they were under way.

Working quickly, Lara removed the blood-soaked towel from the girl's shoulder and replaced it with small 4 × 4 sterile gauze pads. She pressed them into the wound, then tightly bound the child's shoulder with an Ace bandage. The bleeding could be fatal if it wasn't stanched.

Next she began searching the back of the child's hand for a vein. The patient began to retch. Her mother cried out in distress. Calmly, Lara said, "Turn her head to one side so she won't choke on her vomit." The mother did as she was told. The child's air passage was clear, but her breathing was thready, as was her pulse.

The father drove like a madman, honking wildly at every other car on the road, racing through intersections, and cursing through his tears. The mother cried noisily and wetly.

Lara's heart went out to them. She knew how it felt to watch uselessly while your child died a bloody death.

Dissatisfied with the small vein she'd located in the back of the girl's hand, she made a swift decision to do a cut-down. She pulled the child's foot from beneath the quilt and, as the mother watched in horror, used a scalpel to make a small incision in her ankle. She located the vein, made a small nick in it and inserted a thin catheter, through which she connected the IV apparatus. Her fingers moving hastily but skillfully, she closed the tiny incision with a suture to secure the catheter in place.

She was dripping with perspiration and used her sleeve

to mop her forehead. "Thank God," she murmured when she saw that they had arrived at the landing strip.

"Where's the helicopter?" the father screamed.

"Honk the horn."

A rheumy-eyed man in greasy overalls came hurrying out of the corrugated tin hangar and went straight to the driver.

"You Doc Mallory?" he asked.

The father pointed toward the rear of the station wagon. The mechanic bent down and gaped at the gory scene. "Doc?"

Lara opened the tailgate and got out. "Have you heard from Mother Frances Hospital?"

"They had one chopper picking up a man having a heart attack out at Lake Palestine and the other at a wreck on Interstate 20."

"Did they notify Medical Center?"

"Their chopper's at the same wreck. Hell of a pileup, I guess. Said they could dispatch one from somewhere else. They're putting out the call now."

"She's got no time!"

"Oh, God, my baby!" the mother wailed. "She's going to die, isn't she? Oh, God!"

Lara looked at the tiny body and saw the life ebbing from it. "God help me." She covered her face with her gloved hands, which smelled of fresh blood. This was her recurring nightmare. Watching a child die. Bleeding to death. Incapable of doing anything to prevent it.

"Doctor!"

The child's father grabbed her arm and shook her. "What now? You gotta do something! Our baby's dying!"

She knew that all too clearly. She also knew she alone couldn't handle an emergency of this magnitude. She could control the shock temporarily, but the girl would most certainly lose her limb if not her life if she didn't get emergency treatment immediately. The small county hospital wasn't equipped to handle trauma of this magnitude. A nasty cut, a broken radius, yes, but not this. Taking her there would be a waste of valuable time.

She rounded on the awestruck mechanic. "Can you fly us there? This is a life-or-death situation."

"I just tinker on 'em. Never learned to fly 'em. But there's a pilot here who might fly you where you need to go."

"Where is he?"

"In yonder." He hitched his thumb in the direction of the hangar. "But he's feeling right poorly hisself."

"Is there a plane available? Better yet, a helicopter?"

"That pro golfer that retired here a while back? He keeps a chopper here. Fancy one. Flies it back and forth to Dallas once or twice a week to play golf. He's a regular Joe. Don't reckon he'd mind none you using it, considering it's an emergency and all."

"Hurry, hurry!" the mother pleaded.

"Can this pilot fly a helicopter?" Lara asked the mechanic.

"Yeah, but like I said he ain't— "

"Keep the IV bottle elevated," she said to the mother. "Monitor her breathing," she told the father. She was taking a chance by leaving her patient but didn't trust the loquacious mechanic to convey to the pilot the urgency of the situation.

She rushed past him and entered the building at a run. Several disemboweled aircraft were parked inside. She didn't see anyone. "Hello? *Hello?*"

She went through a door on her left, entering a small, stuffy room. In the corner was a cot. A man was lying on his back, snoring sonorously.

It was Key Tackett.

Chapter Eight

*H*e smelled like a brewery. Lara bent over him and shook him roughly by the shoulder. "Wake up. I need you to fly me to Tyler. Now!" He mumbled something unintelligible, shoved her away, and rolled onto his side.

Inside a rusty, wheezing refrigerator Lara found several cans of beer, some foul-smelling cheese, a shriveled orange, and a plastic container of water, which was what she had hoped for. Gripping the handle, she removed the lid and tossed the entire contents into Key's face.

He came up with a roar, hands balled into fists, eyes murderous. "What the *fuck!*" When he saw Lara holding the dripping pitcher, he gaped at her with speechless incredulity.

"I need you to fly a young girl to Mother Frances Hospital. Her right arm is hanging on by a thread and so is her life. There's no time to argue about it or explain further. Can you get us there without crashing?"

"I can fly anywhere, anytime." He swung his legs to the floor and picked up his boots.

Lara spun around and left the building. The father rushed up to meet her. "Did you find him?"

"He's coming." She didn't elaborate. He was better off not knowing that their pilot had been sleeping off a drinking binge. The mechanic was standing beside a helicopter, giving them the thumbs-up signal. "What's your name?" she asked the young father as they hurried across the tarmac.

"Jack. Jack and Marion Leonard. Our daughter's Letty."

"Help me get Letty to the helicopter."

Together they lifted her out of the station wagon and rushed her toward the helicopter. Marion trotted along beside them, holding up the bag of glucose. By the time they reached the chopper, Key was in the pilot's seat.

He'd already started the engine; the rotors were turning. The Leonards were too worried about their daughter to notice that his shirt was unbuttoned and that he desperately needed a shave. At least his bloodshot eyes had been concealed with a pair of aviator sunglasses with mirrored lenses.

Once they were aboard, he swiveled his head around and looked in Lara's direction. "All set?"

She nodded grimly. They lifted off.

It was too noisy to carry on a conversation, but there was nothing to say anyway. The Leonards clung to each other while Lara monitored the girl's blood pressure and pulse. She trusted that Key knew how to reach the heliport at Mother Frances Hospital. He had slipped on a headset; she saw his lips moving against the mouthpiece.

He turned and shouted back at her, "I found their frequency and am talking to the trauma team. They want to know her vital signs."

"Blood pressure fifty over thirty and falling. Pulse one forty and thready. Tell them to alert a vascular surgeon and an orthopedic specialist. She'll eventually need both. I've started an IV."

"Did you give her an anticoagulant?"

She'd debated that but had decided against it. "She's too young. The bleeding is temporarily under control."

Key transmitted the information. Lara continued to check Letty's blood pressure, breathing, and pulse. She strove for objectivity but it was difficult when the patient was this young, this helpless, and this seriously injured.

Occasionally Marion would reach over and touch her unconscious daughter's hair or stroke her cheek. Once she ran her thumb across Letty's plump toes. That distinct maternal gesture wrenched Lara's heart.

As the outskirts of the city slid beneath them, Key spoke again. "The trauma unit is standing by. They've given us permission for a hot landing."

Letty's shallow breathing stopped suddenly. Lara dug her fingers deep into the child's neck but couldn't feel a pulse.

Jack Leonard cried out in alarm. "What is it? Doctor? *Doctor!*"

"She's arrested."

"My baby! Oh, God, my baby!" Marion screamed hysterically.

Lara bent over the girl and placed the heels of her hands just beneath her sternum. She pushed hard several times, trying to stimulate the heart with chest compressions. "No, Letty, no. Fight. Please. How much farther, Key?"

"I can see the hospital."

She sealed her mouth over Letty's nostrils and mouth and blew air into them. "Don't die. Don't die, Letty," she whispered fervently.

"Oh, Christ!" Jack cried hoarsely. "She's gone."

"Letty!" Marion screamed. "Ah, God, please. No!"

Lara didn't even hear their hysterical cries. Her attention was focused on the small body as she pushed rhythmically on the narrow chest and alternately rendered mouth-to-mouth resuscitation.

When she felt a blip of a pulse, she gave a shout of relief. The child's chest rose and fell as her breathing resumed. Lara continued to render CPR. The pulse was feeble but her heart was beating again.

"We've got her back!"

Key set the chopper down.

The trauma team approached, ducking the rotor blades.

Lara relinquished her patient and helped hold Marion back as they hustled the child onto a gurney and into the emergency room. They followed, but a nurse intercepted them and directed them into a waiting area.

"I want to be with my baby." Marion strained toward the disappearing gurney.

"I'm sorry, ma'am, you have to wait out here. She's getting the best medical attention possible."

Lara nodded understanding to the nurse. "I'll see to her. Thank you."

Together, she and Jack got Marion into the waiting area. He spoke to her soothingly. "I've got to go call our folks, Marion."

"Go ahead. I'll stay with her."

"No," Marion said, firmly shaking her head. "I want to be with Jack." She couldn't be dissuaded. Supporting each other, the couple shuffled off to locate the public telephones.

"Is the kid going to make it?"

At the sound of Key's voice close behind her, Lara turned. He was watching the Leonards as they moved down the corridor.

"It'll be touch and go."

"You almost lost her, didn't you?" His gaze shifted to her. "And you fought like hell to get her back."

"That's my job."

After a moment he asked, "What about her arm?"

"I don't know. She may lose it."

"Shit." He slipped his sunglasses into the breast pocket of his shirt, which he'd taken time to button before following them into the hospital. "I need some coffee. Want some?"

"No, thank you."

"Whenever you're ready to go back to Eden Pass— "

Lara was shaking her head. "I'll wait here with them. At least until she's out of surgery. Feel free to leave whenever you like. I'll find a way back."

He gave her a hard look, then said curtly, "I'm going for coffee."

Lara watched him as he moved down the sterile corridor, his gait straight and steady except for a slight limp that favored his right ankle. In spite of his dishevelment, one would never guess she had roused him from a drunken stupor a short while ago.

He'd set the chopper down between a multilevel parking garage and the hospital building. It was tricky piloting. His boast of being able to fly anywhere at any time wasn't an empty one.

The Leonards returned from making their telephone calls and began their long vigil. When Key returned, he brought with him several cups of coffee and vending machine snacks. Lara introduced him to the anxious couple.

"We can never thank you enough," Marion told him tearfully. "No matter how it turns out, if you hadn't gotten us here, Letty . . . she . . ."

He squeezed her shoulder reassuringly, rather than diminish the gravity of the situation with empty platitudes. "I'll be back in a while." With no further explanation, he left.

Reports from the operating room were agonizingly slow in coming. Each time the OR nurse approached the waiting area, the three of them tensed. But her message on these brief and periodic visits was that the surgeons were doing all they could to stabilize Letty and save her arm from amputation.

It was busy in the ER that morning. Several people had sustained serious injuries in the wreck on the interstate. It had involved three vehicles, including a van filled with senior citizens on a field trip. The staff was harried, but from what Lara could see they were competent.

Key returned about an hour later, bringing with him a large shopping bag from Walmart. He extended it to

Lara and Marion. "I thought y'all'd be more comfortable if you got out of those clothes."

Inside the sack they found slacks and T-shirts. Their clothes had grown stiff with Letty's blood. They used the nearest restroom to wash up and change. When Jack tried to reimburse Key, he wouldn't hear of it.

"You're Barney Leonard's son, aren't you? You run the laundry and dry cleaners for your daddy now, don't you?"

"That's right, Mr. Tackett. I didn't figure you knew me."

"You're doing a hell of a job on my shirts. Just the right amount of starch," Key told him. "That's repayment enough."

Jack solemnly shook his hand.

Their kinfolk arrived about an hour later, along with the Leonards' pastor. The subdued group huddled together and prayed for Letty's life. During her medical career Lara had witnessed many such scenes and no longer felt uncomfortable in the face of personal tragedy.

But Key obviously felt out of place. He paced the hallway and frequently disappeared. Each time he left, Lara figured he had flown the borrowed helicopter back to Eden Pass, but he always returned and asked if there had been any news on Letty's condition. During one of these unspecified absences, he had shaved and tucked in his shirttail. The improvements made him look marginally respectable.

Almost seven hours after Letty was wheeled into surgery, a paunchy, middle-aged man in blue scrubs entered the waiting room and called their name. The Leonards stood and grasped each other's hands, bracing themselves for what they were about to hear.

"I'm Dr. Rupert." He introduced himself as the vascular surgeon. "Your little girl is going to be fine. Unless there are unexpected complications, she should pull through."

Marion would have collapsed if her husband hadn't been there to support her. She began weeping in hard, dry sobs. "Thank you. Thank you."

"What about her arm?" Jack asked.

"We managed to save it, but at this point I can't tell you how much use it will be to her. Full circulation has been restored, but there might have been nerve and muscle damage that won't show up until later. Dr. Callahan, the orthopedic surgeon, will be out shortly to speak with you. He'll talk to you about physical therapy. The important thing now is that she's alive and her vital signs are good."

"When can I see her?" Marion asked.

"She'll be kept in an ICU for several days, but you can see her at intervals. The nursing staff will let you know. Dr. Callahan'll be right out."

When their relatives swarmed forward to embrace Jack and Marion, the surgeon turned to Key. "Dr. Mallory?"

"Not me."

"I'm Dr. Mallory." Lara extended her hand. "I'm a GP in Eden Pass."

"You did some fine work considering what you were dealing with. Got her here in the nick of time."

"I'm glad," she said with a weary smile. Lowering her voice, she asked, "Any professional guesses on how much use she'll have of her arm?"

"If I were a betting man, I'd say better than fifty percent recovery. She's young enough to learn to compensate for any disability. If use is fully restored, she won't remember when this happened." He smiled wanly, the strain of the grueling surgery showing in his face. "But I bet she won't be poking her arm through any more open car windows."

They shook hands again. After exchanging a few final words with the Leonards, he retreated down the hallway. The Leonards hugged Lara, then left to phone other relatives and friends with the good news that the crisis had passed.

Awkwardly, Lara looked over at Key. "I guess I'm finished here."

"Ready when you are, Doc."

Once they were airborne, Lara's stress evolved into profound fatigue. The day's events had taken their toll. Her body ached of muscle strain. She rolled her head, trying to work out the knots in her neck.

Viewed from above, the deepening twilight was beautiful, but she couldn't enjoy it for thinking about how close she had come to losing Letty Leonard.

Life's fragility was fully realized when a child died. Any death affected her, but a child's death made a shattering impact because she always equated it with the tragic way in which Ashley had been snatched from her. One moment her sweet daughter had been cooing and gurgling happy baby sounds, the next she lay bloody and limp.

Tears filled Lara's eyes. Her throat felt achy and tight. Had it not been for Key Tackett sitting beside her in the close confines of the cockpit, she would have wept bitterly.

Instead she forced herself to retain control. She remained stoic until he set the helicopter down at the Dabbert County landing field. The mechanic greeted them.

"How's the little girl?" he asked as Lara alighted.

"She's alive, and they saved her arm."

"Praise be. I'd've thought she was a goner. Hey, Key. It's a beauty of a chopper, ain't it?"

"First class, Balky," he conceded, passing the mechanic the keys.

Lara pointed at the Leonards' station wagon. "Would you please see that their car is cleaned up before they come to retrieve it?"

"Already did," the mechanic told her. "Bo done sent a boy from his garage to wash out the blood."

"That was very kind of you, uh . . . Balky, is it?"

He nodded. "Balky Willis. Pleasure, ma'am." He extended his hand to Lara.

She shook it. "Dr. Lara Mallory."

"Yes, ma'am, I figured you was her."

"I'm sure the Leonards will appreciate your thoughtfulness about their car."

"Weren't my idea. Key called from Tyler and suggested it."

Surprised, Lara looked at him. He shrugged indifferently. "Either way it went, I figured they didn't need any unpleasant reminders. Ready to go?"

"Go?" Only then did she realize she was without transportation. "Oh, would it be an imposition— "

He indicated the yellow Lincoln parked on the far side of the hangar.

Lara asked Balky to thank the golfer who had lent them the helicopter. "Tell him to send me a bill for any expense that was incurred."

"Sure thing." He saluted her and bade goodbye to Key.

"I'll expect a bill from you, too, Mr. Tackett," she said as they approached the Lincoln. "How much do you charge?"

He pulled open the wide passenger door and held it for her. "Depends on what service I've rendered."

Unsmiling, she slid into the car and sat staring straight ahead through the windshield.

Once they were on the highway headed toward town, Key remarked, "You know, your sense of humor ain't for shit. Don't you ever laugh?"

"When I hear something funny."

"Oh, I get it. I don't amuse you."

"Sexual innuendoes have lost their charm for me. I've been the subject of too many to find any humor in them."

He stretched his long body, adjusting his bottom more comfortably in the seat. The leather squeaked agreeably. "I guess that's the price one pays when she's caught up in a sex scandal."

"That's only one price she pays."

He gave her a frankly appraising stare, then returned his attention to the road. They drove in silence, the car gliding along the two-lane stretch of highway through the deepening dusk.

"Are you hungry?"

She hadn't thought about it, but now that he'd asked, she realized she was famished. All she'd had that morning before going out to weed her flower bed was some yogurt and two cups of black coffee.

"Yes," she admitted.

"Do you like ribs?"

"Why?"

"I know where you can find the best in the world. Thought we'd stop for some."

She glanced down at the clothes he'd brought to the hospital. "Much as I appreciate the change of clothing, I'm not really dressed for going out."

He barked a laugh. "You're almost overdressed for Barbecue Bobby's."

"He's aptly named."

"He didn't get his name from barbecuing, but for being barbecued." She looked at him quizzically. "See, one night Bobby Sims got on the wrong side of a bull rider named Little Pete Pauley. They were at a postrodeo dance and got in a fight over a woman. Bobby came out on top and humiliated Little Pete—who always was real touchy about being only five feet four standing in his boots.

"Later that night, Little Pete got revenge by setting fire to Bobby's house. Bobby made it out okay, except that most of his hair got singed off. Went around for six months as hairless as a lizard and smelling faintly of wood smoke. Everybody started calling him Barbecue. From there on, his life's work just naturally evolved."

Lara suspected he was spinning a yarn, but before she could express her doubts, he pulled into the parking lot of a tavern. "Hmm. Crowded tonight."

"This is a beer joint," she protested. A single strand of yellow lights, many of them burned out, had been strung along the roof-line. They were the building's only decoration. "I'm not going in there."

"How come?" He turned to her. "Are you too prissy for us?"

He had backed her into a corner. If she refused to go in with him, he would once again accuse her of being a hypocrite, a holier-than-thou snob who couldn't rightfully throw stones when she herself had been caught transgressing.

On the other hand, she didn't want the rumor mill to grind out that she was being squired around town by Key Tackett. How tongues would wag! The lady doctor had corrupted Senator Clark Tackett, people would say, and now she had her hooks in his younger brother.

But facing down the gossip was a future possibility. Key's scorn was a sure thing in the here and now. She opened her door and got out. He was wearing an insufferably smug grin when he joined her at the entrance and pulled open the door.

The interior of the honky-tonk was no sightlier than the exterior. A pall of tobacco smoke clung to the ceiling, making the dim lighting dimmer. The smell of beer was almost as strong as the bass being pumped from the gaudy jukebox in the corner. Several couples were two-stepping around a tiny dance floor. A long bar comprised one entire wall, and tables were scattered around the murky fringes of the room.

Every head turned toward the door when they walked in. The women inspected Key; Lara was a target for the men. Self-consciously she let him lead her to a table.

"Do you drink beer?"

She rose to meet the challenge in his voice. This was another test. "With barbecue? Of course."

He placed two fingers in his mouth and whistled shrilly. "Hey, Bobby, two beers."

"Well, I'll be a cross-eyed billy goat!" the bartender boomed. "Two beers coming up for the long-lost Key Tackett."

Key sat down across from Lara and pushed aside the condiments in the center of the table. "Saving a kid's life and drinking beer with me all in the same day. You really enjoy living on the edge, don't you, Doc?"

He didn't expect an answer, and she didn't have time to offer one before a rotund man wearing a white apron stained with meat juices and barbecue sauce sauntered over carrying two longneck beer bottles in one hand. With the other, he whacked Key between the shoulder blades.

"Long time no see." He set the beer bottles on the table. Lara quickly reached out to catch hers before it toppled over. Bobby didn't notice. He was still greeting Key.

"Heard you just got back from one of them A-rab countries. Heard if you look sideways at their women, they cut off your dick. That true? Wondered how a horny bastard like you could survive over there. Wondered when you were going to get out here to see me, you asshole."

"The place looks great, Bobby. Still doing a land office business."

"Hell, yes. As long as folks eat, drink, and screw, they know the best place to come to find all three. One-stop shopping. That's my business philosophy! Who's this?" He jabbed a finger in Lara's direction.

Key introduced her. The tavern owner didn't even attempt to hide his surprise. "So you're the shady lady I've heard so much about. Son of a bitch." He looked her over with a candor she appreciated after being eyed covertly by so many others.

"You hung your shingle out in town. Old Doc Patton's place, 's that right?"

"That's right." Lara smiled, noticing the burn scars above his eyebrows and along his hairline.

"Will wonders never cease." He shifted his gaze between the two of them. "Didn't reckon y'all would be on speaking terms."

"We're not," Key replied. "But we were hungry at the same time, so here we are. You going to serve us or jaw all night?"

Barbecue Bobby grinned. "Hell, yeah, I'm going to serve you. Can't wait to get my hands on your money. What'll ya have?"

"Two rib platters. No sauce on mine."

"I'll bring the sauce on the side and y'all can suit yourselves. A couple more beers?"

"When you bring the dinners."

"Sure hope I get sick real soon," Bobby said, winking at Lara. Then, shaking his head over the vagaries of life, he lumbered back to his bar.

Key took several long swallows of his beer. Lara sipped hers. "Did you go flying last night?"

He stopped drinking, but held the spout of the bottle against his lips and idly rubbed it across them. "Why?"

Lara looked away from his mouth and the beer bottle. "Just wondering."

"Yeah, I flew last night. Took out a Piper Cub. Know what that is?" She shook her head, although she now had a vague idea of what one looked like. "Nice little kite if you're going out for a spin. Why'd you ask?"

She wouldn't admit that in order to clear her head after their altercation in the school parking lot she had taken a drive in the country, or that she had watched a foolhardy, but highly skilled, pilot flirt with death and destruction.

"I was thinking about your ankle," she said. "Since you're still favoring it when you walk, I wasn't sure you could fly."

"It still gets sore. But I couldn't remain grounded any longer or I'd have gone crazy."

"Then this hiatus is unusual for you?"

"Flying's my business. I fly for hire. For whoever has a job that sounds interesting."

"That's your criteria? Whether it's interesting?"

"And well paying," he said with a grin. "I don't fly for chicken feed."

"You can pick and choose your clients?"

"Pretty much. Some outfits are top notch. Their planes are slick and expensive. They even enforce a few rules and regulations about how many hours a pilot can fly without sleep and how long it's been since his last beer. They expect you to fill out all the paperwork required by the FAA.

"But there are just as many outfits whose planes aren't as well maintained. Sometimes the landing strips at the destination aren't ideal. And about their only restriction on a pilot is that he's able to open one eye."

"You've flown under those conditions?"

"'Under those conditions' I've earned some of my best money."

Having listened to him talk about it, she decided that money was the least of his motivators. "You love it, don't you?"

"Second only to sex. Sometimes it's even better than sex because there's no foreplay and airplanes can't talk."

She didn't take the bait.

He went on. "Up there, everything's so clean. There's no bullshit to cloud your thinking." He squinted as though searching for the appropriate description. "In the sky, things are uncomplicated."

"It looks extremely complicated."

"Flying's a motor skill," he said with a brusque shake of his head. "You're either born a flyer or you aren't. It comes from your gut, not your head. You're either good or bad. Decisions are either right or wrong. You fuck up, you die. It's that simple. There're no gray areas, no time for analysis. Only quick judgment calls that you hope to God are right."

"It wasn't that simple today," she reminded him.

"For me it was. I wasn't involved in the emergency. My job was to pilot the craft. That's what I did."

Lara didn't believe he was as nonchalant as all that. He had been more emotionally involved with saving Letty Leonard's life than he wanted to admit and would have been terribly upset if she had died en route to the hospital.

Barbecue Bobby served their beers and rib platters. On each was a side of succulent baby back ribs, french fries cooked in their jackets, creamy coleslaw, a slice of red onion, two slices of white bread, and a jalapeño pepper the size of a small banana. Key bit into his as though it were a piece of fruit. Just the scent of it brought tears to Lara's eyes, so she avoided it. The ribs, however, tasted as good as Key had promised. The pork, smoked for hours over mesquite wood, virtually melted off the bone.

"Did you always want to be a pilot?" Lara asked between bites.

"Did you always want to be a doctor?"

"I can't remember wanting to be anything else."

He shot her a wicked grin. "When you were a kid and played doctor, you played it for real, huh?"

"Actually yes," she returned with a smile. "Although not as you mean. My friends would eventually tire of the game and wanted to move on to playing 'teacher' or 'movie star' or 'model.' I never wanted to stop bandaging them until they looked like mummies. I took their temperatures with Popsicle sticks and gave them shots with meat basters."

"Ouch."

"It was a preoccupation my parents desperately hoped I would outgrow. I never did."

"They didn't cotton to you going into medicine?"

"Not at all. They wanted me to be a lady of leisure who does lunch with friends, holds office in service clubs, and organizes charity functions. Not that there's anything wrong with doing those things. For a lot of women that represents challenge and fulfillment. But it wasn't the life for me."

"Mama and Daddy couldn't understand that?"

"No, Mother and Father couldn't." He acknowledged the distinction with raised eyebrows. Lara explained. "I came late in their marriage. In fact I was an unexpected and unpleasant surprise.

"But, since they were stuck with me, my parents decided to make the best of the situation and plotted the course of my life. Because I didn't want to follow the path they had carefully chosen, they've never let me forget what a burden I've been to them. And sometimes I was," she added with a reflective laugh.

"I once kept a friend in 'intensive care' for hours until her concerned parents came looking for her. They found her in my bedroom breathing through drinking straws that I'd poked up her nostrils. It's a wonder she didn't suffocate. I prepped another friend for brain surgery by giving her a very short haircut."

Chuckling, Key blotted his mouth with a napkin.

"Then there was Molly."

"What'd you do to her?"

"I cut her open."

He choked on his swig of beer. "You *what?*"

"Molly was our next door neighbor's golden retriever. She was a beautiful dog that I'd played with since I could toddle in the yard between our houses. Molly got sick and— "

"You operated?"

"No, she died. Our neighbor was disconsolate and couldn't bear to bury her the same day she expired. So they wrapped her in plastic and left her in the carriage house overnight."

"Good God. You performed an autopsy?"

"A crude one, yes. I coerced a friend of mine, who claimed to want to be a nurse, to sneak into the carriage house with me. We took along our housekeeper's kitchen utensils."

He laughed, running his hand down his face. "Most girls I knew played with Barbie dolls."

Defensively, Lara said, "As long as Molly was feeling no pain, I didn't see the harm in cutting her open and taking a look inside. I wanted to learn something about anatomy, although at the time I didn't even know the word."

"What happened?"

"As I began to remove Molly's organs, my so-called friend started screaming. Hearing the screams, Molly's owner called the police. They arrived roughly at the same time my parents missed my friend and me. They stormed the carriage house, saw the carnage, and all hell broke loose.

"Naturally, my parents were horrified and began accusing each other of having undisclosed 'bad seeds' in their family trees. The neighbor declared she would never speak to any of us again. My friend's parents told mine that there was obviously something dreadfully wrong with me and that I should have psychiatric care before I became a real danger to myself and others.

"My parents agreed. After weeks of expensive and extensive psychiatric sessions, the doctor's analysis was that I was a perfectly normal eleven-year-old. My only unusual trait was an obsessive interest in human anatomy from a strictly medical viewpoint."

"Bet your folks were relieved to know they hadn't raised a ghoul."

"Not really. They continued to believe that my desire to become a doctor was strange. To some extent, they still do." With her finger she absently traced a bead of condensation that trickled down her beer bottle.

"My parents are very social. Appearances are important to them, and they resent cogs in their well-oiled lives. I've provided many, beginning with my birth and ending— " She raised her eyes to meet his. "Ending with the scene at Clark's cottage. Like you, Mr. Tackett, they didn't chasten me for having an affair. Only for making it public knowledge."

At that moment, a body landed in the middle of their table.

Chapter Nine

Dirty dinner dishes clattered to the floor while rib bones scattered across the grimy planks like clumsy Pick-Up-Sticks. Four bottles of beer toppled. One broke, the others rolled away.

The man's weight had tipped the table to a forty-five-degree angle. He was bleeding from his nose. Grunting curses, he struggled to his feet and charged the man who had punched him.

"Time to go." Key calmly stood up and encircled Lara's upper arm. "Your first time at Barbecue Bobby's ought not to be spoiled with a fight."

She was spellbound by the sudden outbreak of violence. As the two young men continued to slug it out, a ring of onlookers formed an arena for them, shouting encouragement. She watched and listened in horror as blood splattered and cartilage crunched.

"They're hurting each other!" As Key ushered her toward the door, she tried to dig in her heels. He ignored her attempts and moved inexorably toward the exit, pausing only long enough to hand Bobby a twenty-dollar bill. "Still up to standard. Thanks."

"Sure thing. Y'all come back."

Bobby didn't take his eyes off the fight, which had intensified. The fighters were throwing vicious punches and shockingly obscene insults at each other.

"I should stay," Lara protested. "They'll need medical attention. I could help."

Key gave the fighters an indifferent backward glance as

he pushed her through the door. "They wouldn't welcome your help, believe me. Especially those two. They don't appreciate others poking their noses into family affairs."

"They're related?" Lara asked, aghast.

"Brothers-in-law." By now they were in the car, pulling out of the parking lot onto the highway. "Lem and Scoony have always been best friends. A few years back, Scoony's little sister started looking real good to Lem. They began dating. That didn't set too well with Scoony, having seen Lem in action with other girls. Scoony warned him that if he knocked up his sister he'd beat the shit out of him."

He concentrated on passing a loaded logging truck.

Impatiently Lara asked, "Well, what happened?"

"Lem knocked her up, and Scoony beat the shit out of him."

"And they've been enemies ever since?"

"No, they're still best friends. Missy, that's Scoony's sister, heard that Scoony was out to throttle Lem. She tracked them down—at The Palm, I believe it was—and joined the fracas. Kicked them both where they're most vulnerable.

"By the time the sheriff got there, both boys were in tears, cradling their privates, and blubbering like babies. Missy told Lem he could either marry her or she'd permanently emasculate him and told Scoony that if he didn't like it he could . . . Well, Missy never has been known for her ladylike language. Anyway, Lem and Missy got married, had a little boy, and everybody was happy."

"Happy?" Lara exclaimed. "What about tonight?"

"Oh, hell, that was nothing. They were just blowing off steam. By now they're probably buying each other a drink."

Lara shook her head in dismay. "This place. These people. I always thought tales of Texas were exaggerations to perpetuate the state's mystique. Like Barbecue Bobby. What you told me is really the way it happened, isn't it? A bull rider named Little Pete Pauley set fire to his house, his hair got singed, and that's how he got his nickname."

He looked surprised. "Did you think I was lying?"

"I don't know what to think."

She gazed through the windshield as if viewing the landscape of an alien planet. Although she would never admit it to him, she felt bewildered and overwhelmed. Would she ever fit in? Had she been deluding herself that she could? Eden Pass was as peculiar and at times as intimidating as a foreign country.

"It's so different here," she said lamely.

"True enough. Different for you, anyway." He pointed through the windshield at the approaching lights of town. "For every person living in Eden Pass, there's a story. I could spend all night with you and still not get around to all of them."

She reacted, turning her head quickly. His choice of words had been calculated. She could tell that by the way he was looking at her.

In a sexy voice he added, "But I don't guess we'll be spending any nights together, will we, Doc?"

"No, we won't."

"Because you and I don't have a damn thing in common, do we?"

"Only one thing. Clark. We have Clark in common."

At the mention of his brother's name, his sultry gaze instantly turned cold. His expression changed completely.

"Well, he and I didn't have much in common except our two parents and a home address. We loved each other, even liked each other. But Clark obeyed all the rules. I broke them. I grudgingly respected him for being good all the time, and I think he harbored a secret envy for my ability not to give a damn. We were as different as brothers could be and still be kin." His eyes moved over her. "Where we really differed was our taste in women."

"I doubt the two of you would appeal to the same woman," she said stiffly.

"Right. It would either be one of us or the other. For instance, if Clark had taken you to dinner tonight, you wouldn't have had the pleasure of Barbecue Bobby's. You'd have dressed up fit to kill and gone to the country club. You'd have rubbed elbows with the upper crust, the social climbers, pillars of the community.

"They're still drinkers, liars, cheaters, and fornicators, but they're less honest about their failings than the folks out at Bobby's." He angled his head to one side. "Come to think of it, you'd've fit in much better out there at the country club with all those other hypocrites."

Lara took the insult with equanimity. "What is it about me that really bugs you, Mr. Tackett?" Once today she had slipped and called him by his first name. That had been at the height of the crisis with Letty Leonard. Last names seemed more appropriate now. It reestablished the breach.

He brought the Lincoln to a halt in her driveway, barely missing the Leonards' picnic paraphernalia still scattered about.

Laying his arm on the back of the seat, he turned to face her. "What really bugs me is that the whole world knows you're a whore. Your own husband caught you whoring. But you don't own up to what you are. You pretend to be another kind of woman entirely."

"What do you suggest I do, brand a letter A on my chest?"

"I'm sure many would pay for the pleasure. Me, for one."

"How dare you judge me? You don't know the first thing about me, and you know even less about my relationship with your brother." She shoved open the car door. "What do I owe you for today?"

"Forget it."

"I don't want to be obligated to you."

"You already are," he said. "You cost Clark everything that was important to him. He's no longer around to call in the marker, but I am. And when I do, it's going to be expensive."

"You've got it backward, Mr. Tackett. I'm the one who's holding the IOU, and you are the one who's going to pay."

"How do you figure?"

She gave him a level look. "You're going to fly me to Montesangre."

His arrogant grin collapsed, and for a moment he stared blankly at her. Then he cupped his hand around his ear. "Come again?"

"You heard me."

"Yeah, I heard you, but I can't believe it."

"Believe it."

He was incredulous. "Does the expression 'not in this lifetime' mean anything to you?"

"You'll take me there, Mr. Tackett," she said confidently as she alighted. "I'll see to it."

"Yeah, right, Doc." He was laughing as he backed the Lincoln out of the driveway. It fishtailed as he sped away.

"I love you."

"I love you, too."

Heather Winston and her boyfriend, Tanner Hoskins, were entangled on the quilt they'd spread out in the tall grass. Nearby the lazy waters of the lake slapped against the rocky beach. The moon had risen and was reflected on the water.

Even on the hottest evenings there was always a cool breeze around the lake, which made it more comfortable for the young lovers who parked there. In Eden Pass the lake was the most popular make-out spot. If you went to the lake with someone, everyone assumed the relationship was serious.

Heather and Tanner had a serious relationship, now four months old. Previously she'd gone out with Tanner's best friend, who, she came to find out, was fooling around with another girl. Following the much-publicized breakup scene outside the chemistry lab, Tanner went to her house to console her.

He'd been very sweet, calling his friend a stupid jerk-off and taking Heather's side on all points. Heather took a closer look at Tanner and decided that he was much more handsome than the creep who'd cheated on her.

After polling her best friends and discovering that they too thought Tanner was a good catch, she changed the tenor of the time they spent together. Soon it was known around school that she was "with" Tanner. She couldn't have been happier with the way things had turned out.

Since Heather Winston was the most sought-after girl in the junior class, Tanner was also walking on air. The first time he kissed her they'd frenched, and it nearly took the top of his head off. All the guys agreed that she had a body—taking after her mama, who was indisputably the hottest-looking bitch in Eden Pass. There was a lot of good-natured speculation in the locker room as to just how much of Heather's delights ol' Hoskins had sampled.

Tanner's responses to these teasing jeers were deliberately vague. Most of the guys chose to think he was getting all he wanted but was protecting Heather's reputation with gallant silence. Those more cynical figured he hadn't seen or touched anything that a swimsuit would cover.

The truth lay somewhere in between.

Tonight, he had unbuttoned her blouse and gotten his hand inside her brassiere. Heather permitted him to fondle her anywhere above the waist. Below it was where she customarily drew the line.

They were on the brink of a breakthrough, however. The gentle feathering of his tongue across her nipples had pushed Heather to a sexual height she'd never achieved before. Yearningly, she brushed her hand across the fly of his shorts.

He made a strangled, groaning sound. "Please, Heather."

Tentatively she pressed her palm against the bulge in his crotch. Her friends had warned her that "it" got huge and hard. Even so, she was timid of his erection. Yet curious. And desirous. And her friends were going to start believing she was weird if she didn't move things farther along.

"Tanner, do you want me to?"

"Oh God," he moaned and began frantically grappling with his zipper.

He shoved her hand beneath the waistband of his underwear, and before she was quite prepared for it, her hand was filled with pulsing, adolescent lust.

Tanner muttered incoherently as she timorously explored his shape. She knew how this monstrous organ was supposed to couple with her body, although she didn't understand how it possibly could. Still, it was exciting to imagine. Her mind drifted through an array of erotic images, intensified by recollections of some of Hollywood's recent renditions of sex, movies that her mother had forbidden her to see.

Then he ruined it.

"Oh, God!" she cried. "What . . .? *Tanner!* Oh, puke!"

"I'm sorry, I'm sorry," he panted. "I couldn't help it. Heather, I— "

She leaped up and headed for the lake at a run, refastening her bra and buttoning her blouse as she went. When she reached the pebbled beach, she knelt and swished her hand in the water. She was repulsed, not so much by the substance on her hand but by necking in general. It was so juvenile, so common, so unromantic. Nothing like the misty love scenes in the movies.

She moved along the beach until she reached the fishing

pier, then walked out to the end of it, sat down, and stared out over the water. Tanner caught up with her there a few moments later. He lowered himself beside her.

For a moment he said nothing. When he did speak, his voice was ragged with emotion. "I'm sorry. Christ, I didn't mean to. Are you going to tell?"

Heather saw that he was humiliated, and she regretted her adverse reaction to what she knew wasn't entirely his fault. She stroked his hair. "It's all right, Tanner. I didn't expect it and overreacted."

"No, you didn't. You had every right to be disgusted."

"I wasn't. Truly. Anyway, it's okay. Of course I won't tell anybody. How could you think I would? Just forget about it."

"I can't, Heather. I can't because . . ." He hesitated as though to gather courage, then blurted, "Because if we'd been doing it right in the first place, it wouldn't have happened."

Heather returned her gaze to the moonlit water. He'd never come right out and said he wanted to go all the way. He wanted to—she knew that. But knowing it and hearing him say it were two different things. Hearing it was much scarier because it forced her to make a decision.

"Don't get mad," he said, "but hear me out. Please. I love you, Heather. You're the prettiest, sweetest, smartest girl I've ever met. I want to, you know, know everything about you. Get inside you," he added softly.

His words shocked her in a pleasant way. They made her body tingle in secret places. "That's sexy talk, Tanner."

"I'm not just feeding you a line. I mean it."

"I know you do."

"Look around." He gestured back toward the parked cars. "Everybody else does it."

"I know that, too."

"Well, do you think . . . I mean, don't you want to?"

She gazed into his fervent eyes. Did she want to? Maybe. Not because she was passionately in love with him. She didn't see herself spending her life with Tanner Hoskins, the grocer's son, having children and grandchildren with him, growing old together. But he was sweet, and he clearly adored her.

She gave him a qualified yes.

Encouraged, he scooted closer to her across the rough boards. "It's not like you could get AIDS or anything because we're not strangers. And I'd make damn sure you wouldn't get pregnant."

Amused by his earnestness, she took his hand and squeezed it between her own. "I'm not worried about any of that. I'd trust you to take precautions."

"Then what's stopping us? Your folks?"

Her smile faded. "Daddy would probably shoot you if he knew we were even having this conversation. Mother . . ." She sighed. "She thinks we've already done it."

That was the crux of Heather's hesitation. Her mother. She didn't want to validate Darcy's low opinion of her.

Her relationship with her father was uncomplicated. He thought the sun rose and set on her. She was his pride and joy, his precious little girl. He would gladly die for her. She was confident of his unconditional love.

Her relationship with her mother wasn't as clearly definable. Darcy had a volatile and unpredictable personality. She wasn't as easy to love as her unflappable father. If Fergus was as constant as sunrise and sunset, Darcy was as changeable as the weather.

Some of Heather's earliest memories were of Darcy dressing her up and taking her downtown. She would parade her up and down the sidewalk of Texas Street, in and out of shops, making sure that everyone saw them and stopped to speak. Darcy had always liked to show her off.

But once they returned home, her mother's indulgent affection ceased. She withdrew the love she showered on Heather in public and began preparations for their next outing.

"*Practice your piano, Heather. You won't win any blue ribbons in the competition if you don't practice.*"

"*Stand up straight, Heather. People will think you have no pride if you slouch.*"

"*Stop biting your nails, Heather. Your hands look horrible, and besides, it's a terrible habit.*"

"*Wash your face again, Heather. I can still see black-heads around your nose.*"

"*Your jumps need work, Heather. You won't get reelected cheerleader next year if you start shirking.*"

Although Darcy professed to push her because she wanted her to be and to have the very best, Heather suspected that her accomplishments were more for her mother's sake than for her own. She also suspected that underlying Darcy's maternal love was a deep resentment that bordered on outright jealousy. It puzzled Heather. Mothers weren't supposed to be jealous of their children. What had she done or failed to do to provoke this unnatural emotion?

As Heather matured, their riffs had become more frequent and virulent. Darcy imagined that Heather was sexually misbehaving. She persistently made veiled accusations and sly innuendoes.

What a laugh, Heather thought scornfully.

Her mother was the one guilty of sexual misconduct. Everybody knew her reputation, even the kids at school, although no one had ever confronted Heather with it because they didn't dare. She was too popular.

But the whispered rumors reached her. It was a struggle to ignore them, especially at home when her mother was being particularly nasty. Countless times she could have used the latest gossip about Darcy to shut her up. But she hadn't and she wouldn't because of Fergus. She wouldn't do or say anything that might indirectly hurt her father or cause him embarrassment.

So when Darcy railed at her about her relationship with Tanner, and hounded her with questions about the depth of it, she withstood the inquisition in sullen silence.

Beyond petting, she hadn't done anything shameful. The fundamental reason for her abstention was that she didn't want to become like her mother. Obviously she had inherited Darcy's robust sexuality, but she didn't have to act on it. The last thing she wanted was a reputation for screwing around—like mother, like daughter. Nor would she betray her father's love the way her mother did.

Tanner had been sitting quietly at her side, patiently giving her time to sort through her misgivings. "I feel everything you do, Tanner. Honestly," she said. "Maybe not as urgently," she added with a gentle smile. "But I love you enough to want to have sex with you."

"When?" he asked thickly.

"When we feel the time and mood are right. Okay? Please don't pressure me about it."

His disappointment was plain, but he smiled and leaned forward to give her a tender kiss. "I'd better take you home before it gets any later. Your mother will have a shit fit if you're thirty seconds late."

They arrived punctually. Nevertheless, Darcy was waiting for them at the front door with a glare for Tanner and a lecture for Heather on how a girl couldn't be too protective of her good name.

"Good morning."

"Good morning."

Bowie Cato and Janellen Tackett faced each other across the desk in the cramped office at the shop. He was surprised to notice that her eyes were on a level with his. He hadn't realized when they met the first time that she was almost as tall as he. She had looked so dainty, frail even, sitting behind that large desk, looking as nervous as a whore in church.

Now why would an analogy like that pop into his head when he was in the presence of a lady like her? As though he'd spoken his thoughts out loud, he hastened to make amends.

"I'm sorry I wasn't around when you called The Palm. Hap—Mr. Hollister—gave me your message to come by when it was convenient. Is now convenient?"

"Yes, and it was kind of Mr. Hollister to remember."

"He's been real decent to me."

"Well, thank you for coming. Have a seat, please."

She indicated the metal chair behind him. He lowered himself into it as she resumed her seat behind the desk. She carefully smoothed the back of her skirt and sat down in one fluid motion. Some motions like that she carried off gracefully, without thinking about them. At other times, particularly when she was looking directly at him, her movements were as jerky and uncoordinated as a newborn colt's. She had the jitters worse than anyone he'd ever met. If he said "boo!" she'd probably faint dead away.

He couldn't imagine why Miss Janellen Tackett was nervous over this interview. She was the one holding all the aces. He needed her; his future hung in the balance, not the other way around.

"I . . ." She got a false start and began again after clearing her throat. "We've had a job become available."

"Yes, ma'am."

Her large blue eyes opened even wider. "You knew about it?"

When would he learn to keep his fat trap shut? "I, uh, heard you fired a man after accusing him of stealing."

"He *was* stealing!" Her loud exclamation startled them both. She appeared mortified by her outburst. Bowie decided to make it easier on her and in the process chalk up a few points for himself.

"I don't doubt it for a minute, Miss Tackett. You don't appear the kind of person who would make accusations until you were sure you were right."

Bowie had overheard the man everybody called Muley virtually bragging about being fired by "that skinny Tackett bitch." The harsh names the redneck had called Janellen and the unflattering way he'd talked about her hadn't jived with Bowie's memory of the soft-spoken, self-conscious lady he'd met.

He'd asked around, subtly, and found that the Tacketts had a reputation for fairness. They expected an honest day's work from their employees, but paid well. Miss Tackett was known to be especially reasonable and to cut her people a lot of slack. Muley Bill was obviously a liar as well as a thief.

"That Muley character is a loudmouthed bully, Miss Tackett," Bowie said. "So I didn't put too much stock in what he spouted off. I'm only wondering why we're wasting your valuable time talking about him."

"He was a pumper."

"Yes, ma'am."

"I'm offering you his job."

His heart lurched, but he kept his expression unreadable. He'd hoped her summons meant a job offer, but he was suspicious of being handed good fortune, fully expecting the other hand to slap him. "That sounds real fine. When do I start?"

She fingered the buttons on her blouse. "What I have in mind," she said haltingly, "is a probationary position. To see how . . . how you get along here."

There it was. The slap. "Yes, ma'am."

"This is my family's business, Mr. Cato. I'm the third generation and feel a responsibility to protect— "

"Are you scared of me, Miss Tackett?"

"Scared? No," she replied with a lying little laugh. "For heaven's sake, no. It's just that you might not like working for Tackett Oil. Steady employment might require some difficult adjustments since you were recently released from . . ."

She shifted in her seat. "If, after a time, both parties agree that it's working out, I'll offer you a permanent position. How does that sound?" She gave him a wavering smile.

Bowie also shifted in his chair and carefully regarded his hat as he threaded the brim through his fingers. If anybody else had offered him a temporary job until he proved himself worthy, he'd say "screw you" and stomp out. But he recognized the chip on his shoulder for what it was and curbed his temper.

"Do all your new employees go through this, uh, probationary thing?"

She wet her lips and fiddled some more with the buttons on her blouse. "No, Mr. Cato. But frankly you're the first person I've ever considered hiring who is on parole from prison. I'm responsible for the daily operation of the business. I don't want to make a mistake."

"You won't."

"I'm certain of that. If I weren't, I wouldn't have called you for an interview."

"You can check my record with the Department of Corrections. I got a lot of time off for good behavior."

"I've already spoken with your parole officer." His eyes snapped up to hers and she blushed. "I felt I had to. I wanted to know what you . . . what you had done."

"Did he tell you?"

"Assault and battery, he said."

He looked away and pulled his lower lip through his teeth several times. Again, he was tempted to walk out. He didn't owe her a goddamn thing, and surely not an explanation. He didn't feel he had to justify himself to anyone.

But, oddly, he wanted Janellen Tackett to understand why he'd committed the crime. He couldn't pin down exactly why he wanted her understanding. Maybe it was because she looked at him like he was an actual person and not just an ex-con.

"The bastard had it coming," he said.

"Why?"

He sat up straighter, preparing to lay out the facts and let her read them as she pleased. "He was my landlord. He and his wife lived in the apartment below mine. It was a dump, but the best I could afford at the time. She—his wife—was as kind a woman as I ever knew. Ugly as sin but a good heart, you know?"

Janellen nodded.

"She'd do favors for me. Sew on shirt buttons, stuff like that. Sometimes she'd bring me leftover stew or a slice of pie because she said bachelors never ate right and a body couldn't survive only on Wolf Brand Chili."

He bounced his hat on his knee. "One day I met her on the stairs. She had a black eye. She tried to hide it from me, but the whole left side of her face was swollen. She made up an excuse, but I knew right off that her old man had worked her over. I'd heard him yelling at her plenty of times. I didn't know he'd started using her as a punching bag.

"I cornered him and told him if he wanted a fistfight I could give him a hell of a good one. He told me to mind my own business. Then he beat her again a couple of weeks later. That time we had more than words. I slugged him a few times, but she intervened and begged me not to hurt him."

He shook his head. "Go figure. Anyway, I warned him then that the next time he hit her, I'd kill him. A few months went by, and I thought he'd gotten the message. Then one night the racket downstairs woke me up. She was screaming, crying, begging for her life.

"I ran down to their apartment and kicked the door in. He had thrown her against the wall hard enough to put a hole in the sheet-rock and to break her arm. She was cowering against the wall, and he was whipping her with a leather belt.

"I remember sailing through the air and landing square in the middle of his back. I beat the holy hell out of him. Almost killed him. Luckily one of the other tenants called the police. If they hadn't gotten there when they did, I'd've been sent up for manslaughter." He stopped, thinking back. "I'd had to deal with bullies like him all my life. I'd had enough of it, I guess, and just sorta snapped."

He was silent for a moment and stared at his hands. "At my trial, he broke down and cried, made his apologies to God and man and swore he'd never raise a hand to his wife again. My lawyer advised me to tell the jury that I didn't remember the attack, that I'd gone temporarily wacko, that I was too enraged to realize what I was doing.

"But, seeing as how I'd sworn on the Bible to tell the truth, I told them in all honesty that I wished I'd killed the son of a bitch. Any man who beats a defenseless woman like that needs killing, I said, and I meant it." He shrugged resignedly. "So he walked, and I went to the pen."

After another silence, Janellen's chair creaked slightly as she got up and moved to a tall metal filing cabinet. From it she withdrew several forms. "I'll need you to fill these out, please."

He remained seated and looked up at her. "You mean I'm hired?"

"Yes, you're hired." She quoted him a starting salary that flabbergasted him.

"And after hearing your story," she said, "I'm willing to waive the probationary period. It was a silly idea anyway."

"Not so silly, Miss Tackett. You can't be too careful these days."

His smile seemed to fluster her. She hesitated a

moment, then leaned down to lay the forms on the desk in front of him. "These are tax and insurance forms. A nuisance, I'm afraid, but necessary."

"I don't mind the paperwork if it means a job."

As she talked him through the forms, Bowie tried to concentrate on them, but it was tough to do with her standing so close. She smelled good. Not overwhelmingly perfumed like the whores he'd gone to following his release.

She smelled clean, like soap and bedsheets that had dried in the sunshine. Her hands were slender and delicate and pale. They entranced him as she sorted through the documents and pointed out the dotted lines on which he signed his name.

From the corner of his eye, he could see her in profile. She wasn't beautiful, but she wasn't downright ugly, either. Her skin was smooth and fair, practically translucent. There was no wiliness in her expression, not like some women who you could tell were calculating their next move on you. Instead she seemed to be straightforward and honest and kind, qualities he'd rarely run across. He liked listening to her voice, too. It was as soft and soothing as he imagined a mother's lullaby would be.

And her eyes . . . Hell, those eyes could have dropped a man at fifty paces if she'd chosen to use them that way.

He didn't know why Muley, or any other man, would refer to her as a "stick of a woman." Of course, even in profile, it was obvious that she wasn't fleshed out and curvy. She was slender-hipped, narrow-waisted, and small-breasted. Just the same, he took several surreptitious glances at those buttons she had a habit of fiddling with and discovered, to his chagrin, that he wouldn't mind fiddling with them himself. He knew from experience that small-breasted women sometimes had the most sensitive nipples.

Mentally, he yanked himself away from his erotic

thoughts. What the hell was the matter with him, thinking about Miss Janellen's nipples? She was a prim and proper lady. If she could read his mind, she'd probably call the law on him.

"Thank you, Miss Tackett, I think I can handle it from here," he said gruffly and hunched over the desk, blocking his view of her.

When he had completed all the forms, he pushed them across the desk and stood up. "There you go. When do you want me to start?"

"Tomorrow if you can."

"Tomorrow's fine. Who'll I report to?"

She gave him the name of his supervisor. "He's been with us a long time and knows how we like things done."

"Does he know I served time?"

"I thought it fair to tell him, but he's not the kind to hold it against you. You'll like him. He'll meet you here in the morning and drive you to all the wells you're responsible for. He'll probably run your route with you for several days. You'll have use of a company truck, of course. I assume you have a driver's license?"

"Just got it renewed."

"How can we get in touch with you?"

"That could be a problem. I haven't got a permanent address yet. Hap's been letting me sleep in his back room, but I can't do that indefinitely."

She opened her desk drawer and withdrew a large business check-book. "Find a place to live and have a telephone installed so that we can reach you at any time. We never know when an emergency will arise. If the phone company requires a deposit, have them call me." She wrote out the check, tore it from the book, and handed it to him.

Three hundred dollars, made out to him, just like that! He didn't know whether to be elated or affronted. "I don't take charity."

"Not charity, Mr. Cato. An advance. I'll take fifty dollars out of your first six paychecks. Will that be satisfactory?"

He wasn't accustomed to kindness and trust and didn't know how to respond. With Hap it was easy. Generally men didn't have to express themselves to other men. They seemed to understand one another's feelings without having to vocalize them. But with a woman it was different, especially when she was looking at you with crystal blue eyes the size of fifty-cent pieces.

"That's fine," he said, hoping he didn't sound as awkward as he felt.

"Good." Coming to her feet, she smiled and extended her hand. Bowie stared at it for a moment and had an insane impulse to wipe his hand on his pants leg before touching hers. He gave it a swift shake and immediately released it. She quickly reclaimed it. There was a second or two of uncomfortable silence, then they both began to speak at once.

"Unless you— "

"Until— "

"You go ahead," she said.

"No. Ladies first."

"I was just going to say that unless you have any questions, we'll look forward to your reporting to work tomorrow."

"And I was going to say 'until tomorrow.'" He pulled on his hat and moved toward the door. "It'll feel good to be doing real work again. I sure appreciate the job. Thank you, Miss Tackett."

"You're welcome, Mr. Cato."

Halfway through the door, he halted and turned back. "Do you call all the men who work for you by their last names?"

The question seemed to catch her off guard. Rather than speak, she shook her head rapidly.

"Then call me Bowie, okay?"

She swallowed visibly. "Okay."

"And it's Boo-ie, like Jim Bowie and Bowie knife. Not Bowie like David, the rock star."

"Of course."

Feeling dumb for bringing it up—what the hell difference would it make to her how he pronounced his name?—he touched the brim of his hat and made tracks.

Chapter Ten

*I*s the roast too dry, Key?"

Janellen's question roused him from his deep brooding. He sat up straighter, looked across the dinner table at her, and smiled. "Delicious as always. I'm just not very hungry tonight."

"That's what happens when you fill up on whiskey," Jody interjected.

"I had one drink before dinner. And so did you."

"But I'll stop with one. You'll go out and get drunk tonight, like you do every night."

"How do you know what I'll be doing tonight? Or any other night? Furthermore, what do you care?"

"Please," Janellen exclaimed, covering her ears. "Stop shouting at each other. Can't we have one meal together without an argument?"

Knowing his sister's anxiety was deeply felt, Key said, "I'm sorry, Janellen. You've served a great meal. I didn't mean to spoil it."

"I don't care about the meal. I care about the two of you. Mama, your face is as red as a beet. Did you take your medication today?"

"Yes I did, thank you kindly. I'm not a child, you know."

"Sometimes you act like one when it comes to taking medicine," Janellen gently chastised. "And shouting across the dinner table is something you never allowed us kids to do."

Jody pushed aside her plate and lit a cigarette. "Your

father didn't allow arguments at the dinner table. He said it spoiled his digestion."

Janellen brightened at the mention of their father. She had only foggy memories of him. "Do you remember that, Key?"

"He laid down the law about such things," he replied, smiling for his sister. "Sometimes you remind me of him, you know."

"You're kidding?" A blush of pleasure crept up her slender throat and over her face. She was pathetically easy to please. "Really?"

"Really. You've got his eyes. Doesn't she, Jody?"

"I suppose."

She wouldn't even agree with him on an obvious and insignificant point, but he refused to let it bother him. "All three of us kids inherited the Tackett blues. I used to hate it when people said to Clark and me, 'You boys have the prettiest eyes. Just like your daddy's.'"

"Why did you hate it?" Janellen asked.

"I don't know. Made me feel like a sissy, I guess. Being told that anything attached to him is 'pretty' isn't what a little boy wants to hear."

"Your father didn't mind hearing it," Jody said crisply. "He loved having people fawn over him. Especially women."

Ever guileless and naïve, Janellen said, "You must have been very proud to have such a handsome husband, Mama."

Jody rolled the smoldering tip of her cigarette against the rim of the ashtray. "Your father could be very charming." Her face softened. "The day Clark the Third was born, he brought me six dozen yellow roses. I fussed at him for being so extravagant, but he said it wasn't every day that a man had a son."

"What about when Key was born?"

Jody's misty vision cleared. "I didn't get any flowers that day."

After a tense silence, Key said very quietly, "Maybe Daddy knew you wouldn't like them. That you'd only throw them out."

Janellen reacted quickly. "Mama explained why she threw out your flowers, Key. They made her sneeze. She must have been allergic to them."

"Yeah, she must have been."

He didn't believe it for a minute. Earlier in the week, vainly looking for a way to make peace with Jody, he'd brought her a bouquet. Janellen had arranged the flowers for him in a vase and placed it on the dresser in Jody's bedroom while she was out with Maydale.

The next morning, he'd found the flowers in the garbage can outside the back door. It wasn't so much that she'd thrown them out that had rankled him, but that she hadn't even acknowledged them until he presented her with the wilted evidence and asked for an explanation.

Calmly, coldly, she'd told him the bouquet had given her hay fever. She hadn't said that they were pretty and that it was a pity she couldn't enjoy them. She hadn't thanked him for the gesture.

Not that he wanted or needed her thanks. He would survive without it. It just made him damn mad that she thought him stupid enough to accept her lame excuse for rebuffing a gift from him. Rather than give her the satisfaction of seeing him hurt and angry, he acted as nonchalant now as he had that morning he'd tossed the bouquet back into the trash can.

Jody broke another lengthy silence. "How's the new man doing?"

Janellen practically dropped her coffee cup. It clattered noisily against the saucer. "He . . . he's doing fine. I think he's going to work out well."

"I still haven't seen his references."

"I'm sorry. I keep forgetting to bring them home. But his supervisor reports that he's doing the job well. He's never late and is very conscientious. He gets along with the other men. Doesn't make trouble. I've had no complaints."

"I still can't figure why Muley up and quit without giving notice."

Janellen had told Key the circumstances of Muley's severance but had asked him not to tell Jody. Her reaction to a trusted employee turning thief was likely to be volatile and a threat to her high blood pressure. Key had agreed.

He also knew that Bowie Cato was an ex-con who'd barely had time to lose his prison pallor. Even before Janellen introduced them, Key had seen him at The Palm. Hap had given him the scoop on Cato.

Key nursed no prejudice against former inmates. He'd spent a few days in an Italian jail himself a few years back. Cato was friendly but not ingratiating. He kept to himself, did his job, and avoided trouble. That could not be said of very many men who didn't have prison records.

Jody's viewpoint on social reform wasn't exactly liberal. She had a low tolerance for mistakes. She wouldn't welcome having an ex-con on the payroll, so the less she knew about Cato's background, the better for everybody. Muley was gone; Janellen had found a qualified replacement. That was the bare-bones story they'd given her. But apparently Jody smelled a rat. This wasn't the first time she'd broached the subject.

Key kept his expression impassive and hoped Janellen would do the same. But lying didn't come easily to her. Under her mother's incisive stare, she fidgeted with her silverware.

"Cato isn't from around here?"

"No, Mama. He grew up in West Texas."

"You don't know who his people are?"

"I think they're deceased."

"Is he married?"

"Single."

Jody continued staring at her daughter as she puffed

on her cigarette. After what seemed an endless silence, Janellen glanced nervously at Key. "Key's met him. He thought he was all right."

Damn! He didn't want to get caught in the cross fire. But he went to his sister's rescue. "He's a nice guy."

"So's Santy Claus. That doesn't mean he knows an oil well from his asshole."

Janellen flinched at her mother's crude phraseology. "Bowie knows a lot about oil, Mama. He's worked in the business since he was a boy."

As long as he'd already been drawn into it, Key furthered his sister's cause. "Cato is doing his job. Janellen likes him and so do the other men. What more could you want?" He knew, of course, what his mother wanted: Jody wanted to be young, healthy, and strong; she wanted to be at the controls of Tackett Oil and Gas and resented Janellen's hiring an employee without consulting her. If she'd hired a reincarnation of H. L. Hunt, Jody wouldn't have liked him.

"He's been on the payroll for . . . what, Janellen, two weeks?"

"That's right."

"And he hasn't caused a single mishap," he continued. "So it looks to me like Janellen made a sound business decision."

Jody turned to him, her contempt at full throttle. "Like your opinion counts for something where Tackett Oil is concerned."

"I wasn't speaking as an expert on the oil business," Key returned evenly. "Just as a guy who shook hands with another guy. Cato looked me straight in the eye, like he didn't have anything to hide. I met him at the end of the day. He was sweaty and his clothes were dirty, which indicated to me that he'd been working his ass off outdoors in the heat."

Jody sent a plume of cigarette smoke toward the ceiling. "Sounds as though you could learn a lesson or two about the work ethic from this Cato fellow. It wouldn't hurt you to sweat a little, get dirty, do some work around here."

"Key's been working, Mama. He fixed the latch on the gate."

"That's tinkering. I'm talking about sweat-of-the-brow, damned hard work."

"On your oil wells, you mean." Despite his best intentions to hold his temper, Key's voice was rising.

"It wouldn't kill you, would it?"

"No. It wouldn't kill me, but it isn't my gig. It's yours."

"Ah, that's why you never wanted to be part of the business. Because I was there first? You didn't want to play second banana to a woman."

Key, shaking his head, laughed ruefully. "No, Jody. I never wanted to be a part of the business because I'm not interested in it."

"Why not?"

Jody never accepted a simple answer at face value. He didn't remember a time when he hadn't been required to justify, explain, and account for his opinions, especially if they differed from hers. It was no wonder to him that his daddy had turned to other women. With Jody, everything was a contest to see who could best whom. It wouldn't take long for a man to grow tired of that.

Forcing himself to remain calm, he said, "Maybe if we were still drilling for oil, if there was a challenge involved, I'd consider going into the business."

"You crave excitement, is that it?"

"Routine holds no appeal for me."

"Then you should have lived during the boom. It attracted your kind of people. East Texas was crawling with gamblers and con artists and crooks and whores. All living on a wing and a prayer. Taking high-stakes risks. Saying to hell with tomorrow, let the devil take it.

"That's the life for you, isn't it? You're not happy unless you're walking a tightrope with crocodiles on both sides ready to eat you if you fall. Just like your father, you thrive on adventure."

Key was clenching his teeth so tightly that his jaw ached. "Think whatever you want, Jody." Then, leaning forward, he stabbed the table with his index finger to emphasize each word. "But I never did and never will want to baby-sit a bunch of stinking oil wells."

"Key," Janellen groaned miserably.

She could barely be heard over Jody's chair scraping back. Her face was florid. "Those stinking oil wells allowed you to live high on the hog all your life! They provided food for your belly, clothes for your back, bought you new cars, and paid your way through college!"

Key rose, too. "For which I'm grateful. But am I supposed to become an oilman just to pay you back for upholding your responsibilities as a parent? If you and Daddy had been plumbers, would I be obligated to shovel shit the rest of my life? It was never expected of Clark to go into the oil business, so why me?"

"Clark had other plans for his life."

"How do you know? Did you ever ask him his ambitions? Or did he only follow *your* plans for his life?"

Jody drew herself up. "He had his career mapped out and would have followed it, had it not been for that whore of a doctor that you've been jockeying around the countryside."

"That was an emergency situation, Mama," Janellen interjected. "That little girl would have died if it hadn't been for Key."

Letty Leonard's accident had been a headline story in the local newspaper.

"Thank you, Janellen," Key said, "but I don't need you to defend what I did. I would have done it for a dog, let alone a little girl."

Jody was fixed on only one aspect of the drama. "I told you to stay away from Lara Porter."

"I didn't hightail it to the emergency room for her, for chrissake. I did it for the kid."

"Were you thinking of the kid when you bought the doctor's supper?"

Rather than appear surprised or guilty that she also knew about his and Lara Mallory's barbecue dinner, he shrugged. "I hadn't eaten all day. I was hungry. She happened to be along when I stopped."

Jody's stare was hot with wrath. "I'm telling you one last time. Stay away from her. Do your drinking and whoring with somebody else."

"Thanks for reminding me. I'm getting a late start tonight." He strode to the sideboard, poured himself a shot of whiskey, and tossed it back defiantly.

Making a sound of disgust, Jody turned and left the dining room with a militant tread, climbing the stairs to the second story.

"Why can't you two get along?"

Key rounded on his sister, prepared to make a defensive comeback. Her remorseful expression stopped him.

"Jody starts it, not me."

"I know she's difficult."

He laughed sardonically at her understatement.

"Thank you for keeping my secret about Mr. Cato. Mama wouldn't want an ex-con on the payroll, even if he has turned out to be an exemplary employee."

Key cocked an eyebrow. "Exemplary employee? Isn't it too soon to tell?"

"Mr. Cato isn't the subject here," she said primly before switching subjects. "Did you really take her to dinner?"

"Who? Lara Mallory? Jesus, what's the big deal? I popped into Barbecue Bobby's for some ribs. She happened to be along because I was giving her a ride home from the airstrip. That's all there was to it. Is that a hanging offense?"

"She called me."

His anger evaporated. "She what?"

"She called me last week. Out of the blue. I answered the company phone, and she identified herself. She was very gracious. She invited me to lunch."

He laughed. "She invited you to lunch?" The notion was ludicrous.

"I was so taken aback, I didn't know what to say."

"What did you say?"

"I said no, of course."

"Why?"

"Key! This is the woman who ruined Clark's political future."

"She didn't rape him at gunpoint, Janellen," he said wryly. "I doubt if she tied him to the bedpost, either. Unless it was for recreational purposes."

"I don't see how you can joke about it," she said crossly. "Whose side are you on?"

"I'm on our side. You know that." He stared into near space for a moment, bouncing the empty shot glass in his hand. "It might have been interesting if you'd accepted her invitation, though. I'd like to know what she's up to."

"Do you think she's up to something?"

He thought about it for a moment. Admittedly his estimation of Lara Mallory had risen when he witnessed the determination with which she'd struggled to save the Leonard child's life. He'd seen military medics less committed to saving a patient.

However, despite the courage and skill she'd demonstrated in that crisis, she was still the key player in the scandal that had irreparably compromised Clark. She wouldn't have come to Eden Pass without strong motivation. She wanted something. She'd said as much when she told him she was holding an IOU she intended to collect.

You're going to fly me to Montesangre.

He hadn't believed for one second that she was serious.

She'd made clear her low opinion of that country. Wild horses couldn't drag her back there.

So why had she said that? To get a rise out of him? To throw him off track and keep him guessing about her true motives?

"She wouldn't have called you unless she wanted something from you," he told Janellen irritably.

"Like what?"

"Who the hell knows? Possibly something as Mickey Mouse as a keepsake of Clark's childhood. Or something as abstract as public approval. You're a well-respected member of the community. Maybe she thinks that being seen with you would give her the acceptance she needs to make a go of her practice. Next time she calls— "

"If she does."

"I think she will. She's a gutsy broad. When she calls, reconsider. Lunch with her might be interesting."

"Mama would have a fit."

"She doesn't have to know."

"She'd find out."

"So what? You're a grown-up. You're allowed to make your own decisions even if they don't set well with Jody."

She placed her hand on his arm and spoke earnestly. "Please, Key, for both your sakes, make peace with her."

"I'm trying, Janellen. She doesn't want to make peace with me."

"That's not true. She just doesn't know how to give in graciously. She's old and crotchety. She's lonely. She doesn't feel well, and I think she's afraid of her mortality."

He agreed on all points, but that didn't solve the problem. "What do you want me to do that I haven't already tried? I've bent over backward to be polite and pleasant. I even brought her flowers. You see how much good that did," he said bitterly. "I'll be damned if I'm going to bend at the waist and kiss her pinky every time I see her."

"I'm not asking you to pamper her. She'd see straight through any insincerity and only resent you for it. But you could be less prickly. When she began talking about work, you could have told her about some of your recent jobs."

"I shouldn't have to display my achievements like merit badges. I'm not out to impress her. Besides, she's not interested in what I do. She thinks flying is a hobby. If I was the pilot of *Air Force One*, it wouldn't be good enough for her."

He returned the shot glass to the tray, his motions slow and heavy with discouragement. "Jody doesn't want me here. The sooner I leave, the better she'll like it."

"Please don't feel like that. And don't go away with this thing festering between you. She's still devastated over Clark's death, and because she can't tolerate that weakness in herself, she overcompensates by lashing out at you."

"I've always been a convenient whipping boy. She hasn't liked me since the day I was born and Daddy failed to send her six dozen yellow roses."

"He hurt her, Key. She loved him, and he hurt her."

"Loved him?" he repeated with a bitter laugh.

Janellen looked serious and a bit puzzled. "She loved him very much. Didn't you realize that?"

Before he was able to refute her, the doorbell rang.

"It's going to get better between you. You'll see." She pressed his arm before releasing it. "I'll get the door."

Rejecting his sister's optimism, he decided to have another whiskey. He swallowed the shot whole. It stung his throat, seared his esophagus, and in all probability would upset his stomach. He didn't enjoy drinking as much as he once had.

He didn't enjoy most things as he once had. When had taking a woman to bed become more trouble than

it was worth? He was soured on life in general and didn't
know why.

He had blamed his recent disenchantment on his
sprained ankle and the bullet wound in his side. But
his ankle only bothered him occasionally now, and his
wound had healed, leaving only a little tenderness and a
pink scar to remind him of it.

So what was wrong with him?

Boredom.

He had too much idle time in which to think. His
thoughts invariably turned to Clark's accidental drowning
and all the loose ends of the theories dangling like the
ragged hem of a shroud. Key wanted the facts, yet was
cautious not to root them out, afraid he'd learn something
he didn't want to know. Every rock he'd overturned lately
had ugly worms beneath it. He decided that some things
were best left undisturbed.

Thank God he was actively flying again. He hadn't
flown Letty Leonard to Tyler for the publicity it would
generate, but since then his phone hadn't stopped ringing.
He'd already flown some good contracts and had scheduled even more. He didn't particularly need the money,
although it was always welcome. What he desperately
needed was the activity and the sense of freedom that
only flying afforded him.

For his peace of mind, he was in the wrong state, the
wrong town, and the wrong house. He wanted to find a
place that was completely different from anything he'd
experienced, where the language was foreign and the
food was strange. Some exotic place where the people
had never even heard of the Tacketts.

He'd traveled all over the world searching for a place
where nobody knew that he was Clark Tackett's brother.
It was an ongoing quest. Eventually strangers would
put two and two together. "Tackett? Any kin to the
former senator from Texas? His kid brother? Well, I'll
be damned."

Clark had been the measuring stick by which Key had been judged all his life.

"Key is almost as tall as Clark now."

"Key can run almost as fast as Clark."

"Key isn't as well behaved as Clark."

"Key didn't make the honor roll, but Clark always does."

He'd eventually exceeded his brother in height. During adolescence, he'd surpassed him as an athlete. But unfavorable comparisons had followed him into adulthood. Incomprehensible as it seemed, he'd never been jealous of Clark. He'd never wanted to be like his brother, but everyone else thought Clark was the example to which he should aspire. Jody thought so more than anyone.

As a kid, it had hurt him that she so obviously favored Clark. She'd bandaged his skinned knees but never kissed them. Rather, she'd rebuked his recklessness. His small gifts, the pictures he'd colored at school, were glanced at and set aside, never cherished, never taped to her vanity mirror.

When he was a teenager, he resented her coldness toward him. Blatant disobedience and rebellion had been his way of dealing with her favoritism for Clark. She only approved of him when he was throwing touchdown passes for the Eden Pass Devils, but that was self-aggrandizement and had little to do with him personally.

Off the gridiron, he went out of his way to show her just how little he cared one way or another, although deep down he cared a great deal and couldn't understand why he was so unlovable.

But with maturity came the acceptance that his mother simply didn't love him. She didn't even like him. Never had. Never would. He'd given up trying to analyze why, and, frankly, he didn't much care anymore. That's just the way it was. Clark had been caught in a bedroom scandal involving a married woman, but Key was the one accused of "whoring."

Several years ago, having finally reached the conclusion that winning his mother's tolerance, if not her love, was a lost cause, he'd decided that it would be to everyone's advantage if he made himself scarce, a decision that also satisfied his innate wanderlust.

Now, even that was being stymied.

He was restless and bored, and the questions surrounding his brother's death were tethering him to their home. He needed to go looking for anonymity again, but whenever he was tempted to pack up and truck it, a vision of his sister's imploring face saddled him with guilt.

Her concerns were valid and justified. Aging and the loss of control that accompanied it were frightening to a woman as strong-willed as Jody. In good conscience, Key couldn't leave Janellen to handle her alone. He'd come to agree with Janellen's fear that Jody's forgetfulness and confusion were harbingers of something much more serious than senility. If a medical crisis did occur, he'd never forgive himself if he were thousands of miles away and unreachable. No matter that he wasn't her ideal of a son, Jody was still his mother. For the time being, he belonged in Eden Pass.

"Key?"

Lost in thought, he turned at the sound of his sister's hesitant voice.

"There's someone at the door to see you." She was looking at him in a peculiar, quizzical manner.

"Who is it? What does he want?"

"It's a woman."

Chapter Eleven

*L*ara arched her back, stretching the stiff muscles and holding the position for several moments. Gradually she relaxed and rubbed her eyes before repositioning her reading glasses on the bridge of her nose.

After eating an early dinner while watching the evening news, she had forgone watching prime-time TV because it offered nothing enticing. Any enjoyment derived from reading fiction had been sadly reduced since that morning in Virginia. No novelist could conjure up a plot with as many twists, pitfalls, and calamities as those in her life the last five years. It was difficult to sympathize with a protagonist whose dilemma was mild when compared to her own.

With nothing to do for entertainment, she had decided to read through her patient files. The intricacies of medicine never failed to engross her.

While other students in her class had complained all through medical school, for Lara it had been like a vacation. She relished the required hours of study. Having unlimited access to textbooks and perplexing case histories was a luxury. She gorged on them like a gourmand with an endless supply of delicacies.

Unlike her parents, none of her instructors or classmates berated her for her unquenchable thirst for knowledge, or repeatedly told her that the study of medicine was unsuitable for a well-bred young woman and that there were much more acceptable avenues of interest to pursue.

She'd graduated third in her class at Johns Hopkins, excelled as an intern, and had been offered her pick of hospitals in which to serve her residency. Naturally, she'd enjoyed the grudging admiration of her colleagues, but the real reward lay in healing. A grateful patient's simple "thank you" surpassed the accolades of her associates.

Heartbreakingly, those rewards came few and far between now. That's why Lara enjoyed perusing her files, charting a patient's progress from diagnosis to cure.

She was roused by an approaching car. Expecting it to drive past, she watched with puzzled interest when it entered her driveway and wound around to the rear of the clinic. She laid aside her reading material and quickly left her office. As she made her way through the clinic, she experienced a twinge of déjà vu. This was disturbingly similar to the night Key Tackett had appeared on her threshold, his side bleeding from a gunshot wound.

It was so similar that she barely registered surprise when she opened the door to find him standing on her back steps. Only this time he wasn't alone.

Lara gave the girl a curious glance, then looked at him. "I keep regular office hours, Mr. Tackett. That's something you seem to forget. Or ignore. Or is this a social call?"

"Can we come in?"

He wasn't in a mood to spar with her. A frown was pulling his eyebrows together, and his lips were compressed into a stern, narrow line. If he had come alone, Lara probably would have slammed the door in his face. She was on the verge of doing so anyway when she gave the girl a closer look and saw that she'd been crying. Her eyes and nose were moist and red, and her face was mottled. She was clutching a damp tissue so tightly her knuckles had turned white.

Beyond these visible signs of distress, she appeared to be a perfectly healthy girl in her late teens. She was stoutly built, with a deep bosom and full hips. Her face was pretty, or would have been if she'd been smiling. Her shoulder-length hair was straight and dark. Because of the bleak expression in her brown eyes, coupled with her obvious misery, Lara couldn't shut her out.

She stepped aside and motioned them in. "What can I do for you?"

The girl remained silent. Key said, "This is Helen Berry, Dr. Mallory. She needs a doctor."

"You're ill?" Lara asked the girl.

Helen glanced furtively at Key before saying, "Not exactly."

"I can't help you unless you tell me what the problem is. If it's a general checkup you need, you can be the first patient I see tomorrow morning."

"No!" the girl protested. "I mean . . . I don't want anybody to know . . . I can't . . ."

"Helen needs you to examine her."

Lara turned to Key, who'd spoken for the girl. "Examine her for what? If she's not ill— "

"She needs a gynecological examination."

Lara gave him a wide, inquiring stare that demanded further explanation. He remained silent, his expression immutable. The girl was anxiously gnawing her lower lip.

"Helen," Lara asked gently, "were you raped?"

"No." She gave her head a hard shake. "Nothing like that."

Lara believed her and was greatly relieved.

"I'll wait out here." Key executed an abrupt about-face and stalked down the hallway to the dark waiting room.

His exit created a soundless vacuum. It was several seconds before Lara let out her held breath. She gave Helen Berry a reassuring smile and said, "This way, please." The girl followed her into an examination room, where Lara pointed her onto the table.

"Don't you want me to undress first?"

"No," she replied. "I'm not going to do a pelvic

examination until I have more information. Besides, my nurse isn't here to assist me. I never conduct an examination like that without an assistant."

That was for her protection as well as the patient's. In a sue-crazy society, doctors were paranoid about malpractice suits. Because of the scandal that haunted her, she was more vulnerable than most.

Her patient's eyes filled with fresh tears. "But you gotta examine me. I gotta know. I gotta know right now so I can decide what to do."

Obviously distraught, she was shredding the soggy tissue. Lara clasped her hands to keep them still. "Helen." She spoke gently but with authority. Her primary objective was to calm the patient. "Before we can proceed, I must get some information from you."

She reached for a chart and a pen and asked Helen for her full name. The paperwork could have been postponed, but doing it now forced the girl to compose herself. Working her way down the standard form, Lara learned that Helen was a local girl who lived in a rural area. She was eighteen years old and had graduated from high school the previous May. Her father worked for the telephone company. Her mother was a homemaker. She had two younger sisters, one brother. There was no history of serious illness in the family.

"Now," Lara said, setting the chart aside, "why did Mr. Tackett bring you to see me?"

"I asked him to. I had to." Her face crumpled and her lower lip fell victim to more brutalizing. Tears streamed down her plump cheeks.

Lara, believing she knew the cause of Helen's distress, cut to the heart of the problem. "Do you think you're pregnant?"

"Oh, jeez. I'm so stupid!" With that, Helen flung herself onto the examination table, drew her knees to her chest, and began sobbing uncontrollably.

Lara moved swiftly to her side and took her hand again.

"Helen, calm down. We don't know anything for certain yet. You might be crying over nothing. A false alarm."

She kept her voice calm and soothing, but she wanted to grind her teeth. She wished she had a double-barreled shotgun, loaded and aimed at Key Tackett's testicles. Bedding wayward housewives like Darcy Winston was one thing; seducing high school girls was quite another.

Lara smoothed back strands of Helen's hair. "When was your last period?"

"Six weeks ago."

"So you've only missed one? That doesn't necessarily mean you're pregnant."

Helen bobbed her head emphatically. "Yes it does. I'm never late."

Perhaps, Lara thought, but there were myriad reasons for delayed menses, only one of which was pregnancy. Still, she had learned that patients were often the best authorities on their own bodies. She couldn't blithely dismiss Helen's conclusion. "Have you had sexual intercourse?"

"Yes."

"Without using any contraception?"

Helen's head wobbled up and down in answer.

Lara was dismayed that high school students were still negligent in their use of condoms, which were the simplest and least expensive, yet reliable, protection against unwanted pregnancy and sexually transmitted diseases. In a community like Eden Pass, open discussion about these safeguards was certain to generate opposition from conservative parents and religious groups. Nevertheless, it was vital—indeed a life or death matter—to acquaint teenagers with the risks they were taking if they were sexually active and didn't take precautions.

"Any breast tenderness?"

"Some. No more than usual. But anyway, I did one of those home pregnancy tests."

"It was positive?"

"No question."

"They're fairly reliable, but there's always a margin for error in any test." Lara gave her a hand up. "Go into the bathroom and get a urine specimen. I can do a preliminary test tonight."

"Okay. But I know I'm pregnant."

"Have you ever been pregnant before?"

"No. But I know. If I am, he'll kill me."

She retreated into the adjoining toilet. Thinking of Key Tackett sitting complacently in her waiting room made Lara want to confront him immediately and convey her disgust. But her patient came first.

"I left it on the lid of the tank," Helen said when she emerged.

"Fine. Lie down on the table and try to relax."

In a few minutes, Helen's worst fear was once again confirmed. "I knew it," she wailed when Lara told her that the indications were positive. She began to cry again. Lara placed her arms around her and held her until the sobs became dry, racking hiccups.

"Until your pregnancy is confirmed beyond any doubt, I'd rather not give you a sedative. Would you like something to drink?"

"A Coke? Please."

Lara left her alone only long enough to fetch the soft drink. When she returned, Helen was weeping quietly but was more composed. She took several greedy sips of the cola.

"Helen, is marrying the child's father out of the question?"

"Yes," she mumbled. "A baby is the last thing he wants or needs."

Angry heat spread throughout Lara's body. "I see. What about your parents? How supportive will they be?"

"They love me," she said as more tears filled her eyes. "They won't kick me out. But Daddy's a deacon in our church. Mom's . . . Oh, God, they'll just die of shame."

"Do you intend to have the baby?"

"I don't know."

"You could always make it available for adoption."

She shook her head morosely. "I don't think he'd let me. Besides, if I had it, I could never give it away."

"Have you considered abortion?"

"That's probably what I'll have to do." She sobbed and blotted her nose. "Except . . . except I love him, you know? I don't want to kill his baby."

"You don't have to make that decision tonight," Lara said softly as she stroked the girl's hand.

"If that's what I decided, would you do it so nobody would know?"

"I'm sorry, Helen, no. I don't perform D and Cs to terminate pregnancy."

"How come?"

Having watched her own child die, aborting living tissue was something Lara simply couldn't do unless the mother's life was at risk. "That's just my policy," she told the girl. "However, if you are pregnant and that's the alternative you choose, I'll make the arrangements for you."

Helen nodded, but Lara doubted that she was retaining much of this conversation. Dismay had numbed her. Lara patted her hand and told her she would come for her in a few minutes. "Lie quietly and finish your drink."

Stepping into the hallway, she bolstered herself for the coming encounter. As she entered the waiting room, she flipped on the light switch and flooded the area with a cold, unforgiving, fluorescent glare. Key was slouched on one of the short sofas. Blinking to adjust his eyes to the sudden brightness, he slowly came to his feet.

"Why did you bring her to me?" Lara demanded angrily.

"I figured you needed the business."

"I appreciate your thoughtfulness," she said caustically, "but I would rather not have been drawn into another of your intrigues."

He folded his arms across his chest. "From your tone of voice, I gather Helen was right. She's pregnant?"

"It appears so."

His head dropped forward, and he swore elaborately.

"I take it you don't welcome this news."

His head snapped up. "Damn right, Doc. It sucks."

"You should have thought of that before sleeping with an unsophisticated girl like Helen. And why didn't you take precautions? Surely a man of the world like you keeps a handy cache of condoms. Or does using one hamper your macho image?"

"Now just a frigging minute. You— "

"Clark told me all about your satyric reputation. I thought he was exaggerating, but apparently he wasn't. 'Key Tackett's women.' Around here, it's like a club, isn't it? The only requirement for membership is to have gone to bed with you." She looked at him contemptuously.

"Maybe they should change the name to Key Tackett's *girls*," she said with a sneer. "What's the matter with you? Are you losing your boyish charm? Has aging bruised your ego? Are you so insecure over your fading youth that you've resorted to bedding high school girls?"

"What difference does it make to you?" With his eyes half-closed, he added softly, "Jealous?"

Lara drew herself up, angry for having stooped to his level. By doing so, she'd left herself open to counter-attack. In a cool, professional voice she said, "Helen is seriously considering abortion. Until she reaches a firm decision, I'll be happy to give her prenatal care, provided she comes here alone, without you."

"She won't be coming here at all. All we wanted from you tonight was a yea or nay." Angrily, he reached into the hip pocket of his tight, worn jeans and fingered out his money clip. "How much do I owe you?"

"This one's on me, but I want something in exchange."

"Like what? No, let me guess. Let's see . . . a free flight to Timbuktu?"

She had wondered if he would make reference to their last conversation and wasn't surprised that his remark was sarcastic. She didn't take the bait. "What I want is your promise— "

"I don't make promises to women. While Clark was filling your ear about my sex life, did he fail to mention that?"

She strove to keep her voice even. "I don't want you dumping any more of your garbage at my back door. This is the second time I've had to clean up one of your messes. Leave me out of them, please. I want no part of your juvenile, romantic escapades."

"Is that right?"

"That's right."

Menacingly, he came nearer, until he was standing so close that their clothing was touching. She could feel his body heat, feel his breath on her uplifted face. His rage, too, was palpable. Only sheer determination kept her from backing down.

"That's funny, Doc," he whispered huskily. "I'd've thought this kind of romantic escapade was right up your alley."

She held her ground and his blue stare for as long as she could stand them, then backed up a few steps and turned away. "I've tried to make Helen reasonably calm, but she's still upset," she said over her shoulder. "If you have a smidgen of decency you'll be gentle with her tonight. No blame. No recriminations. Until she decides how to resolve this crisis, she's going to need patience and understanding."

"Well that's just fine, because I fairly ooze the milk of human kindness."

Lara shot him a fulminating look, then gave him her back and walked down the hall. She tapped on the examination room door before going inside. Helen was lying on her back on the padded table, staring at the acoustical tiles in the ceiling. Lara was relieved to see that she was no longer crying.

She plastered on a smile she hoped didn't look too false. "How are you feeling?"

"Okay, I guess."

"Good. Key's waiting for you."

She assisted Helen off the table and they moved into the hallway. He was waiting at the back door, as though ready to make a quick getaway. To say he had the morals of an alley cat would be doing alley cats a disservice. It was a pity that his character didn't match his good looks.

The open collar of his shirt provided only a glimpse of what Lara knew was a broad chest. His jeans fit his sex, narrow hips, and long thighs like a second skin. Clark had rarely worn casual clothes, never Levi's. She'd never seen either him or Randall in cowboy boots. Key's were well-worn victims of the elements.

Key Tackett's women, she thought scornfully.

Being so physically attractive, his success with women wasn't surprising. Within weeks, he had slept with Darcy Winston and this eighteen-year-old. How many others were there? His affair with Darcy wasn't as shocking as his dalliance with this girl so much younger and more innocent than he. For some vague and disturbing reason, she was disappointed in him.

To his credit, he opened his arms to Helen, who rushed into his embrace. He held her tightly against him for several moments, his head bent low over hers, whispering so softly into her ear that Lara couldn't distinguish the words. Between sobs, Helen nodded her head against his chest.

Then, setting her away, he said, "Wait for me in the car, sweetheart. I'll be right out."

On her way through the door, she gave Lara a hasty thank-you. Key said nothing until Helen was out of earshot. "I'll see that she gets proper prenatal care, but it won't be from you."

Lara lamented losing a patient, but reasoned that was the price she would pay for giving him a lecture on philandering. In lieu of saying anything she might later regret, she gave him a curt nod. At this point she was willing to leave well enough alone.

Not Key. He got in another parting shot. "On my way over here, I heard something on the radio that might interest you. Late this afternoon, Letty Leonard died."

Key wasn't the only one who had heard of the child's death. Jody had.

Eden Pass was situated midway between the Dallas/Fort Worth metropolitan area and Shreveport, Louisiana. Its location provided it with a large selection of television stations. All three networks had affiliates in those cities, which were carried by the local cable company, along with CNN and other major cable stations.

When it came to regional news, however, Jody relied on the station that broadcast from Tyler. She personally knew the owners and was familiar with the on-air talent. Watching their newscasts was like having a member of her family visit every night to deliver the news.

She was inordinately tired this evening. Her angry exchange with Key had sapped her energy. That, coupled with their conversation about Clark Junior, had taxed her mentally, emotionally, and physically. Even though he'd been dead more than two decades, thinking about her late husband always left her feeling resentful and depressed.

Immediately following her huffy departure from the dining room, she'd retired to her room to watch television and had barely managed to remain awake for the ten o'clock news. In fact she was in bed, propped against the pillows, dozing, when the story about Letty Leonard awakened her.

Instantly alert, she used the remote control to increase

the volume on the set. It wasn't a lengthy story. The only visual was a snapshot of the child and a floppy-eared dog sitting in front of a Christmas tree surrounded by heaps of unwrapped presents.

The anchorman solemnly reminded his viewing audience of the tragic accident that had recently occurred in Eden Pass and of the highly specialized surgery that had temporarily saved Letty's life. Her sudden death had been caused by an embolism that had dislodged and moved to her lung. It had come as a shock to the attending physicians, as well as to her family, who had believed she was on her way to a full recovery. The story consumed no more than twenty seconds of air time.

Jody muted the sound, threw off the covers, and got out of bed. Then she lit a cigarette, and as she drew the smoke deeply into her lungs and exhaled slowly she began to pace.

The news story hadn't mentioned Dr. Lara Mallory or Key. As far as the general public was concerned, their joint involvement was inconsequential. But it was like a pebble in Jody's shoe, an aggravation she was unable to live with.

Dammit, she'd told Key to keep his distance from that woman. Not only had he disobeyed, he'd helped the doctor rescue a dying child. Jody couldn't sit by and let Lara Porter become a local heroine.

But would she be considered a heroine now that the child had died? Exactly what was an embolism? What might have caused it? What could have prevented it? She didn't know, but she would damn sure find out if Lara Mallory Porter was in any way responsible for the girl's death.

She was still mulling over her strategy when Janellen came in to say good night. She didn't return Janellen's embrace. She'd never been comfortable with outward displays of affection, even token ones, and considered sentiment a waste of time.

It was foolish to cling to memories like the six dozen yellow roses Clark Junior had brought her the day Clark the Third was born. Her memory of them should have withered and died just as the petals had. Why didn't she forget them? What good had they done her?

"Good night, Mama. Try to get some rest. Don't get up again and don't smoke any more tonight. It's not good for you."

As soon as she was alone, Jody lit another cigarette. Having one in her hand enabled her to think better. She often lay awake for hours, smoking in the darkness. What Janellen didn't know, she couldn't hound her about.

Janellen. What was going on with her daughter? she wondered. She seemed to be distracted these days, often staring into space for long stretches of time, a goosey expression on her face. At other times, she became upset over the least little thing. Small hazards that wouldn't have ruffled her before now sent her into conniptions. She wasn't acting like herself at all. It was probably something hormonal.

But Jody couldn't waste worries on her daughter when fretting over Key was her full-time preoccupation. He was impossible and had been since birth, even before birth if you counted the twenty-six hours of difficult labor he'd put her through. Twenty-six long, agonizing hours that she'd endured alone because Clark Junior couldn't be located.

Key was born the moment his father, reeking of another woman's perfume, arrived at the hospital. That's when her difficulties with Key had begun. She was mad at him before he had drawn his first breath, and even as a newborn he had sensed it. Their dislike for each other had intensified during his childhood when it seemed that he was incapable of staying out of mischief.

She had wanted him to be a replica of Clark the Third, but two boys couldn't have been more dissimilar. Everything Clark did was motivated by an anxious desire to please her. Her approval was essential to his peace of mind. He was disconsolate if he thought he'd fallen out of favor.

Just as fervently as his brother tried to please, Key tried to provoke. Whatever Jody wanted or expected of him, he was bound and determined to do the opposite. He delighted in her disfavor; he nurtured it. She'd wondered many times if he had driven his car into that tree out of spite, just so he couldn't fulfill her dream of having him play professional football. He was hardheaded enough to risk his life rather than bow to her wishes.

She was secretly proud of his success, but acknowledging it would be tantamount to conceding that he'd made a better life for himself than she could have made for him.

One of the reasons he loved his work so much was because it kept him away from home. Although they'd denied it, she knew Janellen had called him home to watch her die. She resented that. If he didn't give a damn, he didn't give a damn. Never had, never would. It was that simple. Why pretend their relationship was something it wasn't? He and Janellen thought her death was imminent. She could see it in their eyes. They had another think coming!

She chuckled in the darkness, coughing on cigarette smoke. Wouldn't her immortality come as a nasty shock to them? She'd made a career of taking people by surprise. It didn't pay to be caught napping around Jody Tackett. They could ask Fergus Winston if they didn't believe it.

Again Jody laughed, and again she coughed, harder, reminding herself that where her mortality was concerned, she might not have a choice.

Frowning, she viciously cursed fate. She wasn't ready to die. She had things left to do, the main one being to drum that Porter bitch out of Eden Pass. Clark must have been out of his head or under the influence of some mind-altering substance to have purchased Doc Patton's clinic and then deed it to her. What had he been thinking, for chrissake?

More than Janellen and Key guessed, as long as Lara Mallory Porter remained in Eden Pass, she posed a serious threat to them and to all they held sacred.

Jody hadn't yet figured out the doctor's reason for moving here. However, she knew with the same certainty that the sun rose in the east that it was for more than to accept Clark's legacy. Unless she wanted something more, she would have turned that clinic for a quick profit and never set foot in Tackett territory. She was here for a reason. Jody dreaded learning what it was, but must before either she or one of her children walked into a trap laid by Lara Porter.

She, Jody Tackett, had come from poverty and married the richest man around. She hadn't remained at the helm of an independent oil company for years, hadn't become a woman to be feared and revered, by sitting on her ass trying to figure out other people's motives. She acted first, before they were given a chance. A rattler struck before he was stepped on.

Jody remained awake for a long time, smoking and plotting. By the time she'd smoked her last cigarette down to the filter, she had formulated her next move.

Darcy lowered her car windows. The wind punished her hairdo, but it would blow away the odor of tobacco smoke that she'd absorbed in the bar. That might make Fergus suspicious. Smoking wasn't allowed in the nursing home where her mother resided. Visits to the expensive facility provided her excellent excuses to go out at night. She'd been going out more frequently than usual because her ego needed boosting. Thanks to Mr. Key Tackett, her self-esteem was shaky.

Knowing that she'd been dumped gnawed at Darcy, eating away at her self-confidence like a vicious rat.

That's why she wasn't having any fun lately. She couldn't concentrate on any other man and wouldn't until she'd repaid Key for slinging this shit on her.

She hadn't even had the satisfaction of showing him how little she cared. Oddly, he hadn't been hanging out at the popular watering holes. The word around town was that he was flying a lot, chartering flights for clients from Dallas to Little Rock and as far south as Corpus Christi. But he couldn't be flying all night every night. Where was he going in between jobs? How was he spending his free time?

With another woman? She hadn't heard any scuttlebutt, and surely she would have. His name hadn't been linked to any local woman except for . . .

Darcy reacted as though she'd been slapped. "But that's impossible," she protested out loud.

Key Tackett and Dr. Mallory? Their names had been linked when they'd flown that kid to Tyler, but that sure as hell hadn't been a lark.

On the other hand, the doctor was a renowned man-eater. She'd been carrying on with her lover right under her husband's nose. Even Darcy had more morals—and better sense—than to do that.

Some men, however, liked a woman with the spirit of adventure. It added spiciness and suspense. James Bond didn't fuck shrinking violets, did he?

She gripped the steering wheel tighter. If Key was having a secret affair with his brother's mistress, Darcy would make certain that everybody in East Texas heard about it. By the time she got through spreading tales, he'd be a laughingstock. Taking Clark's leftovers? Ha! That would serve the bastard right.

But the rumors should contain at least a grain of truth or the laugh would be on her. How could she make certain that he was sleeping with Lara Mallory? She'd never even met the doctor. Lara Mallory would see right through any friendly overtures. She was no fool.

How could she get close to Lara Mallory without putting her on guard? It warranted some thought, but she was confident that she'd think of a way.

Arriving home, she let herself into the house, tiptoeing and moving around in the dark to keep from waking Fergus and Heather, who were asleep upstairs. She didn't want to account for the lateness of the hour unless absolutely necessary. She hated lying to her husband and avoided doing so whenever possible.

Moving past the door to the family room, she noticed that the television set had been left on. She went in to turn it off. As she rounded the leather sofa, two startled people leaped up. There were exclamations of surprise as they grappled for loose articles of clothing.

Darcy switched on the lamp, took in the situation at a glance, and angrily demanded to know—although she already did—*"Just what the hell is going on here?"*

Chapter Twelve

*T*he pastor of the First Baptist Church commended Letty's soul to the Lord and said a final amen over the small white casket. Marion Leonard's keening cry echoed across the windswept cemetery, raising goose bumps on all who heard it. Jack Leonard was silent, but tears rolled down his gaunt, pale cheeks as he pulled his grieving wife away from their daughter's coffin. It was a heartrending scene that deserved privacy. Mourners began to disperse.

Lara had kept to the fringes of the crowd, trying to be as unobtrusive as possible. As she turned to leave, the white-hot flash of a high-tech camera exploded near her face. Instinctively she threw up her arm for protection. The first blinding flash was followed by another, then a third.

"Mrs. Porter, will you comment on the Leonards' malpractice suit against you?"

"What?" A microphone was thrust against her mouth. She shoved it aside. "I don't know what you're talking about. And my name is Dr. Mallory."

As the violet spots receded, she saw a horde o reporters blocking her path. She switched directions. The band flocked after her. Some were obviously affiliated with TV stations—their video cameramen trotted along beside them, connected by cables. Others were from newspapers; with them were the still photographers and their despised flashes. Five years ago, she'd become well acquainted with the accoutrements of mass communication.

What was the media doing here? What did they want with her? She felt as if her nightmare was being reenacted.

"Please, let me by."

Glancing back, she saw that others attending Letty Leonard's funeral had gathered in clusters and were speaking in hushed but excited voices, gaping at the sideshow. She hadn't created the spectacle but was nevertheless its unwilling star.

"Mrs. Porter— "

"My name is *Mallory*," she insisted. "Dr. Mallory."

"But you were married to the late U.S. Ambassador Randall Porter?"

She hurried across the neatly clipped grass toward the gravel lane where her car was parked in a line of others behind the white hearse and the limousine.

"You're the same Lara Porter who was Senator Tackett's mistress, isn't that right?"

"Please move aside." Reaching her car at last, she fumbled in her handbag for her keys. "Leave me alone."

"What brought you to Eden Pass, Mrs. Porter?"

"It is true that Senator Tackett brought you here before his death?"

"Were you still lovers?"

"What do you know about his accidental drowning, Mrs. Porter? Was it actually a suicide?"

"Did your negligence cause the Leonard girl's death?"

She had been asked the other questions a thousand times before and had become inured to them. They bounced off the armor of repetition. But the last question brought her around. "What?" Looking directly at the young female reporter who had posed the question, she repeated, "What did you say?"

"Did your negligence cause the embolism that killed Letty Leonard?"

"No!"

"You were the first doctor to attend her."

"That's correct. And I did everything possible to save her arm and her life."

"Apparently the Leonards don't think so or they wouldn't be suing you for medical malpractice."

Had Lara not had experience in masking her reaction to personal and probing questions and verbal salvos, she might have reeled under the impact of this one. Instead she gazed back at the reporter without revealing her inner turmoil. The muscles in her face felt wooden, but she managed to move her lips sufficiently to get out the words.

"I took drastic measures to save Letty Leonard's life. Her parents are well aware of that. I haven't been notified of a pending malpractice suit. That's all I have to say."

Naturally the news hounds didn't accept that as her final word. As she drove away, they were still aiming lenses and microphones at her, hurling questions like stones. She gripped the steering wheel with sweating hands, keeping her eyes forward, ignoring the curious onlookers as she drove past them.

It was a warm, humid morning, but she hadn't been uncomfortable with the heat until the reporters had resurrected the ugly past. Now her clothes were sticking to her damp skin, her head was pounding, and her heart was beating at an alarming rate. She felt nauseated.

What had initiated all this media attention? Her move to Eden Pass had gone unnoticed; she'd lived in relative anonymity for more than a year. There had been newer scandals to exploit, more sensational stories to expose, sinners more sinful than she caught sinning. The story of Lara Porter and Senator Tackett had been buried in the graveyard of dead stories ages ago.

Until this morning. Letty Leonard's death had exhumed her. Once again she was a notorious public figure.

Yet, the story of Letty's accident, tragic as it was, hadn't warranted statewide or national media coverage; only the local press had reported it. Naturally, her name would have been in Letty's medical file, but unless a reporter was very astute, he wouldn't have connected Dr. Lara Mallory of Eden Pass with Lara Porter, Senator Clark Tackett's mistress.

In subsequent stories about Letty's surgery and recovery, she hadn't been mentioned at all, for which she'd been glad. The less publicity she generated, the better. She wouldn't have cared if her name never again appeared in newsprint. But it was going to appear now, with the stigmatizing word *malpractice* shadowing it.

Through the entire incident with Clark, through the disaster in Montesangre, her proficiency as a physician had never come under fire. Her reputation as an accomplished doctor had withstood the bombardments to her character. She had clung to that last vestige of pride.

Now, if the Leonards even suggested they might pursue a medical malpractice suit, her work would be placed under a microscope. It would be laid bare and dissected just as her private life had been. Nothing incriminating would be found, but that didn't matter. The examination itself would create headlines. In the public's mind, being suspect was equivalent to being guilty.

Once again she would become fodder for the news mill. Her floundering practice—the only important thing left her—would suffer until it was extinct.

Someone must have tipped the media that the Dr. Mallory who had first attended Letty Leonard was none other than the infamous slut Lara Porter.

As she had feared, parked outside her clinic were cars and vans designated with call letters. When she pulled her car into the rear driveway, reporters swarmed her. She shoved her way through them and entered the clinic via the back door, which Nancy was holding open for her.

"What in hell is going on?" the nurse demanded as she slammed the door behind Lara.

"The rumor is out that the Leonards are suing me for malpractice."

"Have they lost their minds?"

"I'm sure they have. To grief."

"These people," Nancy said, indicating the reporters just beyond the closed door, "and I use the term loosely, showed up about an hour ago and started pounding on the door. I didn't know what to think. The phone hasn't stopped ringing." Sure enough, the phone rang.

"Don't answer it."

"What do you want me to do, Dr. Mallory?"

"Call Sheriff Baxter and ask him to remove these reporters from the premises."

"Can he do that?"

"He can keep them off my property. They can still park in the street, which I'm sure they'll do. For the next several days, we'll be under siege. Maybe you ought to take this week off."

"Not on a bet. I wouldn't desert you to fight off these jackals alone." As Lara slipped out of her suit jacket, Nancy took it from her and noticed the damp lining. "I've never seen you secrete a drop of sweat. I doubted you even had sweat glands."

"That's nervous perspiration. They ambushed me at the funeral."

"Those buzzards."

"Make up your mind. Buzzards or jackals." It was comforting to know she had retained her sense of humor.

"Doesn't matter. They're both scavengers. I ought to get Clem over here with his shotgun. That would scatter them."

"I appreciate the gesture, but no thanks. I don't need the bad publicity," Lara said grimly. "Before I even got a foothold on being Dr. Mallory, a small-town doctor, I'm once again Lara Porter, Clark Tackett's married lover."

Nancy's face reflected her regret. "It's such a damn shame. I'm sorry."

"Thanks. I'll need all the friends I can get." She sighed with consternation. "I wasn't actually in hiding, but I didn't want my whereabouts publicized for fear that something like this would happen. Someone deliberately stirred up this hornets' nest. I don't believe for a moment that it evolved on its own."

"Tackett's the name. Treachery's the game."

Lara looked sharply at her nurse. "Key?"

Nancy shook her head. "Isn't his style. My guess is the old lady. You're making headway here. Not in leaps and bounds, but in baby steps. She can't tolerate that. Jody heard about that little girl dying, knew that you'd been the first attending doctor, and saw a chance to create a ruckus."

"She could have done that when I moved to town."

"But it would have come out that Clark set you up here. That would have implied that he was still emotionally attached to you. Jody didn't want to flatter you that much. This time, Clark's out of the picture."

What Nancy said made sense. Lara headed for her office. "I doubt any patients will even attempt to get in today, but I'll be in my office if I'm needed."

She pulled down the window shades so she wouldn't have to witness the destruction of her lawn under the trampling feet of eager reporters. Once seated at her desk, she consulted the telephone directory. Her personality had undergone some drastic changes since that morning in Virginia. She was older now, tougher, and she wasn't going to take persecution lying down. Reaching for the phone, she dialed a number.

"Miss Janellen?"

"Bowie! What are you doing here?"

She was seated at the kitchen table, staring at the telephone she'd just hung up. He had poked his head around the door. She signaled him in.

"Seems like I'm always sneaking up on you, pulling you out of deep thought. I don't mean to." He moved into the room, looking uneasy. "The, uh, maid told me to come on back. If this is a bad time for you . . ."

"No, it's all right. I'm just surprised to see you here."

"I tried the office first, then the shop. They told me there that you'd knocked off early today."

"My mother wasn't feeling well this morning when I left for work, and I was worried about her." As usual, when in Bowie's presence, she felt tongue-tied. She indicated one of the chairs across the kitchen table from her. "Sit down. I was about to have some tea. Would you like some?"

"Tea?" Dubiously he glanced at the steaming kettle on the stove. "Hot tea? It's a hundred degrees outside."

"I know, but, well, I like tea," she said with an apologetic shrug. "It's soothing."

"I'll take your word for it."

"Something else then? Lemonade? A soft drink? A beer? Key keeps beer in the fridge."

"No, thanks. Besides, I can't sit down. I'm dirty."

He looked wonderful to her. Until he called her attention to it, she hadn't noticed the dirt smeared on his jeans and shirt. Hunks of it clung to the soles of his boots. It was embedded in the grain of his leather work gloves, which he'd stuck into his belt, and his hat, too, was dusty.

"Don't be silly," Janellen said. "Mama made my brothers work during their summer vacations. They used to come in all sweaty and stinky—not that you're stinky," she said hastily. "I just meant that this kitchen was built for working men to . . . you know, to enjoy and relax in."

Realizing that she was blabbering, she forced herself to stop. "You obviously came here to discuss something with me, so sit down, please."

After a moment's hesitation, he lowered himself onto a kitchen chair, balancing his buttocks on the edge of the seat.

"Wouldn't you like something to drink?" she repeated.

"Lemonade, I guess." He cleared his throat.

"You were a million miles away when I came in," he remarked after taking a long swallow of his drink.

"I'd just had a very disturbing telephone call." She debated whether she should discuss the call with him. He was looking at her expectantly, and it would be a relief to talk about it with someone who was uninvolved and therefore impartial.

"Have you been following the story of the little girl from Eden Pass who almost lost her arm?"

"I heard she died."

"Yes. Her funeral was today. Such a tragedy." She paused. "The doctor who treated her for shock and took her to Tyler— "

"Dr. Mallory."

"Yes. Well, she . . . she called just now. See, she was once . . . my older brother was . . ."

"I know."

She gave him a grateful smile. "Then you can imagine how embarrassing and uncomfortable it's been for us to have her here in Eden Pass."

"How come?"

The question was totally unexpected, and for a moment she was taken aback. "Because she brings back such bad memories for us."

"Oh."

He didn't seem convinced, so she felt compelled to explain. "Lara Porter ruined Clark's political career."

Bowie cocked his head to one side and lightly scratched his neck as though ruminating on her point. "She's not a husky old gal by any stretch. I don't figure she could wrestle him down, strip him naked, and force him into bed with her, do you?"

This wasn't the first time Janellen had considered that, but only privately. If she had verbalized her thoughts, Jody would have gone through the roof.

Prudently Janellen avoided further discussion in that

direction. "Somehow the media found out that Lara Porter is in Eden Pass, passing herself off as Dr. Mallory. Apparently she was accosted by reporters at Letty Leonard's funeral this morning and had to call Sheriff Baxter to disperse those who've besieged her clinic."

Bowie smacked his lips with disgust. "Imagine them disrupting that little girl's funeral like that."

"I know. It was ghastly of them." For a moment she reflected on the continuing turbulence caused by her brother's affair with Lara Mallory Porter. "It's believed that the Leonards are going to file a medical malpractice suit against her," she told Bowie, then paused to take a deep breath. "She thinks my mother is responsible."

"Is she?"

"No."

"You don't sound too sure."

Her fingertips brushed her lips once before moving to her blouse. It didn't have buttons, so she fiddled with the fabric, then nervously laid her hand on the table near her untouched cup of tea.

"I don't know if she is or not," she admitted at last. "Dr. Mallory called to speak to her. Maydale told her that Mama was resting. She wouldn't take no for an answer and demanded to speak to whoever was available." She fidgeted with the salt and pepper shakers. "I wish Key had been here. He's a pro when it comes to confrontation. He would have known what to say to her."

"What did you say?"

"That I'm sure our family didn't cause her recent hardships."

"Think she bought that?" Bowie asked skeptically.

"She said she doubts that I would be that spiteful, but that she wouldn't put anything past my mother or my brother." In a small voice she added, "I'd hate to think they could be that cruel."

She stared into space for a moment, then returned her attention to her guest. "I'm sorry, Bowie. I didn't mean to take up your time with my family's problems. What did you need to see me about?"

He rolled his shoulders. "It's probably nothing. In fact, I tried for several days to talk myself out of bothering you with it." He had set his hat on the table. Now he scooted it aside and leaned forward. "You ever notice anything peculiar about well number seven?"

"No, should I?"

"Probably not, but I figured I had to get it off my chest. See, it's not yielding as much natural gas as it should. At least, that's my opinion. Its production doesn't jive with comparable wells."

"All wells are different."

"Yes, ma'am, I know that. They have personalities and they're constantly changing. Kinda like women. Each well has its quirks and you've got to get to know it real good. Stroke it every now and then."

Janellen ducked her head so quickly that she didn't see that Bowie ducked his, too. Her cheeks turned warm, but since this concerned business, she felt it was imperative to keep the conversation going.

"What's the daily MCF?" Gas was measured in hundreds of thousands of cubic feet.

"Two fifty per day. I figure that well's output ought to be higher."

"We allow for a four to five percent loss, Bowie. Even up to ten. There's probably a small leak somewhere in the line and the gas is being absorbed into the atmosphere."

He gnawed his cheek for a moment, then shook his head stubbornly. "I think the loss is higher than the allowance. After recording that well for the last several weeks, I think it should be a high gas producer, especially considering the oil we get out of it. Instead, it's one of our lowest."

"You've spent a lot of time studying it."

"On my own time."

Her heart swelled with pride. He was a conscientious employee who did more than was required. Her decision to hire him had been justified.

Even though she appreciated his concern, she felt it was misplaced. "I don't know what to tell you, Bowie. Well number seven produces as we've come to expect from it."

"Well, I reported it to the foreman, but he just shrugged it off and said its rate of flow has always been low, long as he can remember. Damned if I can figure out why, though. Just one of those worries that grabs hold and won't let go, you know?"

"Yes, I know." She stared into her cup of tea. After a long moment of silence, she raised her head. "There I go again. I can't keep my mind on business. I keep dwelling on that little girl's family. Her daddy does all our dry cleaning. He's a nice, friendly man. I know how devastated he and his wife are, because we felt the same way when Clark drowned. I thought we'd have to bury my mother with him."

"I never had a kid, but if I did, I can't imagine having to put him in the ground."

Janellen looked at him searchingly. He'd never had a child, but she wondered if he'd ever been married. There were a thousand personal questions she wished to ask him, but couldn't bring herself to. Among those questions was where he had acquired his insight into people. He had an uncanny knack for seeing beyond affectations and straight into the heart and mind of an individual.

Trusting his instincts, she asked, "Bowie, do you think Dr. Mallory did something that caused that little girl to die?"

"All I know about medicine is that there's no real cure for either a cold or a hangover."

She smiled. "I've only seen Lara Mallory in person once, but she looked so . . . so . . . put together."

Everything that I'm not, she thought dismally. Having seen Lara Mallory, she was no longer surprised that Clark had risked everything to be with her. She wasn't merely beautiful. Her eyes reflected compassion and intelligence, and she exuded self-confidence and competency.

Janellen wanted to despise her. She knew that she wouldn't be feeling this ambiguity if Dr. Mallory had come across as an empty-headed sexpot, all fluff and no substance. Instead, it was quite the opposite.

"I don't believe the woman I met could be negligent." Her conviction surprised even herself and made her feel disloyal. "I know I'm supposed to hate her, but . . ."

"Who says?"

"My mother."

"Do you always do what your mother says? Don't you ever think different from her?"

"Rarely." The admission made her sound like a wimp. She was probably sacrificing any respect Bowie had for her as an individual and as an employer.

But Lara Mallory's call had upset her terribly. She was past the point of trying to hide her feelings. Propping her elbow on the table, she rested her forehead on her hand. "Oh, God, I wish her affair with Clark had never taken place. He would have enjoyed a successful political career like Mama wanted for him. He even might still be alive. Mama would be happy. And I— "

She caught herself before saying that if events had been different, she wouldn't feel so responsible for holding things together now. Seeing to everyone's happiness and well-being was exhausting. It was also impossible.

Ever since the night that girl had come to the door asking for Key, he'd been even more irascible than before. He and Jody hadn't quarreled any more, but that was because each went out of his way to avoid the other. Key answered direct questions in gruff monosyllables. He was preoccupied with only God knew what, and Janellen didn't dare guess. He stamped through the house with his shoulders angrily hunched, his expression belligerent. He was so unhappy at home that he often left as abruptly as he had appeared.

Now, Lara Mallory had just burdened her with a new source of worry. Before she realized that she was crying, a tear rolled down her cheek.

"Hey, what's this?"

She sensed the movement of Bowie's arm, but she didn't expect him to touch her. When she felt his callused fingertips against her cheek, she raised her head and looked at him, her lips parting in stunned bewilderment.

She was rarely touched by anyone, and, because she was starved for the touch of another, she reflexively raised her hand and folded it around his.

He went incredibly still. Nothing moved except his eyes. They went from hers, to her hand covering his, then back to her eyes. Janellen sat just as still as he, but inside she was all aflutter. Her lower body felt feverish, full, heavy. Her breasts tingled and tightened, making her want to press her palms over them to contain the rush of excitement.

How long they remained staring at each other she never knew. She was held in thrall by Bowie's sad, sweet eyes and the pressure of his fingertips, which were damp with her tears. If he hadn't heard Key's car approaching, she might still have been frozen in that tableau when her brother slammed in.

As it was, she hastily shot to her feet and whirled around to greet him. "Key! Hi!" Her voice was unnaturally high and thin. "What are you doing here?"

"When I left this morning I still lived here." He divided an inquisitive look between her and Bowie, who she hoped could conceal guilt better than she. Her face was fiery hot. She knew she must be flushed from her throat, where her pulse was pounding, up to her hairline.

Key took a beer from the refrigerator. "Hi, Bowie. Want a beer?"

"No, thanks."

Janellen said, "I already offered him one, but he wanted lemonade instead."

"I just stopped by to tell Miss Janellen that— "

"He thinks the MCF on well number seven is low and— "

"It's probably nothing, but— "

"He thought we ought to know in case— "

"So I brought it up with Miss Janellen and— "

"And that's what we've been doing. Talking about that," she finished lamely.

"Uh-huh." Looking amused, Key popped open the beer and tilted it toward his mouth. "Well, don't let me interrupt this high-level business conference."

"No, it's all right." Bowie snatched up his hat as though it were a piece of incriminating evidence. "I was just on my way out."

"Yes, he was about to leave when you came in. I'll . . . I'll just walk him to the door now." Flustered and unable to look at either her brother or Bowie, she fled the kitchen and was waiting for Bowie in the entry, holding the front door open for him. She kept her eyes averted as he joined her there. "Thank you for the information, Bowie."

He pulled on his hat. "Just figured it ought to be brought to your attention. It's your money."

"I'll check into it."

"I don't think that's such a good idea."

At the sound of her brother's voice, she swung around. His shoulder was propped against the arched opening of the dining room as he nonchalantly sipped his beer.

"What's not such a good idea?" she asked.

"You checking into a malfunctioning well."

"Why not?"

"As of today, the Tacketts are in the news again."

"So?"

"So reporters are going to be crawling over Eden Pass like ants on a picnic ham. Until a hotter story comes along, that is. When they don't get anything out of me—and they won't—they're likely to come sniffing after you for a statement. Bowie," he said, looking at the pumper, "keep an eye out for her, okay? If she inspects any oil wells, you go with her."

Bowie glanced uneasily at Janellen. "Meaning no disrespect, Mr. Tackett, but she's the boss."

"Boss or not, do it as a favor to me. I'm asking as her brother." Again Bowie's eyes darted toward Janellen. She was fuming and didn't trust herself to speak. With uncertainty, Bowie said, "Okay, Mr. Tackett."

"Call me Key."

"Yes, sir. Well, 'bye, y'all."

He wasted no time in getting to the company truck and driving away. In fact, he looked grateful to be escaping with his hide intact.

Janellen rounded on her brother. "I don't need a keeper!"

"Well, I do," he replied, unfazed by her anger. "If a reporter pesters you, I'll go after him wanting to kick ass. That'll create more news and make a bad situation worse."

She resented his taking charge of her employee, of making it appear that she was incapable of taking care of herself. But his explanation was well founded. If a reporter did ambush her demanding a statement, and Key found out about it, there was no telling what he'd do. Once, when she was in high school, she'd come home from a date in tears. Key had almost throttled her terrified escort before she could explain that they'd just seen a sad movie.

Knowing that he was looking out for her best interests, she let her anger subside. "The situation is already worse than you know," she told him. "Lara Mallory called here a while ago wanting to talk to Mama. Dr. Mallory thinks she tipped the media about her being here in Eden Pass."

Key ran a hand around the back of his neck. "Well I'll be damned."

"Does that surprise you?"

"No. What surprises me is that the doctor and I are beginning to think alike. I also figured Jody was at the bottom of this. I know plenty of smart reporters, but no more than a handful of them knew Lara was involved in the Leonard girl's case; it would have been a bizarre coincidence if one of them had added two and two and come up with four." He looked toward the second story of the house. "Shrewd old bitch."

"Don't talk like that about our mother."

"I meant it as a compliment. You've got to give her credit for creative thinking."

"Was it so creative?"

"Meaning?"

Worriedly, she said, "You were there, Key. You saw everything. Was Dr. Mallory negligent? Do the Leonards have grounds for a malpractice suit?"

"I was concentrating on flying the chopper, but from what I saw, Lara fought like hell to save the kid's life. According to the autopsy report, that embolism was a freak of nature. Could have happened anytime. And another thing—the Leonards didn't seem the kind of people who'd be vengeful. They're faithful Christians."

"So it surprises you that they're looking for a scapegoat?"

"Right. I wouldn't put it past Jody to circulate a rumor of a malpractice suit, whether or not there's any truth to it. Lara's an easy target." Janellen looked at him quizzically. "What?" he asked.

"Several times you've referred to her as Lara. It sounds odd."

He hesitated, then said querulously, "That's her name, isn't it?"

Janellen had too many other pressing matters on her mind to pursue something so trivial. "She sounded awfully mad, Key. She said to tell Mama and you that she wouldn't be driven out of town like she was before. What did she mean?"

"She's referring to when she and Randall Porter went to Montesangre." He frowned. "She's got it into her head that Clark engineered the appointment for Porter by flexing some muscle in the State Department. His appointment looked and sounded good, but it was practically legalized banishment."

Janellen was stunned. "Do you believe her? Could Clark have been that devious?"

"Devious is a strong word, but our big brother was fairly adept at weaseling his way out of trouble."

"He never really got out of this trouble, though, did he?"

"No, he didn't," Key said slowly. "And as long as Lara's around to remind everybody of it, he never will."

"So you agree with what Mama did. *If* she did."

"No. I want Lara Mallory out of Eden Pass, but I want her to hang herself. Left alone, I think she eventually will." Once again he glanced upstairs. "But you know Jody. She's never been one to let things follow their natural course. If things aren't moving along according to her plan and her timetable, she plays God."

"Please don't be critical, Key. She's sick. Can't you try and talk her into seeing a doctor?"

He barked a laugh. "That'd be a surefire way to guarantee that she wouldn't. But I agree. She should have a complete checkup, have some tests run." He placed his hand on her shoulder. "But I'm afraid that persuading her to do it is up to you, sis. Stay after her." He squeezed her shoulder, then headed for the stairs, taking his beer with him.

"Are you going out tonight, Key?"

"As soon as I shower."

"Are you going out with Helen Berry?"

He stopped dead in his tracks and turned. "Why do you ask that?"

Gauging by his expression, Janellen knew she'd struck a nerve. She also realized why people were sometimes afraid of him. "Helen's been going steady with Jimmy Bradley since they were freshmen. The gossip is that . . ." she paused to wet her lips, "that Helen recently broke up with him, very sudden."

"So?"

"Oh, Key." Taking hold of her courage by both hands, she asked, "Why? Why, when there are so many other women for you to choose from, would you pick her? Helen's half your age."

"Careful, Janellen. If you start digging into my personal affairs, I'll have to start digging into yours." He moved down two steps and lowered his voice to a stage whisper. "For instance, I might ask what's going on between you and Bowie Cato."

Her stomach dropped. "Nothing's going on!"

"No? Then why all the rushed, breathless explanations when I came into the kitchen? I haven't heard such fast talking since Drenda Larson's daddy caught us in his hay barn when we were thirteen."

"Bowie's an employee. We were talking business."

"Okay, I'll believe that," Key said, his cocky grin back in place. "If you'll believe that all Drenda Larson and I were doing in that haystack was looking for a needle."

Lara's prediction proved correct.

A week following Letty Leonard's funeral, the media moved to greener pastures to graze on other personal disasters and dilemmas. During that week, however, Lara had been hounded each time she stepped across her threshold. Sheriff Baxter had done his official duty, albeit grudgingly, and seen to it that the reporters and cameramen stayed off her property. But their presence on the public street made her a virtual prisoner at the clinic.

The TV network affiliates from Dallas and Shreveport

had filed stories that were aired on national newscasts, but Lara Porter and the key role she'd played in the downfall of Senator Clark Tackett five years earlier only rated fifteen seconds of air time in the last few minutes of the newscasts. She'd lost her rank as a lead story.

The Leonards too had been thrust into the spotlight but had hired an attorney to do their talking. He was a wet-behind-the-ears graduate of Baylor Law School who had only recently passed the bar. He rose to the occasion, however, and wasn't intimidated by being in the limelight. Stubbornly and repeatedly, he told reporters that his clients had no statements to make and were trying to deal with their bereavement before addressing the question of liability for their daughter's death.

Lara had done some intensive soul-searching. It had been a judgment call as to whether to use an anticoagulant on Letty. After hours of review and research, she stood by her original decision. However, in order to ease her mind, she conferred with the emergency room doctor who had next tended to the young patient. He backed her decision and assured her he would testify to such if it ever became a matter of litigation.

As days passed and Lara didn't hear from the Leonards' lawyer, she hoped that the rumor of the malpractice suit against her was just that—a rumor. No doubt it had been spawned by one of the Tacketts. Her repeated calls to them had rendered nothing and only increased her frustration. Jody Tackett was either indeed too ill to take a telephone call, or she had good liars protecting her.

Lara had spoken to the housekeeper and to Janellen, but she hadn't seen or spoken to Key since the night he'd brought Helen Berry to her. He probably thought she'd been joking when she mentioned his taking her to Central America. Another opportunity to broach the subject hadn't presented itself, but her determination hadn't wavered one iota. It was just that so many other events had temporarily distracted her.

When she had awakened this morning, the last of the TV vans was gone, but because of the negative publicity, the patients with appointments had called to cancel. It was difficult to remain optimistic about cultivating a practice when she couldn't get people inside her door. She and Nancy went through the motions of working, but they had more idle time on their hands than either wanted to acknowledge.

By midafternoon she left her private office with the intention of dismissing Nancy early. Nancy, surprisingly, was speaking to someone in the waiting room.

"We'd like to see the doctor right away. I know we don't have an appointment, but then you're not exactly overflowing with patients, are you?"

The strident, condescending voice belonged to Darcy Winston.

Chapter Thirteen

May I help you?"

When Lara spoke from the doorway, Darcy turned. She wasn't as flawless close up as she'd appeared on the school auditorium stage. There were faint crow's feet around her eyes and frown lines across her forehead. She had artfully applied cosmetics, but her face bore unmistakable traces of hard living and deep-seated bitterness.

Lara had formed an unflattering opinion of Darcy Winston's character, but knew from experience that such bias was unfair. Trying to keep an open mind, she smiled and extended her hand. "Hello, Mrs. Winston, I'm Lara Mallory."

Darcy raised one carefully penciled eyebrow inquisitively. Lara explained how she recognized her. "I heard you speak at the town meeting. You were extremely convincing."

Again Darcy communicated by using her eyebrow. She gave Lara an arch look, obviously trying to guess how much she knew about her "intruder."

Lara turned to the girl standing beside her mother. "And your name is Heather, isn't it?"

"Yes, ma'am."

"I'm pleased to meet you, Heather."

"Thanks."

"Heather's the reason we're here," Darcy said.

"Oh? What's the problem?"

"I want you to put her on birth control pills."

"*Mo-ther*!"

The girl was mortified, and Lara didn't blame her. Unfortunately, Darcy was living up to Lara's expectations. She was a first-class bitch. Wanting to spare Heather further embarrassment, Lara asked, "Nancy, which examination room is ready?"

Nancy was eyeing Darcy, her expression sour. "Three."

"Thank you. Heather?" Smiling, Lara pulled open the connecting door and held it for the girl. Darcy fell into line behind her.

"Mrs. Winston, you may wait out here where you'll be more comfortable. Nancy will need some information from you in order to start a patient file on Heather. If you like, she'll get you something to drink while you wait."

"She's my daughter." Her tone made it obvious that she was accustomed to intimidating people and getting her way.

"And this is my office," Lara said with matching imperiousness. "Heather is my patient. I respect and protect the privacy of my patients."

Without another word, she closed the door on Darcy's tight, angry frown and showed the girl into the examination room. She left her there with Nancy, who would see that she was undressed, draped, and weighed before taking her blood pressure and collecting specimens of urine and blood.

Nancy summoned Lara from her office with a light tap on the door. As she moved back toward the waiting area, Nancy whispered, "How am I supposed to pacify Bat Lady?"

"Throw her a small rodent."

Nancy gave her a thumbs-up sign. She went into the examination room where Heather was warily perched on the end of the table. "Everything okay?"

"Fine, I guess. I don't like having my finger pricked."

"Neither do I."

"It's better than having blood drawn from your arm, though. I hate needles."

"They aren't my favorite things either."

"But you're a doctor."

"I'm a person, too."

The girl smiled, more at ease now.

"When do you start cheerleading practice?"

"How'd you know I was a cheerleader?"

"The booster club sent me an application for membership." Lara examined her eardrums with an otoscope. "I saw your picture."

"We start practicing next week."

"So soon? Say 'ah.'" Using a tongue depressor, she looked at Heather's throat. "School doesn't start for another month yet."

"Ahhhh. Yeah, but we want to be good. Last year we won several trophies."

"Swallow for me. Any tenderness in your glands here?" Lara asked as she felt Heather's neck.

"No, ma'am."

"Good. Take care of your throat. If you notice any soreness, let me know. Sore throats and hoarseness are inherent to yell leaders."

"Okay. Sure."

Lara lifted the drape and placed the stethoscope beneath Heather's left breast. The girl gasped. "I know it's cold," Lara apologized with a smile. After listening to her heart, she moved to her back to listen to her lungs. "Take several deep breaths through your mouth, please. That's good." After a moment she moved once again to stand in front of the girl. "Are your periods regular?"

"Yes, ma'am."

"Heavy?"

"Usually just the first and second day. Not after that."

"Do you have cramps?"

"Yeah. Really bitchin'."

"Do you take something?"

"Midol, aspirin. Stuff like that."

"Does it help?"

"I'll live," she replied with a grin.

Making Heather as comfortable as possible on the table, Lara summoned Nancy from the waiting room to assist her with a breast check and a pelvic examination.

"This is gross," Heather said as Lara guided her feet into the stirrups.

"Yes, I know. Try to relax as much as possible."

"Right," Heather said sarcastically when Lara opened the speculum.

When she was finished, she left Heather to dress and returned to her office. Heather joined her there a few minutes later. Lara indicated the sofa and sat down beside her, creating a mood that was more friendly than clinical.

"Why do you want to go on birth control pills, Heather?"

"She wants me to."

"Your mother?"

"She's afraid I'll get pregnant."

"Is that a possibility?"

Heather hesitated. "Well, I guess. I mean, I have a boyfriend . . . and we, you know."

"I'm not asking to be nosy," Lara told her gently. "I make no moral judgments. I'm a doctor who needs to decide what's best for my patient. The only way I can do that is to have as much information as possible." She let that sink in, then asked, "Are you having sexual intercourse?"

Heather looked down at her tightly clasped hands. "Not yet." Then she furtively glanced at the closed door. "She thinks we already have. I've told her we haven't, but she doesn't believe me."

Once she began, the words poured from her, crowding one another in their rush to get out. "She caught Tanner and me making out in the living room. We weren't doing anything. I mean, I had taken off my blouse and bra, and

Tanner had taken off his shirt, but by her reaction you'd have thought we were totally naked, that she'd caught us actually *doing* it."

Suddenly her eyes swung up to Lara. "Oh, jeez, I'm sorry. I didn't mean to say it that way. I didn't link it to you and Senator Tackett."

"No offense taken," Lara said quietly. "This is about you, not me. When your mother found you and Tanner, she jumped to the wrong conclusion, is that right?"

"To put it mildly, she went totally apeshit," Heather said, rolling her eyes. "She screeched so loud she woke up my daddy. He ran downstairs, bringing his pistol, thinking the house had been broken into again." She shoved back a handful of glossy auburn hair. "It was awful. Tanner kept telling them that he wouldn't do anything to hurt me, but Mother threw him out of the house and hasn't let me see him since. I've been grounded. She took away my car keys and my phone."

Tears filled her eyes. "I might as well be in Siberia. It's awful! *And I didn't do anything!* She looks at me like I'm a, you know, a whore. Daddy's tried to make peace, but she doesn't easily forgive and forget. I've told her a million times that I'm still a virgin. Technically, that is. Tanner's, you know, used his finger, but not his . . ."

Lara indicated her understanding with a nod.

"But Mother doesn't believe that. This morning she told me we were coming to you, and I was going to start taking birth control pills whether I liked it or not. She said if I was going to screw around, at least she wasn't going to get stuck with a grandkid to raise."

Lara empathized with the girl because Darcy's sentiments echoed those of her own parents. The message had been: Do whatever you want, just don't get caught and thereby inconvenience us. Heather sniffed wetly. Lara passed her a box of tissues. "I miss Tanner so much. He loves me. He really does. And I love him."

"I'm sure you do."

"He's so sweet to me. Not like her. Nothing I do pleases her."

Lara waited while Heather noisily blew her nose, then said, "I see no problem in prescribing the pills for you. You appear to be in good health."

"They'll make me fat, won't they?"

Lara smiled. "Weight gain can be a side effect, but I doubt that will be a problem for a young woman as active and energetic as you." She looked intently into the girl's face. "Aside from the physical aspects, I want you to be psychologically prepared for this step. Are you certain that this is what *you* want, Heather?"

Again, her eyes darted toward the door. "Yeah, it is. I mean, Tanner's promised that he'll use something, but if I was taking pills, too, no way could I get pregnant."

"Just remember that the pills don't protect you from sexually transmitted diseases. If you're going to be sexually active, I suggest using a condom every time, even with a steady boyfriend. Encourage your friends to do the same."

She wrote out the prescription form, then together they moved toward the waiting room. Darcy was impatiently thumbing through a magazine. She tossed it aside as soon as they entered.

"Well?"

"I've given Heather a prescription for oral contraceptives and asked her to come back in six months just to see that everything is okay. Of course, she's to call me if she has any negative side effects or discomfort."

"You were in there an awfully long time."

Lara refused to be defensive. "Your daughter is a delightful young woman. I enjoyed talking with her. Which reminds me, I'm interested in implementing some health education programs at the high school. As president of the school board, would Mr. Winston be open to hearing my ideas?"

"You'll have to ask him."

"Then I will," Lara replied graciously, in spite of Darcy's curtness. "I'll contact him as soon as the semester begins."

"How should I handle the bill?"

"Nancy will take care of it now." Lara turned to Heather. "Good luck with cheerleading. I'll be watching you from the grandstands."

"Thanks, Dr. Mallory. I'll wave at you." She grinned, then added, "It still feels weird calling a lady 'doctor.'"

They were several blocks from the clinic before Darcy broke the antagonistic silence with her daughter. "Well, you two certainly seemed chummy when we left."

"She's nice."

Darcy snorted. "Clark Tackett thought so too, and look where that landed him. She's nothing but trash. And trouble."

Heather turned away to gaze out the window.

Most of Darcy's criticism arose from jealousy. She hadn't expected or wanted Lara Mallory to be so charming. She was cool and classy. Every subconscious gesture bespoke good breeding and social training. She was so damned tidy that she'd made Darcy feel like she needed a bath. She was slender as a reed, and probably had not an ounce of cellulite clinging to her thighs. Her hair was thick and healthy. Her seemingly poreless skin was taut. From a woman's standpoint, there was a lot there to envy.

But what would a man, specifically Key Tackett, see in her? Her figure wasn't voluptuous. She had a candid gaze, like a man's. Or did her eyes assume a sultry mystery when she was with a lover?

After making up her mind to visit Lara Mallory, Darcy had been forced to wait a week before doing so. Heather and Tanner had provided her the perfect excuse, but then the Leonard kid had died and the town had been in upheaval. Everyone was watching Lara Mallory. Darcy decided it would be smart to wait until the dust had settled. She wanted an up-close and personal look at Dr. Mallory, but without the whole town knowing she was curious.

Was Lara Mallory Key's new squeeze? Dammit, she'd come away as mystified as before. The doctor seemed too cool to appeal to Key's lusty nature, but looks could be deceiving. And there was no accounting for taste, particularly a taste for women, which she knew was unique to every man.

So all Darcy had to show for her meeting with Lara was Heather's dewy-eyed admiration for the woman who might have snatched Key away from her. Not that she'd actually been in a position to claim ownership of him. He had picked her up in a bar and slept with her only once, but she believed that they had a future as lovers. Without the interference of another woman, it could happen. Lara Mallory might jinx it.

"Did y'all talk about me?" Darcy asked Heather peevishly. "I'll bet you made me out to be a bitch."

"No, I didn't."

"What did you say about me?"

"Nothing. Except general stuff."

"Then what did you talk about that took so damn long?"

Heather sighed with adolescent resignation. "We talked about cheerleading and my periods and Tanner and becoming sexually active and stuff."

"What did she say about you becoming sexually active?"

"That she didn't make moral judgments."

"At least she's not a hypocrite. That'd be the pot calling the kettle black, wouldn't it?"

"I guess."

"I thought you'd probably hear a sermon against going on birth control pills at your age."

"No," Heather said wearily. "She only lectured about condoms."

"Condoms?"

"Uh-huh. Mom, can I please have my phone back now?"

"What did the doctor say about condoms?"

Heather shot her a mutinous glare, then recited hurriedly, "That they're still the best protection from disease and that if me and my friends are going to sleep with our boyfriends, we should always use them."

"She told you to have a condom handy just in a case a date turned into sex?"

"Something like that," Heather said, shrugging with unconcern. "Can I please have my phone back, Mommy? Please? And my car keys?"

A glimmer of an idea winked on inside Darcy's head. She regarded it from all angles and decided it was worth saving and nurturing. Smiling and feeling more like her old self, she reached across the console and patted Heather's knee.

"Sure you can, sweetie. You can have them back as soon as we get home. But first let's stop and have a piece of pie with Daddy. I've been a perfect grouch all week and want to make it up to y'all, starting now."

Bowie Cato turned off the highway onto the state road that ran along the north end of The Green Pine Motel, where Darcy was alighting from her late model Cadillac.

"'S that Mrs. Winston?"

"Yes." Janellen had turned to wave. "Do you know her?"

"I've seen her. Who's that with her?"

"Her daughter, Heather. She's about the most popular girl at the high school these days."

"Pretty," Bowie commented, glancing back at the two women as they entered the motel lobby.

' Very. She works part-time at the motel for her daddy. I see her whenever we go to the Sunday buffet after church. She's friendly and sweet and well liked."

Bowie wondered if the daughter was as "well liked" as

the mother. He'd seen Darcy Winston in action plenty of times at The Palm, beginning that night Key Tackett had returned to town and as recently as last night when she'd been playing a rowdy game of billiards with three Shriners who were having a night out on the town without their wives.

Darcy was a tramp, and everybody knew it. Just like everybody knew that Janellen Tackett was a lady. That's why folks looked askance at them whenever she was with him. They were wondering what Miss Janellen was doing with a no-account ex-con like Bowie Cato.

He'd been wondering that himself. He both thanked and cursed Key for asking him to keep an eye on her. He thanked him because being near Janellen was about as close to a class act as he was ever going to get. He cursed Key because he was beginning to like being near her too well.

He enjoyed seeing her every day and having a good excuse for it. But it was temporary bliss. Sure as God made little green apples, something would happen to put an end to it. Waiting for the inevitable and wondering what disastrous form it would take was driving him nuts. Right now he was living a fairy tale. Trouble was, he didn't believe in fairy tales. They were for kids and fools. He sure as hell wasn't a kid, but he was beginning to think he was a fool.

He was letting himself in for a fall. No two ways about it.

Damned if he could stop himself, though. Every chance he got to be with her, he took. Like today. When word reached him that she was going out to take a look at the number seven well, he'd jumped into the truck and driven like a bat out of hell to get to the office before she left.

He caught her just as she was leaving and reminded her that Key didn't want her to be alone. He also said that the truck was more suited to the well site than her compact car. She'd conceded and climbed into the cab of the truck with him.

But she wasn't happy about it.

She was as jittery as a chihuahua passing peach pits and wouldn't look him in the eye. She was probably ashamed to be seen riding around with a convicted felon. Hell, who could blame her?

"It gets pretty rough from here," he warned.

"I know," she said acidly. "I've driven it myself plenty of times."

He ignored that and took the turnoff. The dirt track, carved into the earth by tire treads, ran parallel to the highway several hundred yards away. In between was The Green Pine Motel. He'd heard talk of how Jody Tackett, years ago, had swindled Fergus Winston out of his oil lease.

Fergus had come to Eden Pass as a young man, bringing with him a small legacy and big dreams. He bought a patch of land that didn't look like much on the surface but had highway frontage and rumors of oil underneath.

He met Jody, who at the time was working for Clark Tackett Senior and was already reputed as being a knowledgeable land man. Jody befriended him and offered to let a Tackett Oil geologist check out his lease and give him an expert opinion. After weeks of assessment, she sorrowfully told Fergus that it was doubtful his land had any significant deposit of oil.

Fergus, somewhat in love with her by then, believed her, but he decided he needed a second, bipartisan opinion. He retained the services of another geologist who sadly informed him that horny toads were about the only thing his patch of ground was likely to harvest.

Fergus was disappointed but had come to believe that his future lay not in the competitive oil industry but in providing temporary lodging for the folks who wheeled and dealed in it. Jody, still passing herself off as a concerned friend, told him she hated to see him getting stuck with land that wasn't good for anything. She offered to buy his lease for Tackett Oil, which could use it as a tax write-off. Fergus would then have enough capital to begin building his motel.

Relieved to be unloading a white elephant and recovering some of his investment, he sold the land and all the mineral rights for next to nothing, keeping only the strip of property that fronted the highway, on which he planned to build his motel.

But Fergus's white elephant was sitting on top of a black lake of rich crude. Jody knew that, and so did the Tackett Oil geologist, and so did the one Jody bribed to back up the lie of the first. The ink wasn't dry on the deed before Tackett Oil erected a drilling rig. When the well came in, Fergus was fit to be tied. He accused Jody and the Tacketts of being thieves and liars. When she married Clark Junior, he cursed her even louder. But he never legally pursued his allegations of dirty dealing, so folks discounted his grievances as sour grapes and jealousy because Jody had jilted him in favor of Clark Junior.

Fergus built his motel, and it was profitable almost from its opening day. But even if it had been as fancy as a Ritz-Carlton, he'd never be as rich as Jody Tackett. To this day, he carried a grudge.

Bowie parked the truck outside the chain-link fence that formed a neat square around the pumping well. He alighted and went around to offer assistance to Janellen, but she had already hopped down by the time he reached her. He used his key to unlock the gate.

The motor driving the horse head pump was chugging away. He'd been out hours earlier to check on it, which he did every day except for his days off, when the relief pumper ran the route. He and Janellen weren't interested in the pump or the storage tanks, but in the meter box where red, green, and blue pens recorded the line pressure, temperature of the gas, and rate of flow onto circular charts that were changed biweekly. Fortunately the meter box for well number seven was located only yards from the well itself. It could have been miles away.

Fifteen minutes later, he was feeling like a damn fool. There seemed to be nothing wrong with well number seven. The meter box was functioning properly. There were no discernible leaks between the well and the meter box. Everything appeared to be in perfect working order.

"I guess you think I'm crazy," he mumbled.

"I don't think you're crazy, Bowie. In fact, if it would relieve your mind, I'll authorize you to put a test meter between the well and the recorder."

He got the impression that he was being humored. "Okay, I will," he said, calling her bluff. "Do you know if there was ever a flare line off this well?"

"If there was, it was capped off when they became illegal. We don't waste gas that way anymore."

They retraced their steps back to the gate. Bowie locked it behind them. "Did you tell your mama about this?"

"No."

"You didn't think it was important enough?"

By now she had reached the passenger door of the truck and turned to face him, shading her eyes against the sun. "I'll thank you not to put words in my mouth, Bowie. It's just that these days I don't worry Mama with anything that I don't have to."

"You sure look pretty, Miss Janellen."

"What?" she exclaimed. Her hand remained where it was, with her index finger following the curve of her eyebrows and her palm sheltering her eyes.

Oh, hell. He'd gone and done it now. He reached beneath his hat to scratch the back of his head. He hadn't meant to say what he was thinking. The words just popped out. And now an explanation was called for.

"It just, uh, struck me all of a sudden how pretty you look standing there. With the sun shining in your eyes and the wind whipping your hair around."

The hot, arid wind had also plastered her clothes to her body, so, for the first time since meeting her, her shape was clearly defined for him. In his estimation it was a very nice shape, but he didn't indulge his curiosity for long because her face was crumbling and her eyes were filling up with tears that had nothing to do with the sun's glare.

"Oh!" she sobbed. "Oh, Lord! I could just *die!*"

Her reaction alarmed him. All a parolee needed was to have a hysterical woman on his hands, bawling and carrying on and saying she could just die. He anxiously rubbed his damp palms against his thighs.

"Hey, Miss Janellen, don't get yourself all worked up now." Nervously he glanced around, hoping no one was witnessing her distress. "When I said . . . well, I didn't mean anything disrespectful. You're safe with me and that's a fact. What I mean is, I wouldn't— "

"Just because he told you to keep an eye on me doesn't mean you have to shower me with compliments you don't mean."

Bowie squinted his eyes and cocked his head, unsure he'd heard her right. "Come again?"

"I don't need him watching over me, or you either."

"'Him'? Are you referring to your brother? Key?"

"Of course Key," she said with annoyance. "Ever since he asked you to keep an eye on me, I can't turn around without bumping into you."

"Well, I apologize for any inconvenience it's caused you, but I promised Key I'd look out for you, and I keep my promises. I plan to keep on looking out for you until he tells me to stop."

"*I'm* telling you to stop. As of this minute. All the reporters have left Eden Pass. I'm in no danger of being ambushed by them, so you don't need to trouble yourself any longer."

"It wasn't any trouble to drive you around, Miss Janellen."

"I can drive myself! I have since I was sixteen."

"Yes, ma'am, I know that, but— "

"And I can read a meter box the same as any man. Alone, too."

"I'm sure you can."

"While you feel duty-bound to trail me everywhere, I certainly don't need you throwing out empty compliments that— "

"It wasn't empty."

"—that you can laugh over later."

"Laugh?"

"I know what the men think of me. They think I'm a dried-up old maid. Muley told me that they laugh at me behind my back. You're trying to suck up to my brother— "

"Now hold on just a goddamn minute," Bowie interrupted angrily. "I don't suck up to anybody. Got that? And leave your brother out of this, because he doesn't have a friggin' thing to do with why I said what I said. And I don't give a rat's ass about what any of the other men think. I make up my own mind about things, and if somebody disagrees with my opinion, well then screw 'em. When I told you you looked pretty, it's because I really thought so."

"God a'mighty! Most women would have said, 'Why, thank you, Bowie. What a nice thing to say,' and let it go at that. But not you. No. You gotta read something into it 'cause you're prickly and prissy and have a burr up your butt the size of Dallas."

His words reverberated in the air between them before the wind snatched them away.

But not soon enough, Bowie thought dismally. His self-control had snapped, something he'd thought would never happen with her. He'd lost his temper and shot off his mouth. He'd fucked up major big this time. Now she'd fire him, and the fault was all his.

She faced him, wide-eyed, tremulous, and speechless. Tears had made pools of her blue eyes, pools deep enough for a grown man to drown in. A small shudder rippled through her. She drew in a quick little breath that brought her lower lip in fleeting contact with her teeth.

It was too damn much.

Figuring that at this point he'd just as well be hanged for a sinner as a saint, he bent his head and kissed her. It was a hard and swift kiss. It had to be. Any minute now she might start screaming. Besides, he didn't trust himself to linger and taste. He might do something really stupid that would land his sorry ass right back in jail.

The instant he pulled back, he turned her about and shoved her up into the truck. He climbed in on the other side, turned on the noisy motor, engaged the grinding gears, and guided the truck over the deeply rutted track.

They rode in silence all the way back to the ugly company office, where he'd picked her up. After he killed the engine, the silence was as engulfing as the heat that rose from the ground in shimmering waves.

She was probably still too distressed to speak, so it was up to him to say something. For several moments he stared through the dirty windshield, then said, "I'll take the truck back to the shop and turn in the keys. You can mail me my final check."

He heard her swallow, but he didn't look at her. He couldn't bear to see her disgust.

Finally, in a feeble voice, she asked, "Are you leaving Tackett Oil?"

He looked at her then, turning his head so quickly that his neck popped. "Aren't I?"

"Do you want to?"

"Don't you want me to?"

She shook her head and, in a barely audible voice, said, "No."

He didn't dare move for fear of shattering the fragile mood. "Those things I said, Miss Janellen . . . I never should have used that kind of language in front of you."

"I grew up with two brothers. I know all the words, Bowie. And what most of them mean."

She flashed a gamine smile, but he didn't return it. "That, uh, that other—kissing you—well, that's grounds for firing me for sure. But I want you to know that I only did it because I lost my head."

"Oh." After a moment, while the silence and tension and heat thickened, she added, "Then it was purely an impulsive gesture?"

Something in her eyes compelled him to answer truthfully. "No, I can't truly say that it was, Miss Janellen. I'd thought about doing it before."

"I'd thought about it, too."

He couldn't believe what she'd just said, yet he was looking straight at her. He'd watched her lips form the words, and because his loins had filled with liquid fire, he knew he wasn't dreaming.

But it only got better.

He shifted slightly. She tilted her head inquisitively. Then they met somewhere in the middle of the bench seat. Within seconds of her soft declaration, he was holding her against him, her arms were twined around his neck, and they were kissing madly.

Her lips were responsive but shy, which was okay because Bowie wasn't an experienced kisser anyway.

He'd never had a woman of his own, and easy women and whores usually skipped the kissing part. So he and Janellen tutored each other, and when his tongue slipped between her lips and connected with hers, they both murmured in delightful discovery.

Was her mouth actually sweeter than any other woman's he'd kissed, or was it that she was the first he'd french kissed with caring and not only as a hasty prelude to getting laid?

He lowered his hand to her waist and pressed it. Another tiny shudder went through her. God, it was exciting. He wanted to chart that shudder from her breasts, up her throat, and across her mouth. But of course he didn't.

Eventually she angled her head back and gazed up at him with rapidly blinking eyes. She was embarrassed. Her cheeks were flushed. Her breathing was rapid and shallow. She rolled her lips inward, then released a breathy little laugh.

"I'd better go now. If I'm late for supper, Key's likely to come looking for me."

He scooted back behind the steering wheel. "Sure enough."

"I'll see you tomorrow."

There was the slightest inflection of inquiry attached. "Bright and early." He smiled, although it was a strain because his cock was throbbing like a son of a bitch.

She opened the door and was on the verge of getting out when she turned back and said in one gust of breath, "I love you, Bowie."

She slammed the truck's door, ran to her car, scrambled into the driver's seat, and drove away. Bowie watched the cloud of dust she raised until it had dissipated. Even then he sat behind the steering wheel of the truck, staring through crusty insect carcasses and oil-field grime, unable to move, shell-shocked by her parting words.

Well, that explained the kissing spree, he thought. Janellen Tackett wasn't right in the head. In fact, she was plumb crazy.

Nobody had ever loved Bowie Cato.

Chapter Fourteen

Are you awake?"

"I am now." Lara's nightstand clock registered 2:03 A.M. "Who is this?"

"Key Tackett."

She groaned, burrowing her head deeper into her pillow and almost letting the telephone receiver slip from her hand. "Is this another of your emergencies?"

"Yes."

Sensing the strain in his voice, Lara came fully awake. This wasn't a prank. She sat up and switched on the nightstand lamp. "What is it?"

"Are you familiar with the state highway everybody calls the Old Ballard Road?"

"I know where it is."

"Go south on it two miles beyond the Dairy Queen. On your right will be a cutoff. There's an old windmill there, so you can't miss it. A few hundred feet beyond that, on your left, there's a farmhouse. My Lincoln is parked out front. Bring your stuff."

"What stuff?"

"Doctor stuff. Hurry."

"But— "

The line went dead. She flung back the covers; her feet hit the floor running. It was second nature to respond to an emergency call. She didn't pause to consider the advisability of responding to this one until she was speeding down the dark, deserted highway. If the Tacketts really wanted to get rid of her permanently, how better than to trick her into going out in the middle of the night on an emergency call from which she would never return?

She had pulled on the first clothes her hands had touched and shoved her feet into a pair of sneakers. In the clinic, she'd filled her medical bag with supplies that would handle most, but certainly not all, emergencies.

She might very well be walking into a trap, but she could not have said no to the summons. And, strange as it was, she believed the urgency in Key's voice had been genuine.

She sped past the windmill before seeing it. If his directions hadn't included it, she never would have spotted the narrow, unmarked road. She backed up and took the turn sharply. Moments later her headlights swept across a frame farmhouse. As promised, Key's yellow Lincoln was parked in front. She pulled in beside it, grabbed her bag, and alighted.

The dogs went berserk.

Key had been watching for her from the living-room window. As soon as she wheeled in, he pulled open the front door. Unfortunately he didn't reach it in time to call off the hunting hounds who charged out from their various lairs to surround Lara with snarling maws. They raised a horrendous racket.

She jumped onto the hood of her car and thrashed her legs, trying to kick away the howling attackers. Key emitted a shrill whistle that brought a sudden halt to the barking. A few of the hounds whimpered as they slunk back to their hideouts.

"Good Lord! I could have been chewed to pieces."

"All's clear now. Hurry." He pushed open the screen door. Tentatively Lara placed one foot on the ground. Out of the darkness came a menacing growl, but when Key ordered, "Hush!" the dog fell silent.

She picked her way up to the porch. "Whose house is this? Why am I here?"

"Helen lost the baby."

She stopped dead in her tracks and looked at him meaningfully. He motioned her inside with a brusque movement of his head. By the light of the Berrys' homey living room, he noticed that Lara's face was free of makeup. She hadn't taken time to brush her hair. It was still pillow-tousled, reminding him of the first time he'd seen her. That night, she hadn't known his name. She'd smiled at him a couple of times, even when threatening to notify the sheriff of his gunshot wound. She wasn't smiling tonight. Her expression said she wouldn't waste spit on him if he was on fire.

"Where is she?"

"Back here."

"When did the spotting start?"

"Spotting?" he repeated. "She was goddamn near bleeding to death when I got here."

He led her through a long, narrow hallway. The walls were decorated with framed photographs that chronicled the growth of a family. Time had yellowed some of them. The most recent one was of Helen in her graduation cap and gown.

Key stood aside and let Lara precede him into the bedroom where Helen lay in a single bed, clutching a teddy bear to her chest and quietly weeping.

"Helen? The doctor's here." He moved to the side of the bed and took her hand. It was flaccid and cold. He pressed it between his own, trying to restore animation and warmth.

He didn't know which was worse, her abject despondency now or her previous hysteria. She had called him at The Palm. "It's a woman," Hap had said as he passed him the telephone receiver. "Says your sister told her to try and catch you here. She sounds stressed out."

That had been an understatement. He'd hardly been able to hear her above the din inside the bar, but her alarm came through loud and clear. When he reached

her house and rushed into the bedroom, he saw a
copious amount of dark, clotted blood on her sheets.
He'd immediately called Lara Mallory.

"Hello, Helen," she said now, bending down and laying
a gentle hand on Helen's brow. "Everything's going to be
all right. I'll take care of it, okay?"

Her bedside manner was flawless, but Helen didn't buy
it. "I lost my baby."

"You're sure?"

Helen nodded and glanced across the room. Lara
followed her gaze to the soiled sheets which Key had
stripped from the bed and piled up in the corner. Lara
looked at him. "Will you excuse us, please?"

He gave Helen's hand a hard squeeze. "Hang in there,
sweetheart. I'll be in the living room if you need me."

"Thanks, Key."

He backed out of the room. Lara was placing a blood
pressure cuff around Helen's arm as he closed the door.
In the living room he posted himself at the wide picture
window and stared out into the night. Away from the
lights of town, the stars were brilliant. It never failed to
astonish him how many there were. That was one of the
reasons he loved night flying. Only then could he fully
appreciate the vastness of the sky and know peace.

He wished like hell he were up there now.

A hound dog loped up onto the porch, slurped water
from a bowl, yawned broadly, then dropped its head onto
its front paws and went back to sleep. A night bird called
plaintively. Occasionally the old lumber inside the walls
would shift with a groan and a creak. Other than that,
the house was quiet.

He wondered what was going on in the bedroom. How
long would it take for Dr. Mallory to do whatever she
was doing? Time crawled. When the bedroom door finally
opened, he turned away from the window and rushed to
meet her halfway down the hall. She was wearing surgical
gloves and carrying the bloody sheets.

"Seeing these is upsetting her. They need to soak."

He led her to a screened-in back porch that ran the width of the house. It was equipped with a deep utility sink, into which she put the sheets, and then turned on the cold water. "You know your way around the house very well."

"Her daddy's about the best hunter in East Texas. I've gone with him lots of times, ever since I was a kid."

"That's why you know how to call off the dogs."

"Yes. This is where we cleaned up after dressing our kills." He nodded down to the sink now filling with pink water.

The sight of blood had never bothered him. He'd seen ghastly war injuries, men whose flesh was melting off their skeletons following oil-well fires, even the severed head of a Moslem woman caught in adultery. He'd thought he had a cast-iron stomach where violence was concerned, that nothing could make him queasy.

He was wrong. This blood bothered him tremendously. He ran his hand down his face and looked away from the sink.

"I examined the expulsion," Lara said as though reading his mind. "She miscarried the embryo."

He nodded.

"Where are her parents?"

"They took the younger kids to Astroworld today," he answered mechanically as he watched Lara peel off her surgical gloves. "Helen wasn't feeling well and begged off. It's a good thing, too. She hadn't told them about the baby yet. Imagine if this hadn't happened at home, in bed. Jesus," he added grimly, "it doesn't bear thinking about."

"Besides, the fewer people who know about this, the better, right? Especially for you. Look at it this way, you're off the hook now."

Although it took all the willpower he possessed, he let the insult pass.

When the sink was full, she turned off the faucet. "I've given Helen an injection to retard the bleeding and a sedative to help her sleep. In the morning she can come to the clinic and I'll do a D and C."

"Good. Her folks aren't supposed to be back until late tomorrow night."

"By then she'll be home, although I recommend a few days of bed rest. She can tell them she's got a severe case of cramps, which, unfortunately, is true." After a significant pause, she added, "I also highly recommend that sexual intercourse be suspended for several weeks. You'll have to take your fun with someone else."

His eyes homed in on hers. Matching her scorn measure for measure, he said, "Any suggestions?"

They didn't break eye contact until the dogs set up another howl. A car door slammed. There were running footsteps on the porch.

"Helen?"

Key moved around Lara and went through to the living room. Jimmy Bradley was standing there, frantically glancing around.

"Key?" he exclaimed. "What are you doing here? Me and some of the guys went to Longview to knock around tonight. When I got home my brother said you'd called. Said for me to haul ass over here. What's happened? Where is everybody? Where's Helen?"

"She's in her bedroom."

Jimmy noticed Lara, who had just entered the room, gave her a puzzled glance, then cut his eyes back to Key. "What's going on?"

"This is Dr. Mallory."

"A doctor? For Helen?" he asked with mounting alarm.

Key laid a hand on the young man's broad shoulder. "She had a miscarriage tonight, Jimmy."

"A mis—?" He gulped hard, darted another look at Lara, then at Key. "Jesus." He broke away from

Key, ran down the hall, and burst into the bedroom. "Helen?"

"Jimmy? Oh, Jimmy! I'm sorry!"

Key looked at Lara. She was staring at him, whey-faced, her lips parted in surprise. "I hate to disappoint you," he said dryly, "but the baby wasn't mine. Helen came to me for help because she knew she could trust me."

He allowed himself only a moment of self-righteous indignation before turning abruptly and following Jimmy to the bedroom. Jimmy was seated on the edge of the bed, clutching Helen to him, running his hands over her back and shoulders. Both were crying.

"Why didn't you tell me, Helen? Why?"

"Because I was afraid you'd give up your scholarship. I didn't want you to be stuck with me and a baby."

"Honey, as long as I can carry a damn football, I can go to school. That college doesn't care if I've got three wives and six kids. You should have told me. You went through hell all by yourself."

"Key helped." She sniffed. "I knew how much you respected him, so, when I didn't know where else to turn or what to do, I asked him for advice. He begged me to tell you, but he also promised to keep my secret."

"I didn't think I should keep the secret any longer, Helen," Key told her from the open doorway. "I felt Jimmy had a right to know, so I called him tonight."

"I'm glad you did," Jimmy said fervently.

"So am I. Now," Helen added softly as she nuzzled his chest. "I've missed you so much."

"Me, too. When you broke up with me, I got mad for a few days. Then the hurt set in. I couldn't figure why you'd stopped lovin' me all of a sudden like that."

"I didn't stop loving you. I never will. It's because I love you so much that I didn't want to be a burden to you, to hold you back or keep you from taking this opportunity."

"As if you could ever be a burden. You're my second half, Helen. Don't you know that?" Jimmy bent his head and kissed her softly on the lips, then pulled back and whispered, "I'm sorry about our baby."

When Helen began crying again, Key knew it was time to leave the young lovers to work through their reconciliation and regret alone. He stepped into the bedroom only long enough to retrieve Lara's black bag.

"Sometime before her folks come home, see to things on the back porch," he told Jimmy. "Take her to Dr. Mallory's office in the morning. No one else will ever know."

The younger man nodded. "Thanks, Key. You're the best." Key kissed the tip of his finger and pressed it to Helen's temple, then left the room.

He found Lara in the living room, seated on the sofa, hugging her elbows. She looked at him with cold reproach. "You could have told me."

"And spoiled your fun? Think of the hours of pleasure you've had despising me."

"I'm sorry."

Suddenly he was very tired and didn't feel like dragging this out. Every time they were together, they were at each other's throats. The emotional events of tonight had left him feeling drained; the fight had gone out of him. "Forget it."

She stood and reached for her bag. He handed it over to her. It weighed down her arm like an anchor. "You okay?" he asked. "You don't look so hot." She too appeared tired, bone-weary, and dispirited. "You're pale."

"No wonder. You woke me out of a deep sleep, and I didn't take time to use my blusher." She moved to the front door. "Can I get out of here without being mauled by coon dogs?"

Key secured the front door and they left the house together. The dogs were roused, but Key gruffly ordered them to stay where they were. Once Lara was in the driver's seat of her car, she rested her forehead on the steering wheel.

"Are you sure you're all right?"

"Just tired." She raised her head and reached for the door. He moved aside and let her close it, then watched as she drove away. He kept her in sight as he climbed into the pimp-mobile. She drove slowly, as if it were a newly acquired skill.

At the crossroads, he debated over whether to return to The Palm. It was late. Only the drunkest of the drunks would still be there. He didn't feel like carousing. But he wasn't ready to go home, where he always felt claustrophobic.

In the opposite direction, the taillights of Lara's car disappeared behind a rise in the road. "What the hell," he muttered as he turned the Lincoln around.

In spite of her protests, she hadn't looked too chipper. He was responsible for getting her out at this time of night. The least he could do was follow her to see that she got home safely.

Lara didn't notice his headlights in her rearview mirror, so it came as an unpleasant surprise when the Lincoln pulled into her driveway as she was unlocking the clinic's back door.

"I'm closed!" she called. Undeterred, Key joined her on the back steps. "What do you want now? Why can't you leave me in peace?"

Her voice was beginning to fray. If she noticed the weakness, he was certain to hear it too. The tears she had managed to hold back during the drive home filled her eyes, making his image watery.

Turning her back to him, she inserted the key into the lock. At least she attempted to, but her vision was blurry and her hands were unsteady.

Key reached around her. "Let me."

"Go away!"

He took the key from her, pushed it easily into the lock, and opened the door. The alarm began its delay buzzing. He went in ahead of her and moved to the panel.

"What's the code?"

She wanted to tell him to go to hell, wanted to forcibly remove him, but didn't have the strength for either. "Four-o-four-five." He punched in the code and the buzzing ceased. "It won't do you any good to know the code," she told him peevishly. "I'll change it tomorrow."

"Where's your coffeepot?"

"In the kitchen. Why?"

"Because you look like shit, like you could keel over any second now. A cup of strong black coffee would probably be good for whatever's ailing you."

"You're what's ailing me. Leave me alone, and I'll be fine. Can't you do that? Please? It's so simple! *Just go!*"

She didn't want to fall apart in front of him, but the choice was no longer left to her. Her voice cracked on the last two words. She raised her hand to indicate the back door, but it moved to her mouth instead and covered a sob as her knees buckled. She sank into the nearest chair. Tears overflowed her eyes. Her shoulders began to shake. Despite her best intentions, she couldn't contain the racking sobs.

Propping her arm on the back of the chair, she laid her head on the crook of her elbow and surrendered to the emotional outburst. Pride deserted her. Grief, bitterness, and pain had clawed their way to the surface and, having been tamped down for so long, would not be restrained.

To his credit, Key didn't interfere by asking questions or offering banalities. The light remained off; the concealment of darkness lent some comfort. She cried until her head ached. Then, for several minutes, she kept her face buried in her sleeve and suffered the aftershocks of the violent catharsis. The tremors came in waves, significant but not sufficient to produce another tidal wave of emotion.

Eventually she raised her head, expecting to see him standing there gloating. She was alone but noticed that a dim light from the kitchen spilled out into the hallway. Weakly coming to her feet, she smoothed back her hair and went to the kitchen.

He was leaning back against the range. Only the night light above the cook surface had been turned on. It cast dark shadows onto his face as he sipped from a steaming cup of coffee. He'd found her bottle of brandy. It was standing open on the counter. She could smell its pungent bouquet, enticingly mingled with fresh coffee.

As soon as he noticed her, he nodded toward the coffeemaker. "Want me to pour?"

"No, thanks. I can." Her voice sounded rusty from so many tears. It disturbed her that he was on her turf, making himself at home in her kitchen in the hours just before dawn. Key Tackett, her self-proclaimed adversary, had been rummaging through her pantry, handling her things, and was now offering to pour her coffee in her own kitchen.

"Feel better?"

She listened for sarcasm behind his seemingly innocent question but heard none. Nodding, she carried her cup to the kitchen table and sat down. She took a sip. The coffee was scalding and potent, the way a man would brew it. "You can go now. You don't have to stay. I'm not self-destructive."

Ignoring what she'd said, he pushed himself away from the stove and, bringing the bottle of brandy with him, sat down across from her. He added a dollop of the liquor to her cup.

His eyes were steady and disconcertingly watchful. His fingertips moved up and down the glassy surface of the coffee mug cupped between his strong, tanned hands.

She feared that if she watched them too long, they would have a hypnotic effect on her.

"What was that all about?"

Self-consciously, she hooked her hair behind her ear. "That's really none of your business, is it?"

His head dropped forward, and he cursed as he exhaled.

His hair grew in a swirling pattern around the crown of his head. Even in the dim light she could see the cowlicks. The most gifted barber would be challenged by them. Perhaps that's why he wore his hair long and loose and in no particular style.

When he raised his head, his eyes were angry. "You refuse to let me be a nice guy, don't you?"

"You're not a nice guy."

"Maybe I'm trying to change." She gave him a retiring look, which only heightened his anger. "Bury the hatchet for once, okay? And bury it someplace besides my skull. Can't you forget my last name? Even temporarily? I'll try to forget yours. Deal?" He held her stare until she lowered her gaze.

Taking that as concession, he said, "Thanks for what you did tonight. I was out of my element and knew it the minute I saw the condition Helen was in, physically and emotionally. It was a scene out of hell, and you handled it like a real pro. You . . . were terrific."

Again Lara listened for sarcasm, but there was none. Those words, she knew, were difficult for him to say. It would be churlish of her not to accept the compliment. "Thank you." Then, with a self-deprecating laugh, she added, "Actually I'm great during emergencies. I never crack under pressure. Only afterward. Then I collapse."

It seemed a long time before he spoke again. When he did, it was in a hushed voice that invited confidence. "What was the crying binge about, Lara?"

She felt herself respond not only to his tone but to his speaking her name. Still she hesitated, unwilling to bare her soul to him. Although what did it matter now? He'd already witnessed her loss of self-control.

Her throat ached from so much crying. She cleared it before speaking. "My daughter. It was about my daughter."

"I guessed as much. Go on."

She threw back her head, then rolled it around her shoulders. "Sometimes when a case involves a child, it conjures up the nightmare. Ashley dies all over again." She sniffed and blotted her nose with a paper napkin from the dispenser on the table.

"There've been two in the last few days. First Letty Leonard. Now Helen's fetus. Knowing that a small, helpless, innocent life was needlessly lost . . ." She shrugged eloquently. "It still affects me. Deeply." She sipped from her coffee mug, which felt very heavy in her trembling hand. The brandy had been a good idea. It warmed and soothed all the way down.

"Tell me about her."

"Who, Ashley?"

"Pretty name."

"She was pretty." She laughed softly, with embarrassment. "Every mother thinks that about her child, I know, but Ashley *was* pretty. From the day she was born. Blond and blue-eyed, cherubic-looking. She had a perfectly round face and rosy cheeks. Truly a beautiful child. And she was a good baby. Content. She didn't cry much, even during the early months. She had an unusually happy disposition. Her smile was like sunshine. Even strangers commented on it. She . . . beamed. Yes, beamed," she said reflectively.

"She seemed destined to make everyone around her smile, to light up a room when she walked in. She certainly lit up my life." Her coffee was growing cold. She folded her hands around the mug in a vain attempt to retain the warmth.

"Until she was born, I was desperately unhappy.

Randall's job required all his time and concentration. Montesangre is a hideous place. I loathe it. All of it. The climate, the land, the people. Living there in banishment was the bleakest period of my life. Or so I thought at the time. I didn't learn what real despair is until I lost my child."

She paused for a moment to stave off another smothering attack of bereavement. She swallowed with difficulty and briefly mashed her fist against her lips. When she felt it was safe to speak, she cleared her throat again and continued.

"Ashley made even that horrid place bearable. When I nursed her, it was as nurturing to me as it was to her. For weeks after I weaned her, my breasts ached." She covered her breasts with her hands, feeling once again the pain of disuse and remorse. Then, remembering herself, she lowered her hands and glanced at Key. He sat unmoving, watching and listening. "And then she died."

"She didn't die. She was killed."

She sipped her coffee, but it was cold now so she pushed the mug aside. "That's right. There is a distinction, isn't there?"

"Definitely."

She waited for him to say more, but he didn't. "What do you need, a play-by-play account?"

"No," he answered quietly. "I think that's what *you* need."

It was on the tip of her tongue to tell him to go to hell, but the words died unspoken. She didn't have enough energy for defiance. Moreover, perhaps he was right. Perhaps she did need to talk about it.

"We were on our way to a party," she began. "A wealthy local businessman was throwing a birthday bash for one of his seven children. I didn't particularly want to go. I knew it would be an ostentatious affair. The way in which the wealthy Montesangrens flaunted their wealth made you almost sympathize with the rebels. Anyway,

Randall insisted that we attend the party because the host was an influential man.

"I dressed Ashley in a new dress. Yellow. Her color. I put a yellow bow in her hair, on the top of her head where her curls were the thickest." She touched her own hair to demonstrate.

"Randall had arranged for someone on the embassy staff to drive us, thinking it would be more impressive if we arrived with a chauffeur. He was sitting in the front seat with the driver. Ashley and I were in the back. We were playing patty-cake. The car approached a busy intersection. Ashley was laughing, squealing. She was happy."

Lara couldn't go on. Resting her head in her palm, she pinched her burning eyes shut. After a moment, she forced herself to continue.

"The driver stopped for the traffic light. Suddenly, the car was surrounded by armed, masked guerrillas. I didn't realize this at the time. It all happened too fast. I didn't know anything was wrong until the driver fell forward against the steering wheel. He'd been shot through the head at close range. The second bullet shattered the front windshield. It struck Randall.

"The third bullet was intended for him too, but he had slumped to one side. Ashley was hit instead. Here." She touched the side of her neck. "Her blood splattered over my face and chest. I screamed and fell across her to protect her. That's when I was shot, in the back of my shoulder. I didn't even feel it."

She paused and sat staring into space. It was an effort to continue, but she knew that healing processes were customarily painful.

"Bystanders started screaming. People left their cars idling and scattered in every direction, seeking cover. They were safe. It was us the rebels were after. Three of them opened the passenger door and grabbed Randall. He shouted in pain and outrage. I believe one of the gunmen struck him in the temple with the butt of his pistol. Randall lost consciousness before they carried him to their waiting truck. I read all this later in the newspaper, after they had executed him. I knew nothing at the time of the kidnapping. All I knew was that my baby was dying.

"I knew it, but I couldn't accept it," she continued hoarsely. "I was screaming. I couldn't stop the bleeding. I pushed my finger into the bullet hole in her neck to try to stop it. The authorities arrived within minutes of the attack, but I was hysterical. They had to prize Ashley away from me. They dragged me to an ambulance. I don't remember anything after that. I lost consciousness. When I woke up, I was in a hospital in Miami."

She didn't realize that tears were rolling down her face until one ran into the corner of her lips. She licked it away. "The ambush on our car marked the official beginning of the revolution. The rebels attacked the birthday party, too. It was a bloodbath. Only a few survivors lived to tell about it. No doubt we would have been killed there. I don't know why they chose to ambush us en route.

"Because of what happened to Randall, the United States closed the embassy in Montesangre—what was left of it after it was ransacked—and abruptly discontinued diplomatic relations with their new government.

"Following his execution, the revolutionaries returned Randall's body to the States. It was more a gesture of contempt than largess, because they also sent gory photographs of the firing squad to the secretary of state. They didn't send back Ashley's remains, nor any pictures of her body or coffin. No death certificate. Nothing. They ignored all Washington's demands for either more information or the release of her body. After a while, Washington lost interest and stopped demanding. I've continued to badger them, but as far as our government is concerned, the matter is closed.

"Oh, God." She covered her face with her hands. "My

baby is still down there. I never got to touch her. Never got to see her face one last time. Never got to kiss her goodbye. She's somewhere down there in that wretched place. That— "

"Don't, Lara." He was there in an instant, standing beside her chair, smoothing back her hair. "You're right. It's a goddamn nightmare, but for Ashley it was over in a heartbeat. She didn't suffer any fear or pain."

"Yes, the pain has been all mine. I thank God for that. But at times it's so crushing that I don't think I can stand it anymore. There's no relief from it." She pressed her fist against her chest. "It hurts so bad. *I want my baby back!*"

"Shh. Don't do this to yourself. Don't." He pulled her to her feet. His arms went around her.

Instinctively, her fingers curled into the fabric of his shirt, and she pressed her face against his chest. "I'll never forget it. But there are parts of it that I can't remember. Like frames of a motion picture film, segments have been clipped out, and I'm afraid they're important. I want to remember the missing pieces, but my mind blocks them out. Sometimes I can almost grasp a lost memory, then it eludes me. It's as if I'm afraid to grasp it. I fear those things I can't remember."

"Shh-shh. It's all right. It's over and you're safe."

The assurances were whispered into her hair before his lips moved to her brow. Lara became aware of how good it felt to be held by someone physically stronger than herself. There had been no one with whom she could share this grief. Not her parents, who implicitly blamed her for everything that had happened, including Ashley's death. All her friends had deserted her when she made banner headlines for being Clark's mistress. For years she'd carried this burden alone. It was an unexpected luxury to lean on someone else and, for a few moments, relinquish a portion of the cumbersome weight.

Placing his fingertips beneath her chin, Key tilted

her head up and grazed her lips with his. "Don't cry anymore, Lara." The raspy words were lightly ground against her mouth. "It's all right." Again, his lips rubbed hers. "Don't cry."

Then he kissed her, a deep, hot, wet, questing kiss.

Lara's eyes slowly closed. She swirled in a maelstrom of fluid heat. Her will was voluntarily surrendered, and her mind went on a sensuous ride where nothing mattered except the connection—mouth to mouth, tongue to tongue, man to woman. It fulfilled a primal need she wasn't even aware she possessed.

Her response was instinctual. Her hands clutched him yearningly. She tipped her middle up, a gesture purely feminine, a silent solicitation for intimacy.

As though from a distance she heard his soft curse, then felt his hands moving across her shoulders, down her back, over her hips, drawing her against him, pressing her close. Closer.

It was that sudden and shocking familiarity with his body, or perhaps a self-preserving resurgence of sound judgment, that jolted her out of the sensual mist and into cold reality.

She pushed herself away and turned her back to him. Seeking support, she leaned forward against the counter. She took several deep breaths and vainly tried to disregard the desire rioting through her.

"Take me there."

He said nothing.

She let go of the counter and faced him. "Take me there. I've got to know what happened to my child. I've got to see her death certificate, touch the soil in which she's buried. Grasp . . . something."

His face remained impassive.

"That closure, that final goodbye, is essential to one's survivors. That's why we have funerals and eulogies and wakes." Still he said nothing. "Damn you! Say something."

"You weren't bullshitting. You really intend to go back."

"Yes. And you're going to fly me."

He folded his arms across his chest. "Now why would I do something that dumb?"

"Because you're smart enough to realize that I'm right. Clark was instrumental in getting Randall assigned to Montesangre. My baby died as a consequence of your brother's cowardly, political machinations."

"A debatable point at best," he said. "So, in order to make your argument more convincing, you decided to throw in some tongue-twisting kisses, right?"

Heat rushed to her face. "One has nothing to do with the other," she said gruffly.

He made a snide, scoffing sound. "You know, Doc, you've just lived up to all my expectations. In fact, you surpassed them." He whistled long and softly, wagging his hand as though he'd touched something hot. "One little kiss and you're ready, baby."

He snickered insultingly as he looked her over, then started toward the door. "Find yourself another sucker. I'll pass on taking a vacation to a war zone. I'm sure as hell not interested in fucking my dead brother's leftovers."

He was so angry, it was a life-threatening risk to drive, yet he pointed the Lincoln toward home and pushed it through the night like a Sherman tank. He was angry with her, but that was nothing new or surprising.

The surprise was that he was angry with himself. He, who never analyzed his actions or apologized for anything he did, was riddled with guilt because he wanted his late brother's mistress. If circumstances had been different, if she had given him the go-ahead, he'd be tugging off his boots right about now.

Jesus. Didn't he have any more character than to be craving a piece of the woman who'd caused his brother's downfall? Jody was right about him after all. Who better to know a child's character than his mother? He was rotten to the core, just like his old man. Where women were concerned he had no discretion and no conscience. If he did, his cock wouldn't be hard enough to drive nails, and the taste of Lara Mallory's mouth wouldn't still linger on his tongue.

When they were growing up, he and Clark had shared things, sometimes voluntarily, sometimes under parental duress. They swapped sweaters, shaving lotion, skateboards. But they'd never shared women. Not the easy girls at school. Not even whores.

This tacit agreement had evolved out of their adolescence, possibly because romance was one arena in which they didn't want to compete. As brothers, they were constant subjects of comparison, but they drew the line when it came to sexual aptitude. Key had never wanted a girl that Clark had dated before him, and, although he couldn't put thoughts into Clark's head, he figured his brother had felt the same way. That's why his desire for Lara Mallory was so puzzling and infuriating. It violated one of his own commandments.

He knew he had just as well get over this itch for her because he could never scratch it. To want the woman who had tainted his brother's name and destroyed his future was sinful. And while sin had never been a deterrent to his doing anything he wanted to do, stupidity certainly was.

That was the crux of his anger. He felt like a stupid fool for listening like a trusted old fogy while she poured out her tearful story. He'd brewed coffee, for chrissake! Then he'd gone one step farther and held her. Kissed her.

"Shit." He hit the steering wheel with his fist.

She was probably still laughing, knowing that she'd built a fire in his gut that he doubted ten other women could extinguish. A woman didn't let you make love to her mouth like that without knowing damn good and well what it was doing to you. No wonder she'd chosen that moment to make her pitch about a trip to Central America. She figured she had him so wound up he'd agree to take her to Mars if she asked.

Guess again, Doc, he thought with a smirk. He'd been hot for a lot of women, but even in the throes of passion he'd never taken a total departure from his reason.

On second thought, she hadn't looked particularly complacent when he left. She had seemed as confused and humiliated as he felt now. True enough, the story of her daughter's death had been heartbreaking. He still didn't trust her, but when it came to Ashley's murder, who could doubt that her suffering was genuine? The kid's death had shattered her, and she wasn't over it yet.

When I nursed her, it was as nurturing to me as it was to her.

She seemed destined to make the people around her happy.

She had adored that kid and had taken her death harder than Randall Porter's brutal execution. Of course, following the nasty scandal involving Clark, their marriage couldn't have been on solid ground. By her own admission, she'd been miserably unhappy in Montesangre. Only the birth of her daughter had made life there livable. To her, Ashley must have been like a consolation prize, a sign of God's forgiveness. Having lost Clark, she'd transferred all her love and attention to her baby.

Suddenly Key withdrew his foot from the accelerator. The Lincoln began to slow down. He stared sightlessly into the darkness that was gradually lifting on the eastern horizon. But the imminent sunrise didn't register on him. Nor did he realize that the Lincoln was straddling the center stripe as it rolled to a stop.

Other things Lara had said echoed in his head.

Blond and blue-eyed.

Her smile was like sunshine.

She beamed.

Key knew of only one other person who'd been

described in such radiant, solar terms. Clark Tackett the Third.

"Son of a bitch," he whispered as his hands heedlessly slipped from the steering wheel and landed in his lap.

Lara Mallory's beloved Ashley had been his brother's child.

Chapter Fifteen

Ollie Hoskins went to work with his feather duster on the cans of pork 'n' beans, chili, tamales, and tuna in aisle 6. As manager of the Sak'n'Save supermarket, he could have delegated dusting the shelves to one of the stockboys, but he enjoyed doing the menial tasks—pricing, stocking, sacking—because the work was clearly defined and easily dispatched. It was mindless labor that he could do while thinking about something else.

He'd served in the United States Navy for fifteen years before mustering out, and while he didn't miss the months at sea, he looked back fondly on the freedom from responsibility he'd enjoyed as a sailor. He'd never desired to be an officer and was still better at taking orders than issuing them.

One spring while on shore leave in Galveston, he'd met a young woman on the beach, fallen in love, and married her within a month. When it came time for him to reenlist, she urged him not to and relocated them to her hometown of Eden Pass so that she could be close to her mother.

They probably would have been better off staying in the service, Ollie thought now as he moved to aisle 5, where the shelves were neatly stocked with flour, sugar, spices, and shortening. His wife's family had never welcomed him into the fold. Ollie hailed from "up north somewhar," and, in their estimation, the only thing worse than being a Yankee would be to have an ethnic heritage. That he was Anglo made him tolerable—barely.

After twenty years, he still wasn't crazy about his in-laws, and vice versa. The bloom of love had long since faded from his marriage. Now, about the only thing he and his wife had in common was their boy, Tanner.

In their individual ways, they doted on him. His mother frequently embarrassed him with her overt demonstrations of affection. She'd been unable to conceive after Tanner—a condition that she implied was Ollie's shortcoming, not hers—so she fussed over him like a mama bear with her cub. It tickled her pink that he was Heather Winston's steady. Having her son dating the most popular girl at the high school somehow elevated her social standing among her friends.

Ollie had nothing against Heather. She was as cute as a button, friendly, full of pep. He only hoped that Tanner didn't let the romance get out of hand. He'd hate to see his son's future compromised by healthy lust.

Frequently Ollie looked at Tanner and marveled over the genetic quirk that had produced from his seed, and his wife's lackluster bloodline, such a smart, good-looking boy. Thank God he was athletic. If he'd wanted to play an instrument in the marching band, or had aspired to be a chemist or a rocket scientist, his relatives would have shunned him as a weirdo. But Tanner could kick and throw and carry a football, so he was affectionately walloped and jabbed and hugged by his rowdy cousins and uncles. They claimed him as theirs and conveniently forgot that Ollie was physically responsible for his origin.

Ollie didn't mind. Tanner was his, and he nearly busted his buttons every Friday night when number twenty-two charged onto the football field wearing the crimson and black of the Fighting Devils. The approaching season promised to be Tanner's best one yet.

Ollie finished straightening the cans of Crisco, rounded the sale display of Nabisco cookies at the end of the aisle, and entered aisle 4—coffee, tea, and canned beverages. Two women were moving along the aisle. The younger was pushing the cart while the older consulted a shopping list.

"Good morning, Miss Janellen, Mrs. Tackett," Ollie said pleasantly. "How are you this morning?" He'd never quite gotten the knack of saying "y'all." This deficiency in his vocabulary still branded him a Yankee outsider.

"Good morning, Mr. Hoskins," Janellen replied.

"Ollie, have the butcher cut us three T-bone steaks, one inch thick. And I don't mean seven-eighths. Last time they were cut much too thin and were so tough we couldn't chew them."

"I apologize, Mrs. Tackett. I'll make certain it's done to your liking this time." Just as Miss Janellen could always be counted on for a smile, he could depend on Jody Tackett to be a bitch. Lying, he said, "It's good to see you up and about."

"Why wouldn't I be?"

He was only trying make friendly conversation. By the way she snapped at him, you'd think he'd insulted her. "Why, no reason," he said, feeling his bow tie growing tighter around his neck. "I'd just heard you weren't feeling well these days. But you know how gossip travels."

"I'm feeling great. As you can see."

"Mama and I haven't been shopping together in a long time." Sweet Janellen was trying to smooth over the awkward moment. "We thought we'd treat ourselves."

"Well, it's certainly good to see you both. I'll go tell the butcher about those steaks and have them waiting for you at the checkout counter." He poked the handle of the feather duster into his rear pants pocket, turned, rounded the end of the aisle, and bumped into a grocery cart pushed by another woman.

"Dr. Mallory!" he exclaimed.

"Hello, Mr. Hoskins. How are you today?"

"Uh, fine." *Lord have mercy*, Ollie thought; Jody Tackett and Dr. Lara Mallory were on a collision course. He didn't want his store to be the scene of any trouble. "Did you see those watermelons in the produce section, Dr. Mallory? They came in from South Texas early this morning."

"A whole watermelon is wasted on one person, I'm afraid."

"I'll slice one and sell you a portion."

"No, thanks. I'll stick to cantaloupe."

When she smiled, his heart sped up a little. Regardless of the reputation that stereotyped sailors, he'd never been a dedicated skirt chaser. But he'd have to be blind not to notice that Dr. Mallory was a real looker. Her face and figure turned heads. In Eden Pass her name was synonymous with *temptress*.

Frankly, he'd never seen that side of her. She was friendly but never flirtatious. Maybe he just wasn't her type, although a natural flirt usually flirted with everybody of the opposite sex. Like Heather's mother. Now that woman was a tart if he'd ever seen one. He hoped to goodness that Heather didn't take after Darcy in that respect. Tanner was a good boy, but it wouldn't take much encouragement from a pretty girl like Heather for him to do something he ought not.

"Let me know if there's anything you need, Dr. Mallory."

"Thanks, Mr. Hoskins. I will."

Regrettably, he saw no way to avoid disaster. He moved aside and let her pass, thinking that maybe he should warn her that Jody Tackett was in the next aisle. He hoped the doctor didn't need any coffee or tea. Fatalistically he watched as she wheeled her cart into aisle 4. He loitered at the end of it, pretending to rearrange packages of Oreos and Fig Newtons. He prayed that he wouldn't be called upon to referee a cat fight.

The squeaky front wheel on Dr. Mallory's cart rolled

to a stop. For several moments there was silence, then he heard her say, "Good morning."

Janellen replied in her shy little voice, "Good morning, Dr. Mallory."

"I'm glad to see you're feeling better, Mrs. Tackett." Dr. Mallory gave Jody ample opportunity to respond. When she didn't, the doctor added, "I've called your house several times, hoping to speak with you."

"We have nothing to say to each other." Only Jody Tackett could have put that much venom into a few simple words. "Let's go, Janellen."

"Excuse me, Mrs. Tackett, but we have an awful lot to say to each other. I'd like very much to talk to you about Clark."

"I'll see you in hell first."

"Mama!"

"Hush, Janellen! Come along."

"Please, Mrs. Tackett. Mrs. Tackett? Mrs. Tackett!"

At first there was an underlying plea in the doctor's voice. Then inquiry. Then alarm.

"*Mama!*"

Ollie Hoskins knocked over several packages of Nutter Butters in his haste to get to aisle 4 to see what had happened. He arrived in time to see Jody Tackett reel sideways against her cart. She extended her arms at her sides, palms down, as though trying to regain her balance. The cart rolled forward; she lost her support and fell against the shelves stacked with boxes of Lipton's Tea. Several glass jars of instant decaf crashed to the floor, breaking on impact and spilling their fragrant powders. Jody fell backward against the shelf, then slid to the floor. She lay prone upon shattered jars and instant tea.

Janellen dropped to her knees. "Mama! Mama!" Lara Mallory didn't waste a second. She was beside Jody before Ollie could blink. "Call 911," she shouted back at him. "We need an ambulance."

He, in true military fashion, passed the command to

one of his subordinates, a checker who happened to be restocking cigarettes in front of her register. She turned and ran toward the office phone. The aisle was now filling up with other shoppers who'd been alerted by Janellen's frantic screams. Deserting their carts, they converged on aisle 4 from every corner of the supermarket. Ollie ordered them to stand back so the doctor would have room to see to Mrs. Tackett.

"Hold her arms. She could break a bone."

Janellen tried to catch Jody's flailing arms so she wouldn't bang them against the shelves. Even if no bones were broken, she was going to be badly bruised.

Dr. Mallory dug into her handbag and produced a clear, acrylic key ring in the shape of a large key. She thrust it into Jody's mouth and used it to depress her tongue.

"It's okay, it's okay," she told Janellen. "Her breathing passage is clear now. I'm holding down her tongue. She can breathe."

"But she's turning blue!"

"She's getting oxygen now. Keep holding her arms. Mr. Hoskins, did you call for the ambulance?"

"Yes, ma'am," Ollie briskly replied. He turned to the checker, who nodded her head to confirm. "Anything else I can do?"

"Find my brother," Janellen said. "Get him here."

Jody was drooling from the corners of her mouth. Her legs were still thrashing. It took all Janellen's strength to confine her arms. Dr. Mallory kept her tongue depressed with the key ring, but her breathing sounded like a combine. Ollie didn't have a soft spot for Jody Tackett, but he figured the lady deserved some privacy.

"All you people, clear this aisle."

Of course no one moved. He shoved his way through the growing crowd and ran to his open, elevated office at the front of the store.

Knowing that Key Tackett was a pilot, Ollie called the county airstrip first. Key wasn't there, but old Balky Willis gave him Key's portable phone number. "He left here 'bout fifteen minutes ago. He had that hand-held gadget with him."

Twenty seconds later, Key answered his portable phone with a cheerful, "Pimp-mobile."

"Mr. Tackett?" Ollie said nervously. He'd never had a run-in with Key, but he'd heard about the unfortunates who had. Even his brothers-in-law, all of them wild as March hares and ready to draw blood at the drop of a hat, spoke Key Tackett's name with reverence and respect. "This is Ollie Hoskins down at the Sak'n'Save and— "

"Hey, Ollie. I watched that Crimson-Black scrimmage the other night. Tanner's going to give 'em hell this season."

"Yes, sir, thanks. Mr. Tackett, your mother just collapsed here in— "

"Collapsed?"

"Yes, sir. Your sister and— "

"Is she all right?"

"No, sir. We've called for an ambulance."

"I'm on my way."

Ollie dropped the phone and rushed back to aisle 4. Clusters of shoppers blocked it at both ends. "Excuse me. Let me through." It pleased him to discover that he'd regained his military bearing sufficiently that he could make people heed him. "Please, everybody, stand back," he ordered with newfound confidence. He moved to stand directly behind Dr. Mallory.

"Is she having a stroke?" Janellen asked the doctor fearfully.

"Possibly a mild one. Tests will tell. Has she done this before?"

"No."

Dr. Mallory leaned down nearer the fallen woman. "Mrs. Tackett, an ambulance is on the way. Don't be frightened."

Jody had ceased to struggle for breath. Her limbs had relaxed and now were limp. She rolled her eyes from side to side as though trying to orient herself. Lara gradually withdrew the large plastic key from her mouth. It had teeth marks deeply imbedded in it, which explained why Dr. Mallory hadn't used her fingers to clear Jody's breathing passages. She wiped saliva from Jody's chin with a Kleenex from her own purse.

"You had a seizure, but it's over."

"Mama? Are you all right?" Janellen clasped her hand.

"She'll be groggy for several minutes," Dr. Mallory said. "That will pass."

"Let me through. What are y'all gawking at? Don't you have anything better to do? Get the hell away from here."

Key plowed through the crowd of spectators. They parted for him. Ollie stepped forward. "You must have been close to have gotten here so fast."

"Thanks for calling me, Ollie. Clear these people out, will you?"

"Yes, sir!" Ollie barely stopped himself from saluting. Key Tackett had that effect on people. "Okay, everybody. You heard Mr. Tackett. Clear this area."

"Key! Thank heaven!" Janellen cried. "Mama had a seizure."

"Jody?"

"Don' le' 'er touch me."

He knelt beside his mother, but his piercing eyes were on the doctor. "What's the matter with her?"

"Just as your sister said, she had a seizure. Serious and scary, but not fatal."

Key bent over his mother. "They've called an ambulance for you, Jody," he said in a low, reassuring voice. "It'll be here soon. Hang in there."

"Ge' 'er away from me. Don' want 'er to touch me."

Her speech was slurred, but her message was clear.

"Dr. Mallory saved your life, Mama," Janellen said gently.

Jody tried to sit up but couldn't. She fixed a murderous stare on Dr. Mallory. Although she couldn't articulate her animosity, it was effectively conveyed.

Key made a swift motion with his head. "Take off, Doc. She doesn't want you near her. You're only making matters worse."

Janellen said, "Key, if she hadn't— "

"But— " the doctor interrupted.

"You heard me," he barked. "Get out of her sight."

They glared at each other for what seemed to Ollie a long time, as if there was a lot more there than the eye could see. Eventually Dr. Mallory came to her feet. She was visibly shaken and her voice was unsteady. "Your mother is gravely ill and needs immediate medical attention."

"Not from you."

Even though the words weren't directed at him, Ollie quailed at Tackett's fierce expression and bone-chilling tone.

"Thank you, Dr. Mallory," Janellen said quietly. "We'll see that Mama gets the medical care she needs."

Her services having been flatly rejected, she turned her back on the Tacketts and moved down the aisle toward the onlookers. They parted for her as they had for Key. She didn't return to her cart of groceries but headed straight for the exit.

Ollie watched her leave, his respect for her increasing. She had a lot of class. She hadn't slunk past the bystanders but had walked tall and proud. Neither the Tacketts nor the gawkers had daunted her. He resolved to personally deliver her groceries to her once this crisis was over.

The wail of a siren was heard outside and moments later paramedics rushed into the store. Mrs. Tackett was transported by gurney to the waiting ambulance, which

sped away. Key and Janellen roared after it in his yellow
Lincoln.

Long after all the instant tea in aisle 4 had been swept
up and the shelves straightened, store customers lingered
to discuss what they'd seen and heard, and the drama
was re-created for new arrivals who had missed it. The
seriousness of Jody Tackett's condition was speculated
upon. Some said she was too mean to die and would live
to be one hundred. Others surmised that she was only a
breath away from death. Some wondered out loud about
the future of Tackett Oil. Would Jody's death, whenever
it occurred, also mean the end of the oil company, or
would Key stop his globe-hopping and stay in Eden Pass
to manage it, or was Miss Janellen strong and savvy
enough to seize control? Opinions varied widely.

However, the juiciest gossip that day centered around
Dr. Lara Mallory and how, even as she faced death, Jody
Tackett had refused her assistance. The doctor's notorious
affair with Senator Tackett was rehashed for those whose
memories had faded.

Ollie was resentful of the clacking tongues. Not that
his opinion mattered, but he didn't think Dr. Mallory
was getting a fair shake. Hadn't she saved stingy, nasty
Jody Tackett's miserable hide, when she'd probably just
as soon have watched the old woman swallow her own
tongue?

She was almost tearfully grateful when he delivered her
groceries that afternoon. She thanked him profusely and
offered him a cold drink for his effort. She might have
been a fallen woman once, but a nicer lady you'd never
find, was his way of thinking.

"Can you believe it? Old Jody was lying there on the
floor of the Sak'n'Save, foaming at the mouth, they said,
jerking and twitching something awful. But the old girl
had enough fight left in her to refuse medical attention
from Lara Mallory."

The Winstons' housekeeper had prepared a cheesy chicken casserole for dinner. Darcy was doing more talking than eating. Fergus was transferring food from his plate to his mouth with single-minded purpose. To Heather, the casserole looked like something that had already been regurgitated. She pushed the chunks of food around her plate, pretending to eat. Now that she was taking birth control pills, she counted every calorie and wasn't about to waste several hundred on this junk.

Besides, her mother's enjoyment of the gossip that had circulated through town about Mrs. Tackett's seizure had ruined Heather's appetite. Darcy had learned all the gory details at the beauty shop and recounted them with disgusting enthusiasm.

"She peed her pants. Jody Tackett peed her pants. Can you believe it?" Darcy chortled. "Incontinental, they call it."

"It's 'incontinent,' Darcy," Fergus corrected. "And it's hardly something I want to talk about over supper."

Heather reached for her glass of iced tea. "Tanner's daddy said Dr. Mallory saved Mrs. Tackett's life. If I were her, I'd've let the old fart die."

Darcy's fork clattered to her plate. "That's fine language for a proper young lady! And this juvenile crush you have on Lara Mallory has become annoying, Heather."

"I don't have a 'crush' on her. I just think it was stupid of Mrs. Tackett not to let the doctor help her. I mean, if you're dying, isn't any doctor, even one you personally dislike, better than none at all?"

"Not if you're Jody Tackett," Fergus remarked as he paused to blot his mouth. "That woman's heart is the hardest substance on earth. I agree with you, Heather. I'd have let her choke."

"As usual, you two are taking sides against me." Darcy angrily pushed her plate aside.

"Sides?" Fergus asked, bewildered. "I didn't know we

were choosing up sides over this. What's it got to do with us?"

"Not a damn thing," Darcy snapped. "I just fail to see what makes Lara Mallory such a bloody heroine in Heather's eyes."

"May I be excused?" Heather asked in a bored voice.

"You may not! You haven't eaten a bite."

"I'm not hungry. Besides, this casserole is gross. It reeks with fat."

"I should have been so lucky to have a maid cook dinner for me when I was your age!"

"Oh, please." *Here we go*, Heather thought—*another sob story about Mother's deprived childhood.*

"She shouldn't have to eat it if she isn't hungry," Fergus said.

"Naturally, you let her have her way."

"Thanks, Daddy. Tanner and I will get something later."

"You're going out with Tanner again tonight?" Fergus asked.

"Of course." Heather looked at her mother and smiled smugly. "We're officially together now."

"Together?"

"Going steady," Darcy clarified impatiently, never taking her eyes off Heather. "I can't say I'm thrilled about it."

Heather, holding her mother's stare, took another sip of tea. Putting her on birth control pills had been Darcy's doing, but Heather was getting back. She seized every opportunity to remind her mother that whenever she and Tanner went out on a date, they could have sex without suffering any consequences.

Darcy couldn't say anything to her, especially in front of Fergus. He still didn't know about the contraceptives and would have raised hell with Darcy for encouraging them. He clung to the quaint notion that morality was a deterrent to premarital sex.

Heather took pleasure in keeping her mother perpetually miffed. Her sidelong glances and innuendoes conveyed that she was now sexually active. But she hadn't let Tanner go all the way yet. It wasn't because she didn't love him, or that she feared an unwanted pregnancy, and there certainly was nothing to fear in the way of parental reprisal.

Her reason for holding out was the same as it always had been. She didn't want to become a replica of her mother.

Tanner was being very sweet about her abstinence. Since that night at the lake when he had disgraced himself, he was loving and patient, gratefully taking whatever crumbs of eroticism she chose to toss him and asking for nothing more.

Heather was still Fergus's little angel, and when she was with him she strove to maintain his image of her. Her relationship with her mother, however, had deteriorated. They were undeclared adversaries, two women in a silent face-off. The battle lines that had been suggested before were now clearly drawn.

"I didn't realize that you'd made Dr. Mallory an idol, Heather," Fergus observed as he stirred sugar into his coffee. "I didn't even know you'd met her."

"Mother took me to see her. Didn't she tell you?"

"For a checkup," Darcy said hastily. "She needed a physical exam for cheerleading, and it was going to be a month before she could see an out-of-town doctor. I decided it was silly to shun Dr. Mallory just because she was involved with Clark Tackett at one time. Who cares? It's ancient history. Besides, an enemy of Jody Tackett's is a friend of yours, right?"

"I must say Dr. Mallory showed a lot of gumption by moving to Eden Pass in the first place. She shoots straight from the hip, too. I like that."

"When have you talked to her?" Darcy wanted to know.

"Yesterday. She called me and asked for an audience with the school board. She wants to speak to the high school kids about sexual responsibility. I think the idea is a little bit radical for Eden Pass, but I told her we'd hear her ideas at the meeting next week."

For several moments Darcy regarded him without comment. "You're right, Fergus. She's got her nerve. She was caught in adultery. How sexually irresponsible can you get?"

"She emphasized that she wasn't concerned with the moral aspects. She only wants to alert the kids to the health risks involved."

"I doubt that'll go down well with the local preachers. And don't be so sure that morality doesn't figure in there somewhere. Lax morality, that is. She told Heather to make sure she always had a condom handy."

"That's not what she said!" Heather exclaimed.

"Same as," Darcy said curtly. "Before we know it, the kids at the high school will start packing rubbers in their lunch boxes and having quickies between classes."

"Darcy, please!" Fergus harrumphed. "Heather shouldn't be listening to this."

"Wake up and smell the coffee, Fergus. Kids nowadays know all about everything. Once Lara Mallory gives them the green light, they'll be screwing like rabbits."

Fergus flinched. "She's not going to encourage them to have sex. She wants to warn them of the possible consequences."

"Oh, brother! She really snowed you, didn't she? What I think she wants is an outbreak of teenage pregnancies in order to drum up some much-needed business."

"That's ridiculous, Mother."

"Shut up, Heather! I'm talking to your father."

"But you're twisting Dr. Mallory's words around. It's not fair."

"This is an adult conversation, and no one invited you to join in."

At that moment Heather hated her mother and wanted badly to expose her hypocrisy. But her love for her father guaranteed her silence. Darcy knew that and used it. She was the one now wearing the smug smile. Heather scraped back her chair and flounced from the dining room.

On her way out she heard her mother say, "Go ahead and grant Dr. Mallory an audience with the school board, Fergus. It'll be fun to sit back and watch the fur fly."

"I thought I'd . . . I probably shouldn't have come." Now that she was standing on the front porch of Lara Mallory's clinic, spotlighted by the overhead light fixture, Janellen felt like a fool. It wouldn't surprise her if the doctor slammed the door in her face. She wouldn't blame her, either.

"I'm glad you came, Miss Tackett. Come in."

Janellen stepped into the dim waiting room and glanced around. "It's late. I shouldn't have disturbed you."

"Quite all right. How is your mother?"

"Not too well. That's what I came to talk to you about."

Lara indicated the hallway that led to the rear of the building. With Janellen behind her, she moved out of the clinic and into her private living quarters.

"I was having a glass of wine. Will you join me?"

They entered a cozy den where magazines were scattered over tabletops and scented candles flickered in votives. The TV was tuned to a cable station that broadcast classic movies. The one currently being shown was in black and white.

"I'm a fan of old movies," Lara said with a self-deprecating smile. "Maybe because they usually have happy endings." She used the remote control to turn off the set. "Chablis is all I have. Is that all right?"

"I'd rather have a soft drink."

"Diet Coke?"

"Fine."

While Lara was getting her drink from the kitchen, Janellen stood as though rooted to the floor in the center of the room. She had invaded the enemy camp, but it was certainly a comfortable place. Two walls of the room were lined with bookshelves. Most of the reading material was related to medicine, but there was also a collection of hardcover and paperback fiction. Over the fireplace, where once had hung the stuffed head of a ten-point buck, there was now an Andrew Wyeth print. On the sofa table stood a silver-framed photograph of a baby girl.

"My daughter."

Janellen jumped at the sound of Lara's voice as she reentered the room carrying an icy glass of soda. "Her name was Ashley. She was killed in Montesangre."

"Yes, I know. I'm sorry. She was a beautiful child."

Lara nodded. "I have only two photographs of her. That one and another in my office. I have those because I reclaimed them from my parents. None of our personal effects were ever recovered from Montesangre. I wish I had something of Ashley's. Her teething ring. Her teddy bear. Her christening gown. Something." She shook her head slightly. "Please, sit down, Miss Tackett."

Janellen gingerly lowered herself onto the sofa. Lara sat in the easy chair she'd obviously been occupying when her doorbell rang. There was a crocheted afghan bunched up on the hassock in front of the chair and a glass of white wine stood on the end table.

"Is your mother in the hospital?"

Janellen shook her head.

"No?" That was obviously not the answer she had expected. "I thought for certain her condition would require at least one night in the hospital."

"She should be hospitalized." Janellen felt herself on the verge of tears. She picked at the cocktail napkin wrapped around the glass of soda. "I came because . . . because I wanted to hear what you had to say. You were there during my mother's seizure. I'd like to know your professional opinion of it."

"Your mother certainly didn't."

"I'm sorry about the way she behaved toward you, Dr. Mallory," Janellen said earnestly. "And if you ask me to leave, I'll understand."

"Why would I do that? I don't hold you responsible for what your mother said and did."

"Then please give me your opinion of her illness."

"It's unethical for me to second-guess another doctor's diagnosis when I haven't even examined the patient."

"Please. I need to talk to somebody about this, and there's no one."

"What about your brother?"

"He's upset."

"So are you."

"Yes, but when Key gets upset or worried, he . . ." She lowered her eyes to the glass in her hand. "Let's just say he's currently unavailable. Please, Dr. Mallory, give me your opinion."

"Based strictly on what I saw?"

Janellen nodded.

"With the full understanding that I could be incorrect?"

Again Janellen nodded.

Lara took a sip of wine. Looking toward the portrait of her daughter, she pulled in a deep breath, then released it slowly. Her eyes moved back to Janellen. "What treatment did your mother receive at the county hospital?"

"They examined her in the emergency room, but she refused to be admitted."

"That was foolish of her. Were you given a diagnosis?"

"The doctor said she'd had a mild stroke."

"I concur. Did they do a complete blood work?"

"Yes. She was prescribed medication that's supposed

to thin⁻ her blood. Is that what you would recommend?"

"Along with extensive tests and observation. Did they do an ECG?"

"The heart thing?" Lara nodded. "No. They recommended it, but she wouldn't stay that long."

"Was a brain scan done?"

"Yes, but only after Key threatened to tie her down if she didn't consent. The doctor said he didn't find any significant cerebral infarction." She tried to quote him precisely. "I'm not certain what that means."

"It means that your mother has no significant amount of dead brain tissue due to a loss of blood supply. Which is good. However, that doesn't mean that the blood to her brain isn't being interrupted or completely blocked. Did he suggest doing sound wave tests on the carotid artery? They're called Dopler studies."

"I'm not sure." Janellen rubbed her temple. "He was talking so fast, and Mama was complaining so loudly, and— "

"These tests would determine if there's an obstruction in the artery. If there is, and the blockage isn't eliminated, there's a very good possibility for infarction, resulting in permanent disability or even death."

"That's what they said, too," Janellen said hoarsely. "Something like that."

"No angiogram to see where the blockage might be?"

"Mama refused that. She ranted and raved and said she'd had a dizzy spell and that's all there was to it. Said she only needed to go home and rest."

"Did the impairment to her speech and muscle control last very long?"

"By the time we got her home, you couldn't tell anything had happened."

"That quick recovery fools patients into believing they've suffered only a dizzy spell." Lara leaned forward.

"Does your mother frequently forget things? Does she sometimes have blurred vision?"

She told the doctor what she had shared with Key a few weeks earlier. "She never admits to any of this, but the spells have gotten noticeable. I tried persuading her to see a doctor, but she refused. I think she's afraid of what she'll hear."

"I can't be certain without examining her," Lara said, "but I think she's experiencing what we call TIAs, which stands for transient ischemic attacks. 'Ischemia' refers to insufficient blood circulation."

"I'm following you so far."

"When one of these occurs, it interrupts the blood supply to the brain. It's like an electrical blackout. The part of the brain that's affected is turned off. The dementia you described, blurred vision, slurred speech, and the dizziness are all symptoms, warning signals. If they're not heeded, the patient can suffer a major stroke. Today was probably the strongest warning yet. Has she complained of numbness in her extremities?"

"Not to me, but she wouldn't."

"Does she have high blood pressure?"

"Very. She takes medication to control it."

"Does she smoke?"

"Three packs a day."

"She should stop immediately."

Janellen smiled wanly. "Never in a million years."

"Urge her to eat properly and monitor her cholesterol intake. She should do moderate exercise. See that she takes her medication. Those precautions will help prevent a life-threatening stroke, but there are no guarantees."

"There's no complete cure?"

"For selected patients the arterial blockage can be removed surgically. It's a fairly routine procedure. Unfortunately, without the proper tests and your mother's full cooperation, that's not an option." Sensing Janellen's despair, she leaned forward and pressed her hand. "I'm sorry. And remember, I could be wrong."

"I doubt you are, Dr. Mallory. You've said essentially what the emergency room doctor told us. Thank you for discussing it with me. And for the soda." She set the untouched drink on the coffee table and stood to go.

"Under the circumstances, I doubt we can be friends, but I'd like us to be cordial. Please call me Lara."

Janellen smiled but remained noncommittal. When they reached the front door, both were surprised to see that it was raining. It was much easier to talk about something as banal as the weather. Finally, Janellen shook the doctor's hand.

"You had every right to be rude to me. Thank you for inviting me in."

"Thank you for giving my opinion credibility. The next time you visit, let's hope the reason for it won't be so serious."

"Next time? Are you asking me to come back?"

"Of course. Feel free to drop in anytime."

"You're very nice, Dr. . . . Lara. I can understand why my brother was so attracted to you."

Lara shook back her hair and, looking up at the rainy skies, laughed mirthlessly. "You're wrong. Key isn't the least attracted to me."

Janellen was stunned. "Key?" she repeated with puzzlement. "I was referring to Clark."

Chapter Sixteen

*B*owie flipped up the collar of his denim jacket and huddled closer to the exterior wall of the house. The eaves provided scant protection from the blowing rain. He was getting soaked.

He really couldn't say why he was at the Tacketts' place at this time of night, standing outside in the rain. He should be stretched out in front of his secondhand TV set. His rented trailer had few amenities, but at least it was dry.

Whatever the weather, he had no business being here. Jody Tackett's health was a private family matter. They'd hardly want an outsider butting in. None of that had affected his decision to come; he had felt compelled. When he arrived, he noticed that Key's Lincoln was gone and so was Janellen's car. He parked the company truck out of sight behind the detached garage. The only car in the driveway belonged to the housekeeper.

He saw no need to announce his presence to her. What would he say? He supposed he could tell her the truth—that he was worried about Miss Janellen; how she was reacting to her mama's collapse in the Sak'n'Save. Then the housekeeper would probably want to know what business it was of his, and he'd have to say no business of his at all, and she'd shoo him off the porch and probably call the law.

So he lurked in the shadows, standing ankle deep in rainwater. He couldn't adequately justify his reason for being there. He just knew he had to be. Furthermore, he intended to stay right where he was, come hell or high water, until he saw for himself that Miss Janellen was holding together.

He hadn't laid eyes on her since that afternoon of their kiss, followed by her startling declaration that she loved him. He hadn't taken it seriously, of course. Something had caused her to blurt it out—PMS, or too much sun, or maybe an allergy pill that had made her a little goofy. In hindsight, she probably felt like cutting out her tongue.

Because he empathized with anyone who shot off his mouth without thinking, he'd been avoiding Janellen, sparing her the embarrassment of having to face him and offer an excuse for her bizarre behavior. Sure enough, she'd gone out of her way to avoid him, too.

They couldn't keep dodging each other forever, though. Sooner or later they'd meet, so it might as well be tonight when she had something even more terrible to fret over. He couldn't do anything about her mama's failing health, but he could relieve her of one concern. He could assure her that he didn't intend to take advantage of something she'd said during a mental lapse of unknown origin.

Headlights appeared at the end of the private drive. Bowie's gut clenched reflexively as he watched the car turn off the county road and onto Tackett property. He shrank back closer to the wall, not wanting to be seen until he was certain it was Janellen. Reputedly, Key kept a loaded Beretta beneath the driver's seat of his car. It could be gossip, but Bowie would just as soon not have it confirmed the hard way. If Key saw a prowler, he might shoot first and ask questions later.

The headlights, diffused by the rain, approached slowly. Bowie recognized Janellen's car. She parked in the driveway, got out, and dashed through the rain toward the back door. The screen door squeaked when she pulled it open. She had her key in the latch when he softly called her name.

Startled, she spun around. Rain fell on her pale face

as she peered through the gloom. "Bowie! What in the world are you doing out here?"

"Are you okay?"

"I'm okay, but you're soaked. How long have you been out here? Come inside."

"No, I'll go on along home now." He knew he must be a sorry sight, what with the brim of his hat dripping rainwater and his pants wet from the knees down. "I just wanted to make sure you were all right, considering what happened this morning. Word around the shop is that Mrs. Tackett is feeling poorly."

"Unfortunately, that's true." She unlocked the door and insisted he follow her inside. Reluctantly he stepped into the kitchen, but stayed just inside the door.

"Take off your jacket," she said. "And your boots. They're sopping wet."

"I don't want you to fuss."

"No fuss. Let me check on Mama and send Maydale home, then I'll make some coffee." She moved through the dark kitchen, but turned when she reached the doorway. "Don't go away."

Bowie's heart swelled so large he could barely draw breath. She hadn't screamed or shuddered or puked when she saw him. That was a good sign. Now she was asking him, almost pleading with him, to stick around. "No, ma'am. I surely won't."

While she was gone, he removed his hat and his damp jacket and hung them on a wall peg near the back door. Balancing on one leg at a time, he tugged off his boots and placed them beside a pair that obviously belonged to Key. The toes of his socks were damp, but he was relieved to see that they didn't have holes.

He tiptoed across the vinyl tile floor. Leaving the lights off, he gazed through the window over the sink, watching the rain drip from the eaves. After several minutes he heard a muffled conversation at the front door, then watched through the window as Maydale picked her way around puddles to her car while trying to protect her beehive hairdo with a silly plastic bonnet.

At the sound of Janellen's approach, he turned. "How's your mama doing?"

"Sleeping."

"She's all right, then?"

"Not really. She won't follow doctor's orders. She's too hard-headed to heed the warnings, like the one she got this morning. She doesn't believe her condition is serious."

"From what I've heard, she's a stubborn old gal."

"To say the very least."

"Maybe her condition isn't as bad as the doctors say."

"Maybe."

"Sometimes they exaggerate to make their point and justify their bill."

Her wan smile indicated she didn't believe that and knew that he didn't either. "Well," she said, pulling herself up straighter, "I promised you some coffee."

"You don't have to bother."

"No. I want to. I'd like some, too. I won't be sleeping much tonight, so I might just as well."

She moved toward the pantry, but her footsteps were sluggish and her voice unsteady. She didn't turn on the lights, probably because she didn't want him to see the tears in her eyes. He saw them anyway.

The coffee canister almost slipped from her hands before she set it down on the counter. Peeling a single paper filter from the compressed stack proved to be a challenge. Once that was done, she spilled coffee grounds as she scooped them from the canister.

"Oh, dear. I'm making a mess." She began twisting her hands and brutalizing her lower lip by pulling it through her teeth.

He felt about as useless as a teat on a boar hog. "Why don't you sit yourself down, Miss Janellen, and let me make the coffee?"

"What I'd really like you to do . . ." She struggled to get the next words out. "What I'd really like . . ."

"Yes, ma'am?"

She turned and looked at him imploringly. "If it's not too much to ask, Bowie."

"Name it."

She uttered a little squeaking sound, tilted her head to one side, then swayed forward. He caught her, encircled her with his arms, drew her against his chest, and hugged her close. She was so slight, he was afraid he might be holding her too tightly, but trustingly she laid her cheek on his shoulder.

"Bowie, what will I do if Mama dies? *What?*"

"You'll go right on living, that's what."

"But what kind of life will I have?"

"That depends on what you make of it."

She sniffed wetly. "You don't understand. Key and Mama are all that's left of my family. I don't want to lose them. If Mama dies, Key will go on about his business, and I'll be left here alone."

"You'll make out just fine by yourself, Miss Janellen."

"No, I won't."

"Now why would you say that?"

"Because I've never had an identity of my own. People only see me in relation to my family. I'm Clark Junior's daughter. Clark and Key's little sister. Jody's girl. Even though I've been doing most of the work at Tackett Oil the last couple of years, everybody thinks I'm just Mama's puppet. I guess they're not too far wrong. She's always told me what to do, and I've obeyed her, partially because she's usually right, but mostly, I suppose, because I lack the self-confidence to stand up to her and offer a different opinion. I've never really minded answering to her, but when she's gone, what then? Who will I be? *Who am I?*"

He pushed her away and gave her a little shake. "You're Janellen Tackett, that's who. And that's enough.

You're stronger than you know. When the time comes for you to stand up on your own, you'll do it."

"I'm afraid, Bowie."

"Of what?"

"Failing, I guess. Not living up to expectations." She laughed, but it was a sad sound. "Or, more to the point, I'm afraid that I will live up to everyone's expectations and land flat on my backside when Mama's not here to call the shots."

"It won't be that way," he said with a stubborn shake of his head. "You've got years of experience. The men are used to taking orders from you. You're smart as a whip. I always thought of myself as fairly clever. I've got some street smarts, but when I'm with you—and this is the God's truth—I feel dumber than dirt."

"You're not dumb, Bowie. You're very smart. Nobody else noticed the discrepancy in well number seven."

"Which turned out to be nothing."

"We didn't know that until you installed the test meter."

He'd put the test meter midway between the well and the recorder. The data registered had been the same. A leak could be anywhere along the line. In order to locate it, he'd have to move the test meter until a section of line was isolated. That could go on indefinitely. He'd checked the records and, sure enough, that well had had a flare line, but it had been capped off years ago. He felt like a fool for making such a big deal over something his bosses considered insignificant.

Janellen's hands were still riding on his waist, and that's all he could think about now. Finally he said, "I'm sorry about your mama, Miss Janellen, because I know how much you care about her. I hope she lives to a ripe old age so you'll be spared the grief of her passing. But with or without her, you're your own person. You don't have to be anybody's daughter or sister or . . . or wife. You're good enough all by yourself. You've got plenty on the ball and don't let anybody make you think different."

"You're good for me, Bowie," she whispered.

"Aw, hell, I'm not good for much of anything."

"That's not true! You are! You're very good for me. You make me focus on my strong points instead of my weaknesses. Don't get me wrong. I know my limitations. I've lived with them all my life. I know I'm intelligent, but not exceptionally so. I'm not self-assertive, I'm timid, and I lack confidence. I'm not pretty. Not like my brothers."

"Not pretty?" Bowie was baffled, so baffled he didn't stop to wonder when he'd begun thinking of her as beautiful. "Why, you're the prettiest thing I've ever seen, Miss Janellen."

Flustered and confused, she ducked her head. "You don't have to tell me that. Just because of what I said the other day."

He cleared his throat uncomfortably. "I want you to know right now that I'm not holding you to that."

"You're not?"

"No, ma'am."

"Oh." The features of her face worked emotionally. Then she lifted her gaze back to his. "How come?"

He shifted his weight from one foot to the other. "Well, 'cause I know you didn't really mean it, that's how come."

She wet her lips and took a quick breath. "In fact I did, Bowie."

"You did?"

"I meant it from the bottom of my heart. And if you, well, you know, if you ever wanted to kiss me again, it would be all right."

The buzzing inside Bowie's head almost drowned out the pounding rain on the roof. His heart was beating so hard and fast that it hurt. His throat was tight, but he managed to strangle out, "I do want to kiss you again, Miss Janellen. I surely do."

He slipped his hands beneath her hair and cupped her jaw, then drew her mouth toward his. Her parted lips responded warmly. This time they needed no warm-up, no rehearsal. They skipped getting reacquainted and picked up right where they had left off, engaging in a kiss that left them breathless when they at last pulled apart.

He pressed his mouth against her throat while her hands clutched at his back. "I never knew it could feel like this, Bowie."

"Neither did I. And I've been doing it for some time now."

They kissed again and again, each kiss piercingly sweet and increasingly intimate. They kissed until their lips were swollen, their passions brimming.

He longed to nestle his erection in the cleft of her long thighs, but he curbed the impulse. However, with an eagerness that was instinctual and almost childlike in its innocence, she arched her body against his, in effect accomplishing what he wouldn't do for himself.

The contact was erotically shattering. It would have evoked the animalistic urges of a saint, and that was something Bowie Cato had never claimed to be.

He fumbled beneath her skirt and grabbed a handful of her bottom, kneading the silk-covered flesh once, twice, while mashing his distended fly against her mound. It wasn't premeditated. He didn't weigh the benefits against the consequences. If he'd thought about it at all, he'd never have done it. It was an unthinkable thing to do.

Janellen's soft exclamation brought reality crashing down on his head, and along with it shame and self-disgust.

He released her immediately. Without a word, he crossed the kitchen in three strides, grabbed his boots, his hat, and his jacket, and stomped out the kitchen door and into the downpour.

The moment he reached the truck he'd left parked behind the garage, a jagged fork of lightning rent the darkness, connecting the firmament and the earth with a hot-white brilliance that crackled with wrath and seared the air with ozone.

Bowie figured it was God, meaning to strike him dead. His aim was just a little off.

Thunder rattled the liquor bottles and glassware behind the bar. "Brewing up a real storm out there," Hap Hollister observed as he poured Key another drink.

"Grounded me. I was supposed to be flying to Midland tonight, taking an oilman and his wife home."

"I'm right proud of you, Key. You've got better sense than to fly in this weather."

"Wasn't me who chickened out. It was the wife. Said she didn't want to die in a plane crash."

Hap, shaking his head over the younger man's derring-do, moved away to serve the other customers who had braved the storm to come to The Palm. Some were playing billiards, leaning on their cues and drinking longnecks as they awaited their turns. Others were watching a late-season baseball game on the large-screen TV mounted beneath the ceiling in one corner of the bar. Drinkers were grouped in twos and threes.

Only Key drank alone at one end of the bar. His dark expression and hunched shoulders signaled his mood. News of the incident at the Sak'n'Save had reached every ear in town, and so his silent request to be left alone was sympathetically honored by everyone in the tavern.

Jody was the subject on Key's mind as he sipped his fresh drink, but his thoughts weren't running toward the sympathetic. He'd like to give his mother a good swift kick in the butt. At the hospital and later, when he and Janellen had taken her home against the doctor's recommendation and their own better judgment, Jody had griped and complained and staved off all their attempts to make her comfortable.

"I'm hiring a live-in nurse for you, Jody," he'd told her as Janellen urged her to get into bed. "Janellen keeps office hours. I'm away a lot. Maydale's a good housekeeper, but we can't count on her to handle a medical emergency like the one that occurred this morning. You should have someone with you constantly."

"That's a wonderful idea, Key!" Janellen exclaimed. "Isn't it, Mama?"

Disregarding Janellen, Jody blew smoke at him from her fresh cigarette. "You took it upon yourself to hire me a nurse?"

"She'll be here around the clock to fetch and carry for you."

"I can fetch and carry for myself, thank you very much. I don't want a busybody fussing over me, bossing me, meddling in my things, and stealing me blind when I'm not looking."

"I went through a top-notch agency in Dallas," he patiently explained. "They won't send us a thief. I specified our requirements. I made it clear that you're not an invalid, that you're independent and value your privacy. They're checking their files to see who's available, but promised a nurse would be here no later than noon tomorrow."

Jody's eyes narrowed to slits. "Call them back. Cancel. Who the hell gave you the authority to make my decisions for me?"

"Mama, Key's only doing what he thinks is best for you."

"I'll tell him what's best for me. I want him to butt out of my life. And you too," she said, snatching her jacket away from Janellen, who had assisted her in taking it off. "Get out of my room. Both of you." At the risk of bringing on another attack, they had left her.

He was worried sick about her. When he'd seen her

lying on the floor of the Sak'n'Save, spittle on her chin, her dignity gone, he'd almost passed out himself. But he could hardly remain compassionate when his every attempt at kindness was met with a scornful tongue-lashing.

Hell, he could take Jody's crap. He'd been taking it all his life. When weighed against her precarious health, their verbal skirmishes seemed petty. At issue now was that his mother refused to accept the seriousness of her illness. She could die if she didn't undergo the treatment prescribed for her. Only a fool would flaunt mortality like that.

Then, smiling wryly, Key reminded himself that he'd been willing to fly into a stormy cold front and would have done so if the passengers who'd chartered the plane hadn't nixed it.

But that was gambling, a game of chance with risks involved, the outcome uncertain. It wasn't like being told by medical experts that you were a time bomb with the clock ticking and that if you didn't take care of the problem you could die or, what to Key's mind would be worse, live in a vegetative state for the rest of your life.

The doctor at the county hospital had bluntly laid out the sobering facts of Jody's diagnosis to Janellen and him. He would have liked a second opinion. He would have liked having Lara Mallory's opinion.

"Shit." He signaled Hap for another hit.

The last thing he wanted to think about was Lara Mallory. But, like the intoxicating whiskey, she had a way of infusing his head, permeating it, saturating it. Silent and invisible, she was always there, fucking with his mind.

Had his brother sired her child? Had her husband known? Had *Clark* known? Had knowing that his child died violently precipitated Clark's suicide?

If so, didn't he owe it to Clark—and to Lara—to

go to Montesangre and find out the details of the child's death?

Hell, no. It was none of his business. Nobody had appointed him Clark's custodian. It was her problem. Let her deal with it. It had nothing to do with him.

But the more he thought about it, the more convinced he became that Ashley was his niece. He'd tried not to think about it at all, but that was impossible. Just as impossible was forgetting how devastated Lara had been when she recounted her daughter's violent assassination. God, how did anyone retain his sanity after experiencing something like that?

A few weeks ago, he would have bet his last nickel that he would never waste a charitable thought on Lara Mallory. After hearing her story, he would have to be a real bastard not to feel charitable. So he had held her. Comforted her. Kissed her.

Angrily, he drained his drink, then stared into the glass as he twirled it around and around over the polished surface of the bar.

He'd kissed her all right. Not a little, meaningless, charitable peck, either. He'd kissed his brother's married lover and the scourge of his family like it counted. She had accused him of taking advantage of her emotional breakdown, but she was wrong. Oh, he'd pretended that she had his motives pegged perfectly, but, honest to God, when he was kissing her, the last thought in his head was that she was a lying, cheating adulteress who had beguiled Clark. In his arms, with her mouth moving pliantly beneath his, she became only a woman he desperately wanted to touch. He'd abided by the ground rules he himself had stipulated—he'd forgotten her name.

"Haven't you got anything better to do than watch ice cubes melt? Like, for instance, buy a lady a drink?"

Frowning over the unwelcome interruption, Key lifted his gaze to find Darcy Winston seated on the barstool beside his. "Where'd you come from?"

"Just stopped to get in out of the rain. Do I get that drink or not?"

Hap approached. Key nodded tersely, and the bartender took Darcy's order for a vodka and tonic. Key declined when asked if he wanted another.

"Making me drink alone? How rude!" Darcy's carefully painted lips formed a pout.

"That was the idea. To drink alone. You didn't take the hint."

She sipped the drink Hap slid toward her. "Worried about your mama?"

"For starters."

"I'm really sorry, Key."

He doubted that Darcy gave a damn about anybody's well-being except her own, but he nodded his thanks.

"What else is on your mind?"

"Not much."

"Liar. You're sulking. Does it have anything to do with Helen Berry going back to Jimmy Bradley? I hear they're more in love now than they were before you broke them up."

He lowered his head until his chin almost touched his chest. The breakdown of communication was so absurd that he chuckled.

"What's so funny?"

"This town. The other side of the world could blow up, stars could collide and cause another Big Bang, and folks here would still be scurrying around to find out who was screwing who."

"Who are you screwing?"

"That's my business."

"Bastard."

She glared at him with such ferocity that he laughed again. "You sure are dressed up for a Tuesday night, Darcy," he observed, taking in her conservative dress and plain high-heeled pumps. Of course nothing looked conservative or plain on Darcy. The dress was made of flaming pink silk, which she wore well despite her red hair. Her chest filled out the bodice and then some. She'd left the top three buttons undone to provide an enticing peek at cleavage. The high heels added length and shape to her already long and shapely legs. She looked hot—there was no doubt about that.

"I was on my way home from the Library Society meeting," she told him.

"Eden Pass has a Library Society? I didn't even know we had a library."

"Of course we do. And the society has forty-two members."

"No shit? How many of them can read?"

"Very funny." She finished her drink and slammed the glass onto the bar. "Thanks for the drink. Call me if you ever get your sense of humor back. You're a real drag these days."

"What'd you say to piss her off?" Hap asked after she had stalked out. He reached for her glass and dunked it in a basin of soapy water.

"Does it matter?" Key asked testily.

It was still raining, but Key didn't even duck his head as he walked to his car. His mind was on so many other things, the inclement weather was inconsequential.

He got into the Lincoln on the driver's side and had inserted the key into the ignition before he noticed her. She slid across the yellow leather seat and placed her hand high on the inside of his thigh.

"I know what's wrong with you."

"You don't have the foggiest notion, Darcy."

"I'm an expert at these things, you know. I was born with a sixth sense. I can tell what a man wants and needs just by looking at him."

"'S a fact?"

"That's a fact. When a man wants it, he gives off an odor just like a woman does."

"If that's true, there ought to be a pack of dogs after you."

Taking that as a compliment, she moved her hand to his crotch. "You want me, Key. I know you do. You're just too stubborn to take back the ugly things you said that night at the town meeting." She stroked him, and he had to admit that her technique was excellent.

"This is silly. Neither of us wants to make the first move to reconcile. There's no point in both of us being miserable over a little pride, is there?"

She began unbuttoning his jeans. Key, assuming the role of an impartial observer, let her. He was curious to gauge his response. She lifted him out of his jeans and massaged him between her hands. His cock began to grow hard.

"Oh, baby," she said with a sigh. "I knew that all you needed was Darcy's magic touch."

She smiled at him seductively, then lowered her head to his lap. Her tongue was alternately quick and light, then languorous and lazy. She licked him delicately and sucked him hard. Her teeth threatened pain before her lips kissed soothingly. She knew what she was doing.

Key rested his head against the seat and squeezed his eyes closed. He didn't desire Darcy and was therefore amazed that his body was functioning as it should. On the other hand, why should that surprise him? he wondered. He'd bedded women without ever learning their names. He'd forgotten more women than he remembered. They'd only done for him something he could have done just as well for himself. His body could do it without involving his mind.

He was glad that Darcy hadn't kissed him. That would have made it personal. He would have had to share a part of himself with a woman who meant nothing to him. He didn't even like her.

If Darcy had kissed him, her avaricious tongue might have swept away the taste of another kiss, which he wasn't ready to forget. He kept the memory of it under lock and key like an old man hoarding victory ribbons. On occasion, Key let himself think about that kiss, recall its sweet sexiness, just as that old man would take out his ribbons and finger them sadly while remembering past glories. Then, annoyed with himself and feeling like a fool, Key would shut out the memory, as the old man, ashamed of his sentimentality, would slam the drawer in which he kept his treasured ribbons.

It was pathetic, Key thought, the way individuals longed for something that could never be.

Now he let his mind go blank, disassociating himself from the act but granting his body permission to respond. He didn't touch Darcy, not even when he came. Instead, he clenched his hands around the steering wheel until his fingers turned white. As soon as it was over he calmly rebuttoned his jeans.

Darcy sat up and opened her purse to get a tissue, then daintily blotted her lips. "You know how we know God is a man?" Key said nothing; he'd heard the joke. "Because if God were a woman, come would taste like chocolate."

"Charming."

Either she failed to catch the disgust underlying his comment or she chose to ignore it. Laughing, she rubbed her breasts against his arm. "Where do you want to go? Or should we use that lovely backseat?" she suggested, glancing behind her. "Pity they're not making big cars like they used to. Some of the best fucking I ever did— "

"Good night, Darcy. I'm going home."

"The hell you are! We're not finished."

"I'm finished."

"You mean to tell me that I— "

"You did exactly as you pleased. I didn't ask you to,"

he reminded her softly. "Now will you kindly haul your carcass out of my car so I can go home?"

She spat in his face.

As quick as a striking cobra, he grabbed a handful of her hair and yanked her head back. "I didn't kill you for shooting me, but I just might for doing that."

Chapter Seventeen

*D*arcy believed him. She was well aware of the murderous temper for which Key was famous. However, it went against her nature to back down once the die was cast.

"Let go of me, you son of a bitch."

He relaxed his fist, releasing her hair. "Get out," he said succinctly.

"I'm going. But not before I tell you exactly what I think of you. You're sick. Not just mean, *sick*."

"Fine. Now that we've established what's wrong with me, get out of my car."

"You're fucked in the head, and it's not that fat Berry girl who's doing it to you. It's Lara Mallory." His right eye twitched, but the rest of him went dangerously still. Knowing she'd struck a chord, she plucked it again. "Don't you feel just a teensy-weensy ridiculous, falling for your big brother's ex-bimbo?" She laughed derisively.

"Shut up, Darcy."

"The notorious lady doctor has big bad Key Tackett by his short-and-curlies. He didn't learn a thing from his brother's experience with her, did he?"

She knew she should stop while she was ahead, but she couldn't resist making him squirm. Since adolescence, she'd been able to manipulate every man she'd met. Except Key. That had wounded her ego severely, but she knew it wouldn't prove fatal.

"Have you fucked her yet, Key?" she taunted, pushing her face close to his. "When she came, did she cry out your name or dearly departed Clark's? Who's the better lover, I wonder, Senator Clark Tackett or his baby brother? Is that what attracts you to her? Do you want to prove that you're every bit as good in the sack as Clark was?"

Key moved so suddenly, she flinched. He shoved open the driver's door and got out. Then, reaching in, he grabbed the front of her dress and pulled her out. The pink silk soaked up the rain. Her heels sank into the muck.

He ignored her screaming curses as he got back into his car and started the engine. When he reached for the door, Darcy grabbed the handle and wouldn't let go. "Where are you going, Key? To visit your brother's mistress? You're going to be a laughingstock when word of this gets around. And you can bet both balls on it getting around. I'll see that it does. As if it's not funny enough that she's a whore, she's your late brother's whore."

"At least whores put a price on it, Darcy. You can't give yours away." He jerked the car door closed, pushed the gear stick into reverse, and peeled away. The wheels slung wet gravel and mud onto Darcy's shoes and designer stockings.

She shouted dirty names after him. Then, standing there in the drenching rain, she resolved to teach the bastard a well-deserved lesson. She would find Key's greatest weakness and devise a way to pierce it. Only not tonight. She would wait until her anger cooled down and she could approach the problem analytically.

As she slogged toward her car, she was adamant on one point—nobody treated Mrs. Fergus Winston the way Key had and got away with it.

"Thank you, gentlemen," Lara said in conclusion to her address to the seven members of the Eden Pass school board. "I hope you'll give my proposal for some informal sex education seminars careful consideration.

If you want any further information to facilitate your decision-making, don't hesitate to call me."

"You've made some very convincing arguments and raised some interesting points," Fergus Winston said. "It's a touchy topic. We've got a lot to mull over. It might take a week or two before we reach a decision."

"I understand. Thank you for allowing me— "

She broke off when the door behind her opened. All eyes swung to it, astonishment registering on every face. Lara swiveled around. Darcy Winston had entered the conference room. Accompanying her was Jody Tackett.

Lara almost recoiled from the malice in Darcy's eyes when she looked at her. She also had an air of complacency, although she wasn't actually smiling. Jody didn't even deign to glance in Lara's direction.

Hastily the seven board members came to their feet. Only Fergus spoke. He addressed his wife by name, but his eyes were fixed on Jody Tackett.

"What are you doing here, Darcy? This is a closed session."

"Not anymore." Jody still looked unwell, but her voice was strong enough to penetrate matter.

"She insisted on coming," Darcy explained. Fergus finally tore his baleful stare from Jody and looked at his wife. "I'm sorry, Fergus. I know you asked me not to discuss the items on the school board's agenda until they were ready to be made public, but I felt so strongly about this particular issue that I had to do something."

Lara rose from her seat. "I presently have the floor, Mrs. Winston. If you want to address the school board, I suggest you go through the proper channels and petition for an audience the way I did. Or aren't the rules the same for everyone?" She turned and looked pointedly at Fergus.

He had been glaring at Jody Tackett as though she were poison. He looked ready to strangle his wife for bringing her into a chamber where he was in charge.

"Dr. Mallory's right," he said. "If you and Jody have something to call to this board's attention, do it in the proper manner. You can't just bust in like this and interrupt a meeting."

"Ordinarily we wouldn't," Darcy agreed. "But— "

"I'll speak for myself." Impatiently Jody approached the conference table. When she was certain she had the undivided attention of each board member, she asked bluntly, "Have y'all lost your senses?"

Eyes were averted. No one spoke. Finally Fergus stiffly invited her to take a chair.

"I'd rather stand."

"Suit yourself."

"I always have."

The animosity between them was palpable. The others seemed embarrassed by it and looked away, but Lara didn't let the awkwardness prevent her from speaking. "Mr. Winston, I insist that the board extend me the courtesy of concluding our meeting."

She was patently ignored.

Jody turned to Reverend Massey, pastor of a local church. "I can't understand you, preacher. Every Sunday you preach against fornication. Yet you're thinking of letting an adulteress talk to our young people about sex?" She sniffed with incredulity and disdain. "Makes me wonder why I'm giving my tithe to your church."

He smiled sickly. "We haven't reached a decision, Jody. We've merely listened to Dr. Mallory's proposal. Rest assured that she's not advocating sin."

"Is that right?" Jody looked toward Darcy. "Tell him what you told me."

She stepped forward, making certain to stand directly beneath the overhead light like an old pro of the boards locating center stage. In a rushed, breathless voice she said, "I took Heather in for a checkup a few weeks ago. Afterward, she told me that Dr. Mallory urged her to start having condoms handy whenever she went on a date."

"That's not what I said!" Lara cried. "I warned Heather about being sexually active without using condoms. Obviously what I told her was misconstrued. Either she didn't fully grasp my meaning, or Mrs. Winston is rearranging the words to suit her purpose here."

"I'm doing no such thing," Darcy shot back. Then, to the board, "Not only that, she told Heather to tell all her friends the same thing. Now if that's not goading teenagers to fool around, I don't know what is. All they need is the power of suggestion and they run with it. You know how kids are. Telling them to take rubbers on their dates is like handing them a license to . . . you know." Chastely she lowered her eyes.

Lara wanted to retaliate, to tell them that Darcy had brought Heather to her specifically to get a prescription for birth control pills. But she couldn't do so without violating patient confidentiality. The secret smile Darcy flashed her indicated that she was well aware of that.

"I cautioned Heather about promiscuity and a multiplicity of partners," she admitted. "I suggested she share the information with her friends. I in no way advocated sexual misconduct."

"Even though you're an expert on the subject?"

"Darcy, please," Fergus said with a soft groan. "Let's keep personalities out of this. Our focus here should be on the young people of our community."

"Amen," the reverend intoned. "Frankly, I have misgivings about holding such open discussions on human sexuality. Our youth have enough temptations to withstand as it is. Their minds are fertile. We should plant seeds that would yield strong spiritual fibers, not doubts and confusion over the devil's handiwork."

"Save the sermons for Sunday, preacher," Jody said. "But I'm glad to know I can count on your vote against this idea."

Her gaze moved down the long the table, pausing on

each member of the board. She looked straight through Lara as though she weren't there.

"Once you've had time to think about it, I'm sure all of you will come to the same conclusion. If you don't, I'll have to reconsider my own plans."

"What plans?" one of the board members asked.

"My son Clark loved every day he spent in the Eden Pass school system and often credited it for preparing him for his political career. He would have liked having his name on a school facility. Something like the Clark Tackett the Third Gymnasium. It's getting to where I'm scared to go to the basketball games anymore, afraid I'll break my neck climbing into those rickety bleachers. Those computerized scoreboards are nice, too, aren't they? Wouldn't it be something if Eden Pass were the first school in the area to have one? We'd put the bigger schools to shame, wouldn't we?"

Lara lowered her head. In her mind she could hear the tap-tap of a hammer nailing the coffin shut on her proposal.

Jody let their greedy minds devour the bait before continuing. "I was born in Eden Pass. Lived here all my life. Went through twelve grades of public school here, and so did my three children. I've always boasted that our school system is one of the best in the state."

She leaned on the table and thumped it with the knuckles of her blunt, freckled hand. "I'll change my opinion in a New York minute if you let this woman speak one word under the schoolhouse roof. Why in God's name would you even consider it, knowing what everybody in the country knows about her? Do you want a woman like her having any influence over your kids?" Her face had turned red. She was laboring to breathe.

"I would rather die than let her lay a hand on me. And I'm not just throwing words around. Ask anybody who was in the Sak'n'Save last Tuesday morning."

"You've made your point, Mrs. Tackett." Lara was

afraid that Jody was building up to another stroke. She didn't want to be blamed for bringing on the fatal one. "I'm sure everyone here knows that you resented my efforts to save your life. I'm not going to fight you on this because engaging in a contest like that is beneath my dignity. Secondly, I know I can't win. I don't have the resources to bribe the school board with new gymnasiums and state-of-the-art scoreboards."

"Now see here," the minister blustered, "I resent that implication."

Lara ignored him. "Primarily, I'm backing down because I'm afraid the fight might kill you."

Jody focused on her for the first time since entering the room. "Well you're wrong. I won't die until I see you on your way out of town. My town. Clark's town. I won't rest until you're gone and the air is fit to breathe again."

Lara calmly stacked the typed pages of her presentation and zipped them into a black leather portfolio, tucking it and her handbag under her arm. "Thank you, gentlemen, for giving me your attention this morning. Unless I hear from you otherwise, I'll assume that my proposal was rejected."

None of them had the guts to look her in the eye. She derived some satisfaction from that as she turned and walked from the room.

Darcy followed her out. Lara didn't stop until she had reached the main entrance of the building. There, she turned to confront Darcy. "I know why Jody Tackett hates me," she said. "But why do you? What have I ever done to you?"

"Maybe I just think people ought to stay where they belong. You had no business coming to Eden Pass. You don't fit in. You never will."

"What do you care whether I fit in? How am I a threat to you, Mrs. Winston?"

Darcy made a scoffing sound.

"That's it, I'm sure," Lara said. "For some unfathomable

reason, you regard me as a threat." Could Darcy's hatred for her relate to Key Tackett? It was an uncomfortable thought, which she kept at arm's length. "Believe me, Mrs. Winston, you've got nothing that I want."

Darcy licked her lips like a cat over a bowl of cream. "Not even a daughter?"

Lara reeled, unable to grasp the extent of the other woman's cruelty. "I didn't give you enough credit," Lara said. "You're not only selfish and spiteful, you're deadly."

"Fucking-A, Dr. Mallory. When it comes to getting what I want, I pull no punches. I have absolutely no scruples, and for that reason I'm dangerous. You can pack up that bit of information and take it with you when you leave town."

Lara shook her head. "I'm not leaving. In spite of what you or Jody Tackett or anybody else says about me, no matter how vicious your threats become, you can't drive me out."

Darcy's lips broke into a beautiful smile. "This is going to be fun."

Laughing, she turned and retraced her steps to the administrative offices. Her laughter echoed eerily in the cavernous foyer.

Darcy blew her nose into a monogrammed handkerchief. "I can't stand having you mad at me, Fergus."

After seeing Jody Tackett home, she returned to her house to find Fergus lying in wait for her. She'd seen him this angry with other people, but never with her. It alarmed her. Fergus was her safety net. He was always there to fall back on if things went wrong.

"Please don't yell at me anymore," she begged tremulously.

"I'm sorry. I didn't mean to raise my voice."

Darcy sniffed, then blotted her running mascara. "What I did, I did for you."

"I fail to see that, Darcy."

"Dr. Mallory had placed you in an impossible situation. Because you're president of the school board, you had to be nice to her and honor her request for an audience. Right?"

"Right," he answered warily.

"But I knew you didn't want her conducting sex seminars and handing out rubbers to the high school kids, including our daughter. I was only trying to help you out of a tight spot."

"By dragging Jody Tackett into it? Jesus." He ran his hand over his pointed head. "Haven't you learned anything about me in the years we've been married? I want nothing to do with Jody. I sure as hell don't want her bailing me out of a jam. She's the last person on earth I want to be beholden to."

"I know. I know, Fergus." Her voice had taken on a wheedling tone. "But desperate times call for desperate measures."

"I'll never get desperate enough to send for Jody Tackett's help. The one time I trusted her, I was screwed, blued, and tattooed. For years afterward folks laughed over the way she'd duped me."

"They're not laughing at you anymore."

"That's because I've worked my ass off to make a success of my business. My name means something in this town in spite of Jody Tackett."

"So, relax. You've showed her up."

"It's not enough. It'll never be enough."

She exhaled with exasperation. "The feud is over, Fergus, and you've won. She's old."

"Only a few years older than me."

"Compared to you, she's in her dotage. Besides, she's incidental. Dr. Mallory is responsible for this mess."

"Most of what she said made good sense."

Darcy bit back a crude retort. In a measured tone, she said, "I'm sure it did. She's smart. She's got degrees and diplomas hanging on her office walls." She wiped her nose with the hankie. "I, on the other hand, am just an ignorant housewife. What do I know?"

"Oh, honey, I'm sorry."

Fergus lowered himself beside her on the edge of their bed and clasped her hand. Over the years she had led him to believe that she was more sensitive to her lack of higher education than she actually was. When the occasion called for it, she used it as leverage.

"I wasn't implying that Dr. Mallory was smarter than you."

One eloquent tear rolled down her cheek. "Well, she is. She's a manipulator, too. It probably comes from being around people in politics. She's maneuvered Heather into thinking that she hung the moon. Now you're taking her side over mine."

"No, sugar. That's not it at all. The point is that I hated your calling in Jody for reinforcement."

"It's not because I thought you needed it." She reached out and stroked his face. "God as my witness, that's not the reason I went to her."

"Then why?"

"Because I wanted to put Dr. Mallory in her place. And who better to do it than her archenemy? Don't you see, Fergus? Jody did the dirty work for you, but you, as president of the school board, will get the credit for warding off that Yankee doctor and her so-called progressive ideas."

Deep furrows appeared on his forehead as he reasoned it through. "I never thought of it like that."

Darcy glanced up at him from beneath her eyelashes. "Do you think Dr. Mallory's pretty?"

"Pretty? Well, yeah, I guess she is."

"Prettier than me?"

"No, sugar pie," he said, smoothing back her hair. "There's not a woman alive as pretty as you."

"And I belong to you, Fergus." Snuggling against him,

she whispered, "You're the best husband in the whole world." Her hand curled around his neck. "Would you think I was terrible if I wanted to make love right now?"

"In the daytime?"

"It's naughty, I know, but, gosh, Fergus, I just love you so much right now, I want to show it."

"Heather might— "

"She'll be at cheerleading practice for another hour. Please, honey? When you show your strong side and shout at me a little, I get all weak inside. Seeing that macho side of you makes me so hot. I get . . . wet. Down there. You know."

His large Adam's apple slid up, then down. "I . . . I had no idea."

"Feel." She guided his hand beneath her skirt and pretended to swoon when he touched her between the thighs. "Oh, my, God!" she gasped.

Within minutes, Fergus had forgotten all about their quarrel and the reason for it. Darcy kissed and stroked and thrust and panted her way back into his good graces.

If Fergus knew he'd been had, he was content to ignore it.

It took a fortnight for Lara to admit that Darcy Winston and Jody Tackett's threats might have substance. After twenty-one days, she cried uncle. Following the Tuesday morning of Jody Tackett's collapse in the supermarket, Lara didn't see a single patient.

Nancy dutifully reported for work each day, creating busy work for herself to pass the sluggish hours until it was time to go home. Lara filled the days by reading current medical journals. She told herself that this time was valuable, that she was fortunate to have time to keep abreast of new developments and research. But she couldn't completely delude herself.

Doctors with full patient loads rarely had time for reading.

She heard nothing from the young attorney retained by Jack and Marion Leonard. If they were pursuing a medical malpractice suit against her, she hadn't yet been notified. Should it come to that, she was confident that once the facts were known, she would be exonerated. However, the negative publicity generated by the litigation would be professionally devastating and emotionally demoralizing. She clung to the hope that they had reconsidered.

The school board never contacted her. Darcy had rallied friends and PTA members to petition the school board against allowing any offensive persons or projects to filter into the school system. Daily, the newspaper was filled with letters to the editor, written by parents and community leaders who were incensed by the proposal recently submitted to the school board by Dr. Lara Mallory. The consensus of the letters was that Eden Pass wasn't ready for such immoral programs to be incorporated into its school curriculum and never would be. The disapproval had been vocal and vehement.

Everywhere she went she was either ignored, sneered at, or leered at by rednecks who assumed she had loose morals because she'd openly discussed such a racy topic with the school board.

She was an outcast. Eden Pass's Hester Prynne. If she hadn't experienced it, she wouldn't have believed shunning this absolute was possible in contemporary America. She began to believe that Jody's prophecy might be fulfilled: she would live to see Lara Mallory leave town.

But not before she got what she came for.

The Tacketts had made her a pariah. They had sabotaged her medical practice. But she'd be damned before she let Key ignore her demand. He would take her to Montesangre. Now.

Chapter Eighteen

*I*s he here?"

The yellow Lincoln was parked outside the hangar.

"No, Doc, he ain't," Balky said, earnestly trying to be helpful. "But he was s'posed to come back sometime this evenin'. 'Less he decided to stay in Texarkana. Can't never tell 'bout Key."

"Do you mind if I stick around for a while?"

"Not at all. Might be a waste of time, though."

"I'll wait."

He shook his head in a way that suggested people were mysteries to him. He had a much deeper understanding of engines and what made them tick. Muttering to himself, the mechanic ambled back to the gutted airplane he'd been working on when Lara arrived.

She preferred waiting outside the hangar where the air was slightly less stifling. It was half an hour before she saw the blinking lights of the approaching aircraft and heard the drone of its motor. The sky was clear, deep blue on the eastern horizon, lavender overhead, crimson fading to gold in the west. Key once had tried to explain the peacefulness he derived from flying. On nights like tonight, she could almost relate to his mystical bond with the sky.

He executed a faultless landing and taxied the twin-engine Beechcraft toward the hangar. She was standing on the tarmac when he climbed out of the cockpit. He saw her immediately, but his expression registered neither surprise, gladness, disappointment, nor anger, making it impossible for her to gauge his mood.

Flexing his knees and arching his back, he sauntered toward her. "In Hawaii when your arrival is greeted by a pretty girl, you get *leied*." He smiled, his teeth showing white in the gathering dusk. "L-e-i-e-d, that is."

"I get it," Lara said dryly.

"Smart lady like you, I figured you would."

She fell into step with him as he moved toward the hangar's wide entrance. "What do you do now? I mean, now that you've landed and your job is finished."

"Hand the keys to Balky and walk away."

"That's it?"

"I'll pick up my money first."

"Who did you fly today?"

"A cattle rancher and his foreman from Arkansas came to look at a bull. I picked them up in Texarkana this morning. They spent most of the day negotiating a price with the owner of the bull, a man named Anderson who owns a large spread near here. It's his plane. He hired me to ferry them back and forth."

"It's a very nice plane," she said, glancing back at it.

"Worth about ninety-five grand. A Queen Aire."

"Sounds like a mattress."

"It does, doesn't it?" Grinning, he entered the building. "Hey, Balky." The mechanic turned and Key tossed him the keys to the airplane.

"Any problems?"

"Smooth sailing. Where's my money?"

Balky wiped his hands on a rag as he moved into the small room where Lara had found Key asleep the morning of Letty Leonard's accident. He went to the desk in the corner opposite the cot and switched on a gooseneck lamp. From a drawer he withdrew a standard white envelope and handed it to Key.

"Thanks."

"Sure 'nough."

Balky left them. Key opened the envelope and counted

the bills inside, then stuck it in the breast pocket of his shirt.

"He paid you in cash?" Lara asked.

"Uh-huh."

"No invoice? No record of the transaction?"

"I struck a verbal agreement with my client. Why involve anybody else?"

"Like the IRS?"

"I pay taxes."

"Hmm. The FAA?"

"Mounds of paperwork for every little trip. Who needs it?"

"Don't you have to file a flight plan, stuff like that?"

"Up to twelve hundred feet is uncontrolled airspace. The 'see and avoid' rule applies."

"You always keep to the twelve-hundred-foot ceiling?"

He had tired of the patter. "Interested in flight instruction, Doc? I've got my instructor's license and could have you soloing in no time. I'm expensive, but I'm good."

"I'm not interested in flight instruction."

"You just happened by to shoot the breeze?"

"No, I wanted to talk to you."

"I'm listening." He took a beer from the refrigerator, propped one elbow on the top of the outdated appliance, tilted his head back, and took a long draft.

"It's about a job."

He lowered the can and looked at her with interest. "We've eliminated flying lessons, and I gather it's not another emergency flight to the hospital."

"No."

He regarded her for another long, silent moment before tilting the beer toward her and asking, "Want one?"

"No, thank you."

He took another swig. "Well? My curiosity's killing me."

"I want you to fly me to Montesangre."

He calmly finished his beer and tossed the empty can into the trash can with an accurate hook shot. He sat down in the swivel chair, leaned back, and propped his feet on the corner of the desk, pushing aside the gooseneck lamp with the heel of his boot.

Lara remained standing. There was no place for her to sit except on the cot. He didn't offer it to her, and even if he had, she would have declined.

"You've asked me that more than once, and I've said no. Is there something wrong with your hearing?"

"I'm not joking."

"Oh, you're not joking," he said, tongue-in-cheek. "Excuse me. Hmm. Well. Then are you figuring on parachuting out?"

She folded her arms beneath her breasts. "Of course not."

"Surely you aren't suggesting a landing on Montesangren soil. 'Cause to be suggesting that, you'd have to be plumb crazy."

"I'm serious."

"So am I, Doc. How's your Spanish? Maybe you need to brush up on it. Do you know how Montesangre translates?"

"Yes. 'Mountain of blood.' I know firsthand that it's a literal translation. I felt my daughter's blood running warm and wet over my hands."

He swung his feet to the floor and brought the chair upright. "Then why in hell do you want to go back?"

"You know why. I've been trying to go back for years, ever since I regained consciousness in that Miami hospital. I can't get into the country through proper channels. They're blocked."

"So you're looking at me as an improper channel."

"In a manner of speaking."

"In a manner of speaking, folks are getting blown away down there."

"I'm fully aware of that."

"And you still want to go?"

"I have to go."

"But I don't."

"No, you don't. I was thinking you might regard it as an adventure."

"Well, think again. I've been called many things, but never a fool. If you want to go down there and get your ass shot off, that's your business, but I'm kinda fond of my ass, so you can X me right out of your plans."

"Hear me out, Key."

"I'm not interested."

"You owe me this."

"As you've said. I don't buy it."

"You'll be gratified to know that I haven't had a single patient in the clinic since the morning of your mother's seizure. Jody fought off my attempts to help her. You brusquely denounced me in front of the crowd."

"I didn't have time to use tact. My mother was near death."

"Precisely. And when word got around that the Tacketts preferred death over my medical assistance, the few patients I had cultivated disappeared. Months of hard work was destroyed. The confidence that had been so hard won was invalidated with a few harshly spoken words. Since then I've twiddled my thumbs."

"You're breaking my heart."

She took a deep breath to curb her temper. "I wanted to conduct sex education seminars at the high school. They're vitally important, something that would have benefited the young people of the community."

"Yeah, I read all about it in the newspaper."

"What they didn't print is how Jody bribed the school board to disallow the program."

"You really know how to get folks fired up, don't you?"

"Compared to your mother, I'm an amateur. Once she

got finished with me, what little credibility I had left, your lover Darcy ravaged."

"You know, I've heard about mental cases like yours. They're called persecution complexes."

She let that pass. "I've officially closed the doors of the clinic. I dismissed Nancy today. My career has been temporarily suspended. So, you got what you wanted. Your family has effectively demolished any chance I had of practicing medicine in Eden Pass. All things considered, I believe you owe me a concession."

"I owe you zilch."

"I've closed the clinic, but that doesn't mean I'm preparing to leave town." She was down to one final ace. She had to play it. "Your mother vowed she would live to see me leave Eden Pass in disgrace. I doubt she will. I can remain here without working until my savings run out, which, if I live frugally, could be several years."

"That's bullshit. You love medicine too much. You wouldn't give it up."

"I wouldn't want to, but I would."

"Just to spite us?"

"That's right. However, I'm willing to bargain. I'll spare your family any more discomfort and embarrassment, provided you fly me to Central America. As soon as we return, I'll leave. Believe me, I won't be that sorry to go. I'm tired of constant strife and petty gossip. I'm tired of examining myself every time I go out, hoping I'll pass muster.

"Let me tell you something," she said, leaning across the desk, "as far as I'm concerned, the people of Eden Pass have failed to pass muster. They're judgmental and narrow-minded hypocrites, cowards bending to the will of an embittered old woman.

"Take me to Montesangre, Key, and I'll leave this town to you, not because I'm not good enough for it, but because it's not good enough for me."

He said nothing for several moments, then spread his arms out from his sides. "Is that everything?"

She gave a terse nod.

"Good," he said, rolling off his spine and coming to his feet. "I gotta run. I'm hungry as a bear, and Janellen is expecting me for supper."

Lara caught his sleeve as he rounded the desk. "Don't patronize me, you son of a bitch. You've trashed me and my practice, but I won't let you ignore me."

He flung off her hand. "Look, I don't give a damn about local politics and gossip. What my mother does with the school board or anybody else is her business. Unless it involves me directly, I stay out of the boiling pot.

"I guess you're a pretty good doctor, and your clinic has come in handy on occasion, but I couldn't care less if you do brain surgery there, or twiddle your thumbs, or shut it down entirely. Darcy Winston is *not* my lover. And if you've got a hankering to sneak into a country that's on our government's shit list, fine. But count me out."

"How conveniently you turn ethical," she said heatedly, indicating his shirt pocket. "You run illegal charters on a daily basis!"

"Turning you down has nothing to do with ethics. I'm not looking to get killed. Beyond that, I don't trust your motives any farther than I can throw you. So you wasted— "

"What if Ashley is still alive?"

He fell silent and regarded her with piercing intensity.

"Uh, 'xcuse me, Key?" Balky was standing in the doorway, his rheumy eyes darting between them with uncertainty. "I'm leaving for the night. Will you lock up?"

"Sure thing, Balky. Good night."

"Night. Night, Doc."

"Good night."

They listened to his departure. The interruption defused the tension, but only marginally. Key turned his back on her and ran his fingers through his hair. "Is that a possibility?"

"Probably not. The point is that I don't *know*. I guess in the back of my mind I've clung to the faint hope that she somehow survived. Her body was never shipped back like her father's." Wearily, she rubbed the back of her neck. "Of course, as a physician and considering the severity of her wound, I know that's highly improbable. She died and was buried. Somewhere alien and unknown to me. I can't live with that. If nothing else, I want to bring back her remains and bury them in American soil."

He turned to face her, but said nothing.

"I need you to do this," she pressed. "One way or another I want to take my daughter out of that place and bring her home. But I can't get into the country. Even ally nations have very few airlines that serve Montesangre because the government is in such constant upheaval. When and if I did get through, as an American citizen I'd be denied entrance into the country and shipped out on the next flight."

"I'd say that's a fairly accurate guess."

"More than a guess. I've been in contact with people in similar circumstances. Many Americans have loved ones in Montesangre whose fates are unknown. Their fact-finding missions have been futile. If they got as far as Ciudad Central, they were dealt with harshly. A few were imprisoned for hours, even days, before being returned to the airport to await the next outbound plane. Some claimed they barely escaped with their lives, and I believe them."

"That's why I don't want to fly over the place, much less land, get out, and walk around," Key said.

"If anyone can get an airplane in and out of there, it's you. Clark constantly bragged about your flying skills. He told me how you've flown into impossible situations to deliver supplies or make rescue attempts, and that you thrive on taking risks—the more dangerous the circumstances, the better." She paused for breath. "Supposing you agreed to do it, could you get an airplane?"

"That's a broad supposition."

"Go with it for the sake of discussion. Could you get a plane?"

He thought it over for a minute. "I know a guy who once asked me to crash a plane for him so he could collect the insurance. He was that badly in debt. He offered to give me thirty percent of his take. If I lived."

"Can you do that? Deliberately crash a plane and live?"

"If you do it right," he said with a fleeting grin. "His offer was tempting. Hell of a chunk of cash. But it wasn't worth the risk."

"Is he still in financial straits?"

"Last I heard."

"Does he still have the airplane?"

"Last I heard."

"So he might be agreeable to your flying it into a potentially dangerous situation. If it never came back, he could collect his insurance money and keep one hundred percent of it. If we did make it back, he'd have the money we paid him to use the plane. How much would he charge to lease it?"

"It's a sweet plane. Cessna 310. Not that old. Taking into consideration the distance . . . say twenty thousand."

"Twenty thousand," she repeated softly. "That much?"

"Ballpark. In addition to my fee."

"Your fee?"

"If my ass is going to be target practice for a guerrilla with an automatic rifle, you're damn right there's a fee."

By the expression on his face, she knew she wouldn't be able to afford him. "How much, Key?"

"One hundred grand." At her shocked expression, he added, "Payable the day before we leave."

"That would be almost every cent I've got."

He shrugged. "Tough luck. Guess we won't have to get shots after all. I'm glad. Hate needles."

Once again he tried to go past her. This time she blocked his path and placed her hands on his arms. "I really hate that. I think you know how much I hate it or you wouldn't do it."

"Do what?"

"Act cavalier. Talk down to me. Damn you! I won't let you joke about this. You know how important it is to me."

Using her restraining hands to his advantage, he moved forward until he'd backed her into an army-surplus file cabinet. "Just how important is it to you?"

"Extremely. Otherwise do you think I would have asked a Tackett—any Tackett—for a favor?"

The pressure of his body against hers was exciting. So were his smoldering eyes. But she wouldn't give him the satisfaction of knowing that. She kept her chin defiantly high, her gaze steady.

"You could even go so far as to say that I'm your last resort, couldn't you, Lara?"

"You're the reason I came to Eden Pass." The statement took him aback, as she had guessed it would. "Clark handed me a golden opportunity to reestablish a medical practice, but I would have turned it down if not for you. I wanted to meet his daredevil brother, the one who could 'fly anytime, anywhere,' to quote you.

"I knew you were away most of the time, but I also knew you'd return sooner or later. I resolved to get you to take me to Montesangre, one way or another. In a very real sense, yes, you're my last resort."

He had listened with rapt attention, obviously stunned by her admission. He recovered quickly. A slow grin spread across his mouth. "So I can name my price, right?"

"You already have. One hundred thousand dollars."

He reached and idly stroked her cheek. "Which I'd be willing to waive in exchange for fucking you."

Her hand flew up to bat his away from her face, but instead she gripped his wrist, closing her fingers tightly around it as far as they would reach. "I should have known you would turn this into something ugly. I tried to appeal to your decency, but you have none. You feel no sense of responsibility to anyone except yourself."

"Now you're catching on, Doc," he whispered. "You can't imagine how liberating it is to be completely free from obligation."

"Free from obligation? Your brother is partially responsible for Ashley's death. Out of all us sinners, my daughter was the only blameless victim of the whole mess. I hold Clark accountable. Just as I hold myself responsible."

She dropped her hand from his wrist. "Where Ashley's concerned I have no pride. I won't ever see her turn a cartwheel, or hear her run scales on a piano, or kiss her skinned knees, or listen to her bedtime prayers. I want only what I can have, and that's to see her buried in American soil. If sleeping with you is the only way I can accomplish that, then it's a small price to pay."

The passionate glow in his eyes cooled to a cynical frostiness. He backed away, but in slow degrees, so that it seemed to take forever before they were no longer touching.

"As you said, Doc, I have no sense of decency. I'd help an old lady across the street if a Mack truck were bearing down on her, but that's about as noble as I get. I'm not my brother in any way, shape, or form. I left all the good deeds to him. Curious as I am to know what made your snatch so irresistible to him, I'll pass."

As he moved through the door, he called over his shoulder, "Lock up on your way out, will ya?"

"You're late."

"I know."

"We didn't hold supper."

"I'm not hungry anyway."

Key and Jody exchanged words like gunfire. He went straight to the sideboard and poured himself a stiff drink.

"We're having black-eyed peas and ham, Key," Janellen said. "You love black-eyed peas. Please sit down and let me fill you a plate."

"I'll sit down, but I don't feel like eating."

He'd been in a rotten mood since Lara Mallory had asked him to help her retrieve the remains of a little girl, who was probably his own flesh and blood, from Montesangre. Could Clark's guilty conscience have driven him to take his own life? Key had previously denied the rumors of suicide. They no longer seemed so farfetched.

He brought the liquor decanter to the table with him. Defying Jody's critical glare, he poured himself another drink. "How was your day, Jody? Feeling better?"

"There's nothing wrong with me. Never was. I got short-winded and everybody made a big deal of it."

He declined to argue with her at the risk of raising her blood pressure. Since her stroke, he'd walked on eggshells around her, doing whatever was necessary to placate rather than provoke her.

He still thought having a live-in nurse was a good idea, but he hadn't broached the subject again. He'd dodged every verbal missile she'd fired at him, knowing that her rotten disposition stemmed largely from fear. Hell, if he'd had a seizure like the one she'd suffered, he'd be on edge, too.

"How about you, Janellen? Anything exciting happen to you today?"

"No. Business as usual. What did you do today?"

He told them about the rancher from Arkansas. "Anderson paid me well. It was easy work. Boring as hell, though."

"And to you that's the most important thing, isn't it?" Jody said. "God forbid you ever get bored."

Raising his glass of whiskey, Key saluted her accuracy.

"Just like your father." Jody sniffed contemptuously. "You're always looking for adventure."

"What's wrong with that?"

"We've got tapioca pudding for dessert, Key. Would you like some?"

"I'll tell you what's wrong with that." Jody ignored Janellen's desperate attempt to avoid a quarrel. "You're a big baby, living in a dream world. Isn't it time you grew up and committed yourself to something worthwhile?"

"He's flying for one of the timber companies, Mama. They're using him to spray the trees for pine beetles. Saving forests is worthwhile."

Jody didn't hear her daughter. She was focused on Key. "Life isn't made up of adventures. It's working at something day in and day out, rain or shine, good times or bad, whether you feel like it or not."

"That doesn't sound like 'life' to me," he said. "That's my definition of drudgery."

"Life isn't always fun."

"Exactly. That's why you have to look for it. Or make it."

"Like your father did?"

"Yes. Because he couldn't find it at home." By now his temper was at the breaking point. "He searched for it in other places, with other women, in other beds."

Jody came out of her chair like a shot. "I won't have you talking that filth at my dinner table."

Key stood, too, squaring off across from her. "And I won't have you bad-mouthing my father."

"Father?" she said scornfully. "He was no father. He left you for months at a time."

It hurt, that reminder of the countless times he'd watched his father's car disappear around the bend in the road, knowing in his breaking young heart that it would be endless days before he would see him again.

He wanted to hurt her back. "He left to escape you, not us kids."

"Key!" Janellen cut in.

Again, she went unheeded. Now that the well of his resentment had been tapped, he couldn't control the gush of angry words. "You never offered me a kind word or a soft touch. Did you treat Daddy any differently? Did you ever talk to him without making it a goddamn lecture on his faults? Did you ever stop thinking about crude oil long enough to laugh with him, to tease and act silly just for the hell of it? When he was depressed, did you draw him to your breast and comfort him? Not that your bosom would have been comforting, or even yielding. It's as hard as a drill bit."

"*Key!*" Janellen cried. "Mama, sit down. You look— "

"Your father didn't need my love. He got it from whores all over the world. And he flaunted them in my face. He was with one the day you were born." She drew herself up and took several labored breaths. "The only good thing that came out of my marriage to Clark Tackett Junior was your brother."

"Saint Clark," Key said with a sneer. "Maybe he wasn't as saintly as you think. Tonight I was talking about him with his former mistress. Seems Dr. Mallory blames Clark for packing her and her family off to Central America and getting them shot. She asked me to take her down there and help bring back her daughter's remains. Ain't that a bitch?"

"You aren't considering it, are you?" Janellen looked at him aghast.

"Why shouldn't I? Her money's green."

"There's still a revolution going on down there. People are being slaughtered every day."

Although he'd responded to Janellen, his eyes never left Jody. "Dr. Mallory thinks we Tacketts owe her this.

In exchange for my services, she's agreed to leave Eden Pass and never come back."

"You are not to do it, do you understand me?" Jody's voice quivered with wrath.

"Even if it means ridding us of Lara Mallory?"

"You can't trust her to keep her word. Under no circumstances are you to even consider going to Central America with her."

He placed his hand over his heart. "Why, Mother, your concern for my safety is touching."

"I don't give a goddamn about your safety. My only concern is to protect the remaining shreds of Clark's reputation. If you go anywhere with that whore, you deserve no better than to get your damnfool head blown off."

Janellen covered a gasp with her hand and sank back into her chair.

"Why don't you go ahead and say it, Jody?" Key shouted. "If you can't have Clark, you'd just as soon see me dead, too."

Jody swept up her pack of cigarettes and lighter, turned, and marched from the dining room.

For the longest time his rigid arms braced him against the back of his chair. His knuckles turned white against the polished oak, as though at any second he might pick up the chair and heave it through the dining-room window.

Until she spoke, he'd forgotten that Janellen was there. "What you said was so . . . so horrible, Mama was too angry to refute you."

He looked at her bleakly. The muscles in his arms relaxed, and his hands dropped to his sides. Turning on his heel, he started for the door. "You're wrong, Janellen. She didn't refute me because I spoke the truth."

The lamp on the nightstand came on. Lara woke up instantly and rolled toward the light, then sprang to a sitting position, her heart in her throat. "What are you doing in here? How'd you get in?"

"I picked the lock on the back door," Key replied. "You forgot to change the code on your alarm."

His eyes were drawn down to her bare breasts. Lara, still trying to orient herself, didn't scramble for cover. His gaze remained fixed on her for several moments. Then, swearing softly, he snatched up the robe lying across the foot of her bed and tossed it to her.

"Put that on. We need to talk."

Still dazed from awakening to find him in her bedroom, she followed his instructions without argument. She sat on the edge of the bed.

Key paced along the footboard, gnawing on his lower lip. Suddenly he stopped and looked at her. "We'd never get clearance to land. Have you thought of that?"

She was muzzy from the abrupt manner in which she'd been awakened. "No. I mean, yes." She drew a head-clearing breath and pushed her hair off her face. "No, we'd never get clearance to land, and yes, of course I've given it a lot of thought."

"Well?"

"I've got a map marking a private landing strip."

"A WAC?"

"A what?"

"A World Aeronautical Chart. A map specifically for pilots."

"I don't think so. It looks like an ordinary map."

"Better than nothing," he said. "Where'd you get it?"

"It was sent to me."

"By someone you trust?"

"A Catholic priest. Father Geraldo. He befriended us while we where there. Randall made him the official embassy chaplain."

"I thought the rebels had executed all the clergymen."

"They've murdered many of them. He's managed to survive."

Key ruminated on that as he sat down in an easy chair beside the bed, so close to her that their knees almost touched. "Sounds to me as though your priest might being playing both ends against the middle."

"Very possibly," Lara admitted with a weak smile. "He claims to be bipartisan."

"He goes with the flow."

"That's the only way he can continue to do the Lord's work."

"Or save his own skin."

"Yes," she admitted reluctantly. "But I have no reason to mistrust him. Anyway, he's all we've got."

Key blew out his breath. "Okay. Let's temporarily shelve that and move to point B. Do you know if they have radar?"

"I'm sure they do, but it couldn't be very sophisticated. Nothing there is. Technologically they're decades behind the rest of the world."

"How far from Ciudad Central is this landing strip?"

Mentally she converted the kilometers. "About forty miles."

He whistled. "That'd be close. How am I supposed to avoid their radar?"

"There must be ways. Drug smugglers do it all the time."

He looked at her sharply. "I've never smuggled dope."

"I didn't mean to imply— "

"Sure you did." He held her gaze, then shrugged impatiently. "Fuck it. Believe what you want to."

He left the chair and began to pace again. Lara had a thousand questions to ask but didn't dare. She mainly wanted to know why he'd changed his mind. Like a caged animal, he restlessly prowled her bedroom.

"*If* we can slip through their radar, *if* this landing strip is where it's supposed to be . . ."

"Yes?"

"How do we get around?"

"I can make arrangements for Father Geraldo to pick us up."

"Go on."

"There's an underground organization that manages to slip supplies, letters, and such into and out of Montesangre. That's how the map got to me. I waited a year for it, but I've had it for several months. Utilizing this underground, I can have Father Geraldo notified when to meet us."

"It'll take another year?"

"No. I put everyone on alert. They're standing by."

"You were that sure I'd agree?"

"I was that sure I'd do anything to see that you did."

They paused, watching each other.

Key was the first to shake himself free. "Does this priest speak English?"

"Actually his name is Gerald Mallone. He's an American."

He swore. "Which means he's doubly suspicious and is probably being tailed everywhere he goes."

"I doubt it. He's steeped in Montesangren culture, more Latin than Irish in temperament. Besides, he's fully aware of the dangers. He's been living with them for years and knows how to avoid them. The landing strip should be fairly safe. I've been told it's on the coast, at the foot of a heavily vegetated mountain range."

"Safe! Jesus. I'll have to fly in at night, over open sea, dodging radar, and set that puppy down in the middle of a goddamn jungle, hoping all the while that we won't run into a mountain or get blown out of the sky." He saw her about to speak and raised both hands. "I know, I know. Drug smugglers do it all the time. No doubt on this very strip."

He paced another few minutes. She didn't interrupt his thoughts.

"Okay, say we land without crashing and burning, say we manage to leave the plane without having an army of rebels or contras shooting us on sight, say

this semitrustworthy priest is there, where does he take
us?"

"Ciudad Central."

He dragged his hand down his face. "I was afraid you'd
say that."

"That's probably where my daughter is buried."

His eyes moved to her tousled tawny hair. "You'll stick
out down there like a polar bear in the Sahara. Aren't you
afraid of attracting someone's attention when you take a
shovel into the graveyard and start digging?"

She took a swift breath.

"I'm sorry. Strike that for insensitivity." He returned
to the chair and continued in a kinder tone of voice. "I
doubt very seriously they'll let you exhume the casket,
Lara. Do you know which cemetery your daughter would
be buried in?"

"No."

"How about Father what's-his-name?"

She shook her head. "The last word I had from him
is that he's checking into it. Civil records have been
haphazardly kept the last several years. By the time we
get there, I hope he's uncovered a clue." She smiled
apologetically. "That's the best I can do."

"What if he can't obtain any more information?"

"I'll do the detective work myself."

"Christ. That's impossible."

"It's not as hopeless as it sounds," she said with as much
conviction as she could garner. "There's a Montesangren
who worked in the embassy, a savvy young man who
knew his way around. He was initially hired to do
clerical work, but soon became invaluable to Randall
by translating official documents. Randall had only a
rudimentary understanding of Spanish. Emilio is smart
and intuitive. If I can find him, I know he'll help us."

"If you can find him?"

"He might not have escaped the attack on the embassy.
His name didn't appear on the casualty lists, but I doubt

the lists were complete. If he wasn't killed, he's probably in hiding. Anyone who'd worked in the American embassy would be regarded as a traitor by the rebels."

"Suppose he's dead or otherwise unavailable. What then?"

"Then I'm truly on my own."

"You're willing to take that risk?"

"I'll go to any lengths to bring Ashley back."

"Right," he said. "You're even willing to offer your sweet body to dirty old me." He was staring at her thighs, where the robe had parted a few inches above her knees.

Lara said nothing and sat very still.

Abruptly he stood. "Tap in to this underground network. Gather all the information you can. Don't discount anything. Don't trust your memory, either; take copious notes. I want to know everything. Time of sunrise, sunset, temperature, population, the speed limit, every frigging fact you can think of. Let me be the judge of what's significant and what isn't. In situations like this you never know what scrap of information might mean the difference between living and dying.

"We'll travel light. Take only one bag you can carry easily. Don't take anything you value, nothing you couldn't drop and run away from, literally. Keep in mind that if we're successful, we'll be carrying out a casket. That may be all we can handle. Questions?"

"What about the airplane?"

"I'll arrange for it and the weapons."

"Weapons?"

"You didn't think I'd go to a turkey shoot without a gun, did you? Can you shoot?"

"I can learn."

"We'll start lessons as soon as I've got the guns. I'll handle the transactions alone, but I expect to be reimbursed for all expenses."

"Of course."

"There's only one condition: Don't ask me any questions about the arms or the plane. If the feds get curious
and start asking questions, you can honestly say you don't
know."

"What will you say?"

"I'll lie. Convincingly. When do you want to go?"

"As soon as you can get an airplane."

"I'll be in touch."

Lara stood. "Thank you, Key. Thank you very much."

He came to stand directly in front of her, his movements
and speech no longer brisk. "As to my fee, does your offer
still stand?"

She gazed into his dark, brilliant eyes and tried to
convince herself that the weakness in her knees was
caused by relief over his agreeing to make the trip, that
it wasn't a reaction to the sexual energy he radiated.

Lowering her head, she pulled apart the ends of her
sash. The robe separated. She waited only a moment
before peeling it from her shoulders and letting it fall
onto the bed behind her.

She stood before him naked.

The silence was dense, the tension tangible. Although
she wasn't looking at him, she felt his eyes moving over
her. Her skin tingled, as though his gaze were actually
touching her, leaving brush strokes of heat. Breasts, belly,
sex, thighs, all were touched with his eyes.

She turned warm. She grew damp. The tips of her
breasts tightened and strained. Her earlobes pulsated
feverishly. And somewhere deep inside her she throbbed
with carnal awareness.

"Look at me."

She raised her head.

"Say my name."

"Key." At first a whisper, she repeated it. "Key."

He slid his hand around the back of her neck and
lowered his head. His kiss was rough and possessive.
Behind each thrust of his tongue was a hint of anger . . .

at first. Then it seemed to be searching for something it couldn't find. Perhaps a desire as thick as his own.

He found it. Only he never knew. Because as abruptly as it began, it ended.

"I'll take ten thousand now." His voice was amazingly calm, but there were lines of strain around his lips, which moved woodenly. "We'll negotiate the balance of what you owe me when and if we come back alive." He turned away.

She whipped the robe from the bed and held it against her. "Key?"

He stopped on his way through the door and, after a long hesitation, turned around.

"I know why I'm doing this, but why are you?" She shook her head with misapprehension. "What changed your mind? What have you got to gain?"

"Except for a measly ten grand, absolutely nothing. The point is, like you, I haven't got a goddamn thing to lose."

Chapter Nineteen

Did you love my brother?"

The question came out of nowhere.

Lara had closed her eyes, but she wasn't dozing. She was too nervous to sleep, though her eyelids were gritty from lack of it. She hadn't slept well for the last several days before their departure.

It had been at least a half-hour since Key and she had exchanged a word. There'd been no sound in the cockpit except the drone of the two engines. They'd left Brownsville, Texas, late that afternoon. For hours thereafter, the rugged terrain of the interior of Mexico had stretched to the horizon. After crossing the Yucatán peninsula, Key had flown out over the Pacific Ocean and made a wide U-turn. No land was yet in sight as they approached Montesangre from the sea.

There was only a sliver of moon; Key had planned their trip around the lunar cycle. He'd eliminated the lights on the wingtips of the craft. The stygian darkness was relieved only by the muted illumination of the instrument panel.

She had sensed his mounting tension as he mentally prepared for the difficult landing and hadn't distracted him with meaningless conversation. They'd left Eden Pass at noon and flown to Brownsville, where they'd eaten. She'd had no appetite, but Key had insisted she clean her plate. "You don't know how long it'll be before your next meal," he'd said.

He'd refueled the airplane, which she assumed belonged

to the man in serious debt since it was a Cessna 310. As agreed, she didn't ask. In preparation for the trip, Key had removed all but two of the five seats—in order to make room for the casket, she assumed. He'd also equipped the plane with a navigation aid radio.

"It's called 'loran,'" he explained. "I can set the latitude and longitude of the landing strip and this baby finds it for me. Can you get me the coordinates?"

Through the underground, she had obtained this vital information, but they had experienced some anxious days before it arrived. "We can't go during a damned full moon," Key ranted. "If your priest doesn't come through by the twenty-fifth, we'll have to wait another month."

They could have waited a month, but mentally they were geared up to go. Waiting longer would have increased their stress. They had talked the topic to death. Their nerves were raw. Fortunately, barely making it under the deadline, the priest came through with the coordinates Key needed.

Behind their seats he'd stowed the duffel bags in which they'd packed a few changes of clothes and toiletries. Her doctor's bag had been packed to capacity. Key had also brought along a camera bag carrying a 35mm camera and several lenses. If they were questioned by anyone in authority—and he assured her that wasn't likely—they would pretend to be a couple on their way to Chichén Itzá to photograph the pyramids.

There was a hidden compartment in one of the wing lockers. He'd placed a rifle there. He'd kept the two handguns in the cockpit. She had recoiled the first time she saw the weapons.

"This one's yours." He held a revolver.

"I can barely lift it."

"You'll be able to if you have to, believe me. Grip it with both hands when you fire."

"Randall wanted to teach me to fire a gun when we moved to Montesangre, but I didn't want to learn."

"You don't have to be a good marksman with this. It's a Magnum .357. Just point it in the general direction of your target and pull the trigger. Consider it a hand-held cannon. Whatever you shoot at, you'll destroy or severely damage."

She shuddered at the thought. Ignoring her aversion, he'd given her a crash course on how to fire and load the revolver.

They were as prepared as they would ever be. Now they were close to their destination. A million things could go wrong: some of them he'd shared with her, many he had probably kept to himself, she thought.

Was his unheralded question about her loving Clark his way of diverting his mind from the dangers they faced?

She turned and looked at him in profile. He hadn't shaved in a week. "Built-in camouflage," he'd said when she mentioned the darkening stubble. The beard only intensified his good looks, adding the dubious charm of disreputability.

"Did I love Clark?" she repeated. Facing forward again, she stared through the windshield into the unrelieved blackness. She tried not to think about this flying island of technology being all that was between her and the Pacific Ocean. To her mind, aerodynamics defied logic. The craft seemed awfully small and terribly vulnerable in this vacuum of black.

"Yes, I loved him." She felt the sudden movement of his head as he turned to look at her. She kept her gaze forward. "That's why his betrayal was so devastating. He threw me to the wolves and watched from the safety of his elected office while they ripped me to shreds. Not only did he fail to come to my rescue, but, by his silence, he denounced me. I wouldn't have thought that Clark was capable of such disloyalty and cowardice."

"He showed no lack of courage when he took his lover into his bed while her husband slept down the hall," he observed. "Or was that stupidity? Sometimes there's little distinction between bravery and ignorance. What made you do it when there was such a good chance of getting caught?"

"Love is a powerful motivator. It makes us its victims and causes us to do crazy things, things we wouldn't ordinarily do. During that weekend at the cottage, the atmosphere was . . . charged. Expectant."

She looked down at her hands, rubbed her palms together. "Desire that strong obscures conscience and better judgment. It overpowers the fear of discovery." She sighed and raised her head. "I should have read the warning signs. They were glaringly apparent. In hindsight, I realize that disaster was inevitable and imminent. I just wasn't paying attention."

"In other words, you were so eaten up with animal lust that common sense didn't stand a snowball's chance in hell."

"Don't sound so superior. Your 'animal lust' for a married woman got you shot! Besides, that's ancient history. Why bring it up now?"

"Because if I don't make it out of this godforsaken banana republic, I'd like to think I died for a noble cause. I'd like to believe that you were more than a roll in the sack for my horny brother, and that for you he wasn't just a convenient diversion from an unhappy marriage."

It was on the tip of her tongue to tell him to go to hell. But, in effect, she had placed her life in his hands. Without him, her chances of surviving this trip were nil. Like it or not, they were comrades with a common goal. Infighting should be kept to a minimum.

"Despite the way our relationship ended, I loved Clark," she said. "I believe with all my heart that he loved me. Does that make this mission noble enough for you?"

"Was he Ashley's father?"

She hadn't seen that curveball coming. For a moment

she was dumbstruck. She had never hinted that Clark had fathered her child. Not even the news hounds with the sharpest teeth had sunk that particular fang into her. On second thought, she realized, she shouldn't be surprised that Key was the first to raise the question. It was characteristically shocking.

"I can't answer that."

"You mean you don't know? You were screwing them at the same time?"

"I'll rephrase," Lara said heatedly. "I *won't* answer. Not until we've done what we came down here to do."

"What difference does it make?"

"You're the one who asked about Ashley's parentage. You tell me if it makes a difference."

"Oh, I see. You think I might try harder to find her remains if she was a Tackett." He made a disagreeable sound. "Your opinion of me must be even lower than I thought. Exactly where do I rank on your scale of life forms? A notch above pond scum? Or a notch below?"

Anger was a supreme waste of energy considering the ordeal facing them. "Look, Key, we've certainly had our differences. We've both slung more than our share of mud. Some of it was warranted. Some of it was spiteful. But I trust you. If I didn't, I wouldn't have asked you to bring me down here."

"You had no other options."

"I could have hired a mercenary."

"You couldn't afford the going rate."

"Probably not, but shortage of funds wouldn't have stopped me. Eventually I would have gotten the money, even if I'd had to wait for my inheritance."

"But you felt that we Tacketts owed you this."

"That wasn't it entirely." She hesitated; he looked over at her. "True, I came to Eden Pass specifically to coerce you into bringing me down here. But I didn't expect to feel this confident about my choice."

Their eyes locked and held for several moments. Finally

Lara turned away. "Once we're safely on our way back home, I promise to tell you anything you want to know. In the meantime, don't throw any more poison darts, okay? I won't throw any either."

He said nothing for several minutes. When he did, he spoke in a gruff voice on a topic unrelated to Ashley's origins. "One way or another, we'll be going down soon."

"One way or another?"

"We'll either reach the coast and find the landing strip, or we'll run out of fuel and ditch into the ocean. In the meantime, why don't you try to get some sleep."

"Is that supposed to be a joke?"

He grinned. "Yes."

"Not funny."

She searched the horizon but didn't see even a seam in the darkness. Key carefully monitored the instruments. She noticed the decrease in their altitude.

"You're going down?"

"Below five hundred feet, just in case their radar is more sophisticated than you think. You're sure the priest will be there?"

"I don't have an ironclad guarantee." He'd grilled her on this a thousand times. She was as sure as she could be under the circumstances. "He's been given our estimated time of arrival. When he hears the airplane approaching, he's to light torches on the landing strip."

"Torches," he said scoffingly. "Probably tomato soup cans filled with kerosene."

"He'll be there and so will the torches."

"The wind's picked up to twenty knots."

"Is that bad?"

"Less than ten would be ideal. Forty would be impossible. I'll settle for twenty. Crosswinds are always a factor along a seacoast. I wonder how close the jungle is to the shore?"

"Why?"

"This late at night it could produce ground fog, which could mean that we'd miss not only the torches but the mountain. Until we ran into it, of course."

Her palms began to sweat. "Can you think of anything encouraging?"

"Yes."

"What?"

"If I die, Janellen will be doubly rich."

"I thought you were the fearless pilot," she said with exasperation. "The Sky King of the nineties. You told me you could fly anything, anywhere, anytime."

He wasn't listening. "There's the shore." He checked the loran. "We're here. Start watching for the lights. It's up to you."

"Why me?"

"Because I've got to keep us from crashing into those goddamn mountains while keeping below five hundred feet. It's dicey. At least there's no fog."

The rocky shore could vaguely be detected on the horizon. Eons ago, a chunk of mountain had broken away from the strip of Central America that is now Montesangre. That chunk had drifted into the Pacific Ocean where it became an island three hundred and eighty miles offshore. In a geological time frame, this had been a recent event. The jagged tear in the mountain range hadn't had time to erode into sandy beaches. Thus, the mountains dominated Montesangre's coast and formed an inhospitable shore.

Consequently, the country had not enjoyed the healthy tourist trade of its more fortunate neighbors who depended on vacationers from North America and Europe to support their national economies. Such economic deprivation had caused more than one armed conflict between Montesangre and surrounding Central American republics.

From the air, the mountain range resembled the letter

C, which curved from the interior of the country, forming a northern border with the neighboring nation, then running parallel to the shore for miles before tapering off. In the hollow of that C nestled the capital city, Ciudad Central. Ninety-five percent of Montesangre's population was concentrated in the city proper or in scattered villages surrounding it.

Beyond those villages in all directions stretched miles of dense jungle, populated only by wildlife, vegetation, and several tribes of Indians who lived very much as they had for centuries, without the enlightening, or corrupting, elements of modern civilization.

Lara had flown into Montesangre only once before; after her arrival she hadn't left the country until the day she was transported out, injured and unconscious. As the shore became hastily more distinguishable, she was filled with a sense of dread. She recalled how miserably unhappy she had been when she arrived with Randall. On that day, she'd had only the knowledge of the life growing inside her womb to sustain her and buoy her ravaged spirit. Ashley was the only reason she ever would have returned.

"Also keep an eye out for other aircraft," Key said. "I can't do any sightseeing."

"No one knows we're coming."

"You hope. Just in case, I don't want an army helicopter flying up our ass, do you?"

Lara glanced at him. The cockpit's temperature was comfortable, but a trickle of sweat was running down his bearded cheek. Her skin too was damp with nervous perspiration.

"We've got nowhere else to go but down," he muttered as he read the gauges. "I couldn't even make it out of Montesangren airspace. We're shit-out of fuel. Where're the goddamn torches?"

Frantically Lara leaned forward and scanned the coastline. She saw nothing but a narrow stretch of beach that bled into the tree line. The mountains loomed darkly above it.

What if Father Geraldo wasn't there? What if he'd been tortured until he divulged information? What if it was known by the rebel commanders that the widow of the late U.S. ambassador was returning? Not only her life but Key's would be in peril. There would be no one to help them. They would be at the mercy of their captors and, as Lara knew, the Montesangrens were not a merciful people. Their best hope would be to crash and die instantly.

"Shit!"

"What?"

"I've got to pull her up. Hold on." He pushed forward on the throttle quadrant and the craft went into a hard climb. Lara looked below. They barely cleared the crest of the mountain. Key banked to the left and skimmed the steep, vegetated walls before swinging back out over the surf.

"Where's the padre, Lara?"

"I don't know." Anxiously she pulled her lower lip through her teeth. She'd been confident that their escort would be there.

"See anything?"

"No."

"Wait! I think I see— "

"Where?"

"Four o'clock."

He executed another drastic maneuver that sent her stomach plunging. She closed her eyes to regain her equilibrium. When she opened them, the horizon was back in place and three small dots of light were glimmering below and ahead of them. Then a fourth flickered on.

"That's him!" she cried. "He's here. I told you he would be."

"Hang on. We're going in."

He leveled the aircraft and decreased their altitude and air speed. Sooner than Lara anticipated, the spots of light were rushing toward them. They landed with a hard bump. The plane bounced along the uneven dirt strip. Key put all his strength into pushing the throttle forward. He practically stood on the foot pedals. The landing strip was built on an incline to assist slowing them down and facilitating a short landing. Still, it seemed to take forever to stop. They came breathtakingly close to the trees at the end of the crude runway.

He turned off the motor. They sighed with relief. Key placed his hand on her knee. "Okay?"

"Okay." Since she had to alight before he could, she reached for the door.

"Wait." He sat tense and still, his eyes sweeping the black curtain of darkness outside the airplane. "I want to see who our welcoming committee is."

They sat in silence. Behind them, the six torches, three on each side of the landing strip, were extinguished one by one.

Key kept his right hand on her knee. With his left, he reached for the handgun beneath his seat. He'd told her it was a Beretta 9mm. He slid back the top, automatically loading the first bullet into the chamber. It was now cocked and ready to fire.

"Key!"

"We're sitting ducks. I'm not going to be snuffed out without putting up at least token resistance."

"But— "

He held up his hand for silence. She heard it, too—an approaching vehicle. Looking back, she saw a jeep emerging from the darkness and slowly taking shape. It pulled up behind the aircraft and stopped. The driver stepped out and moved toward the plane.

Key aimed the Beretta at the shadow figure.

Lara released a gasp of relief. "It's Father Geraldo. He's alone."

"I hope to hell he is."

Lara opened her door and gingerly stepped out of the

plane, climbing down using the footholds in the wing.
"Father Geraldo," she said as she jumped to the ground.
"Thank God you're here."

He extended his hands. "Indeed. It's good to see you
again, Mrs. Porter."

She extended her hand, and he enfolded it in a warm,
damp clasp. "You're looking well," she said.

"And you."

"Have you learned anything about where my daughter
is buried?"

"I'm afraid not. I've made inquiries, but to no avail.
I'm sorry."

The news was disappointing but not surprising. "I knew
it wasn't going to be easy." Just then Key stepped off the
wing. "This is Key Tackett."

"Father," he said in a clipped voice. "Thanks for
sending those coordinates. Without them, we'd never
have found you."

"I'm glad they were useful."

"Are you sure you weren't followed?"

"Reasonably sure."

Key frowned. "Well, let's get this baby out of sight
before we attract company."

"I assure you," the priest said, "for the time being,
we're safe."

"I don't like to take chances. Which way?"

"Because of the revolution, the drug traffic has slacked
off considerably. The strip hasn't been used in a while. I
brought along a machete, and while I was waiting for you
I cleared out some brush." He indicated what appeared
to be an impenetrable wall of jungle.

"Let's get to it."

After hacking away some of the densest brush, the
three pushed the airplane off the landing strip. They
retrieved the few items they'd brought with them, including the hidden rifle, then covered the plane with the
brush.

"This is a remote spot," the priest said to Key, who was surveying the camouflaged aircraft from every angle. "Even in daylight I don't think it'll be detected. Allow me, Mrs. Porter."

He picked up Lara's duffel and the camera bag and headed for the jeep. Hoisting his own duffel and the rifle to his shoulder, Key spoke to Lara in an undertone.

"You failed to mention that the padre is a drunk."

"He's been conducting Mass. That's sacramental wine on his breath."

"Like hell. It's Jamaican rum. I've vomited up enough of it to know how it smells."

"Then you're in no position to judge."

"I don't care if he guzzles horse piss, so long as he's reliable."

Before she could defend the charge, they reached the jeep. Father Geraldo, who wore his forty years as though they were sixty, helped Key stow their gear in the back. "If you don't mind riding back here, it will be more comfortable for Mrs. Porter in front."

"I don't mind," Key said, easily swinging himself up into the backseat. "From here I can guard our rear."

"Well said." The priest smiled at him. "We live in turbulent times."

"Right. Over drinks some time I'd love to philosophize with you. Now, I think we'd better relocate. Pronto."

If the priest took umbrage at Key's reference to drinks, he didn't show it. After assisting Lara into the passenger seat, he climbed behind the steering wheel. "Best to leave the lights off until we approach the city. The roads are sometimes patrolled at night."

"By whom?" Key wanted to know.

"By whoever wants to patrol them. It changes on a daily basis."

"What's the political climate like now?" Lara asked.

"Volatile."

"Terrific," Key muttered.

"The old regime wants to regain control. President Escávez is still in hiding, but rumor is that he's trying to assemble an army and reclaim his office."

"The rebels won't allow it without a bloodbath," Lara said.

"No doubt," the priest agreed, "but Escávez isn't their primary concern. He believes the people still love him, but he's wrong. No one wants to return to the days of his despotism before the revolution. He's just an old man deluding himself, more a nuisance than a threat. The rebels have bigger problems to worry about."

"Such as?" Key asked. He'd worked up a sweat swinging the machete and moving the plane. He removed his shirt and used it to mop his face, neck, and throat. Lara envied him that freedom. She was sweltering. Her blouse clung to her skin.

"Lack of money is their primary problem," the priest replied to Key's question. "Lack of supplies. Lack of zeal. The men are disenchanted. After living in armed camps in the jungle for years, revolution isn't nearly as exciting as it seemed in the beginning.

"They're tired of fighting, but they fear their leaders too much to return home. They're hungry, diseased, and homesick. Some haven't seen their families since Escávez was overthrown. They hide in the jungle and come out only to wreak havoc on small villages and scavenge for food. Mostly they fight among themselves. Since Jorge Pérez Martínez was assassinated— "

"He was? We didn't hear about that in the States," Lara said, surprised. Pérez had been a general in Escávez's army who had staged the military coup to overthrow him. The rebels had regarded him as a savior of an oppressed people.

"He was killed by one of his own men more than a year ago," the priest told her. "For months the leadership was up for grabs. First one lieutenant, then another proclaimed himself Pérez's successor, but none could hold the rebels together. There were many factions with no cohesiveness. As a result, the counter-revolutionaries, among them Escávez, began to make inroads.

"Then, one of Pérez's protégés emerged and declared himself the new general of the rebel army. Over the last several months he's gained support, I think chiefly because his men fear him. He's supposedly ruthless and will stop at nothing to cement his position as leader. *El Corazón del Diablo*. The Devil's Heart. That's what they call him." He glanced sideways at Lara. "He passionately hates Americans."

Saying anything more would have been superfluous. She looked back at Key to find his eyes on her, piercing and intent. "It's no worse than we expected," she said defensively.

"No better, either."

"I brought some clothes," Father Geraldo said, gesturing at the soft bundle at Lara's feet. "Before we reach the outskirts of the city, you'd better put them on."

They'd been following a rutted dirt road that snaked through the jungle, seemingly without destination. Each time a night bird screeched, Lara's skin broke out in goose bumps, though the humidity was stifling. Her hair felt heavy on her neck, more so when she placed a scratchy scarf over her head as was customary of the matrons of Montesangre, except for the progressive generation of women who fought alongside their male comrades in arms.

In the bundle of clothing she also found a shapeless cotton print dress. She gathered it into her hands and stepped into it, working it up her legs and over her hips before placing her arms through the sleeves. She tied it at her waist with a sash.

For Key the priest had brought the muslin tunic and pants of a farmer and a straw hat. As he placed it on his head, the jeep topped a hill. Ciudad Central was spread out below them, a blanket of twinkling lights.

At the sight of the city she despised, fear and loathing filled Lara's heart. If she'd had a choice at that moment, she might have given up her insane objective and returned to the airplane. But somewhere in that urban sprawl her daughter was buried.

As though sensing her trepidation, Father Geraldo pulled the jeep to a halt. "What you intend to do will be extremely dangerous, Mrs. Porter. Perhaps you should reconsider."

"I want my daughter."

Father Geraldo engaged the gears and switched on the headlights. They started down the curving road. The narrow shoulder dropped off into nothingness. Fearfully Lara wondered how much rum Father Geraldo had consumed that evening. Whenever the wheels sank into the soft shoulder, she gripped the edge of her seat.

As it turned out, the condition of the road and Father Geraldo's level of inebriation were inconsequential. As they came around a bend, they were impaled by blinding spotlights and deafened by a chorus of shouting voices. "*Alto!*"

A platoon of guerrillas surged forward to surround them, guns aimed and ready to fire.

Chapter Twenty

Jody knocked on Janellen's bedroom door.

"Mama?"

Jody opened the door but remained standing on the threshold. She didn't remember the last time she'd been in Janellen's room, and some of the furnishings were unfamiliar to her. However, she recognized the cherrywood fourposter bed, chest of drawers, and dresser; they'd belonged to her daughter since she graduated from the crib.

The drapes and wallpaper were new, or at least it seemed they were. The pale gold and china-blue print combinations were too festive and feminine for her taste. She vaguely recalled granting Janellen permission to redecorate but couldn't remember when that had been. Five years ago? Yesterday?

Janellen was lounging in an easy chair upholstered in floral chintz, her feet resting on the matching ottoman, a paperback novel lying open in her lap. A small brass lamp at her elbow cast soft, flattering lighting over her. It came as an unpleasant shock that Janellen looked almost pretty.

During her childhood Jody realized that her daughter was not going to be a raving beauty. Rather than finding this regrettable, she was glad and had done everything possible to guarantee Janellen's homeliness. She'd never dressed her in anything bright or sassy and she had styled her hair in the least becoming way.

She firmly believed that desexing her daughter was the

best thing she could do for her. Wishing to attract a man was a weakness inherent to women. Jody aimed to see that Janellen never fell into that trap.

Compliantly, Janellen had conformed to the mold her mother designed for her. She'd become an intelligent, competent woman who could never be accused of frivolity or flirtation. She'd been too reasonable to fall in love. Her plainness had spared her the deviousness of playboys, fortune hunters, and men in general. In that respect, Jody considered her daughter most fortunate.

There was one major drawback. Janellen had the Tackett eyes. *His* eyes. He'd been dead for years, but that living legacy, which all her children had borne, never failed to disconcert her. It was as if Clark Junior were in the room with her, watching her from behind their daughter's face.

"Mama, what is it? Are you feeling all right? Is anything wrong?"

"Of course I'm feeling all right. Why wouldn't I be?"

Janellen's curiosity was understandable. Jody never sought her daughter's company and certainly not at this hour. It was almost midnight. Janellen had tucked Jody in hours ago, but she'd been unable to sleep. Smoking heavily, she'd paced the floor of her bedroom. Her body was tired, but her mind wouldn't relax and allow her to rest.

She'd always been an insomniac, even as a girl when frustration over her family's poverty had affected her sleep patterns. Night after night she had lain awake between two snoring siblings, scheming ways to free herself of poverty's stranglehold.

The tornado that had destroyed her house and killed her family had been a godsend.

Once she began working for Tackett Oil, the challenge of the job kept her clever mind too energized for sleep. Later, she'd spent years pacing the floor of her solitary bedroom while conjuring up infuriating, devastating scenarios of Clark Junior with other women.

Pushing that embittering thought aside, Jody said, "Where is your brother?"

"Key?"

She shot Janellen a retiring look. "Of course Key."

"He's out of town."

The problem with Janellen was that she'd learned her lessons too well. She'd conformed, she'd done what was expected of her, she'd never been rebellious, never created unpleasantness of any kind, but she was a titmouse. Sometimes her eager-to-please expression was too much to stomach. This was one of those times. Jody wanted to shake her hard.

"He's gone to Central America, hasn't he? He took that bitch down there just to show me that he didn't give a damn how I felt about it."

"Yes, he went to Montesangre with Dr. Mallory, but not because— "

"When did he leave?"

"Today. They planned to arrive tonight. He said he would call if he had a chance, but he didn't think it was likely."

Jody's posture remained rigid. The folds of her housecoat hid her hand from Janellen. Otherwise her daughter would have seen how hard she was gripping the crystal doorknob.

"He's a goddamn fool. She crooked her finger at him and he went running." Her lips curled contemptuously. "Just like your father, he can't resist a chance in a woman's bed, no matter who she is or what it costs him."

"Key went because Dr. Mallory wants to bring back her baby girl's remains."

The sentimental implications didn't soften her. "When are they due back?"

"He didn't know." Janellen's eyes filled with tears. "He

left some papers with me. I'm supposed to open them if he doesn't . . . if they don't . . ."

If she hadn't been holding on to the door with such determination, Jody might have collapsed from the impact of her emotions. She had to get out of there before she made a fool of herself.

Without a word, she backed into the hallway and pulled the door shut with a decisive click. Only then did she give vent to her inner turmoil. Her shoulders slumped forward. Bowing her head, she raised her fist to her lips and mashed them hard in order to keep from uttering an anguished sound.

After a time, she returned to her bedroom feeling alone and very frightened.

Reaching between the front seats of the jeep, Key thrust the Magnum against Lara's side. "Take it," he whispered. "Don't be skittish about using it if you have to."

She didn't argue. The guerrilla fighters had completely surrounded them. Their expressions were menacing. She clutched the revolver and placed it in her lap, hiding it in her voluminous skirt.

"*Buenas noches, señores.*" Father Geraldo spoke pleasantly to the band of armed men. Key counted a dozen. Three times that many were probably keeping cover in the foliage. He didn't like the odds.

"*¿Quién es?*" One of the soldiers separated himself from the others. He was dressed in camouflage fatigues and armed to the teeth. His stance and tone were belligerent, his eyes hostile and suspicious.

The priest introduced himself. The soldier spat in the dirt. Unruffled, Father Geraldo said in fluent Spanish, "You know me, Ricardo Gonzáles Vela. I conducted your mother's funeral Mass."

"Years ago," the soldier growled, "when we still believed in such foolishness."

"You no longer believe in God?"

"Where was God when women and children begging for food were slaughtered by the swine under the command of Escávez?"

Father Geraldo was disinclined to engage in a theological or political debate, especially since the other soldiers cheered and raised their weapons to reinforce their comrade's opinion.

The angry young rebel glared at the priest, then his eyes shifted to Lara, who'd had the good sense to keep her head down to hide her Anglo features. "Who is this woman?" Ricardo jabbed the barrel of his rifle in her direction. "And him?"

"They live in a small village in the foothills. Her husband was killed defending the village from contra forces. She's pregnant. Her brother-in-law," he said, hitching a thumb toward Key, who'd remained slumped down and seemingly disinterested, "already has four sons. He cannot afford to feed two more mouths. I offered to bring her to the city and provide food and shelter in exchange for housekeeping duties at the rectory until she can find someone else to take care of her."

One of the soldiers made a crude comment about the kind of "housekeeping duties" she would be performing for the priest. Key had a basic understanding of Spanish. He didn't catch all the words, most of which were slang, but these duties had something to do with her getting onto her knees.

Ricardo smiled hugely in appreciation of his comrade's ribald wit, then instantly sobered. He gave Key a contemptuous once-over. "You look strong and tall. Why aren't you fighting? El Corazón's army needs fighters."

Key's stomach tensed, but he pretended not to understand that the question had been directed to him. Thankfully Father Geraldo took his cue.

The priest motioned Ricardo closer. He approached warily, his military accoutrements making sinister jingling sounds in the darkness. Key heard several guns being cocked and wondered if he should do the same with the one hidden in the sleeve of his peasant shirt.

Lowering his voice to a confidential pitch and tapping his temple with his index finger, Father Geraldo whispered, "He's an idiot, good for milking goats and planting beans, but otherwise useless." He shrugged eloquently.

"But you said he has four sons," Ricardo argued.

"All of them nine months and ten minutes apart. The poor fool doesn't realize that rutting makes babies."

A roar of laughter went up from the guerrillas. Ricardo relaxed his vigilance. "When will he return to his village?"

"In a few days."

Ricardo leered. "Perhaps we should pay a visit to his village while he's away. Maybe his wife will be lonely."

The others laughed, including Father Geraldo. "I am afraid you would find her unaccommodating, *amigo*. She was grateful for these few nights of rest."

Ricardo swept his arm toward the road ahead. "We will not detain you. You are no doubt eager to have the widow begin her housekeeping duties."

"*Gracias, señores*," he said, addressing the laughing group. "God's blessings on you and on El Corazón del Diablo."

He put the jeep into first gear. Key's gut muscles began to unknot. The jeep had rolled forward only a few yards, however, before Ricardo commanded them to halt again.

"What is it, comrade?" Father Geraldo asked.

"An airplane was sighted tonight, flying low over the mountains from the coast. Did you see it?"

"No," the priest replied, "but I heard it. Unmistakably. About an hour ago. Back there." He pointed toward the mountains, but in a direction several degrees off the spot where they'd hidden the aircraft. "I thought it was delivering supplies to your army."

"And so it was." Ricardo lied as nonchalantly as the

priest had. "The army of El Corazón del Diablo lacks nothing, especially courage. We'll fight with our bare hands if we must, to our deaths."

Father Geraldo saluted him and let off on the brake. They were allowed to proceed without further delay. None of them breathed easily until they were well away from the reconnoitrers.

"Very well done, padre," Key whispered from the back-seat. "I couldn't have lied more convincingly myself."

"Unfortunately this isn't the first time I've had to break a commandment in order to save lives."

"Lara, you okay?"

She nodded her covered head. "Do you think we'll be stopped again?" she asked the priest, her voice muffled by the scarf.

"Probably not, but if we are, we'll stick to the same story. Keep your head down and try to look like you're grieving."

"I am grieving," she said.

From the backseat Key told her to keep the pistol ready to fire if necessary. She nodded acknowledgment, but said nothing more.

At one time the population of Ciudad Central had exceeded one million. Key doubted that half that many lived there now. Even taking into account the lateness of the hour, the city appeared deserted. The streets were dark, as most city streets would be past midnight. But these streets were beyond dark and sleepy—they were dead.

Structures that had once been thriving businesses and gracious homes were now battle-scarred shells. Nearly every window in the city had been boarded up. No light shone through those few that hadn't been. Lawns that marauders hadn't completely trampled were in a sad state of neglect. Vines and undergrowth grew unchecked. The jungle was reclaiming territory that had belonged to it long before man had striven to tame it.

On walls and fences and every other conceivable surface had been scrawled graffiti advocating one junta or another. The only point on which all sides seemed to agree was their hatred for the United States. Cartoons depicted the president in all manner of disgusting and humiliating postures. The American flag had been desecrated in countless ways. Key had been in many countries hostile to the United States, but he'd never felt the antipathy as strongly as here, where it was as powerful as the stench of raw sewage.

"Oh, my God!"

Lara's gasp drew Key's attention forward. A woman's body was hanging by the neck from a traffic-light cable. Her mouth was a gaping, black, fly-infested hole.

"Some of El Corazón's handiwork," the priest explained to his horrified passengers as they passed beneath the swaying corpse. "Montesangren women are valued as soldiers. They're not spared military duty because of their gender. When they're found guilty of an offense, they're dealt with just as harshly as their male counterparts."

"What was her crime?" Lara's voice was husky with revulsion.

"She was exposed as a spy who carried secrets to Escávez. They cut out her tongue. She drowned in her own blood. Then they hung her body in that busy intersection. It's a warning to everyone who sees it not to cross El Corazón del Diablo."

Considering the risks Father Geraldo was taking to help them, Key didn't blame him for his closet drinking.

"Here we are," he said as he pulled the jeep into a walled courtyard. "You'll find it changed since you were here, Mrs. Porter. The few Montesangrens who are still faithful to the church are afraid to have it known. I hold daily Masses, but more frequently than not, I'm the only one in attendance. That makes for empty offering plates."

Key alighted and looked around. The courtyard was

enclosed on three sides by stone walls covered with bougainvillea vines. When Father Geraldo noticed Key's interest in the arched opening through which they'd entered, he said, "Until three years ago, there was a very beautiful and intricate wrought-iron gate. It was requisitioned by the rebels."

"Sounds like the Civil War when the Confederate army made cannonballs from iron fences. What'd the rebels use your gate for?"

"Pikes. They severed the heads of the generals of Escávez's army, impaled them on the pikes, and left them in the city square until they rotted. That was shortly after you left, Mrs. Porter."

She didn't quail or turn pale or faint. "I'd like to go inside," she said in a level voice. "I'd forgotten how ferocious the mosquitoes here can be."

Key admired her fortitude. Maybe the danger they'd experienced tonight, coupled with seeing evidence of so many atrocities of war, had inured her. Then he reminded himself as they carried their gear toward the entrance of the rectory that she'd experienced an atrocity firsthand.

One of the encompassing walls of the courtyard doubled as the exterior wall of the church. It was taller by two-thirds than the other two walls. Typical of Spanish architecture, the sanctuary had a bell tower, although the bell was missing.

Another of the walls formed the exterior of the school, which Father Geraldo sadly explained was no longer used. "I wished to teach catechism, but all the various juntas wanted the children indoctrinated to violence and retaliation, which are incongruous with Christ's teachings. The nuns were faithful, but feared for their lives. Parents, under the threat of execution, were afraid to send their children to class. Eventually the enrollment dwindled to nothing. I closed the school and requested that the nuns be reassigned to the States. There had been so many clergymen executed that all elected to leave.

"For a while the vacant school was used to house orphans. There were dozens of them, victims of the war. Their parents had either been killed or had abandoned them to join the fighters. One day soldiers arrived in trucks and transported the children to another place. No one would ever tell me where they were taken.

"This," he said, unlocking a heavy wooden door, "is where I live and do what little work I'm still permitted to do."

To Key, the rectory was extremely claustrophobic, but he was accustomed to having the sky as his ceiling. The priest's quarters were a warren of small rooms with narrow windows and low, exposed-beam ceilings. Key had to duck his head to pass through the doorways. His shoulders barely cleared the walls of the dim corridors. More than once the toes of his boots caught on the seams of the uneven stone floor.

"I'm sorry," the priest said when Key tripped and bumped into a wall. "The rectory was built by and for European monks much smaller than you."

"No wonder they prayed all the time. They didn't have room to do anything else."

Father Geraldo indicated that they precede him through a connecting doorway. "I have refreshments in the kitchen. You'll be glad to know that it was modernized in the late fifties."

By contemporary American standards, the kitchen was woefully outdated, but it was centuries ahead of the other rooms of the rectory. They sat down at a round table while Father Geraldo served them fruit, cheese, bread, and slices of a canned ham one of his relatives in the States had smuggled to him. Out of deference to his meager hoard, they ate sparingly.

"The water is supposed to be sterilized, but I boil it anyway," he said as he removed a pitcher from the refrigerator. He placed lemon slices in their glasses. There was no ice. He also set a bottle of Jamaican rum on the table. Only after Key had helped himself to it did the priest pour a glass for himself.

"It helps me sleep," he said sheepishly.

Lara was polite enough to wait until they'd finished the meal before broaching the subject of her daughter's grave. "Where do we start our search, Father Geraldo?"

He looked at them uneasily. "I thought you might have a plan. All my inquiries have led to dead ends. This doesn't mean that no information exists. It simply means that no one is willing to impart it."

"The result is the same," Key said.

"Unfortunately, yes."

Lara, however, seemed undaunted. "I want to start by searching the American embassy."

"There's no one there, Mrs. Porter. It was looted and has remained vacant these past years."

"Do you remember my husband's aide and interpreter, Emilio Sánchez Perón?"

Key had traveled extensively in Central and South America and was familiar with the custom of tacking on the mother's maiden name to establish an individual's identity.

"Vaguely," the priest answered. He refilled his glass from the bottle of rum. According to Key's count, this was his third drink. "As I recall, he was a quiet, intense young man. Slight in build. Wore glasses."

"That's Emilio. Have you seen or heard from him?"

"I assumed he was killed when the embassy was raided."

"His name didn't appear on the casualty list."

"That could have been an oversight."

"I realize that," Lara said, "but I'm clinging to the hope that he's still alive. The embassy library fascinated him. He spent most of his off-duty hours there. Do you know if the library was ransacked along with the rest of the building?"

Father Geraldo shrugged. "The rebels have very little time for recreational reading," he said with a wry smile. "But I wouldn't expect to find anything there intact, including the library. I haven't seen it, but from what I've heard, the building was destroyed."

The discouragement that settled on Lara's face was heartbreaking to see. "What about Ashley's death certificate?" Key asked. "Wouldn't a doctor have signed one before she was buried?"

"That's a possibility," the priest conceded. "If the certificate wasn't destroyed, if the doctor's name was recorded, and if we can locate him, he might know where her body is buried."

Lara sighed. "It seems hopeless, doesn't it?"

"Tonight it does." Key came to his feet and assisted her out of her chair. "You're exhausted. Where is she sleeping?"

"I need a bathroom first, please."

"Of course." Father Geraldo indicated a narrow passageway. "Through there."

While Lara was in the bathroom, which fortunately had plumbing, Key and the priest shared another drink. "If you're so limited in the work you can do here, why don't you return home?" Key asked. "Getting reassigned shouldn't be a problem considering the number of missionaries who've been slaughtered."

"I made a commitment to God," he replied. "I may not be very effective here, but I doubt I'd be much more effective elsewhere."

He raised his glass of rum and drank deeply. Father Geraldo knew that in the States he would be committed by the Church to an alcohol-addiction rehab facility. Staying in war-torn Montesangre was his self-imposed penance for his weakness.

"You might die here if you stay."

"I'm well aware of the possibility, Mr. Tackett, but I'd rather die a martyr than a quitter."

"I'd rather not die at all," Key said somberly. "Not yet."

The priest looked at him with renewed interest. "Are you Catholic, Mr. Tackett?"

Key chuckled at the notion. There wasn't even a Catholic church in Eden Pass. The few Catholic families in town traveled twenty miles to worship. They were treated with only a little more tolerance than the Jewish families and were looked at askance by the Protestants of his hometown, where most folks erroneously assumed that if you were American-born you were automatically Christian.

"I was raised a Methodist, but don't hold that against them. They did their best. I was the scourge of every Sunday-school teacher unfortunate enough to have me in class. I eliminated any doubts they might have had as to the devil's existence. I'm living proof that Lucifer is alive and well. When it comes to righteousness, I'm a lost cause."

"I don't believe that." The priest raised his glass and looked through the rum as he spoke. "I'm not much of a priest, but I haven't forgotten all my training. I can still see into a man's heart and judge his character with a fair degree of accuracy. It took a man of courage and compassion to bring Mrs. Porter here, particularly when one considers her relationship with your brother."

Key let that pass without comment and leaned across the table so he could whisper. Water was running in the bathroom, but he didn't want to take a chance on Lara overhearing. "Since you claim to be a fairly good judge of character, would you say the soldier on the road was fooled by that crock of shit you fed him?"

The water in the bathroom stopped running.

The priest drained his glass. "No."

Father Geraldo and Key exchanged a stare rife with unspoken meaning. Lara rejoined them, fatigue weighing down her small frame.

"Bedtime," Key said, coming to his feet.

The priest led them through a maze of hallways. Entering a cloister, he smiled at Lara encouragingly and indicated the window. "It opens onto the courtyard. I thought you'd like that. But be sure to use the mosquito netting."

She didn't seem to notice that the cot beneath the crucifix was narrow, that the only lighting was a weak, bare bulb suspended from the ceiling, that the chamber was airless and hot, and that in lieu of a closet there were three wooden pegs extending from the wall.

"Thank you very much, Father Geraldo. You're placing yourself at tremendous risk in order to help me. I won't forget that."

"It's the least I can do, Mrs. Porter. More than once this church benefited from your generosity even though you aren't Catholic."

"I admired the work you were doing here. It superseded the arguable points of dogma."

He smiled poignantly. "I remember when your daughter was born. I happened to be visiting the hospital wards that day, heard you had just given birth, and stopped by your room to extend my congratulations."

"I remember. We had met socially on a few occasions, but you were wonderfully kind to visit me that day."

"That was the first time I'd ever seen you smile," he remarked. "And so you should have. Your Ashley was a beautiful baby."

"Thank you."

The priest took her hand. After giving it a brief squeeze, he said good night and left the room. Having been reminded of her daughter's birthday, she looked forlorn and small, as though grief were shrinking her. Key wanted to alleviate her bereavement, to touch her with compassion and understanding as the priest had, but his hands remained at his sides.

"Do you still have the pistol?" he asked.

"I put it in the camera bag."

The bag was hanging by its strap from one of the wall pegs. Key removed the large revolver and handed it to her. "Sleep with it. Don't be without it."

"Did Father Geraldo tell you something I should know? Are we in danger?"

"I think we should be prepared for our situation to get worse before it gets better. If we have no trouble, it'll be a lucky break." He nodded toward the cot. "Try to get some rest. Tomorrow will be a long day. We'll start at the embassy."

She held him with a puissant stare that made him increasingly uncomfortable. "Tell me the truth, Key," she said softly. "Don't talk down to me as though I were a child. You think this is a wild goose chase, don't you?"

He did, but he didn't have the heart to tell her so. Father Geraldo had confirmed what he'd guessed—that the soldiers had let them into the city because they were curious to find out more about them and what they were doing there, not because they'd believed the priest's tale about a widow and her idiot brother-in-law.

Key believed they'd be lucky to escape Montesangre with their lives. He doubted very much that they'd fly away unscathed with the casket bearing Ashley Porter's remains.

But while he didn't have the heart to tell her the truth, he wouldn't insult her intelligence with a fatuous lie. Compromising by avoidance, he said, "Get some rest, Lara. I plan to."

Rather than go to bed, he returned to the kitchen, where he kept Father Geraldo company while the priest drank himself into a stupor. Leaving him slumped over the table soundly snoring, Key found a cot in the tiny room across the hall from Lara's. He stripped to his underwear, lay down between the scratchy muslin sheets, and dozed fitfully, his ears attuned to any noise.

He must have slept more deeply than he'd thought,

because he awakened with a jolt when someone shook his shoulder. Reflexively he grabbed the Beretta, released the safety, and sat upright.

Lara stood beside the cot, washed and combed and dressed, her hand arrested in midair near his shoulder. The muzzle of the gun was only inches from her face.

"Jesus." Key exhaled shortly. "I could have killed you."

She was shaken and pale. "I'm sorry I startled you. I called your name several times. It . . . it wasn't until . . . I touched you . . ."

They stared at each other through the morning gloom. It became increasingly difficult to breathe the heavy, humid air. Her breasts rose and fell with the effort.

Sometime during the night, he'd kicked off the top sheet. Sweat trickled through his chest hair, rolled over his ribs, down his belly, and collected in his navel. An erection like a telephone pole had distended the front of his briefs.

"It's seven o'clock." She sounded as though she'd just run a mile uphill. "I've made coffee." She turned and fled.

Key dropped the gun and covered his face with both hands, dragging them down his haggard, bearded cheeks. Morning erections weren't uncommon, but this one was unusually hard.

As he pulled on his clothes, he stared at the open doorway through which Lara had hastily retreated.

"You were right. There's nothing here."

Lara kicked a chunk of ceiling plaster out of her path. What had been done to the American embassy library defied description. The crystal chandelier lay shattered on the quarry tile floor, which had been robbed of the Aubusson rugs that had once adorned it. The bookshelves had been stripped. Piles of ashes were mute testimony to the fate of the volumes.

The flag that had once stood in the corner was in tatters. Epithets to the United States had been spray-painted on the paneled walls. None of the tall windows remained intact. Apparently guns had been fired into the ceiling, because loose plaster and sections of molding were scattered over the floor. The furnishings had been confiscated. Rodents and birds now nested in the rubble.

"I'm sorry, Mrs. Porter."

"It's not your fault," she told Father Geraldo, who was hovering nearby. He was wan; his skin looked pasty, and his eyes were bloodshot. His hands were shaking so badly that he could barely drink the coffee she'd brewed before their departure from the rectory. She pretended not to notice when he laced his coffee with rum. "You tried to warn me that this was what I'd find."

"Is there anything else you'd like to see?"

"Randall's office, please."

"Make it quick," Key said.

He stood near a window, flattened against the wall. He could see out while remaining hidden. They had dressed in the clothing the priest had provided the night before and had parked the jeep off the main street before entering the building. Nevertheless, both he and Lara doubted that their disguises could fool anyone who looked closely at them.

Key was carrying the rifle. His handgun was tucked into the waistband of his pants. From the moment they'd entered the ravaged building, he'd been more interested in what was going on in the streets than in what she might discover inside.

He turned his head away from the window. "The same jeep has driven past three times. There are two soldiers in it. They're flying El Corazón's flag. I don't trust their nonchalance."

"We'll be quick," she promised as she and the priest picked their way through the litter to the doorway of the library. Key followed but continued to glance over his shoulder as they made their way up the staircase to the room that had been the ambassador's office.

"Wait!" he cautioned as Lara reached for the closed door. She yanked back her hand, and he approached with the rifle. "Stand aside." She and the priest stood with their backs against the wall, out of the way of the door. Key pressed himself against Lara, then used the butt of the rifle to nudge open the door.

He hesitated a moment longer, then explained. "It was the only door in the building that was closed. It could have been booby-trapped."

Stepping around him, she moved into the office. At one time furnished to befit a United States ambassador, it had been ransacked as completely as the library. The desk was still there, but it had been bashed until it was barely standing. The top had been scarred by a knife, probably the same one used to slash the leather chair. White cotton stuffing sprouted from the gashes. The liquor cabinet had been raided; Waterford decanters and glassware had been shattered against the far wall.

Father Geraldo heaved a sad sigh. "It appears that your husband's office suffered the same fate as the other rooms." He headed for the door, but Lara reached out and caught his sleeve.

"Wait. Maybe not." She moved to the far wall where there was a credenza that appeared not to have been disturbed. She opened one of the compartments and uttered a small exclamation.

"Look. Papers and files." She scanned one of the documents. "They're written in Spanish, but they look official."

Father Geraldo read them over her shoulder. "It's a trade agreement." He read further. "Basically, unrefined sugar in exchange for weapons. But it's dated several months before the coup was staged, so it can't be of much interest."

"It is to somebody." Reaching deeper into the credenza, she pulled out a pair of reading glasses and held them up for the priest to see.

"That looks like— "

"The kind that Emilio wore," she finished, her voice excited. "I knew it! I knew that if he was alive— "

Suddenly Key stepped forward and covered her mouth with his hand. He also motioned the priest to silence and angled his head toward the door, which they'd left open.

"Someone's out there," he mouthed.

He signaled Lara to crouch behind the credenza. She adamantly shook her head and headed for the door. He grabbed the back of the loose dress and brought her up short. Furious, she spun around and glared at him. But her glare fizzled beneath his, so she did as he instructed and crouched down at the end of the credenza. Father Geraldo knelt beside her.

By now she too heard the faint rustling of footsteps beyond the door. Key crept closer to it. He had propped the rifle against the desk, but was holding the handgun out in front of him as though he fully intended to use it.

What if they had caught Emilio off guard? What if he'd heard their approach and, fearing for his life, had hidden in another room? He was barely more than a boy, and he'd been loyal to Randall and her. *He* might know the location of Ashley's grave. Key, with his trigger-happy reflexes, could shoot him the instant he appeared in the doorway.

Lara held her breath and listened. Unmistakably the footsteps were coming nearer, although the one making them was trying to go undetected. His approach was halting, as if he, too, was pausing occasionally to listen. Finally the footsteps ceased. Unless her ears were playing tricks on her, the person had stopped just beyond the door, exactly as they had done before Key forced open the door with the butt of his rifle.

Lara watched in dread as he aimed the gun at the doorway.

There was movement in the opening.

Lara surged to her feet and rushed forward. "Emilio, look out!"

Chapter Twenty-One

Startled by her shout, Key spun around and backhanded her, knocking her to the floor. Then, hearing a sound in the doorway, he dropped, rolled, and fired three times.

The blast echoed in the empty building, causing Lara momentary deafness. She tasted blood. Woozy and stunned, she struggled to a sitting position and looked toward the doorway. On the threshold, one side of his body opened by gunshots, lay a goat.

"Fuck!" Key yanked Lara to her feet and shook her hard. "What the hell were you thinking?" He shoved her toward the door. "Let's get the hell out of here. Come on, padre. In a minute or less this place is going to be crawling with troops."

Stumbling from the room, she barely avoided stepping in the gore. Key splayed his hand on her back and pushed her ahead of him down the staircase and through the formal reception halls on the ground floor. Her lip was throbbing; she knew it was rapidly swelling.

When they reached the rear door through which they'd entered, Key jerked her to a halt. Cautiously he poked his head outside and surveyed the immediate area. Lara glanced at Father Geraldo. Breathing heavily, he was supporting himself against the doorjamb. Sympathetically he passed her a handkerchief. She blotted her lip with it; it came away stained with blood.

Key said, "Let's go. But keep your head down and be ready to run for cover. There could be snipers on the roofs."

He gripped her hand and made a dash for the jeep. He hoisted her into the passenger's seat, then ran around to the driver's side, taking over Father Geraldo's position as driver. The priest didn't seem to mind. Without argument he scrambled into the backseat only seconds before the jeep lurched toward the nearest alley.

Key stayed off the main roads, driving at a breathtaking speed down one alley and up another, dodging heaps of garbage and warfare debris, unpredictably switching directions like a crazed animated character in a video game.

"Did I hurt you?" He gave Lara a swift glance.

"Of course you hurt me. You hit me."

"If you'd kept your butt where I'd told you to keep it, it wouldn't have happened." He swerved to avoid colliding with a youth on a bicycle. "Jumping up and hollering like that. Jesus Christ!" He banged his fist on the steering wheel. "You were a prime target for whoever was outside that door. I didn't have time to ask you nicely to duck. I knocked you down to save your life."

"From a *goat*?"

"I didn't know it was a goat and neither did you."

"I thought it was Emilio."

"And what if it had been? Were you hoping he'd kill me?"

"I was trying to keep you from killing him."

"I've got more self-control than that."

"Do you?"

He stopped the jeep so suddenly that she was pitched forward. "Yes, I do. And you, better than anybody, ought to know that." His eyes held hers for several telling seconds.

Finally she turned away.

Key whipped his head around. "Well, padre, what do you think of the day so far?"

Father Geraldo lowered a flask from his mouth and wiped it with the back of his hand. "It's a shame we had to leave the goat. It would have fed several families."

Key looked ready to throttle him, but the priest's droll comment struck Lara as funny, and she began to laugh. Father Geraldo laughed too. Eventually Key acknowledged the macabre humor of the moment with a taut smile.

"Ah, hell." He sighed, throwing back his head and gazing up at the patch of sky visible above the two buildings between which they were parked. "A god-damn goat."

Once their laughter subsided, he turned to Lara and touched her lower lip. He winced with regret when his fingertip picked up a bead of fresh blood. "It was reflex. I didn't mean to hurt you."

"It's nothing." She dabbed the cut with the tip of her tongue and tasted not only her blood but the slightly salty spot where his fingertip had been. "I don't want to stop the search now."

"'Now'?"

"It's incredible to me that the credenza was spared. Either it's a miracle, or Emilio is alive and has recently been in that office setting things right. Those were his eyeglasses. I'd swear to it. He's been there recently."

"Well, he won't be back today. If he was lurking around somewhere, we surely scared the hell out of him."

He was probably right, Lara thought. Emilio was her best chance of gleaning information—if he was indeed still alive and if she could coax him out of hiding. She intended to return to the embassy later, with or without Key and Father Geraldo, and stay through the night if necessary in order to make contact with her husband's former aide. Key would have a litany of objections against that strategy, so she decided to postpone telling him her intentions for as long as possible.

There were, however, other avenues she could explore

in the meantime. "Father Geraldo, wouldn't Ashley's death be a matter of public record?"

"Perhaps. Before the revolt, this nation made stabs at being civilized. If the records haven't been destroyed, they would be on file at city hall."

"What kind of red tape would you have to cut through to get to them?" Key asked.

"I won't know until I try."

"If it's known what you're looking for, we'd just as well raise a red flag."

The priest thought about the dilemma for a moment. "I'll tell them I'm looking for the records of someone named Portales. Portales, Porter. If the death certificates are filed alphabetically, Ashley's name should be in the same volume."

"Volume? Aren't they computerized?" Key asked.

"Not in Montesangre," Father Geraldo replied with a rum-induced smile.

It turned out to be remarkably simple. After the incident at the pillaged embassy, they almost didn't trust their good fortune.

Not quite half an hour after Father Geraldo had left them in the jeep, parked on a side street a couple of blocks from the courthouse, he returned, walking jauntily and wearing a happy grin. "God has blessed us," he told them as he climbed into the backseat.

Although he'd been gone only a short while, to Lara it had seemed like an eternity. She feared that no records would be found and that this errand would produce no new information. Key, pretending to take a siesta beneath his straw hat, had kept careful watch, fearing that they would attract attention.

Ciudad Central was a city in turmoil, but a fair amount of commerce was still being conducted. People moved from place to place in the lumbering city buses, in private cars, on bicycle, and on foot. For all the movement, however, one didn't get a sense of bustling activity.

The pervasive mood was one of wariness. People didn't collect in clusters to chat, lest their reason for gathering be misinterpreted by the soldiers in the military vehicles that imperiously sped along the thoroughfares. Children were kept near their nervous, cautious mothers. Shopkeepers transacted business without engaging their customers in lengthy conversations.

Lara and Key were relieved to see Father Geraldo return. "You found out where Ashley's buried?" Lara asked eagerly.

"No, but there was a death certificate. It was signed by Dr. Tomás Soto Quiñones."

"Let's go," Lara told Key, motioning for him to start the jeep.

"Hold on. This Soto," he said, turning to Father Geraldo, "whose side is he on?"

Lara was impatient to follow up on the clue. "It doesn't matter."

"The hell it doesn't."

"He's a doctor. So am I. That takes precedence over political affiliations. He'll extend me a professional courtesy."

"Will you grow up?" Key said with exasperation. "For all you know he's El Corazón's brother-in-law or a spy for Escávez. Either way, if we go barging in there and say the wrong thing, we're screwed."

"Excuse me." Addressing Key, Father Geraldo played peacemaker. "In my work, I've crossed paths with Dr. Soto several times. I've never known him to profess allegiance to any particular faction. He treats the wounded of all sides, much as I do."

"See? Now can we go?"

Key ignored Lara. "Even if he's sympathetic, he'd be risking his neck to help us. The potential danger could make him reluctant to talk. He might outright refuse.

Worst-case scenario is that he'll sic El Corazón's death squads on us."

"I'm willing to take the chance," Lara said adamantly.

"You're not the only one involved."

"If you won't go with me, I'll go alone."

Key tried to intimidate her with his stare. When she held her ground, he turned to Father Geraldo. "What's your gut instinct on *el doctor*?"

Indecision flitted in the priest's dark eyes. Finally he said, "Whether or not he consents to help us, I think we can trust him to secrecy."

Lara agreed.

"Okay, you two," Key said softly. "Have it your way, but we're going to go about it my way."

Lara and Key waited in the doctor's cramped hospital office while Father Geraldo once again acted as their mouthpiece. Even though Key had closed the blinds against the afternoon sun, the room, without air-conditioning, was stifling. Lara's bodice clung to her damp skin. Perspiration had formed a dark wedge in the center of Key's shirt. He frequently used his sleeve to wipe his sweating forehead. They didn't waste either oxygen or energy on conversation.

Silence was also an added precaution. They didn't want their voices to attract anyone on the hospital staff to the doctor's private office. Explaining their presence there could prove tricky.

The waiting became interminable. Lara folded her arms beneath her head and laid it on the doctor's desk. They'd been there over two hours. What was taking so long? Her imagination began to run wild: They'd been discovered. Armed troops had been summoned and were taking up positions around the hospital. Key was probably right; Dr. Soto used his medical profession as a cover. He was actually a spy. He'd seen through Father Geraldo's ruse, tortured him into telling the truth and—

The instant she heard the approaching Spanish-speaking voices, she sat up. Key had heard them, too. He moved into position behind the door and signaled her to remain quiet and out of sight until the doctor was inside the room.

Her heart beat hard against her ribs. A trickle of sweat slid between her breasts. The doorknob turned and Dr. Tomás Soto Quiñones preceded the priest into his office. He reached for the light switch and flipped it on. "It was a routine birth, but these things can take— "

He spotted Lara and looked at her quizzically.

"Forgive me, Doctor," Father Geraldo said humbly as he ushered the doctor across the threshold. Still in Spanish, he explained, "I've been less than truthful. I do wish to discuss with you a soup kitchen for the starving. Perhaps at a later time?"

Key reached around them and closed the door, posting himself between it and the dumbfounded physician.

Father Geraldo apologized to Lara and Key for the delay. "He agreed to see me as soon as he delivered a baby. The labor stalled and took longer than he had estimated."

"You're Americans?" the doctor exclaimed in flawless English. "How did you get across the border? Please tell me what is going on." Uneasily he glanced at Key's stern visage and at the pistol tucked into his belt. He gaped at the priest, then at Lara, who was now standing at the edge of his desk. "Who are you?"

"My name is Dr. Lara Mallory." Although it hadn't bled for hours, her lip felt like it had an anvil attached. "Three years ago, I was living in Montesangre with my husband, Ambassador Randall Porter."

"Yes, of course," he said as recognition dawned. "Your picture was in the newspapers. Your husband was kidnapped and executed. Such a tragedy. Senseless violence."

"Yes."

"The medical community has continued to mourn the ambassador's death. Since diplomatic relations with the United States were suspended, it has been difficult to obtain pharmaceuticals and medical supplies."

"As a physician, I can appreciate your problem." She took several steps forward. "Dr. Soto, I'll personally see to it that you'll receive an abundance of supplies if you'll help me now."

The doctor glanced over his shoulder at Key, gave the priest another inquisitive look, then turned back to Lara. "Help you in what way?"

"Help me locate my daughter's grave."

Dr. Soto regarded her in stunned surprise, but he said nothing.

"When my husband was taken, she was killed in the gunfire. She was buried here. My government, and several Montesangren regimes, have ignored my repeated requests to have her remains exhumed and sent to the United States. I'm here to do it myself. But I don't know where she's buried."

Far down the corridor, rubber-soled shoes were squeaking on the vinyl floors. The clatter of metal servers and china announced that the dinner carts had arrived. But in this cubbyhole office next to the emergency exit door there was nothing but silence.

Finally the doctor cleared his throat. "You have my deepest sympathy. You're to be admired for undertaking such a dangerous mission. But I am at a complete loss. How would I know where your daughter is buried?"

"You signed her death certificate." Lara moved closer to him. Key tensed and reached for his weapon, but her quick glance ordered him not to interfere. "Do you remember the incident?"

"Naturally."

"Her name was Ashley Ann Porter. She died on March fourth of that year, just hours before the revolution was officially declared."

"I remember distinctly when your daughter was killed and your husband taken captive. You too were injured."

"Then you must remember signing Ashley's death certificate and releasing her body for burial."

Sweat had popped out over his face. He was a stout man, solidly built, shorter than she. His face was square, with a broad, flat nose indicative of some Indian blood in his lineage. His hands looked too large and blunt to perform surgery, although Father Geraldo had said that he was well respected as a surgeon.

"Regrettably, I do not remember signing such a document."

She uttered a despairing cry. "You must!"

"Please understand," he said hastily, "those hours and days following the ambassador's abduction were the most turbulent in this country's history. There were hundreds of casualties. Our president and his family barely escaped with their lives. Anyone who had served his administration in any capacity was publicly executed. The streets ran with blood."

Lara had read the newspaper accounts from her hospital bed in Miami. She didn't doubt the accuracy of the doctor's description of the chaos.

Speaking for the first time since the doctor's arrival, Key was more skeptical. "You don't remember one little Anglo girl among all those other corpses?"

Soto shook his bald head. "I am sorry, señor. I know it comes as a disappointment."

Lara took several deep breaths to fortify herself, then extended her right hand to him. "Thank you, Dr. Soto. I apologize for the theatrical way in which we approached you."

"I understand the necessity for caution. Your husband was unpopular with the rebels who are now in power."

"My husband represented the United States, and they had taken a position that favored President Escávez. Randall was only doing his job."

"I understand," Soto said quietly. "Nevertheless, I can almost guarantee that the families and friends of men who were tortured and killed by Escávez's henchmen will not be so generous in their thinking."

"Can we trust you to keep your mouth shut about this?" Key asked abruptly.

"*Por supuesto.* I would not betray you."

"If you do, you'll regret it."

Father Geraldo stepped between them. "I think we'd better leave Dr. Soto to his duties."

"Yes," Lara agreed. "There's no point in involving you further."

Father Geraldo gave the doctor his blessing and asked forgiveness for tricking him. Dr. Soto assured the priest that he understood. As Lara moved toward the door, Soto laid a hand on her arm. "I am sorry, Señora Porter. I wish I could have been of more help. *Buena suerte.*"

"*Muchas gracias.*"

Replacing the scarf over her head, she followed Father Geraldo from the doctor's office. Key brought up the rear as the priest led them out the way they had come in, through a wing of the hospital that had been closed because the unstable government could no longer afford to keep it open. He knew the layout of the hospital very well, having spent years visiting sick parishioners there.

They emerged undetected. Lara was surprised to see that darkness had fallen while they'd been inside. Not that she cared whether it was daylight or dark. She could barely muster the energy to place one foot in front of the other and probably would have stopped dead in her tracks if Key hadn't herded her along.

After having her hopes raised by the discovery of Ashley's death certificate, the outcome of her meeting with Dr. Soto was a crushing disappointment. Fate had trampled her, and she lacked the initiative to continue.

She still planned to return to the embassy in the hopes of finding Emilio Sánchez Perón. First, however, she must rest. Rest would boost her morale. She knew that once she'd slept several hours, reviewed her options, and charted another course of action, she'd feel much more optimistic.

That was the pep talk she gave herself as she trudged toward the jeep.

She never made it that far. Key dragged her behind a dumpster at the rear of the hospital. "Pst! Padre!"

Father Geraldo turned. "What is it?"

"There's no reason for the cloak-and-dagger act," Lara complained. "No one spotted us."

Key motioned Father Geraldo closer. "What time will Soto be leaving the hospital?"

He shrugged. "I have no idea. Why?"

"Our doctor friend is lying."

"But I've known him— "

"Trust me on this, padre," Key interrupted. "You might be a good judge when it comes to saints, but I know sinners. He's lying."

"How?" Lara asked

"I don't know, but I want to find out. He said he didn't remember your daughter. That's bullshit," Key declared. "That ambush made headlines all over the world. I was in Chad when it happened and it made the front pages there. It started a revolution, yes. Bodies passed through the city morgue like shit through a greased goose, yes. He might have been up to his armpits in corpses, but no way could he forget signing a death certificate for a U.S. ambassador's daughter killed in a bloody shootout. No way, José."

It was amazing how instinctively and completely Lara trusted Key. With the dark scruffy beard, he looked like the meanest of desperadoes, a man who attracted danger and thrived on it. His startling blue eyes moved like quicksilver as they surveyed the surrounding buildings. They didn't miss the smallest movement. His voice was quiet, urgent, compelling, and convincing.

"What are we going to do?" she asked.

Her unqualified trust must have silently communicated itself to him, because his alert eyes stopped their surveillance and fell on her.

"We wait."

At the sound of the fatal click, Dr. Soto came to a sudden standstill. Key thrust the barrel of the Beretta behind the doctor's ear and yanked his left arm behind his back, shoving his hand up between his shoulder blades.

"If you make a peep, you're history." His voice was a hiss in the darkness, so low it could have been mistaken for the rustle of leaves stirred by the faint breeze. "Walk."

The doctor didn't argue. He moved toward the jeep that rolled out from the deep shadows of the alleyway. Behind the wheel sat Father Geraldo, looking both excited and apprehensive. Lara was balanced on the edge of the backseat, gripping the seat in front of her, watching as Key approached with their hostage.

"Frisk him, Lara." She jumped to the ground and ran her hands over the outside of the doctor's clothing.

"I am unarmed," he said with dignity.

"You're also a goddamn liar," Key said. With a nod, Lara confirmed that the doctor wasn't concealing a weapon, then returned to her place in the jeep. "Get in."

Soto did as Key ordered and climbed into the front seat. Key vaulted in to sit beside Lara, digging the muzzle of the gun into the hollow at the base of the doctor's skull. Father Geraldo put the jeep in gear and they took off.

"Where are you taking me? For God's sake, please . . . I don't know why you are doing this. What do you want from me?"

"The truth." Lara leaned forward so she could be heard. "You know more than you're telling about my daughter's death, don't you?"

Key nudged the back of Soto's head with the pistol. "No!" the doctor protested in a high, thin voice. "I swear I know nothing. As God is my witness,"

"Careful," Key warned. "There's a man of God present who tells Him everything."

"I cannot help you," he whimpered.

"Cannot or will not?" Lara asked.

"Cannot."

"That's not true. What do you know that you're holding back?"

"Mrs. Porter, I implore you— "

"Tell me," she insisted.

Father Geraldo drove down a dirt lane that ended in a remote clearing above the river. The river began as a clear, rushing stream in the mountains, but by the time it had snaked its way down through the jungle and cut a swathe through Ciudad Central, where it swept up garbage and pollutants, it emptied sludge into the ocean. He brought the jeep to a stop but kept the motor idling.

"Were you on duty at the hospital that day our car was ambushed?" Lara asked.

He tried to nod but couldn't because of the revolver. "Sí," he whispered in fear.

"Did you see my daughter?"

"Sí. She was critically wounded."

Lara swallowed, remembering the amount of blood gushing from the wound on Ashley's neck. The carotid artery had no doubt been severed. She closed her eyes in an attempt to stamp out that mental picture. Later she could grieve. Now, she didn't have the luxury of time. "What happened to my daughter's body?"

"Father," Soto pleaded, rolling his eyes toward the priest, "I beg you to intercede. I have a family to protect. God knows my heart goes out to Mrs. Porter, but I am afraid of reprisals."

"You damn sure should be." Key spoke in a near growl.

"El Corazón isn't here, but I am. We haven't come a thousand miles to fuck around with you. Tell her what she wants to know, or you're no use to us. ¿*Comprende*? In other words, you're dispensable."

Lara didn't approve of Key's fear tactics. They had agreed that he would use them only when all else failed, or—and this was doubtful—when they became convinced that Soto was telling the truth and that he didn't know anything about Ashley's burial. She was reasonably sure he wouldn't make good on his implied threats, but hopefully Soto would fall for them before she had an opportunity to put it to test.

"Padre?" Soto begged, his voice cracking as he glanced fearfully at the murky, polluted waters below. "¿*Por favor*?"

Father Geraldo crossed himself, bowed his head, and began to pray softly. He couldn't have been more convincing.

"I'm tired of this shit." Key jumped over the side of the jeep and motioned with his head for the doctor to alight.

"*Cementerio del Sagrado Corazón*," he blurted.

"Sacred Heart. She's buried there?" Lara asked.

"*Sí*." The doctor expelled his breath and seemed to deflate like a balloon. "During those early days of fighting, they took most of the casualties there. Take me there, and I will show you."

Father Geraldo stopped praying and put the jeep in reverse. Key climbed back in. He had a warning for the doctor: "You'd better not be bullshitting us."

"No, señor. I swear it on the heads of my children."

The cemetery was located on the other side of the city. It would have been a long drive under normal circumstances. The distance was increased by the circuitous route the priest took. He doubled back several times to make certain they weren't being followed. To avoid roadblocks and military convoys, he zigzagged through seemingly abandoned neighborhoods where streetlights remained dark and only alley cats were brave enough to show themselves.

Lara's nerves were jangling by the time they reached the cemetery gates. "It's locked!"

"But it's a low wall. Come on." Key was the first one out of the jeep. He motioned Soto down. "Keep both hands on your head. If you lower them, I'll shoot you."

"You cannot shoot me or you will not know where to look for the girl's grave."

The bluff didn't work on Key. He flashed a grin that showed up extraordinarily white against his black beard. "I didn't say I'd kill you. I just said I'd shoot you. For instance in the hand. You wouldn't be able to change a Band-Aid, much less do surgery." He stopped smiling. "Now move."

The four of them had no difficulty getting over the low stone wall. Soto indicated the direction in which they should go. They didn't risk using a flashlight. There was no moon, so they had to pick their way carefully around tombstones and over uneven ground.

The cemetery was situated on a hillside and offered a commanding view of the city with the mountains rising behind it. It had not escaped the effects of war. The grounds were no longer maintained. Very few graves appeared to have been tended since the revolution began. It broke Lara's heart to think of her daughter being buried in this desolate place that was overrun with weeds and inhabited by jungle reptiles that slithered unseen in the underbrush.

Ashley won't be here for long, she vowed silently.

Indeed, Dr. Soto had reached a shelf of land that rimmed a wide depression. There he stopped. Moving slowly so he wouldn't incite Key to make good his threat, he turned toward Lara. She was taken aback by the ghoulish appearance of his eyes until she realized that the wavering sheen in them was actually unshed tears.

"I would not have had you know this, but you insisted," he said. "It would have been much better if you had not forced me to bring you here. Better yet that you had forgotten what happened to you in Montesangre and stayed in America."

"What the hell are you jabbering about?" Key demanded.

Lara, more mystified than angry, moved closer to the edge and looked down into the depression. It was about twenty yards in diameter, roughly round in shape, and resembled a meteor crater, although vegetation had cropped up in spots.

Still perplexed, she turned to Father Geraldo. He was staring into the shallow bowl of earth. His shoulders were hunched forward, and his arms hung loosely at his sides. He had a listless grip on his flask, but he wasn't drinking from it. Seeing the depression had stupefied him and supplanted his preoccupation with rum.

Key too was staring beyond the ledge as though demanding it to offer up an explanation. Then suddenly his whole body twitched as though a string coming out the top of his head had been jerked hard. He dropped the pistol in the dirt and grabbed the doctor by the lapels of his linen suit, lifting him until his toes dangled inches from the ground.

"Are you telling us— "

"*Sí, sí.*" Key had shaken the tears from the doctor's eyes. They coursed down his face. "*Doscientos. Trescientos. ¿Quién sabe?*"

"Two hundred or three hundred what?" Lara's voice rose in panic. "Two hundred or three hundred— "

When the answer struck her, she lost her ability to breathe. Her mouth remained open, but she couldn't exhale or inhale.

Key released the doctor and rushed toward her. "Lara!"

The most bloodchilling sound she had ever heard rose above the sepulchral silence of the cemetery. At first she didn't realize that the wail had been ripped from her own throat. Spreading her arms wide, she flung herself toward the rim of the depression and would have plunged to the bottom if Key's extended arm hadn't caught her at the waist. She bent double over it. He hauled her backward, but she fought him with the abnormal strength of the demented.

Finally managing to tear herself free, she crawled toward the edge, inexorably, clawing at the earth, uprooting clumps of grass, and all the while making that unnatural keening sound.

"No! God no! Please no! *Ashley!* Oh, Jesus, no."

Dr. Soto was blathering about the day the mass grave was ordered. It had been dug by bulldozers specifically to accommodate the enormous number of casualties. Morticians couldn't keep up with the demand, he said. When the morgue had filled to capacity, they'd begun placing cadavers wherever they could find space. Hundreds had died in the streets, where their bodies had been left to decompose. It became a health hazard to the living. There were outbreaks of typhoid and other contagious diseases. The rebel commanders dealt with the problem the most expeditious way they could devise.

"Lara, stop this!" Key's hands were on her shoulders, trying to pull her up, but she dug her fingers into the earth and wouldn't let go.

"I am sorry. So sorry," Dr. Soto repeated.

She understood now why he had been reluctant to tell her about this mass grave. He had feared reprisals, but not from El Corazón. From her.

"Leave me alone." As Key tried to pull her away from the brink of the macabre pit, her fingernails left bloody tracks down his forearm. He grunted in pain but only redoubled his efforts to bring her under control.

"Lara." Father Geraldo knelt beside her, speaking gently. "God in His infinite wisdom— "

"*NO!*" she screamed. "Don't talk to me about God!"

Then in the next breath she entreated the deity for mercy.

"Who did this?" Key's hard hands were still bracketing her shoulders but he had fixed a murderous glare on Dr. Soto. "Who ordered that little babies be shoveled into a mass grave? Good God, are you people barbarians? I want a name. Who gave the order? I want that motherfucker's name."

"I am sorry, señor, but it is impossible to know who gave the order for a mass burial. Everything— " Dr. Soto's next utterance was a soft gasp. He dropped to his knees, clutching his chest, then collapsed onto his side.

Father Geraldo was into his third Hail Mary when he pitched forward and landed flat on his face in the damp soil near Lara's right hand.

In fascination and horror she watched a dark pool form beneath his head.

"Christ!"

Key reached for the Beretta he'd dropped earlier but wasn't fast enough. For his failed effort he got a boot in his ribs and went down with a grimace and a groan.

Crabbing backward, Lara tried frantically to move away from the gelatinous mess that had once been Father Geraldo's head. She was yanked to her feet so swiftly that her teeth crashed together.

"*Buenas noches*, *señora*. We meet again."

It was the guerrilla leader from the roadblock outside Ciudad Central. Ricardo.

The military transport truck hit a chuckhole. Lara was thrown against the steel side of the "deuce and a half," which was the American slang for the tonnage of the truck. They'd been traveling for hours.

Almost before her brain had registered that they were surrounded by armed men, her hands had been roughly tied behind her. They were still bound, making it impossible to maintain her balance as the truck bounced along. She'd been thrown from side to side so many times, she would be covered with bruises. If she lived.

That was still open to speculation.

Father Geraldo was dead. Dr. Soto had died in midsentence. Key was very much alive. Thank God. He had kept up a litany of abusive curses as they were dragged from the cemetery and forced into the truck. Several soldiers had been riffling through their belongings left in the jeep. One had been fiddling with the camera and lenses in the camera bag. Key shouted at him. "Keep your goddamn hands off that!"

Like Lara, his hands were tied behind him, but he rushed forward and kicked the bag out of the soldier's hands. The hotheaded soldier cracked the butt of his pistol against Key's temple. Key staggered and dropped to his knees, but he wasn't cowed. He looked at the soldier and, with blood dripping from the wound on the side of his head, grinned and said, "Your mother got you by fucking a jackass."

Whether he understood English, the soldier interpreted the comment as an insult and lunged for Key. Before he could get retribution, Ricardo ordered the younger man to get them into the truck.

There was some discussion among them as to whether they should bring the jeep along or leave it at the cemetery gate. Ricardo decided to let one of the guerrillas follow them in it.

Lara and Key were hoisted into the back of the truck. Their belongings, including the camera bag and her doctor's bag, were tossed in after them. The soldiers climbed aboard, then lowered and latched the canvas canopy. They could see nothing, but their captors insisted that they be blindfolded. Naturally, Key didn't submit. It took three men holding him down before they could secure the dirty bandanna over his eyes.

Lara knew that physical resistance would be futile, but

her eyes conveyed the full extent of her contempt before she was likewise blindfolded.

The road was virtually impassable. The soldiers were unwashed. In the airless confines of the truck, the smell was overpowering. She was thirsty but knew that any request for water would go unheeded. Her butt was sore, as were her arms and legs. The bindings around her wrists were beginning to chafe.

She wanted to know where they were taking them and why. How much longer until they reached their destination? Did they even have a specific destination? When they reached it, what then?

She conserved the strength it would take to ask. No one would answer her. They had attempted to communicate only once. Key had been punished for it.

"Lara?" His throat had sounded as raspy and dry as hers. "You okay?"

"Key?"

"Thank God." He sighed. "Hang in there and— "

"*Silencio!*"

"Fuck you."

There was a scuffle, then a moan, and Key hadn't spoken to her since.

She tried self-hypnosis to remove her mind and body from the present situation. But each time she tired to conjure up mental pictures of a desert sunset, or a rolling tide, or drifting clouds, her focus returned to the mass grave in the cemetery where her daughter would be interred forever.

Accomplishing what she had set out to do was an impossibility. Why then didn't she try to escape, and let a soldier's bullet be her deliverance? Father Geraldo and Dr. Soto had felt no pain. Instant extinction. How lovely.

Why did she still have the will to survive?

No, it was stronger than will. It was a resolve to see the ones responsible for such an atrocity punished. Burying the daughter of a U.S. ambassador in such an unspeakable manner violated universally acknowledged human rights. If she lived, she would see to it that the world knew about the disgrace.

Lara had dealt with many terminally ill patients. Until tonight she had not understood their unwillingness to surrender life. How could one hang on, stubbornly clinging to life, knowing that the situation was hopeless? She'd often contemplated the human spirit's refusal to accept death. Now she understood that one could survive even the worst possible circumstances.

The survival instinct was stronger than she had believed. It preserved life, even when the mind had given up. If that were not so, she would have died upon seeing that mass grave and learning that her baby girl was buried there. That innate determination to live sustained her through the long night.

She must have dozed because she came awake when the truck ground to a halt and she heard sounds of activity outside the truck. She smelled wood smoke and cooking food.

"Here already?" Key quipped sarcastically.

She was brought to her feet and lifted out of the truck. Her limbs were stiff and sore. She stumbled when she was shoved forward, but the fresh air on her skin and in her lungs was welcome. She breathed deeply and tried to work circulation back into her legs.

Suddenly the blindfold was ripped off. Ricardo was standing close, smiling broadly. "*¡Bienvenido!*" She recoiled from his rancid breath. "El Corazón is anxious to welcome his special guests."

She was surprised at his command of English. "I have plenty to say to El Corazón, too."

He laughed. "A woman with a sense of humor. I like that."

"I wasn't being funny."

"Ah, but you were, señora. Very funny."

Just then a woman dressed in dirty fatigue pants and a sweat-stained tank top launched herself against him. After an embarrassingly passionate kiss during which he openly fondled her, she purred,

"Come inside. I have food for you."

"Where is El Corazón?" he asked.

"Waiting inside."

Still groping each other, they ambled toward a crude shack and climbed the rickety steps to a shallow porch and a curtained doorway. The other soldiers were being similarly greeted by women in the camp and given bowls of food dished from a communal cooking pot suspended over the campfire. They drank fresh coffee from tin cups. Lara would have settled for a drink of water. Her lip was still tender and swollen.

Two men with semiautomatic weapons were standing guard over her and Key. When Lara first saw him, she gasped. He was sitting on the ground near her, but the guards stood between them. The wound on his temple had coagulated. It looked nasty and needed to be cleaned and disinfected, probably sutured. She wondered if she'd be given access to her doctor's bag, but thought not.

His eyes were ringed with shadows of fatigue, as she knew hers also must be. His clothes, like hers, were filthy and perspiration-stained. It was barely daylight, so the sun wasn't yet a factor, but the humidity was so high that a mist as dense as fog clung to the tops of the trees in the jungle that surrounded the clearing.

Key was looking at her with a stare that penetrated, but she didn't need this silent communiqué to realize how precarious their situation was. While he had her attention, he cut his eyes toward the camera bag. One of the soldiers had unloaded it and their other bags from the truck and dropped them near where she stood.

Lara cocked her head inquisitively, knowing he was trying to tell her something but unable to decipher what.

Then he mouthed, "Magnum." She glanced quickly at

the camera bag. When she looked back at him, he nodded almost imperceptibly.

"Senōra, senōr." Ricardo swaggered from behind the curtained doorway and propped himself against one of the posts supporting the thatched roof. "You are very fortunate. El Corazón will see you now."

A respectful silence descended over the camp. Those who were eating set aside their food. All eyes turned to the front of the shack. Even the children who'd been chasing one another and dodging toy machine-gun bullets ceased their play. The rebel soldiers stopped trying to impress the women with exaggerated tales of their exploits. Everyone's attention was focused on the porch of the shack.

Ceremoniously, the curtain was drawn aside, and a man emerged. Lara sank to her knees. In a voice almost soundless, she exclaimed, "Emilio!"

Chapter Twenty-Two

Excuse me, Miss Janellen?"

At the sound of Bowie's voice she almost jumped out of her skin, but she gave no sign of it. With the cool condescension of a Russian royal, she raised her head. "Hello, Mr. Cato. What can I do for you?"

He was standing in the doorway that connected the shop with the tiny office in its rear. The ugly, ill-formed building was quiet and, except for the two of them, deserted.

Bowie had brought in with him the scent of outdoors. The first hint of autumn was in the air, and she could smell it on his clothes. His hair had been mashed flat by his hat, the brim of which he was nervously threading through his fingers. His lips were chapped. She looked at him with concealed yearning.

"I was just wondering if you'd heard anything from your brother and Dr. Mallory?"

"No," she replied, feeling a pang of guilt. It was selfish of her to be so wrapped up in her heartbreak over Bowie when their lives could be in danger. Key had promised to call home if he was able, but there had been no communication from him since their departure three days ago. Janellen was sick with worry, and, although, her mother hadn't admitted it, she was, too. She stayed in her bedroom except at mealtimes, when it seemed that even polite conversation was an effort.

"That's too bad," Bowie said. "I was hoping they'd be

on their way back by now." He fiddled with a loose straw in the brim of his hat.

"Was there something else, Mr. Cato?"

"Uh, yes, ma'am. My paycheck. It wasn't in my box this morning. Any other week, I wouldn't bother you about it, but my rent's due tomorrow."

Knowing full well that he spoke the truth, she looked toward the empty pigeonhole labeled with his name. "My goodness, I apologize for the oversight, Mr. Cato. I must have left your paycheck in the safe."

The official company safe was a monstrosity that easily outweighed three pianos. It dominated one corner of the cramped room. The black steel facade was ornately trimmed with gold swirls and curlicues. It dated back to the days when her grandfather had paid his roughnecks in cash.

As she moved toward it, Janellen felt Bowie's eyes on her, and it was unnerving. Thankfully, the combination to the safe was second nature to her. She opened it and withdrew his check from the drawer where she'd intentionally left it that morning. Since he hadn't taken the initiative to approach her since the night they'd embraced in the kitchen, the night following Jody's seizure, she'd made it necessary for him to seek her out.

He'd fled during a thunderstorm, preferring the cold company of lightning and torrential rain to the warmth of her arms. Bowie might have been disappointed in her kisses, might have been disgusted by her eager response to his caresses, but she was not going to let him simply ignore her and pretend that they hadn't shared some degree of intimacy.

"There you are, Mr. Cato." As she handed him the check, she was careful not to let her fingers touch his. "I'm sorry I overlooked it."

She resumed her seat behind the desk and returned to the paperwork she'd been doing when he came in. Her heart was thudding so strongly and so loudly that she could count each beat against her eardrums. Whatever happened next was up to him. The next few moments were critical. If he turned and left without another word it would break her heart. Her nonchalance was a pose she'd affected to hide her despair. If that tempestuous kiss at her kitchen sink was the extent of their love affair, she'd just as soon stop breathing.

Ten seconds ticked by. Twenty. Thirty.

Bowie shuffled his feet.

Janellen waited, making small notations in red ink on the invoice while her entire future and self-image dangled by a thread.

"How, uh, how come you've stopped calling me Bowie?"

Janellen looked up, feigning surprise to find that he was still there. She pretended to ponder her answer. "I didn't think we were on a first-name basis any longer."

"Why's that?"

"When two people address each other by first names, it implies friendship. Friends don't avoid each other. Friends call, drop by, pass the time of day together, make a point to see each other. Friends wave when they drive past; they don't turn their heads and pretend not to see." This last referred to the day before. He'd deliberately ignored her when they'd accidentally met on Texas Street.

"Now, Miss Janellen, I know you thought— "

"Even former friends don't pretend that the other person no longer exists." Her voice began to quaver and for that she hated herself. Whatever the outcome, she had vowed not to cry in front of him.

"Friends don't act like they've never been . . . friendly. Like they've never . . . Oh!" To her mortification, tears filled her eyes. She stood and turned her back to him, cramming a tissue beneath her nose.

"I'm no good at this," she said mournfully, blotting her eyes. "I can't play games like other women. That trick with your paycheck was stupid and juvenile. I know you saw right through it. I just didn't know any other way to force you to see me alone."

She turned to face him, knowing that she looked her worst. She didn't cry prettily like the actresses in movies. When she cried, the whites of her eyes turned pink, her nose turned red, and her complexion got blotchy.

"I'm sorry, Bowie. I know this must be terribly embarrassing for you. Feel free to go. You don't have to stay. I'm fine. Honest."

But he didn't move. In fact, if there was anything redeemable in the last couple of minutes, it was that he appeared as miserable as she. "Truth is, Miss Janellen, I'm the one who's sorry that I put you through a scene like this."

She reasoned that since she had already made a fool of herself and had nothing more to lose, she might as well get to the bottom of it. "Why have you been avoiding me?"

"'Cause I didn't think you'd want to see me after . . . Shit." Mumbling the expletive, he turned his head away. But when his gaze landed on a voluptuous calendar nude, he hastily looked back at Janellen. "I didn't think you'd want to see me after what I did to you. I didn't show you any respect, and I do respect you a hell of a lot."

Her cheeks grew warm as she recalled his hand moving beneath her skirt, clutching her bottom with what she'd thought was uncontrollable lust. It had been shocking, yes, but thrilling.

"Well, I wasn't behaving very respectfully myself, was I?" she asked a bit breathlessly. "But I assumed that our respect for each other had been well established. I thought that our friendship had moved to another level. I thought you might want to, uh, maybe, you know, to fuck."

His hat landed on the top of the desk. He dropped into the chair facing it and planted his elbows among the invoices, holding his head between his hands. His cheeks puffed out, then his lips pursed as he blew out a gust of breath.

"I know that's the right word," Janellen said timidly. "Key says it all the time to mean . . . that."

"Yes, ma'am, it surely is the right word. It gets the message across, all right."

"Well then? Was I wrong?"

Bowie massaged the back of his neck. After what seemed to Janellen an eternity, he raised his head. "Fact of the matter is, it isn't the right word. If that's what I wanted, we could have done it on your kitchen linoleum. But I think too much of you to toss up your skirts and go at you like you're no better than a ten-dollar whore. See, Miss Janellen, you're quality and I'm trash, and nothing's ever going to change that."

"You're not trash!"

"Compared to you I am. Besides which, I'm an ex-con."

"You served time for doing something that needed to be done. In my opinion, the beast you assaulted deserved prison, not you."

He smiled indulgently at her vehemence. "Unfortunately, the state of Texas didn't agree." Turning serious again, he said, "Neither would the people of Eden Pass. If you were to take up with me, how do you think folks would react?"

"I don't care." She rounded the desk and knelt in front of the chair in which he sat, trustingly placing her hands on his thighs. "Bowie, all my life I've lived according to what other people wanted for me. I've done everything that was expected of me and nothing that would be looked upon with disfavor. But not too long ago, Key reminded me that life is passing me by." She inched closer. "I didn't realize how right he was until you kissed me. Then, for the first time in my life, I experienced a sense of bursting free. I don't want to grow old and then discover that I missed the best things life has to offer because I was afraid of offending someone else. For thirty-three years I've been the prim and proper Miss Janellen, and frankly I'm bored with her. The only fun and excitement she's ever had was with you.

"So what if the hometown folks raise their eyebrows over us? They've been tsking for years over my spinsterhood, pitying me because I didn't have any beaux. Between pity and disapproval, I choose disapproval." Taking a deep breath, she added, "If you like me—even a little—don't back off because you're afraid of damaging my reputation."

"If I like you even a little," he repeated, smiling his sad smile. He pulled her up and settled her on his lap. "I like you so much my heart goes to aching every time I think about you, which is all the time."

He took her hand and stroked the back of it, his touch light, as though he feared breaking the fragile bones. "Folks aren't going to cotton to us being a pair, Janellen. You stand to lose so much. Me, I got nothing to lose. No money, no name, no family or friends or a position in the community. But you could be hurt bad."

She laid her fingers against his lips. "I won't be hurt, Bowie."

"Yes, you would. I'd hurt you, and I can't hardly bear to think about it."

Their faces were very close. His eyes were dark and intense, and she knew that he was no longer referring to the effect that their being together would have on her social standing. He was talking about the physical pain their coupling would cause her.

She whispered, "I wish for that hurt. I wish for it right now."

She fell against him softly. A low moan escaped her as his arms enfolded her. She tilted her head back against his biceps and welcomed his urgent kiss. They kissed hotly and hungrily, their mouths melding.

He stroked the side of her face, trailed a finger along the line of her jaw, touched her neck. Between fervent kisses Janellen whispered encouragement. When his hand moved to her breast and gingerly covered it, she lovingly murmured his name.

"I can't go on with that or I'll do what I swore I wouldn't do."

She opened her eyes and sat up straight. "What are you saying, Bowie?"

"That I'm not going to fuck you." She uttered a small sound of protest and dismay. He hastened to add, "What I want to do is make love to you. I want to do it proper, on a bed with sweet-smelling sheets, in a place that's clean and worthy of you."

She relaxed and laughed softly. "That doesn't matter to me, Bowie."

"It matters to me. I still think I'm the worst thing that's ever happened to you, but you're the best thing that's ever happened in my life, and that's for damn sure. I won't treat you like any old gal I could get off with."

While Janellen was disappointed that he'd stopped the foreplay, her heart filled with tenderness.

"I'm fairly certain you're a virgin." He glanced up and she nodded. "I can't imagine why that is, but I'm damned glad no other man beat me to you. It's an honor I don't take lightly, so when it happens, I want it to be like the first time for me, too. And in a way it will be. I've never done it with a woman I'd share my toothbrush with."

She giggled and nuzzled his shoulder. "Will you share your toothbrush with me?"

In reply he kissed her, pressing his tongue deep into her mouth. "I'll be looking for a place where we can go," he said hoarsely when the kiss ended.

"Your trailer," she suggested enthusiastically. "I'll come tonight after supper."

"That trailer is fine for me, but it's not fit for you to set foot in."

"Bowie!"

He stubbornly shook his head. "It's got to be someplace special. When I find it, you'll be the first to know."

"But when?"

"I don't know yet." His eyes burned with desire. "As soon as possible."

"Until then, you can come to the house every night after Mama goes to bed."

"I'd never sleep with you—sneaky like that—under your mama's roof."

"I didn't mean we'd sleep together, just be together. I can't leave Mama alone. Maydale would get suspicious if I asked her to stay late every night. I'd soon run out of excuses to be away from the house. If we're going to see each other, you have to come there."

He frowned. "That's tempting fate, Janellen. If we take chances like that, something terrible could happen."

"That's silly. Nothing's going to happen."

"Your mama could catch us together. Then the shit would hit the fan."

He was right on that score. But even her mother's disapproval wouldn't keep Janellen from seeing him. "We'll make doubly sure we don't get caught until we're ready to make our 'friendship' public." She grinned happily. "I'm ready to tell the whole world."

"I'd postpone that if I were you." He was as grim as she was ebullient. "Sooner or later, something's bound to go wrong. I'm unlucky like that."

"Everything's changing for both of us."

"Janellen." He held her face between his hands again and peered closely into her eyes. "Are you sure about this? Are you absolutely sure? 'Cause being with me isn't going to be a picnic for you. In fact, it's likely to be hell."

She covered his hands with hers. "Being without you would be hell. I'd sooner die. I love you."

"I love you too. And you can believe it or not, but I've never said that to another living soul."

They kissed again, and she wore him down until he gave her his promise to come to her back door at midnight that night.

Heather Winston had absolutely no interest in the search for the Northwest Passage. Irritably, she set aside her American history textbook and gave her mind over to the much more important matter of keeping Tanner Hoskins in line.

She was on duty at the check-in desk of The Green Pine Motel, as she was every weekday night from seven till ten. It wasn't hard work. It allowed her time to do homework and study for exams. But it also kept her from spending time with Tanner. Between cheerleading practice, the football team, and all their other extracurricular activities, they had very little time to be together except on weekends.

She didn't like it any better than he did, but he complained the most. "Lately your mother's got you on such a short leash, it's hardly worth going out at all."

Heather was afraid he would soon tire of their situation and seek the companionship of a girl with a lighter schedule and a more lenient curfew. Just that morning she'd caught him flirting with Mimsy Parker at her locker between second and third periods. Everybody had seen them together. By the time school was dismissed for the day, it was all over campus that Heather was on the verge of being dicked.

She wouldn't have it.

Recently Tanner had been elected student body president. He'd scored two touchdowns last Friday night. He was the most popular boy at school this year. She wasn't about to let Mimsy Parker have him.

As she was devising various methods of keeping him faithful, a bowlegged man entered through the automatic doors, removed his hat, and surveyed the lobby.

"Hi. Can I help you?"

"Evenin", Miss Winston."

"You know me?"

"I've seen you with your folks. My name's Bowie Cato."

She recognized his name. He was the ex-convict now working for the Tacketts. Heather experienced a thrill of fear. Was he about to rob her? His darting eyes were wary and nervous. She was the only one on duty in the lobby. A waitress and a short-order cook were keeping the restaurant open, but they wouldn't be of any help to her if Bowie Cato had armed robbery and murder in mind.

"You might think this is a peculiar request," he said, after self-consciously clearing his throat. "But, well, I got, uh, kinfolks coming to spend the weekend. My trailer isn't big enough to sleep them and me, too, and anyway, these kin are kinda persnickety. So what I'm looking for is a place for them to stay. One night, maybe two."

"I'll be happy to make a reservation for you, Mr. Cato. Will they be here this weekend?"

"No, no, I don't need a reservation. What I mean is, I'm not sure what day they'll be getting here. They're sorta unpredictable."

"Oh." Heather was at a loss. He appeared harmless. She saw no sign of a weapon, although he could have a gun concealed inside his denim jacket, she supposed. He wasn't menacing, but she couldn't account for his jitters. "When you find out their date of arrival, you could call us and reserve a room. This time of year, we usually have vacancies."

"Yes, ma'am." Seeming reluctant to go, he looked through the brochures and state maps in the cardboard rack on the counter. "Uh, actually, I wondered if it would be possible for me to see a room. Like preview it, check it out. Your nicest room," he added quickly. "They like things fancy."

Heather laughed. "You want to see if our rooms are fancy enough for your relatives?"

"Meaning no offense, Miss Winston." He raised his hands and looked so disarming that Heather felt silly for being afraid of him. "These folks are like that. Uppity. Always wanting everything just so. I promised to check out the motel situation before they commit to a visit."

Heather moved to the drawer where keys were filed according to the room number. "The honeymoon suite is our nicest room."

"The honeymoon suite? I like the sound of that."

Heather put a sign on the counter that said BACK IN TEN MINUTES and hid her smile as she motioned him through a pair of wide glass doors. He didn't have relatives coming to visit any more than she had wings. He was planning a rendezvous with a lady friend. It was kind of sweet, Heather thought, the way he was making special plans for it.

"The suite is convenient to the swimming pool." She called his attention to it as they walked through a landscaped courtyard.

"Bit nippy for a swim."

"It's heated year-round."

"No foolin'?" He glanced dubiously at the water.

"No fooling. That pool is my daddy's pride and joy. My mother talked him into installing it when they expanded and added this new wing. But it was Daddy's idea to heat it. The honeymoon suite was also my mother's idea. It's not as elaborate as ones you'd find in Dallas or Houston hotels, but it's pretty. Here we are."

She unlocked the door for him and stood aside. He hesitated on the threshold. "If you feel uneasy coming inside with me, Miss Winston, I can take a look-see by myself."

His eyes were so apologetic and earnest that Heather would have followed him into a dark alley wearing all Darcy's diamonds. "After you, Mr. Cato."

The "suite" was decorated in mint and peach, the quality of materials a notch above what was used in the other rooms. It had a sitting room and a bedroom with a king-size bed. The bathtub had a built-in whirlpool. Otherwise it was standard motel fare. Heather wouldn't want to spend *her* wedding night in it, but she supposed it would seem luxurious to the hicks in Eden Pass.

Bowie Cato nodded appreciatively to every amenity she pointed out, but remained noncommittal. "Where does that go?" he asked, indicating a door on the far side of the bedroom.

"The parking lot. If a guest wants to rent just the bedroom, we lock the door that connects to the parlor."

"Hmm. So you can come into the bedroom using the parking-lot door without having to go through the lobby and around the pool?"

"That's right," she answered, suppressing another grin. Mr. Cato was having a secret affair. "The TV in the bedroom has a VCR, so you can bring your own movies to watch."

"Oh, I doubt we'll be watching— "

He broke off when he realized that he'd given himself away. Embarrassed, his ears turned red and he swallowed hard. She smiled to let him know that his secret was safe with her. "Like doctors and lawyers, people in the hotel business are very discreet."

"Yes, ma'am. Well, I think I've seen all I need to see. Thank you kindly. Can I go out through this door?" He moved to the one that opened directly onto the parking lot.

"I'll lock it behind you. Should I make a reservation for you?"

"Not tonight, thanks. I'll be in touch when, uh, a date's been set. Is that okay?"

"Sure."

Still looking sheepish, he replaced his hat and waved goodbye. Heather locked the suite and returned to the lobby. As far as she could tell, no one had been there during her absence, nor had the search for the Northwest Passage grown more interesting. She couldn't concentrate for thinking about Tanner. He'd told her he would be at home studying tonight, but was he?

On impulse, she dialed his number, asked his father if she could speak with him, and was relieved when Ollie told her to hold on while he called Tanner to the phone.

"Hi, it's me. Whachadoin'?"

"Studying history."

"Me, too. It sucks." She twirled the phone cord. "I'm sorry I totally bitched you out after school today."

"It's okay."

Heather could tell by his tone of voice that it wasn't. "Everyone was saying— "

"Don't believe everything you hear."

That was a little too glib a response, she thought. Why wasn't he denouncing the rumors and denying any interest in Mimsy Parker? *I'm losing him*, she thought in panic. She knew she'd never live it down. "Tanner, why don't you come drive me home when I get off at ten? Please? I want to see you."

"Don't you have your car?"

Since when did he need an excuse to see her? "I can tell my folks that it wouldn't start, so I called you."

"I guess I could."

"Okay." She consulted the clock. "I'll see you in thirty minutes. Unless you want to come now and keep me company until the night clerk gets here."

"I'll be there at ten."

Peeved, Heather hung up. She used the remaining thirty minutes of her shift to primp. The reflection in her compact mirror was reassuring. Mimsy Parker might have boobs the size of cantaloupes, but Heather still had the best hair, the best clothes, the best smile, the best eyes. Nor were her boobs anything to scoff at. Any bigger and they'd sag like Mimsy's in a few years.

Anyway, possession was nine-tenths of the law. Tanner was still hers. She just needed to guarantee that she kept him.

The night clerk, a pimpled geek who had a mad crush on her, arrived a few minutes early. When Tanner pulled his car into the porte cochere, in order not to appear overanxious she pretended to be busy behind the desk with the geek. After letting him wait a full five minutes, she joined him in his car.

"He's so dumb!" she exclaimed in exasperation as she slid into the passenger seat. "Honestly! He's in the National Honor Society but hopeless when it comes to common sense. Hi." She leaned across the console and kissed his cheek.

"Hi."

Heather pretended that the spat had never taken place and that Mimsy Parker didn't exist. She chatted nonstop about school and teachers, inconsequential things. "I've got to get something to wear for the homecoming game. I think Mother and I are going to Tyler Saturday to shop. If we can't find anything there, we'll go to Dallas the next Saturday. You're so lucky you don't have to worry about what you'll wear for the coronation during half-time. You'll be in your football uniform."

That was a subtle reminder that she had been nominated for homecoming queen and that he was damned lucky to be her official escort. "Your football jersey will be all muddy, and when you take off your helmet, your hair will be sweaty. You always look so sexy like that. It makes me hot just thinking about it."

When she dropped her hand into his lap, she made it appear a casual gesture. She felt his instantaneous response. *What a goose I've been*, she thought. *What an idiot!* Sex was power. Look at how much mileage her mother got out of it: all she had to do was whisper something to Fergus and look at him seductively, and she got whatever her heart desired.

From the time Heather had been old enough to recognize that kind of manipulation for what it was, she'd been scornful of it. Maybe it was time for a change of heart. Her sexuality was an unlimited and as yet untapped resource.

What was she saving it for? Why not use it? Now. When it was needed. Every other woman did. Her mother. That slut Mimsy Parker. If she wanted to keep Tanner . . .

"Stop here," she said suddenly. They were still a block from her house. "I want to talk to you for a minute."

Tanner pulled the car to the curb, killed the engine, and cut the headlights. "What about?"

She wanted to slap that surly smirk off his face. Instead, she smiled beguilingly and drew him close. "I don't really want to talk." She pressed her open mouth to his and reached for his tongue with her own.

He was taken off guard but quickly recovered. After a few tongue-twining kisses and some carefully choreographed moves, his erection was well defined behind his fly. She ran her hand up and down it, massaging.

He reached beneath her sweater and seized her breast. "What got into you?" he panted as he unsnapped the front closure of her bra.

Mimsy Parker, she thought. "I just love you so much. Oh, yes." When he lightly pinched her nipple, she placed her hand on the back of his head and guided it down to her. "Tanner, I had the best idea tonight. Listen." She outlined her plan as she slid her hand inside his jeans. "Doesn't that sound wonderful?"

"Yes. Oh, Jesus, oh God. Wait. I have a rubber. Want me to— "

"No. I want to see it."

"Faster, babe. Yes. Yes."

"Touch me, Tanner." She opened her thighs and guided his palm to her center.

After several steamy minutes of dual masturbation, he dropped her at her front walk. His eyes were still lambent, his face flushed; he was pathetically grateful and newly besotted.

Her confidence restored, Heather skipped up the steps of her house. Mimsy Parker didn't stand a snowball's chance in hell of stealing her boyfriend.

As she went inside, ready with an elaborate lie as to why Tanner had brought her home, she silently thanked that ex-con for giving her the idea that had saved her romance.

Chapter Twenty-Three

*E*l Corazón del Diablo gave his prisoners his most ingratiating smile. His eyes flickered to Key, but after one curious glance they returned to Lara. Key doubted that she realized she had sunk to her knees.

No sooner had the thought crossed Key's mind than she slowly came to her feet. "I can't believe it. Emilio, what— "

"I am no longer Emilio Sánchez Perón," he snapped, his glassy smile vanishing. "I have not been that naïve, idealistic youth in a long while. Certainly not since the revolution and your return to the United States." He almost snarled the last two words. "A nation I hold in utmost contempt."

Key hated what the young man said, but he was impressed by the manner in which he said it. He spoke fluent English without a trace of a Spanish accent, although he didn't use contractions.

The squalid backdrop made his neatness even more pronounced. He was smooth shaven and immaculately clean, not an easy condition to maintain in the middle of a jungle. His black hair had been pulled back so tightly that his head was as sleek and shiny as a bowling ball. He had a short queue at the nape of his neck. The style accented his high cheekbones, the lean angularity of his face, the hard, angry slash of his mouth. His eyeglasses had thin gold-wire frames.

Key had tangled with tough customers from all parts of the world. He couldn't recall one who had looked more chilling than Emilio Sánchez. He was slightly built, but the cold, dead quality in his eyes was symptomatic of unmitigated cruelty. The eyes of a snake.

"If you hate the United States so much, why were you working for my husband at the embassy?" Lara asked.

"My position there allowed me to receive information which others found very useful."

"In other words you were spying."

He flashed another grin. "Between you and your husband, I always considered you the more intelligent."

"You were using the embassy as a source of information. For how long?"

"From the beginning."

"You bastard."

A murmur arose from those around them who understood English. El Corazón's smile slowly dissolved, as though it were melting in the heat. "Having narrowly escaped with your life once, you were a fool to return to Montesangre, Mrs. Porter."

"I came to retrieve my daughter's remains. I wished to return them to the United States."

"You came in vain."

"I know that now. I condemn the Montesangrens who buried her in a pit." Tears formed in her eyes, but her posture was now unbowed. "God damn you all."

"You'll find it difficult to attract God's attention from here, Mrs. Porter. He hasn't listened to the people of Montesangre for decades. We no longer believe he exists."

"Is that why you found it so easy to murder Father Geraldo?"

"The drunken priest?" he said scornfully. Ricardo slapped him on the shoulder as though he'd told a joke. "He had outlived his usefulness long ago. He was merely another mouth to feed in a country of starving people."

"What about Dr. Soto? Surely he was useful to your regime."

"And also to Escávez."

"You are unforgivably wasteful. Dr. Soto was a healer. When it came to saving lives, he didn't think politically."

"Which was his downfall," El Corazón replied blandly. "In Montesangre one cannot have divided loyalties. Speaking of which," he said, his eyes moving to Key, "I'm curious about your loyalties, or lack thereof, Mr. Tackett. My curiosity alone has kept you alive."

"My life's an open book."

The soldiers guarding Key had allowed him to stand. His ribs hurt like hell. A couple of them had probably been cracked when he was kicked during the attack at the cemetery. His head hurt worse. The wound on his temple had scabbed over, but his whole cranium throbbed. He itched from having had so much sweat dry on his skin, leaving a salty, gritty residue. On top of everything else, he was hungry.

Sánchez said, "You are assisting the whore who unraveled your brother's political career. I find that peculiar. What would compel you to risk your life for her?"

"Not her. Her daughter. I believe she might have been my brother's child."

"Indeed?" El Corazón removed a folded white handkerchief from the rear pocket of his trousers and blotted his forehead. Even despots were victims of the jungle heat.

Key enjoyed knowing that the other man wasn't immune to discomfort. It made his own aches and pains more bearable. "Now that I know what happened to Ashley's body, I agree with Lara in her opinion of your country."

"Which is?" Sánchez asked as he meticulously replaced the handkerchief in his pocket.

"Montesangre is a shithole and El Corazón del Diablo is the toilet paper."

With lightning speed, Ricardo whipped a pistol from

the holster around his hips and aimed it at Key. Languorously Sánchez raised his hand. Ricardo lowered the pistol but glared at Key murderously.

"You are either very foolish or very brave," Sánchez said reflectively. "I prefer to believe you are brave. Only a brave man would have dared fly an airplane into my country without permission." He smiled his chilling, reptilian grin. "In spite of your clever piloting and the ridiculous charade enacted by you and the priest when my men stopped you on the road, we knew exactly where you landed your aircraft. I haven't seen it for myself, but Ricardo tells me that it is an excellent airplane. Well equipped. It will be useful as we continue our fight. Thank you very much for contributing it to our cause."

Key looked at Lara. When their eyes met, the best he could do was shrug helplessly. He had no tricks up his sleeve. Even if he could get to the Magnum pistol in the camera bag, he'd be gunned down before he could use it. Then they would murder Lara, too, and her death might not be so mercifully quick.

"Untie their hands."

Considering the gravity of Key's thoughts, El Corazón's brusque order came as a surprise. Ricardo voiced his objections, but Sánchez cut them short. "We are not savages. Give them water and something to eat."

Ricardo delegated the unwelcome responsibility to his subordinates, who roughly shoved Lara and Key to the ground. With heart-stopping ferocity and quickness, they severed the cords binding their hands. Key's wrists had been chafed raw. Lara's, he saw, were worse. The skin had cracked opened and she was bleeding.

They were brought crude bowls of a stew comprised mostly of rice and beans. The chunks of meat were scarce and unidentifiable. Key figured he was better off not knowing what it was. A young boy with a body as slender and tough as a jungle vine and eyes as hostile and flat as El Corazón's brought him a crockery pitcher of water. He drank greedily.

When he lowered the pitcher, he became aware of the nearby scuffle. Lara had dumped her portion of food onto the ground and was being jeered for pouring out the water that had been offered.

"How very childish, Mrs. Porter," El Corazón remarked. Someone had brought a chair for him. As he sat in the shade of the porch, two girls, one on either side, fanned him. "It surprises me that you would be so demonstrative. I remember you as a woman who displayed very little emotion."

"I would never accept your charity after what you did to Father Geraldo and Dr. Soto."

"As you wish."

She looked at Key, her irritation with him plain. He shrugged, knowing the insolent gesture would only increase her annoyance with him for eating and drinking what their captor had offered. If they stood a ghost of a chance to escape, they would need physical strength.

He wasn't as principled as Lara, maybe, but he was a hell of a lot more practical. Only moments before he'd been sympathetic to her physical discomfort. Now he could easily have throttled her for squandering food and water, which she desperately needed.

At a signal from Sánchez, several guerrillas detached themselves and moved out of sight behind the hut. Key finished his food and drank the remainder of the water. As the empty utensils were being taken from him, the soldiers returned, leading a man and a woman. Both had their hands tied behind their backs.

They were filthy. The stench of body odor and excrement was overpowering, a threat to Key's full stomach. The man had been beaten about his head. His hair was matted with dried blood. His features were so distorted by swelling, bruises, and abrasions that Key doubted his immediate family would have recognized him.

The woman had probably suffered more. As she was shoved forward, several of the soldiers in the camp whistled and called out Spanish insults that Key had learned as a boy in Texas. It was easy to conclude how she had been brutalized. The trauma had rendered her insentient. Her eyes were vacuous. She didn't respond to anything going on around her.

Sánchez left his chair in the shade and moved to the edge of the porch, where he looked beyond the bedraggled pair and addressed Key and Lara. "This man and woman were having sex while they were on watch. As a result of their carelessness, troops loyal to Escávez raided one of our camps. All of them died in the ensuing fight, but not before they killed two of my finest soldiers."

"*Por favor*," the man blubbered through swollen, discolored lips.

"*El Corazón, lo siento mucho. Lo siento.*" He repeatedly muttered the apology. She was his betrothed, he said. They had loved each other since they were children. Having explained that, he acknowledged that they were wrong to have jeopardized the lives of their comrades.

"She's a whore," Sánchez calmly countered. "She lay with fifty men last night."

The man sobbed but didn't argue. He begged for mercy, swearing on the graves of his mother and father that he would never be so negligent in his duties again. He dropped to his knees and crawled forward until he was inches from the toes of Sánchez's polished boots, appealing to his commander to grant them forgiveness and mercy.

"You admit that it was lust which cost the lives of your comrades? You are weak. A stupid lecher, a slave to your selfish passions. She is a whore, a bitch in heat who would offer herself to anyone."

"*Sí, sí.*" The accused bobbed his head rapidly.

"The liberation of Montesangre is the only thing for

which one should feel such unrestrainable ardor. We must all be willing to make personal sacrifices."

"*Sí, El Corazón, sí.*"

"I could have you castrated."

The sly, softly spoken threat sent the man into a paroxysm of pleading and promising, spoken in such rapid Spanish that Key had difficulty following it.

"Very well, I will not emasculate you." The man began to cry and whimper with relief, croaking elaborate accolades to El Corazón's greatness. "But such carelessness cannot go unpunished."

As a surgeon would extend his hand for a scalpel, Sánchez thrust out his hand. Ricardo slapped a pistol into his palm. El Corazón leaned forward, pressed the barrel of the gun against the groveling man's forehead, and pulled the trigger.

The woman jumped reflexively at the sudden racket but seemed impervious to the splattering of her fiancé's blood and brain matter. At a signal from El Corazón, Ricardo stepped off the porch and moved behind her. He lifted her head by her long hair and, with a deft motion of his arm, cut her throat with a wicked-looking knife. When he released her hair, she crumpled to the ground beside her slain lover.

Key cut his eyes to Lara. She sat unmoving and silent. He admired her stoicism. This sideshow was for their benefit, but, like him, she refused to give El Corazón the satisfaction of seeing her react with revulsion and fear.

I might be next, Key thought, *but the tightassed little bastard won't see me on my knees begging for my life*.

A hush of expectation fell over the camp. Activity was suspended. Key guessed that the anticipation had nothing to do with the two grisly corpses being dragged away, but rather with what would be his and Lara's fate. Executions of enemies and traitors like those they'd just witnessed were probably commonplace, daily occurrences to enforce discipline and discourage disobedience. The camp followers, even the children, were inured to them. But having two American citizens to punish was a unique diversion that had captured everyone's imagination.

It was Lara, however, who began the offensive.

"You were an intelligent young man, Emilio Sánchez Perón." Her voice was soft with fatigue, but it carried to every ear in the camp. "You could have become a great man, an excellent leader, the leader who could have boosted Montesangre out of its rut of poverty and antiquity and into the twenty-first century. Instead you have regressed to what you accused me of being—a child. A petulant, cowardly, self-serving brat.

"You talk about freedom from oppression," she continued. Scornfully her eyes swept the camp. "This community is the most oppressed I've seen in Montesangre. You aren't a leader, you're a bully. One of these days one of your followers is going to tire of your bullying and show you no mercy. You're not to be feared but pitied."

Those who understood English gasped at her temerity. Those who didn't could accurately interpret the expression on El Corazón's face. It became suffused with color. His eyes glinted malevolently.

"I am not a coward," he said stiffly. "I killed General Pérez because his resolve was weakening."

"I'll be damned," Key whispered. Sánchez was the usurper to whom Father Geraldo had referred. He was the soldier who'd murdered his own commander in order to seize control of the rebel forces.

"Yes, Mrs. Porter," Sánchez was saying. "I see you are surprised. I want you to understand how determined I am to become the undisputed leader of my country. I will do whatever is necessary, although sometimes the tasks are unpleasant." He glanced down at the fresh blood drying in the sun.

"Like shooting your own man point-blank?"

"Yes." He broke a smile that was so confident, so smug,

that it was actually more bone-chilling than the brutal act had been. "Like that. And like organizing the ambush on Ambassador Porter's car."

Lara's body jerked. She blanched. Even her lips turned white. "You?"

"Under General Pérez's orders I coordinated the operation because I was familiar with the ambassador's agenda. You were not scheduled to attend the birthday party. You and Ambassador Porter quarreled over it. He insisted that you go with him.

"You should have followed your instincts and refused. He was our target, not you. If you had stayed at the embassy I might possibly have sneaked you out before it was attacked. As it turned out, my hands were tied. It was too late to call off the ambush."

"Ashley."

Key didn't actually hear her speak the name, but he saw her lips form it.

"Ashley." As the implications sank in, her voice gained strength and she screamed, "You killed my daughter!"

"I did no such thing," he said. "She was an unfortunate casualty of war. Actually I was rather fond of the child."

His cavalier dismissal of her daughter's violent death sent Lara into a frenzy. Suddenly she spun into motion, transforming into a whirling, ducking, rolling blur of limbs. The violent conversion was so instantaneous that it caught even her guards unaware. When they regained their wits, they naturally expected her to rush forward, toward Sánchez. They weren't prepared for her to move backward.

By the time she stopped moving, the contents of the camera bag had been dumped into the dirt and she was aiming the Magnum revolver at Sánchez. At least two dozen rifles and pistols were cocked and aimed at her.

"*No!*"

Key leaped to his feet and threw a body tackle at Lara,

knocking her to the ground. The searing pain in his ribs almost caused him to black out, but he held on to her, trying to restrain her thrashing arms and gain possession of the weapon. Cruel irony that it was, Sánchez was their only hope of survival. If Lara killed him, they would be as good as dead, too. As long as they remained alive, there was hope of their getting out of Montesangre.

With surprising strength, she fought like a hellcat. "Let me go! I'll kill him!"

Several of the soldiers had joined the mêlée. Key was pulled away from her. He didn't know why the guerrillas hadn't opened fire on the two of them and dispatched the threat to El Corazón. Not until he saw him calmly approaching did Key realize that he was probably protected by a bulletproof vest. And, it seemed, unless the camp was under direct attack, no one fired a single round without a direct order from him.

"Release her."

At the sound of his voice, the guerrillas released Lara and backed away from her. She surged to her feet and, holding the Magnum in remarkably steady hands, pointed it at Sánchez.

"Lara, no!" Key hissed. He struggled with his captors, but to no avail. "Don't do it. For God's sake, don't."

"She will not kill me, Mr. Tackett." Although he was speaking to Key, Sánchez's eyes were fastened to Lara's.

She pulled back the hammer of the pistol. "Don't belittle me, Emilio. At this moment I'm capable of anything. Because of you, my baby died that morning. I'm going to kill you. Then I don't care what your ragtag band of butchers does to me."

"You will not pull the trigger, Mrs. Porter, because that would make you what you accuse me of being—a cold-blooded killer. You are a healer, someone sworn to extend life, not end it. You cannot kill me. It goes against everything you are."

You smart son of a bitch, Key thought. Sánchez was grandstanding for his troops. This was the stuff legends were made of, and the little prick knew it. He was gambling that Lara would not pull the trigger, and the odds were strongly in his favor. He'd had years to study her while working at the embassy. He knew the kind of woman she was, knew of her dedication to healing. The ability to kill wasn't within her.

"You bastard." Tears left muddy trails in the grime on her face. The heavy pistol began to waver in her hands. "My baby's dead because of you."

"But you cannot kill me."

"They put her sweet little body in a mass grave and covered it with dirt. I hate you!"

"If you hate me so badly, pull the trigger," he taunted. "An eye for an eye. I should think that your killing me would be just retribution."

Key refused to let Lara be made a fool. It would cost them their lives if she pulled the trigger, but he figured them for dead anyway. He decided to take out Sánchez with them.

"Call his bluff, Lara!" he shouted. "Blow him away. Aim for his smug puss."

Her trembling had become uncontrollable. Even if she had been able to pull the trigger, her aim would have been off. Sánchez moved closer. "Stay where you are!" she yelled. "I'll kill you."

"Never."

"I will!" Her voice cracked with hysteria.

"You never could."

Confidently, Sánchez reached out and closed his hand over the gun. Lara put up token resistance, but he easily yanked it from her clutches. She covered her face with her hands and began to sob. Sánchez, smiling complacently, placed the barrel of the Magnum against the crown of her bowed head.

Key's savage bellow was a torturous cry, the kind

one would imagine coming straight from the bowels of hell.

Sánchez grinned. "Your sentiment is touching, Mr. Tackett. I'm afraid this disproportionate respect for human life, any human life, will eventually be the downfall of America. How typically, sadly American you are. You choose to save the life of your brother's whore."

"If you kill her, you're history." He spoke the warning through clenched teeth.

"You are in no position to issue threats, Mr. Tackett."

"If I don't get you in this lifetime, watch your back in hell."

He struggled against the soldiers restraining him. He kicked backward and caught one in the kneecap. It crunched satisfyingly. He elbowed the other in the gut. Like his comrade, he went down. Freed, Key charged forward, but watched in impotent outrage and horror as Sánchez squeezed the trigger of the Magnum.

The empty chamber clicked.

Key skidded to a halt. Inertia propelled him off balance as his knees turned to gelatin. He pitched forward, landing hard in the dirt.

Sánchez laughed at the spectacle. "I am not a fool, Mr. Tackett. The bullets were removed when the gun was discovered in the camera bag. Your attempts to hide it were woefully amateurish."

He tossed the revolver back into the bag, then used the pristine handkerchief once again to wipe off his hands. "I am indebted to you and Mrs. Porter for providing us with a morning of entertainment."

"You fucking son of a bitch." Key struggled to his feet and staggered toward Lara. No one stopped him, which in itself was an insult. He must have seemed too pathetic to pose any real threat.

Little did they know.

He had been destructively livid many times. He'd used

his fists in brawls, bashing bodies and furniture. But he didn't recall a single instance when he'd felt as though he could actually take another's life.

Until this moment.

Given the chance, he could have literally torn Sánchez apart with his bare hands. He wanted to sink his teeth into his throat, taste his blood. It was an animalistic, primordial reaction that he would never have thought himself capable of experiencing, and it was frightening in its intensity.

"Why don't you just kill us and get it over with?"

"I have no intention of killing you, Mr. Tackett. Is that what you thought?"

"You're going to keep us here indefinitely? Why, so we can provide you with entertainment every morning?"

Sánchez smiled. "That is a tempting proposal, but I cannot be that self-indulgent. Actually I am releasing you. You will be returned to Ciudad Central and given accommodation in the finest hotel. Tomorrow at noon, you will be placed aboard a commercial jet bound for Bogotá. From there you will make your own travel arrangements."

Key eyed him skeptically. "What's the hitch?"

"When you reach the United States—I will make certain that the media and proper authorities are apprised of your illegal visit to Montesangre—you can make plain my message to your government."

"Message?" By now Lara had stopped crying and was listening. Key had placed his arm around her shoulders, and she was leaning against him.

"The message is that I will stop at nothing to gain control of this country. President Escávez has neither the military muscle, the personal endurance, nor the public support to defeat me. His power is a thing of the past. In a few months his diminishing army will be completely destroyed. By the end of the calendar year, I plan to establish my government in Ciudad Central."

"What makes you think the United States gives a shit about you and your pissant government?"

Sánchez bared his small, sharp teeth in a gross travesty of a smile. "My countrymen are in dire need of supplies, food, medicine. I would like to reestablish diplomatic relations with the United States."

"I bet you would. What's to make the offer attractive to us?"

"I could also make the same request of several South American countries who need an impartial corridor through which to transport drugs. Montesangre's policy has been to resist this lucrative method of revenue, but these are desperate times."

"How trite. You're not going to say desperate times call for desperate measures, are you?"

Again Sánchez smiled his obnoxious smile. "We must consider all our options. Montesangre would be a convenient stopover between South America and the United States, and the dealers are willing to pay well for the privilege."

Key thought about the landing strip designed specifically for drug runners. He'd told Lara the truth when he said he'd never flown drugs, but that didn't mean he hadn't been asked or hadn't been tempted. Percentages were strongly in favor of never getting caught, and the money couldn't be topped.

But the thought of profiting creeps who turned adolescent girls and boys into prostitutes to support their habits went against his moral code. Contrary to what most people thought about him, he wasn't entirely without conscience.

"What makes you think that anyone will listen to Lara and me?"

"Your trip here will be well documented by the media. Even if the government slaps your hands, your courage will be lauded. The public will be sympathetic to your mission and its regrettable failure. You will be in the spotlight.

"Unfortunately, Mrs. Porter's reputation is dubious, therefore she does not inspire trust. But you are Senator Tackett's surviving brother. No doubt he still has some loyal colleagues in high places. They will listen to you."

"If I have an opportunity, I'll pass along your message," Key agreed tightly.

"You must do better than that, Mr. Tackett. You must give me your word."

He had no intention of getting involved in Montesangren politics even from a distance. Once Lara and he were safely out, the whole damn country could slide into the Pacific for all he cared. But until that time, he would promise Sánchez anything he wanted to hear. "You have my word."

Lara spoke for the first time. Some of her spirit had returned, though it was obvious she was functioning on adrenaline. "You'll burn in hell, Emilio."

"Still delusional," he said retiringly.

"Oh, hell is real, all right. I've been there. The day my husband was kidnapped and my daughter was killed, and again last night when I saw the place where she is buried."

"Such accidents occur during war."

"War?" She sneered. "You're the one nursing delusions. This isn't war, it's terrorism. And you're not a warrior, you're a hoodlum. You have no honor."

Honor was a sacred thing in the Montesangren culture. Key feared Lara might have gone too far, insulting Sánchez in the most offensive way before a crowd of disciples. He held his breath, thinking that El Corazón might rescind his offer to release them. But with a brusque motion of his hand he ordered that they be returned to Ciudad Central.

Key didn't give him time to change his mind. He

climbed into the truck, then leaned down to assist Lara up. To his relief their hands were left unbound. The camera bag, their duffels, and Lara's medical bag were tossed in behind them. Two soldiers took up positions on either side of the rear opening.

Key sat down and leaned against the interior wall. He guided Lara down beside him. "Where are the others?" she asked in a whisper. "He's sending back only two to guard us?"

"Seems so."

The truck's noisy engine was coaxed to life. With a screech of gears, it moved forward. Through the opening in the back, they watched the camp roll past. When they last saw Emilio Sánchez Perón, the dreaded El Corazón del Diablo, he was seated on the porch of his ramshackle hut, consulting with his lieutenants while being fanned by adoring young girls.

"He's so damn smug," Lara angrily observed. "He thinks we no longer pose a threat to him."

Key cupped her chin and brought her head around. "Do we?"

She considered the question, then slowly shook her head as tears began to slide down her cheeks. "No. Even if I'd been able to kill him, his death wouldn't have brought back Father Geraldo, or Dr. Soto, or Randall, or Ashley."

He whisked a tear off her cheek. "No, it wouldn't."

"Then what would be the point? I'd be a killer, no better than he."

"I haven't had a chance to say anything about what we found last night. I'm sorry, Lara."

She nodded her thanks, but hadn't the strength to say more. Within moments, she succumbed to exhaustion. Her eyes closed, and her head fell back against the wall of the truck. Almost immediately she was breathing evenly, having found release in sleep.

One of their guards approached with blindfolds. "Bug

off, Bozo," Key said to him. "We're going to sleep. Our eyes will be closed."

The guerrilla consulted his comrade. The other shrugged indifferently. The blindfolds were withdrawn and the soldier returned to sit near the tailgate with his counterpart. They lit cigarettes.

Despite his aching ribs, Key slipped his arm around Lara so her head wouldn't bump against the truck. He positioned her against his side. She turned and settled her head on his shoulder.

One of the soldiers made a crude comment about the instinctive way she nestled the cleft of her thighs against his hip. The two laughed, flashing Key lewd grins.

He gave them the finger before surrendering to his own exhaustion.

Chapter Twenty-Four

*A*t sunset they arrived at the hotel. It once had been a showcase, but, like everything else in Ciudad Central, it had suffered the effects of war. Lara had attended diplomatic receptions and parties held in its ballrooms in bygone days. Now the staff was inadequate and unfriendly, acting more like surly soldiers obeying orders than like hosts.

After spending hours in the back of the bouncing truck, Lara was so relieved to have reached her destination that the hotel's notable lack of amenities didn't bother her. The formality of registering was waived. She and Key were promptly escorted under armed guard to the third floor.

The hallways were deserted. There was only silence behind the numbered doors. Lara guessed that this floor was reserved for "special guests," and that it could rightfully be called a detention center. Essentially, anyone given a room on the third floor was under house arrest.

"Señora Porter." The bellman handed Lara a room key. He gave Key another. "I trust your stay with us will be comfortable." Under the circumstances, his hospitality was a parody. Nevertheless, he bowed to them, then he and the two guards retreated to the elevator. Only the bellman got in. The guards posted themselves outside the sliding doors. There were also soldiers at the emergency exit doors at both ends of the corridor.

Lara unlocked the door to her room. Key followed her inside. The room was clean but tacky. Through an open door she saw the flamingo-pink tiles of the bathroom and a plastic shower curtain with lurid hibiscus blossoms. She dropped her doctor's bag and duffel at her side and stood in the center of the room, too dispirited to take another step.

Key was behind her. He touched her gently. Turning, she looked at him, and, for the first time since leaving El Corazón's camp, she really saw him. He looked battered and beleaguered. She reached up to touch the wound on his temple, then, realizing that the gesture wasn't professionally motivated, she lowered her hand.

Softly he said her name. As they stood facing each other, he asked, "Are you all right?"

"Yes." Her voice was hoarse from screaming at Sánchez, whose only reaction to her accusations had been a gloating smile. He'd demonstrated no remorse for Ashley's death. Remembering, tears came to her eyes. She inclined toward Key and began shaking her head mournfully. "No, no, I'm not all right. My baby is dead, forever lost to me."

His arms encircled her and held her protectively. "Shh. Don't cry. He can't hurt you anymore. We're safe."

Suddenly she wanted very badly to be convinced of that. Her fingers curled inward, digging hard into the muscles of his chest. She desperately needed to touch, to be touched, and apparently Key was just as eager to allay his own fears.

He tipped her head up as his descended. Simultaneously a violent hunger was unleashed, and they aggressively sought to satisfy it. He claimed her mouth with a frantic, needful thrust of his tongue.

Lara arched against him and locked her arms around his neck. He pulled her shirttail from the waistband of her pants and impatiently tore the buttons from their holes. Reaching behind her, he unfastened her bra, then slid his hands forward to cover her breasts. His strong fingers pressed into her flesh.

His name drifted across her lips—a question, a profession, a prayer.

Responding, he lowered his head and took her nipple between his lips. Her head fell back upon her shoulders, and she gave herself over entirely to the hot urgency of his caress. He pulled her deeply into his mouth, the flexing of his jaws strong and possessive. Then he kissed her mouth again, moving his head from side to side, changing angles, testing positions, tasting her completely.

At last he raised his head and looked at her, his eyes feverish and painfully blue. His eyebrows were pulled into a frown of determination above his straight, narrow nose. His lips were a thin, firm line of resolve set between his bearded cheeks.

Lara wanted him with the purest, most undiluted sexual desire she'd ever experienced. Yet she closed her eyes, shaking her head in denial. "I don't want to be one of Key Tackett's women."

"Yes, you do. Tonight you do."

He carried her to the bed and laid her down against the pillows. He must have known her mind better than she knew it herself, because she reached for him eagerly when he followed her down. His lips tasted salty with sweat and were slightly gritty, but she couldn't get enough of them.

He pushed aside her blouse and the cups of her brassiere and moved his hand across her breasts, lightly grinding her nipples beneath his palm until they were stiff and so sensitive that his merest touch caused her back to arch above the bed.

She did nothing to stop him from unfastening her pants and pushing them down, along with her panties, until they were gathered around her ankles. He undid his trousers, but it was Lara's hands that shoved them over his buttocks.

He entered her.

She received him.

He was incredibly firm. She was wet and snug. His head sprang up, and he looked down into her flushed face. She could feel the color in her cheeks, hear her own quick, soughing breath. His eyes locked with hers as he pushed deeper. She clamped her lower lip between her teeth to keep from crying out.

When he was fully seated inside her, he grimaced with pleasure. Then, with a moan, he pressed his forehead against hers. "Oh, Christ. A fantasy fuck."

He began to move; she raised her hips to meet his smooth thrusts. Each one took her breath, but she couldn't deny herself the overwhelming sensations they evoked.

He waited for her. When she climaxed, he sank all ten fingers into her hair and held her head between his hands, kissing her mouth as thoroughly and intimately as their coupling. Her orgasm was long and strong and more than he could endure. Allowing himself to come, he buried his face in her neck and drew a patch of her skin against his teeth.

It was a long time before either of them moved.

They did move, eventually, from the bed and from her room into his. Their dirty clothes and muddy boots had made a mess of her bed. Defying the curiosity of their guards as they crossed the hall, Key led her into his room, a mirror image of hers except that the tiles in his bathroom were turquoise and the shower curtain was decorated with smiling seahorses.

They removed their clothing and stepped beneath a shower from which they coaxed only rusty, tepid water. Scanty bars of soap were wrapped in green cellophane. They used up three of them to wash the grime off each other.

The water cooled but they stayed beneath the spray, exploring. She examined the gash on his temple and told him that she could put a butterfly clamp on it.

He said, "Don't bother. I'll live."

She examined his bruised ribs and told him that several were probably cracked.

He admitted that they hurt but wouldn't consent to her binding them. "The night we met, you mummified me. Damn bandage nearly drove me crazy. I took it off the next day."

She called him hardheaded as she combed her fingers through his chest hair. She cupped his weighty sex in her palms and sipped water from the delta-shaped hollow at the base of his larynx.

He covered the scar on her shoulder with tender kisses and called it beautiful when she demurred and tried to hide it. "Besides, it's hardly a scratch compared to mine."

With her finger, she followed the raised, red surgical scar that ran up his left leg from knee to groin. "What happened?"

He told her about the car wreck that had ruined his leg and all hopes for a career in the NFL. "Were you terribly disappointed? Is that what you wanted?"

"It's what Jody wanted. We'd never been pals. But after the accident . . ." He shook his head. "I don't want to talk about Jody."

He touched her everywhere, giving and taking pleasure in equal portions. He was indulgent and sensual, more so than she would ever have believed. She thought that surely she was dreaming, although she had never dreamed this erotically about her husband. And never about Clark.

They finally left the bathroom and were foraging through their duffel bags for clean clothes when someone knocked on the door. "What do you want?" Key asked brusquely.

"Tengo la comida para ustedes."

Cautiously he eased open the door. A soldier held a room-service tray perched on his shoulder. *"Gracias."*

Key took the tray of food from him and, without giving him time to argue, slammed the door in his face and slid the chain back into the track.

He set the tray on the table. "I hope it's better than the fare at Sánchez's camp."

"It could be poisoned." Lara approached the table, pulling her hairbrush through her wet hair.

"Could be, but I doubt it. If he wanted to kill us, he wouldn't be that subtle. He'd have done it when he had an audience."

On the tray were an assortment of fruits and cheeses, cold roasted chicken, and bottled water. Key got a drumstick from the platter and without much interest took a bite. "Wonder why he let us go."

She began to peel an orange. "Odd, isn't it?"

"Damned odd. I don't know what I expected, but not this." He used the drumstick to point out their surroundings. "Not exactly The Plaza, but better than a bamboo hut with a dirt floor."

He chewed thoughtfully. "Bottom line. Our lives in exchange for my taking his 'message' to the States? Nope. Doesn't jive. Too easy. If he wanted to convey a message to our government, he could have used someone more influential than us, the head of state of an ally nation, for instance." He tossed aside the chicken bone and opened a bottle of water. "Why didn't he kill us, Lara?"

She returned the half-peeled orange to the tray. "I don't know." Moving to the windows, she parted the drapes and gazed out over the city.

"That orange would do you good. You haven't eaten all day."

She glanced back at the table with revulsion. "I don't want to feel obligated to Emilio Sánchez for anything."

"Don't cut off your nose to spite your face. You should eat."

"I'm really not hungry, Key. My mind isn't on my stomach." There was an edge of impatience in her voice, most of it self-directed. "I've been trying to sort through things."

"What things?"

"I don't know. Things. Everything. About what happened here three years ago. Randall. Ashley. If I dwell on that . . . that mass grave she's buried in, I'll probably go mad." She clutched a handful of drapery. "So I can't. I must concentrate on my memories of when she was alive. I must remember how bright and happy she was, how much joy she gave me during the short time I had her."

Her hoarse voice began to waver. She paused to compose herself. "My daughter is lost to me, but if I focus on her life rather than her death, it doesn't matter so much where her body is buried. Her spirit is still alive. In that respect, this isn't a failed mission after all."

"You had to return here in order to come to terms with it."

She nodded. "Yes. That episode of my life—all of it, beginning with the scandal—has been governing my life for far too long. I accused everyone else of identifying me with tabloid headlines, but I'm the most guilty. I can't continue regarding myself a victim. It's time I got on with the rest of my life."

"In Eden Pass?"

"I haven't had much success there," she remarked as she turned to face him.

"Not because you aren't a good doctor, but because of us Tacketts. We've given you a hell of a hard time."

Suddenly reluctant to look at him, she averted her head.

"Key, why did this happen between us?"

"The animosity? Or the other?"

"The other."

He took a deep breath and held it, saying nothing for several moments. Finally: "You're the doctor. Got any theories?"

She did, and indicated so with a slight motion of her

shoulders. "People who've survived a life-threatening ordeal," she began slowly, "frequently want sex directly afterward." He raised one eyebrow, either with inquisitiveness or skepticism. She wasn't sure. "It makes sense. Sex is the ultimate release of emotion, a means of unequivocally affirming life.

"I've had shamefaced patients confess to me that immediately following a funeral, they made love. With extraordinary passion. Human beings have an innate fear of death. Sex is instant confirmation of survival.

"After the harrowing experiences we've been through the past few days, it follows that we'd expend our pent-up fears and emotions with sex. Fierce, aggressive sex. We're a classic example of this psychological phenomenon."

Key had listened politely. Now he walked to her, coming so close that she had to tilt her head back in order to look into his face. "Bullshit. It happened because we wanted it to." He kissed her hard and quick, stamping an impression of his lips on hers. "Damned if it needs any more justification than that."

The clothes they had so recently put on were discarded as they made their way to the bed. When the backs of his knees touched it, he sat down and guided Lara to stand between his thighs. He lifted her breast to his mouth and flicked the nipple with his tongue.

Her eyes fluttered closed and choppy little breaths issued from her throat. She wound strands of his hair around her fingers but allowed his head to move freely over her breasts and down the center of her body. His beard rasped her belly, eliciting exciting and forbidden sensations. Between her thighs she began to ache, deliciously. The lips of her sex became swollen and warm.

Key splayed his hands over her bottom and tilted her middle up against his face. He nuzzled her. He kissed her navel. He kissed the soft skin beneath it. With little puffs of heat, his breath stirred her pubic hair.

Then he turned her, and she landed on her back on

the bed, the juncture of her thighs forming a cradle for his lowering head. He kissed her with unapologetic carnality. His mouth gently drew on her while his nimble tongue taught her things about herself she didn't know. As though inside her head, taking directions from her thoughts, he knew exactly when to probe, when to stroke, when to sink his mouth into her, and when to withdraw and caress her with the very tip of his tongue.

By the time he rose above her, she was sated, replete, dewy with perspiration, and drunk with passion. Nevertheless, her slack lips awakened beneath his searching kiss. When he entered her, it was a beginning, not a benediction.

Tenderly he traced the scar on her shoulder with his fingertip. "It was bad, huh?"

"Very bad. For a while the doctors believed that I'd be extremely lucky to regain only partial use of my arm."

"Knowing you, you were determined to prove them wrong."

"After the wound healed, I spent months in physical therapy."

For a moment he watched her reflectively. "I think you should stop punishing yourself for not dying with the rest of your family, Lara."

"Is that what you think I'm about?"

"To an extent, yes."

She came up on an elbow and surveyed his lean, naked body. In addition to the scar on his leg, there were many on his torso. "What about you? You're reckless. You take senseless chances. What are you punishing yourself for?"

"It's not the same thing," he answered crossly. "I'm a thrillseeker for the sake of the thrill, that's all."

She gave him a look that said she wasn't buying it. Her eyes wandered from one scar to the next. There was a particularly wicked one cutting a jagged line across his ribs beneath his right arm.

"Knife fight," he said when she looked at him with a question in her eyes.

"Obviously you lost."

"Actually I won."

As to the fate of the loser, she was afraid to ask. "And this?"

"Plane crash. I walked away, but tore open my arm on a piece of fuselage."

She marveled at his nonchalance. "Other than today, have you ever been in real danger of losing your life?"

"Once."

"Tell me about it."

"I got shot. Here," he said, touching his newest scar, the one she was familiar with. "Nearly bled to death."

Laughing, she tossed her hair over one shoulder. "It was more than a scratch, but certainly not a mortal wound."

"I know that. But I wasn't talking about the wound itself," he said. "See, I stumbled into Doc Patton's place, expecting him, but finding someone else. A woman."

Lara became transfixed by his eyes and the hypnotic quality of his voice. "How was that life-threatening?" she asked huskily.

"I turned around and looked at her and thought, 'Shit, Tackett, you're a dead man.'"

She swallowed with difficulty. "We're grown-ups, Key. Beyond the age of consent and too old to play games. I don't expect hearts and flowers from you. You don't have to profess— "

He laid his index finger vertically against her lips. "I'm not telling you this to get you into bed. You're already here and I've already had you. I'm telling you because it's the truth, and you know it as well as I do. We're here together, like this, because we've wanted it from the beginning. We've both known that it was only a matter of time."

He reached up to stroke her cheek. "Once we looked

at each other, I didn't stand a chance and neither did you. I wanted to fuck you on the spot."

"Until you discovered who I was."

"I wanted to fuck you anyway." Reaching behind her head, he clutched a handful of her hair and drew her face close to his. "Damn me to hell, I still do."

Key reached for her as she scooted off the bed and began gathering her clothes. "Where are you going?" he mumbled sleepily.

"To my room."

"What for?"

"A bath."

"We have a tub in here."

"But we used all the soap. Besides, I need to organize my things so that when they come to take us to the airport I'll be ready." She dressed hastily.

"What time is it?"

"Nine."

"Nine! We slept that long?" He sat up and ran his fingers through his shaggy hair.

"You don't have to get up. We've got plenty of time before noon."

"No, I'm getting up. I don't want to give the bastards any reason to delay our departure. As soon as I shower, I'll see if they'll bring us some coffee."

"I'll have everything ready by then." She smiled at him, checked to make certain she had her key, then unlocked the door and stepped into the hall.

Contrary to what he'd said, Key didn't get up immediately, but lay back down and stared sightlessly at the ceiling. Last night Lara had confessed to some confusion. Being less straightforward then she, he hadn't admitted to his own ambiguity.

To assuage her conscience, she had dredged up a psychological explanation for going to bed with him, although he doubted that she believed her own sales pitch.

He didn't think lust needed analysis or rationalization. It was a call to action all by itself.

His confusion was centered not on why it had happened but on how he felt about it—about her—now that it had.

He'd never enjoyed a woman more. Physically, they were a good fit. She had matched him in passion and skill. Despite all the tabloid journalism written about her, he hadn't expected her to be so sexually liberated. Memories of their love-play now sent heat surging through his loins. Even after their marathon of sex, he was far from satisfied. He wanted more of her.

That, too, was unexpected and disconcerting. Usually the chase was most of the fun. Once caught, a woman's charms rapidly diminished. It bothered him greatly to realize that Lara had become only more intriguing. She had layers and dimensions he was eager to explore. Customarily, women were as disposable as razor blades. When one got dull, he threw it away and replaced it with another. He wasn't eager to dispose of and replace Lara.

Not that she was his to do with as he pleased.

Ah! He'd finally acknowledged the crux of all these niggling misgivings. She didn't belong to him. Furthermore, if circumstances had been different, she might still belong to his brother.

Clark had had her first.

That alone had prevented last night from being the most satisfying night of sex he'd ever engaged in. Inadvertently he must have conveyed his uneasiness about it. Either that or Dr. Mallory was damned perceptive.

She brought it up, after they had nibbled on the remainder of the food and decided that they should try to sleep. She lay on her side, facing away from him, her folded hands supporting her cheek. He'd been absently rubbing a strand of her hair between his thumb and index finger, thinking that she'd been luckier at falling asleep than he. He was surprised to hear her drowsily say, "I know what you're thinking about."

He moved his knee against the back of her thigh. "Okay, smarty, what am I thinking about?"

"Clark."

His smile receded and the strand of hair sifted through his fingers. "What about him?"

"You're wondering if I'm comparing the two of you, and, if so, how you measure up."

"I didn't know you were a shrink, too."

She turned her head and gazed at him over her bare shoulder. "I'm right, aren't I? Isn't that what you were thinking?"

"Maybe."

Smiling sadly, she gave her head a small shake. "You and Clark . . . you're two different people, Key. Equally attractive, both charismatic, each of you a natural leader, but so very different. I loved your brother, and I believe he loved me." She reduced her voice to a whisper. "But it was never like tonight." She rolled away from him and returned her cheek to her hands. He had thought she was finished, but she repeated, "Never."

He'd lain there for a while, steeped in jealousy, wanting desperately to believe her. Soon, however, desire superseded envy. Or maybe it wasn't so much desire as jealous possessiveness.

Moving suddenly, he placed his arm around her and roughly pulled her closer until her bottom was firmly pressed against his belly. He entered her with one hard thrust. He took a love bite from the back of her neck and held it between his teeth, feeling the need to dominate and control.

There was no need for it. She was receptive and giving and so erotically charged that he had only to press his open palm against her mound and the inner walls of her body contracted around his cock like a magic fist, massaging him, milking him of semen and of doubts.

It took a while for their breathing to return to normal. Their bodies glistened with a fine sheen of sweat. When he finally withdrew from her, she turned to face him and nuzzled his chest with her open mouth.

She said, "Shameless."

"I've never claimed to be otherwise."

"Not you. Me."

He'd fallen asleep with her in his arms, secure in the knowledge that their lovemaking had gone beyond mutual satisfaction. It had been in another league.

But now it was day, and his doubts were encroaching like the tropical humidity that accompanied the rising sun. He thought back to all that she'd said, to all her sensual responses, to her bold caresses. Surely it couldn't have been any better for her with his brother.

Had she ever ridden Clark until she collapsed, exhausted, on his chest?

Key's fists clenched at his sides.

Had she blissfully tortured Clark to climax with her sliding, kneading hand?

He cursed obscenely.

Had she permitted Clark to kiss her between her thighs, to separate and taste . . .

A bloodcurdling scream brought him bolt upright.

By the time the second one shattered the morning stillness, he had put on his pants and was at the door, all but pulling it from its hinges in his haste to get it open.

"*Buenos días*," Lara said to the guards as she left Key's room. Undaunted by their leers, she crossed the hall and entered her room, carefully locking the door behind her.

Their boots had tracked mud onto the carpet, and, as Key had pointed out, they'd ravaged the bed. He'd joked, telling her that regardless of what she might have heard about Texans, that was the first time he'd ever made love with his boots on.

Made love? Had he used those exact words, or was her memory being kind?

She shrugged off the disturbing thought, having had enough self-analysis for one twenty-four-hour period. The conclusions she'd reached last night had been positive. The rest of her life had begun when she fell into Key's embrace. The experience had been cathartic. Why try attaching a name to it? Her mood and her body spoke for themselves. She felt wonderful. For once, why not let it go at that?

Taking her duffel with her, she went into the bathroom. When she saw her reflection in the mirror over the basin, she laughed with self-deprecation. She had on no makeup, and, though her hair was clean, it had been washed with bar soap and looked it.

He hadn't seemed to notice. Or care.

A blush spread up from her chest to her neck and face. Unbuttoning the first few buttons of her blouse, she glanced down at her breasts and, as expected, saw that they were whisker-burned. Before they slept together again, she'd insist that he shave.

If they slept together again.

To her chagrin, she found herself hoping desperately that they would. Soon.

Smiling with anticipation, she pulled back the shower curtain and reached for the water taps.

Her scream reverberated off the flamingo-pink tiles.

Lying in the bathtub, beaten and bleeding but very much alive, was Randall Porter.

Her husband.

Chapter Twenty-Five

*H*ow charming you look." The former United States ambassador to Montesangre stood as his wife entered the parlor. "Although I liked your hair better when you lightened it. When did you stop?"

"While I was recuperating in Miami. Those were difficult months for me. Hair color wasn't a priority."

Lara glanced at Key. Declining to stand when she came in, he was slumped in an upholstered chair, one ankle balanced on the opposite knee, his foot rapidly jiggling up and down. His steepled fingers tapped his lips in time to the movement of his foot. The posture would have looked insouciant on anyone else, but Lara sensed that he was on the verge of exploding.

If Randall noticed Key's tenuously controlled rage, he gave no indication of it. "Would you like something to drink, darling? We have a few minutes before going downstairs."

"No, thank you. I don't want anything to drink. And I don't see why it's necessary for me to participate in this news conference."

"You're my wife. Your place is by my side." At the bar, Randall poured himself a club soda. "Mr. Tackett? Anything?"

"No."

Randall returned to the sofa where he'd been sitting when Lara joined them from the bedroom of the Houston hotel suite. The well-appointed rooms were a considerable improvement over the accommodations in Montesangre.

Well-wishing floral arrangements crowded every available surface. Their mingled scents were sweet and cloying and had given Lara a dull headache. She thought these expressions of congratulations ludicrously hypocritical, having been sent by many of the same bureaucrats and political figures who, five years ago, had been relieved to see Randall and his cheating wife shuttled off to Montesangre, thereby sparing Washington the embarrassment of having them underfoot.

Technically, Randall was still a United States ambassador. When the media was notified by news services in Colombia of his shocking resurrection, the story took precedence over all others and earned the banner headline of virtually every newspaper in the world. His return to life sent the entire nation into a tailspin, the press into a frenzy.

In Bogotá he'd been treated for his wounds, which were more superficial than they'd first appeared. Key had relented and had his ribs X-rayed. Three were cracked, but he'd sustained no internal injuries.

Lara's injuries were as severe, but not as evident. For fatigue she was prescribed hot, healthy meals and two nights of drug-induced sleep. She'd eaten and slept but continued to look shell-shocked. Her movements were disjointed, her speech distracted. A husband she believed dead had suddenly returned to life. Her entire system had been thrown into shock.

Neiman Marcus had generously offered to outfit her for her first public appearance following her return to American soil. For the newsworthy occasion the store had donated a silk and wool blend two-piece suit, matching Jourdan pumps, and suitable accessories and costume jewelry. The hotel salon had sent the staff to her suite to do her hair, nails, and makeup. On the surface, she was well turned out and appeared ready to accompany her husband to the news conference that was scheduled to begin in half an hour in the hotel's largest ballroom.

She'd just as soon face a firing squad, she thought.

In a very real sense that was exactly what it would be. Too jittery to sit, she moved aimlessly about the room among the furniture cluttered with floral bouquets. "You know what they'll dredge up, Randall."

"Your affair with Clark," he replied without a qualm. They had informed him of Clark's death on the flight from Montesangre to Colombia, but he already knew about it. World news filtered in, although little was filtered out.

"I'm afraid that's unavoidable, Lara," he continued. "I'll try to distract them with my story of the last three years."

"You don't look all that worse for wear." Key ceased wagging his foot and tapping his lips. "You look tan, fit, and well fed."

Lara too had noticed Randall's superior physical condition. He looked even better than when she'd met him seven years ago, as if he'd enjoyed several months' vacation in Hawaii rather than three grueling years as a political prisoner.

He pinched up the creases of his new suit trousers, also a gift from Neiman's. "After the first few months of my captivity, I was treated very well.

"At first, the rebels beat me unmercifully," Randall told them. "For several weeks they ritualistically whipped me with pistols and chains. I thought this was preliminary to their killing me."

He finished his soda and checked the time. Seeing that he still had a few minutes, he continued. "One day they hauled me into General Pérez's quarters. I say 'hauled' because I couldn't walk. They carried me like a sack of potatoes.

"Pérez was pleased with himself. He showed me photographs of my 'death,' as they'd staged it. They'd executed a man, God knows who, shooting him in the head so many times it was little more than pulp."

Lara hugged her elbows. The room was frigid. After sweltering in the tropics for three years, Randall had said he wanted to keep the air conditioning as high as possible.

"You can imagine how devastating it was for me to see those photographs. They also showed me American newspapers reporting my death. They had photos of my funeral. I realized the hell you must be going through." He looked at Lara with commiseration. "I thanked God you were safe but knew you would be agonizing over the violent way in which I'd died. Knowing that no one would be sent to rescue me was the worst torture of all. As far as anyone knew, I was dead."

"Did they tell you about Ashley?"

"No. I didn't learn that she'd been killed in the ambush until I read the newspaper accounts of my funeral. The only comfort I could derive was knowing that you had miraculously survived. If it hadn't been for the priest— "

"Priest? Father Geraldo?"

"Of course. He got you on one of the last American-bound planes to leave Montesangre. I thought you knew."

"No. I didn't," she said in a subdued voice. "I should have thanked him."

"It was certainly an act of bravery," Randall said. "Emilio harbored a grudge against him for facilitating your escape. I suppose that's why he ordered Father Geraldo's murder."

Key cursed beneath his breath. "So good of you to tell her that."

"Lara's a realist, aren't you, darling? Nevertheless it's a pity about the priest. And about Dr. Soto."

"I can never atone for involving them," she said quietly. "I'll always feel partially responsible for their deaths."

"Don't do that to yourself," Key said insistently.

"They'd been pegged for elimination, with or without us. Sánchez said as much."

She threw him a grateful look for the sentiment but knew she would carry the guilt of their murders to her own grave.

"You were incredibly brave to return to Montesangre, Lara," Randall said. "Thank God you did. If you hadn't, I'd still be a hostage."

Key surged to his feet. He'd shaved his dark beard, but his hair was still overly long and contributed to his look of a caged wild animal. Disdaining the role of national hero in which he now found himself, he'd declined Neiman's offer to provide him with new clothes. On his own, he'd bought new jeans, a sport coat, and cowboy boots.

"I don't get it," he said. "Lara and I arrive unannounced in Montesangre, and thirty-six hours later your captors up and decide to let you go?" He spread his arms away from his body. "Why? What does one have to do with the other?"

Randall smiled indulgently. "Obviously you have something to learn about the mind-set of these people, Mr. Tackett."

"Obviously I do. Because your story sounds like a big pile of *caca* to me."

Randall's eyes narrowed marginally. "You saved my life and Lara's. Therefore I'll extend you the courtesy of overlooking your unnecessary vulgarity."

"Don't do me any favors."

Randall dismissed him and addressed his next words to Lara. "Emilio likes to play mind games. Remember the chess tournaments we hosted at the embassy?"

"This is more serious than chess, Randall."

"To you and me. I'm not so sure Emilio makes the distinction between a board game and the little dramas he plays out for his own amusement using human lives as the stakes. He thanked you for providing entertainment to his camp that morning, remember?"

"*I* remember," Key said. "And I'm glad you brought that up because something else has been bugging me. You said you were inside the shack while all that was going on, right?"

Randall nodded. "I was bound and gagged, unable to alert you to the fact that I was still alive. That was Emilio's inside joke."

"When did you first learn that I was in Montesangre?" Lara asked.

"The morning following your arrival. I knew something was afoot because my guards were brusque and wouldn't look me in the eye. We'd developed a grudging respect for one another over the years. Suddenly they were hostile and taciturn again.

"After Ricardo intercepted the jeep on the road, it was only a matter of hours before they deduced who the 'widow' was. There was some speculation about the idiot brother-in-law." He looked pointedly at Key. "But once Emilio learned your name, he put two and two together. He knew about Lara's . . . friendship with Clark.

"The more you snooped around, the more volatile the situation became. The night before you were brought to the camp, I was transported there. Emilio taunted me with the threat of killing you slowly and painfully while I watched. I was beaten, but not severely. He wanted me conscious for the next morning's theatrics.

"After you were taken away, I was beaten again, then driven to Ciudad Central. We were probably only an hour behind you, but my guards and I spend the night in the truck. The last thing I remember is being knocked unconscious shortly after dawn. Your scream when you found me in the bathtub roused me. I was as shocked as you to find myself still alive."

He stood and slipped on his suit coat. "Well, I think it's time to go."

"I still can't comprehend Emilio's strategy," Lara argued, making no move to join him at the door.

"We'll talk about it later."

"No, we'll talk about it now, Randall. If you insist that I face the press, I need to fully understand the situation. They'll ask me about my dealings with El Corazón del Diablo. I'll gladly tell them everything I know about the slender, bookish young man who worked as a translator at the embassy, and about the cold-blooded murderer I met this week. But I can't expound on foreign policy without having a clearer picture of what was in Emilio's mind. Why did he let us go? Why did he keep you alive but imprisoned for three years and then suddenly release you?"

Randall gnawed the inside of his cheek, apparently annoyed by her confusion. He decided to humor her. "I've had three years to ruminate on why my death was staged. The savagery of it was to demonstrate how much Montesangre resented the United States' intervention into its internal affairs."

"Why didn't they kill you for real?" Key asked.

"I assume they wanted to keep me as a trump card. Had the U.S. decided to send troops into Montesangre, as they did into Panama, they could have used me as a hostage."

"So why were you released now?"

"That's simple, Lara. They're starving. Montesangre relies entirely on imports for virtually everything. Under the embargo enforced by the United States, and adhered to by the nations who are either allied with or fearful of us, their resources were quickly exhausted. Frankly, I'm amazed that they've held out this long. They probably wouldn't have if Pérez were still their leader. They would have relaxed their political position long before now without someone as ruthless as Emilio at the helm. He's made himself into a demigod."

"What are you, president of his fan club?" Key asked caustically.

"Certainly not," Randall coldly countered. "He was my jailer for three years. However, I've witnessed firsthand the suffering of the Montesangrens. I have tremendous sympathy for them and wish to help their plight. For all his ruthlessness, Sánchez is the best hope for pulling the country together, feeding the hungry, ending the chaos, and establishing some semblance of order. And, putting personal considerations aside, I must admire his tenacity.

"He's inordinately determined and patient. Using your venture to release me was a brilliant stroke of ingenuity. He knew the human-interest value of this story, knew it would gain the attention of the American people. It's his invitation to the United States to reopen diplomatic dialogue."

"That's the message he gave me to deliver. Why use his ace in the hole?"

Randall smiled as though amused by Key's naïveté. "He knew I would have more credibility in Washington than a cowboy."

"I'm not a cowboy."

"Of course you are." His eyes slid over Key's jeans and boots, making plain his low opinion of them. "The only difference is that you ride airplanes instead of horses. Otherwise, you're a range bum. Even your brother thought so."

Key lunged for him, but Lara stepped between them. Putting her back to Key, she angrily faced Randall. "Clark thought no such thing! He loved Key very much."

Randall smiled and said softly, "I bow to your superior knowledge of whom and what Clark loved." He extended his hand. "We really must go, darling. Ready?"

Disregarding his proffered hand, she moved stiffly toward the door. Sensing that Key wasn't following, she turned to him. "Coming?"

"No."

She panicked. The only thing that would hold her together during this press conference was knowing that Key was beside her. He couldn't lend her physical support, of course, but she'd relied on his strong presence to bolster her.

Gauging by the resolve in his expression, she knew arguing would be futile, but still she had to try. "You're expected."

"They'll just have to be disappointed. The newspapers are hinting that I took you to Montesangre to rescue him." He hitched his head toward Randall. "That's not why I went, and I'm not going to pretend that it was."

"They'll think you're only being coy, Mr. Tackett."

Key glared at her husband. "I can't control what they think. The only thing I have any real control over is myself, and I'm not going to be carrion for a flock of vultures with cameras. If you want a quote, write that one down." Looking at Lara again, he said, "You don't have to go either. No one can force you."

She fought the magnetic pull that would have drawn her to him. There were so many things to say, so many explanations to make, but in order not to cause more damage than had already been done, she had to remain silent.

Naturally she was glad that Randall hadn't died a brutal death. She celebrated his release from a long and hellish captivity. From a very selfish viewpoint, however, his deliverance couldn't have come at a worse time. Randall had been liberated, but her imprisonment was just beginning.

Tears filled her eyes. One rolled down her cheek. Seeing it, Key started to say something, but obviously thought better of it. They gazed at each other in mute misery.

"Well, well," Randall said around a dry little cough. Not knowing that he was echoing Lara's thoughts, he said, "It appears that the husband's resurrection from the dead has come at an inopportune time."

She quickly turned away from Key. "As you said, Randall, we're going to be late. Let's go."

He held up his hand to forestall her. "They'll wait. This, on the other hand, demands immediate attention."

"There is no 'this.'"

"You always were a terrible liar, Lara." He chuckled. "Out of deference to the shock you've sustained, I haven't imposed my marital rights these past few nights. It's a good thing I didn't. Undoubtedly I would have found your bedroom door locked."

She gave him a fulminating look but said nothing.

He laid his finger lengthwise against his lips and fixed an appraising gaze on Key. "He's such a contrast to Clark, I'm amazed you find him attractive. He's certainly not as polished as his older brother. Still, he does emanate a hot-blooded, animalistic quality that I suppose a woman like you would find appealing."

"I'm not deaf and dumb, you son of a bitch," Key said. "If you've got something to say, say it to me directly."

"All right," he said pleasantly. "Didn't you feel the least bit foolish fucking a woman known nationwide as your brother's whore?"

Even Lara couldn't have stopped Key then. He side-stepped her and encircled Randall's throat with his hands.

"Key, no!" She tried to pry his fingers off Randall's neck, but they were unyielding. He backed him into the door; Randall's head made connection with a solid *thunk*. Frantically, he clawed at Key's fingers, but they squeezed tighter.

"Please. Key!" she cried. "Don't make matters worse! Don't make me another tabloid headline!"

Her shouted plea registered. She saw him blink rapidly as though to dispel a fog of rage. When her words sank in, his fingers began to relax. He released Randall with an abrupt gesture of contempt.

Randall recovered himself and, with a semblance of dignity, straightened his coat and necktie. "I'm glad cowboys no longer carry six-shooters. I could be dead."

Key was still breathing hard and looking dangerous.

"You talk about Lara and me that way again, and I'll kill you."

"How chivalrous," Randall said scornfully. He turned to her. "Well, Lara. For the final time, shall we go?"

Key rounded on her and gripped her by the shoulders. "You don't have to do what he says." He gave her a little shake. "You *don't*."

"Yes, I do, Key." She spoke quietly but with steely conviction.

At first he was incredulous. Then his bafflement turned to anger. She watched his face grow taut with fury. She knew he wouldn't understand her decision, and she couldn't explain it. So she had no choice but to withstand his disgust.

He released her, turned on his heel, yanked the door open, and stalked out. Hopelessly, she watched him go.

"I thought it went very well, but after all that talking, I could stand a drink." Randall slipped out of his suit jacket and carefully laid it across the back of a chair as he moved to the bar. "Want something, darling?"

"No, thank you."

He mixed a scotch and soda and smacked his lips appreciatively after the first sip. "One of the many things I missed during my captivity." Sitting on the sofa, drink in hand, he unlaced his shoes. "You're subdued, Lara. What's wrong?"

"What's wrong? I'm fair game and this is the first day of hunting season." She rounded on him. "I hate being put on display, and I bitterly resent you for forcing me to reopen my life to public scrutiny."

"You should have thought of the consequences before you finagled Key Tackett into taking you to Montesangre."

"I tried every other resource I knew of before asking Key. He was my last hope. I've explained why I went. Why I had to go."

"And your noble motivation was duly noted by the

press. You were quite effective when you described the mass grave. You'll probably be nominated for Mother of the Year." He took another sip of scotch. "I honestly don't know why you're so upset."

"Because to even recount the incident at the cemetery is an invasion of my privacy, Randall. And while my motives were pure, the reporters' weren't. They were only politely interested in the events of our trip, and the ruthless despot, El Corazón, and what effects your release might have on foreign policy.

"What they really wanted was dirt. 'Why did you team up with Senator Tackett's brother, Mrs. Porter?' 'Does Key Tackett resent the role you played in Senator Tackett's downfall?' 'Was his death a suicide?' 'How did you feel when you discovered your husband is still alive, Mrs. Porter?' What kind of questions are those?"

"Profound, I would say." With deceptive calm, he set his drink on the coffee table. "How *do* you feel about your husband's return from the dead, Mrs. Porter?"

She avoided his goading glance. "I prefer being addressed by my professional name, Randall. I've been Dr. Mallory for a long time. 'Mrs. Porter' has negative connotations for me."

"Yes, like the fact that you're married," he said with a snide laugh. "You aren't very lucky, are you, Lara? It was so damned untimely for you to fall in love. And with Clark's brother, no less." He threw back his head and laughed harder. "The irony of it is so rich."

She refused to give him the satisfaction of denying or confirming his assumption. Her relationship with Key, which was indefinable even to herself, was none of Randall's business, except insofar as she was still legally his wife. Emotionally, she hadn't felt conjugally linked to him since before that disastrous weekend in Virginia.

He finished his drink. "It's getting late. We'd better get some rest. We're booked on a ten o'clock flight to Washington tomorrow morning."

"I'm not going to Washington."

He had bent down to pick up his shoes. Slowly he straightened. "The hell you're not. It's all arranged."

"Then unarrange it. I'm not going."

"The President of the United States is scheduled to receive us in the Oval Office." His face had become flushed.

"Extend him my regrets. I won't be able to make it."

She headed for the bedroom. Randall stormed off the sofa, grabbed her arm, and brought her around. "You'll be there with me every step of the way through this, Lara."

"No, I won't, Randall," she averred, pulling her arm free. "Frankly, I'm surprised you want to share the limelight. When you left Washington, you were a cuckold, a laughingstock. You're returning a hero. You'll probably be invited to appear on all the TV talk shows, to write a book—there might even be a movie-of-the-week in your future. Your credibility has been fully restored and once again you've got the ear of the president. Why would you want me there, stealing a few rays of your spotlight and reminding everyone of that large, dark blot on your career?"

"To keep up appearances," he said with a cold smile. "You are still my wife. I'm willing to overlook your sleeping arrangements with Key Tackett. After all, you thought I was dead."

"Don't assume that moral posture with me, Randall. The martyred husband who continues to forgive his wayward wife." Her words were laden with contempt. "That's the pose you struck when photos of me being hustled from Clark's cottage hit the newsstands. Little did anyone guess that you'd been having affairs almost from the day we married."

"I've never confessed to that," he replied blandly. "You surmised it for your own benefit."

"I also surmise that you didn't live a celibate life in

Montesangre. If you were chummy with your guards, I'm certain they made arrangements for you."

"A very astute guess, Lara. In fact I did enjoy a satisfying physical relationship while I was in captivity. She was a beautiful girl, petite and delicate with ebony eyes. She was pathetically willing to please me no matter what I asked of her. She was hardly suited to guerrilla warfare, although she was dedicated to the cause and to her second cousin, Emilio Sánchez Perón.

"When he found out she'd become my lover, he had her disemboweled. I believe he was jealous. During their youth they'd been very close. Or maybe he was afraid that her devotion to me would divide her loyalties. Either way, he brought an end to a very gratifying diversion."

Lara was sickened by the story and the cavalier manner in which Randall related it. She said, "I should have divorced you before we went to Montesangre."

"Possibly. But by then you were pregnant. That made things difficult for you."

"Yes, because you threatened to take the baby away from me unless I stayed with you."

"I could have, too. You were an adulterous wife, hardly a model parent. What court in the land would have awarded custody of a newborn to Clark Tackett's whore?"

He'd posed the same question five years earlier. She'd known it wasn't an empty threat. Had she pursued a divorce and refused to go with him when he left the country, he would have exhausted every effort to win legal custody of the child. She would have fought him to the Supreme Court, except for one major consideration—Ashley. During the years most vital to her development, she would have been shuttled between them, more an object under dispute than a human being. That would have made it almost impossible to raise a contented, well-adjusted child. She hadn't wanted that for her baby.

"Your insults can't hurt me, Randall, because I don't love you. You don't love me. Why perpetuate this myth any longer?"

"Appearances are very important in my line of work," he said with exaggerated patience. "You are garnish, Lara. You always have been. Most wives are. The smarter and prettier they are, the better, but all are little more than what parsley is to prime rib."

Disgusted, she backed away from him.

"Your objections have been noted," he said in a condescending way that further infuriated her. Then he smiled. "Actually I find this new rebellious streak of yours rather exciting, but I'm tiring of it. Save it for a more convenient time, hmm? You'll follow me to Washington and stand meekly by my side just as you followed me to Montesangre and fulfilled your duties as my official hostess."

"The hell I will." She confronted him defiantly and fearlessly. "Because of the terrible ordeal you'd been through, I gave you the benefit of the doubt. But your three years of confinement haven't changed you, Randall. You're as selfish and manipulative as you ever were. Maybe even more so because you now feel the world owes you for what you endured.

"I'm glad you're alive, but I want nothing to do with you. Don't think you can persuade me otherwise. It's over and has been for years.

"I went to Central America with you in exchange for Ashley. I agreed to stay for one year following her birth. We were only weeks away from the deadline when she was killed. I lost her anyway," she said with rancor. "Now that she's dead, your threats are worthless. You have no bargaining power because I've already lost everything that was valuable to me."

"What about Tackett brother number two?"

"You can't harm Key."

"No?" he asked silkily. "Reading between the lines, I'd

say he held his brother in very high regard. Think about it, Lara."

The threat was very subtle, but very real. She schooled her features not to give away her alarm. "You wouldn't say anything to him."

He laughed. "Just as I guessed. He doesn't know. It's still our little secret."

She regarded him for a moment, then snickered. "This time, Randall, I'm calling your bluff." She moved toward the bedroom but at the door turned back. "I don't give a damn what you do so long as you stay away from me. Go to Washington. Make headlines. Rub elbows with the president. Become a celebrity. Have all the affairs you want. The divorce I threatened you with years ago is going to become a reality. I'm filing for it immediately. And from now on, if you want a response, address me as Dr. Mallory. I won't answer to your name."

She slipped into the bedroom and slammed the door.

Chapter Twenty-Six

*J*anellen shielded her eyes from the sun as she impatiently kept a lookout for the pimp-mobile. When she spotted it turning off the main road, she cried, "Mama, he's here!"

Key had called from the landing strip to notify them that he'd just flown in and would be home shortly. The evening before, he'd called from Houston. "The prodigal has returned. Kill the fatted calf."

Janellen hadn't gone to quite that extreme, but she'd told Maydale to prepare a special dinner. Key was alive and well! He was back!

She skipped down the steps and planted herself directly in the path of the approaching Lincoln, forcing him to stop. Flattening her hands on the hood, she smiled at him through the windshield, then ran to the driver's side and launched herself into his arms as he alighted.

"Whoa, there! Watch those cracked ribs." He regained his balance and gave her a hug, then held her at arm's length. "Damn my eyes! You look gorgeous!"

"I do not," she coyly protested.

"I know gorgeous when I see it. What's new? Something."

"I got a haircut and body wave, that's all. In fact I was under the dryer at the beauty parlor when somebody thumped on it and pointed at the TV. They were doing a news bulletin about you, Dr. Mallory, and her husband leaving Montesangre and returning home via

Colombia. When I saw y'all on that screen, my heart nearly stopped."

His smile faltered. "Yeah, it's been an eventful week." Then, tweaking her cheek, he said, "I like the new hairdo."

"Mama hates it. She said it's too frivolous for a woman my age. Do you think so?" she asked worriedly.

"I think it's sexy as hell."

"Why, thank you kindly, sir." She bobbed a curtsy.

"Hmm. You've learned to flirt, too." He placed his hands on his hips and tilted his head as he eyed her up and down. "Is there something going on that I should know about?"

"No." Her answer had been too quick and too emphatic. If her cheeks looked as hot as they felt, her brother would know instantly that she was lying.

"Cato's still sniffing, huh?"

She tried to keep from smiling but was helpless to contain the joy that infused her at the very mention of his name. It conjured up memories of the hours they'd spent necking in the parlor late at night, arguing in whispers over the rightness and wrongness of their romance—she advocating the former, he the latter—planning on a future that she insisted they had and he insisted they didn't.

For all their quarrels about the nature and life span of their affair, it *was* an affair. Short of having it consummated and being with Bowie twenty-four hours a day, Janellen couldn't have been happier.

That happiness was transparent, especially to her intuitive brother. He broke a wide smile. "He'd better treat you right. If he doesn't and I hear of it, I'll chase him down, tear off his nuts, and feed them to a dog. You can tell him I said so."

"I wouldn't tell him any such thing!" she declared. "It'd be unladylike." Then she laughed at her private joke, remembering the shocking vocabulary she'd used with Bowie to assure that she got his attention. She didn't regret it. It had worked.

Linking arms with Key, she turned him toward the house. "You must be exhausted. I had Maydale put fresh linens on your bed. You can climb between them as soon as you've had dinner and a long, hot bath."

When he came to a sudden standstill, Janellen glanced up. Jody was watching them from the porch. She looked very well. Apparently the doctors had been alarmists after all, and, as usual, Jody had been right. She was getting better in spite of their dire prognosis.

In the last few days there'd been visible signs of improvement. She claimed to feel better and had more energy. She'd been alert and hadn't fussed when it came time to take her medication. She'd even cut back to two packs of cigarettes a day. Yesterday she'd resumed her standing appointment at the beauty shop.

Janellen doubted it was coincidental that Jody had begun perking up on the day they learned that Key had left Montesangre. Despite their frequent quarrels, her mother and brother cared deeply for each other.

"Hello, Jody."

His tone was reserved, cautious. He was remembering the hurtful, thoughtless things Jody had said to him before he left. Jody too must have been remembering her searing words. Her thin lips twitched once, as though she experienced an uncomfortable twinge.

"I see you made it back in one piece."

"More or less."

Janellen's eyes darted between them, wanting desperately to keep this unspoken truce in force. "Let's go inside and have a drink together before dinner."

Jody preceded them into the parlor. She declined a drink but lit a cigarette. "I read that the rebel army confiscated your airplane." She aimed a plume of smoke toward the ceiling.

"That's right. Thanks, sis." He took the scotch over

rocks his sister had poured for him. "Doesn't matter. The guy who rented it to us was hoping we'd crash or that something catastrophic would happen so he could collect the insurance. He needed the cash more than the airplane."

"I figured it was something like that. You deal with such unscrupulous characters."

"Speaking of unscrupulous characters," Janellen said, trying to avoid any nastiness, "Darcy Winston was at the Curl Up and Dye the day I got my perm. She was going on about her daughter Heather and how she and Tanner Hoskins can't keep their hands off each other. She said before it was over, she might have to turn the garden hose on them."

Key laughed. Janellen looked at him with perplexity. "Everyone else laughed when she said that. I don't get it."

"Oh, for heaven's sake, Janellen," Jody said impatiently.

"What?"

"Never mind," Key said. "Go on. What else did Mrs. Winston have to say?"

"When the news bulletin about you and Dr. Mallory came on, she elbowed everybody else out of the way and hogged the TV. When they announced that Mr. Porter wasn't dead after all, she made a spectacle of herself."

"In what way?" Key was no longer smiling.

"By laughing. No one else thought it was funny. She crowed. Honestly, that woman gives 'tacky' a bad name."

"She's a hot little tramp," Jody said as she flicked ashes into the ashtray. "Fergus thought that marrying a white-trash slut would automatically make her respectable. It didn't, of course. Underneath her fancy designer clothes, she's still trash. Fergus has always been a fool."

Maydale called them to supper and served Key his favorite foods: chicken-fried steaks and roast beef with all the trimmings. For dessert there were two pies—one peach, one pecan—and homemade vanilla ice cream.

Janellen expected him to wolf down the banquet she'd ordered for him, but he ate sparingly. He smiled when talking to her and answered all her questions, but with little elaboration. He was polite to Jody and said nothing to goad or provoke her. For a man who had narrowly escaped death at the hands of guerrilla rebels, he was abnormally subdued.

During lapses in conversation, he stared broodingly into space and had to be forcibly drawn back into the present when talk resumed.

Following the meal, Jody excused herself to go upstairs to watch TV in her room. Before she left the dining room, she looked at him and said, "I'm glad you're all right."

He stared after her thoughtfully.

"She means it, you know," Janellen said quietly. "I think she was more worried about you than I was, and I was crazy with it. She had a real turnaround the day we heard that you were alive and on your way home."

"She looks better than when I left."

"You noticed!" she exclaimed. "I think so, too. I think she's getting well."

He reached out and stroked her cheek, but his smile was sad.

"There's something else, Key. Something about Mama. Yesterday when I came home from work, I couldn't find her and went looking through the house. Guess where she was. In Clark's room, going through his things."

No longer distracted, he was suddenly alert and interested.

"To my knowledge she hasn't been in that bedroom since we picked out his burial suit. What possessed her to go in there now?"

"She was going through his things?"

She nodded. "Papers, certificates of merit, yearbooks,

memorabilia, memos he'd written while he was a senator. And she was crying. She didn't even cry when he was buried."

"I know. I remember."

It struck her then that Key looked very much now as he had at their brother's grave site. Although his actions and verbal responses appeared normal, she got the sense that he was only going through the expected motions, just as he had following Clark's death. He wore a shattered and lost look, as though something incomprehensible had happened.

During the days following their brother's funeral, she'd been too engulfed in her own sorrow to deal with Key's, although even if she'd tried, he probably would have rebuffed her. Besides, she would have felt inadequate. She still did. Nevertheless, she laid her hand on his arm and pressed it compassionately.

"I read a book on bereavement to help me get through Clark's death. According to the author, who's a psychologist, grief can be a delayed reaction. Sometimes a person can deny it for years. Then one day it hits them, and they let it all out. Do you think that's what happened with Mama?"

Key remained thoughtful and didn't say anything.

"I think it's a breakthrough," Janellen said. "Maybe she's finally come to grips with losing him. Now that she's sorted out her feelings, maybe she won't be so angry anymore. You two got along well at dinner. Did you notice the difference in her attitude?"

Key smiled at her affectionately. "You're the eternal optimist, aren't you?"

"Don't make fun of me," she said, wounded.

"I'm not making fun of you, Janellen. It was an observation meant to compliment. If everyone were as guileless as you, the world wouldn't suck nearly as bad as it does."

He playfully tugged on one of her new curls, but his

grin was superficial. "Who knows what compelled Jody to pick through Clark's things? It could mean anything or nothing. Don't expect too much from her. Things don't change that drastically, that quickly. Some things never change. You're in love. You're happy and want everybody else to be."

She laid her head on his chest and hugged him tightly. "It's true, Key. I'm happier than I've been in my entire life. Happier than I believed possible."

"It shows, and I'm damned glad for you."

"But I feel guilty."

Roughly he pushed her away. "Don't," he said angrily. "Milk it for all it's worth. Squeeze every single drop of pleasure from it. You deserve it. You've put up with shit from her, from me, from everybody for years. For chrissake, Janellen, don't apologize for finding happiness. Promise me you won't."

Stunned by his vehemence, she bobbed her head. "All right. I promise."

He pressed a hard kiss on her forehead, then set her away from him again. "I gotta go."

"Go? Where? I thought you'd want to stay home tonight and get some rest."

"I'm rested." He fished in his jeans pocket for his car keys. "I've got a lot of catching up to do."

"Catching up on what?" He shot her a telling look and headed for the door. "Key, wait! You mean like drinking?"

"For starters."

"Women?"

"Okay."

She intercepted him at the front door and forced him to look her in the eye. "I haven't asked because I figured it was your private business."

"Asked me what?"

"About Lara Mallory."

"What about her?"

"Well, I thought, you know, that the two of you might . . ."

"You thought I might take Clark's place in her bed?"

"You make it sound so ugly."

"It was ugly."

"Key!"

"I gotta go. Don't wait up."

Before she opened the door, Lara peered through the blinds to see who had rung the bell, then hastily undid the locks. "Janellen! I'm so glad to see you. Come in." She stood aside and ushered her unexpected guest into the waiting room.

"I hope I'm not disturbing you. I always seem to drop in without calling first. I acted on impulse again."

"Even if you'd called, you wouldn't have been able to get through. I took my phone off the hook. Some reporters don't take 'no' for an answer."

"They've been calling Key, too."

Hearing his name was like getting an arrow through her heart. Trying to ignore the pain, she removed a box of books from the seat of a chair. "Sit down, please. Would you like something to drink? I'm not sure what's in the house— "

"I don't care for anything, thank you." Janellen glanced around at the disarray. "What's all this?"

"This is a mess," Lara said with a wry smile as she sat down on a crate. Wearily, she pushed back a loose strand of hair. Since her return, even involuntary motions seemed to require a tremendous amount of energy. "I'm packing."

"What for?"

"I'm leaving Eden Pass."

Janellen was possibly the only person in town who didn't welcome the news. Her expression was a mix of dismay and despair. "Why?"

"That should be obvious." There was a bitterness in

Lara's voice that she couldn't mask. "Things didn't work out here as I had hoped. Clark was wrong to deed me this place. I was wrong to accept it."

She was touched to see tears in Janellen's eyes. "The people in this town can be so stupid! You're the best doctor we've ever had."

"Their opinion of me had nothing to do with my qualifications as a physician. They bowed to pressure." It was unnecessary to cite Jody Tackett as the party responsible for the shunning.

Janellen already knew, and felt guilty by association. "I'm sorry."

"I know you are. Thank you." The two women smiled at each other. If circumstances had been different, they could have become very good friends. "How is your mother doing? Has the medication been effective?"

Janellen told her about Jody's marked improvement. Lara didn't want to dampen her optimism, but felt it was her professional duty to interject some realism. "I'm glad to hear that she's feeling better, but stay vigilant. She must continue taking the medication until her doctor instructs otherwise. I recommend frequent, periodic checkups. And before you completely reject the idea of angioplasty to dilate the carotid, I recommend another round of extensive testing."

"I don't think Mama would agree to it, but if I notice signs of stress or—heaven forbid—another seizure, I'll insist."

They chatted for a few minutes more, then Janellen rose to leave. At the door she said, "I saw your husband on *The Today Show* this morning. They had videotape of him being greeted by the president."

"Yes, I saw it, too."

"The interviewer asked why you weren't with him. He said you were so overwrought from your experiences in Montesangre that you were unable to accompany him to Washington."

It rankled that Randall was serving as her mouthpiece and giving out false information. She had made her position unequivocally clear to him when they were in Houston and had remained locked in her bedroom of the suite until she was certain he had left the hotel for the airport to catch his Washington flight. They hadn't said goodbye.

His excuses for her absence in Washington were self-serving, but, other than confronting him about it, there was nothing she could do to stop him. The issue wasn't worth having another private encounter. Their next one would be in a divorce court, and then she would have an attorney speaking for her.

"It must have been . . ." Janellen hesitated, then plunged ahead. "Well I can't even imagine how you felt when you discovered that he had been alive all this time."

"No, I'm sure you can't imagine."

Introspectively, Lara again saw Randall lying in the bathtub. She heard her screams echoing off the gaudy tile walls, heard the crunch of breaking wood as Key kicked his way through the door, felt his arms closing around her. She had buried her face against his chest. At first they had thought Randall was dead.

But he'd come back to life.

Key hadn't touched her since, not even casually.

There were no words to describe the enormity of the shock caused by Randall's resurrection, so she simply said, "I was astounded to see him alive."

"I'm sure you were, but you don't appear overwrought. Why didn't you go to Washington with him?" On the heels of her blunt question, Janellen quickly withdrew it. "I'm sorry. That was unforgivably rude."

"No need to apologize. You asked a legitimate question. The answer is simply that I chose not to go. Politics is Randall's arena, not mine. What he does with his recent celebrity is up to him. I want to ignore mine, and I wish that everyone else would."

"So does Key."

The arrow in her heart twisted. "He seemed extremely uncomfortable to find himself suddenly in the spotlight."

Janellen's sweet face puckered with anguish as she blurted out, "He's going away again. To Alaska. He told me this morning. He's been offered a job as a spotter along the pipeline. That's a pilot who checks for leaks."

Lara nodded vaguely.

"He says it's good money and that he needs a change of scenery. I reminded him that he'd just had a change of scenery, but he said the trip to Central America didn't count. I don't want him to go," she said, her anxiety plain. "But now that Mama's in better health, I guess there's nothing to keep him here."

"I guess not." Her voice had a hollow ring.

"I'm so worried about him," Janellen went on. "At first I thought he was just tired from the ordeal, but you've been back a week and he hasn't snapped out of it yet."

Lara was instantly alarmed. "Is he ill?"

"No, he's not sick. Not physically. He's withdrawn. His eyes don't sparkle anymore. He doesn't even yell when he gets mad. That's not like him."

"No, it isn't."

"It's like somebody pulled the plug on the electricity that kept him charged."

Lara didn't know how to respond.

"Well," Janellen concluded awkwardly. "I just thought I'd tell you."

She hesitated, as though there was more she wanted to say. Lara wondered if she knew that they'd slept together. Surely she couldn't know . . . but maybe she'd guessed.

"Well, uh . . . When are you leaving town?"

"I don't have a timetable, just whenever I get everything packed. I haven't yet made arrangements with a realtor to handle the sale of this building."

"Will you be moving to Washington?"

"No," she answered sharply. Ameliorating her tone, she added, "I haven't made any specific plans."

"You're going to pack up and leave, and you don't even know where you're going?"

"That's the gist of it," Lara replied with a weak smile.

Janellen was flabbergasted, but common courtesy kept her from prying further. "When you know your new address, would you please send it to me? I realize there's bad blood between you and us Tacketts, but I'd like to stay in touch."

"You had nothing to do with the 'bad blood,'" Lara said gently. "I'd love to hear from you."

Janellen seemed to debate whether it was the proper thing to do, but in the end she gave Lara a quick hug before rushing down the walk to her car.

Lara watched until she drove out of sight. Slowly she closed the door, symbolically ending a chapter of her life. This visit with Janellen was probably the last contact she'd have with the Tacketts.

Later, Janellen and Bowie were cuddled up on the parlor sofa. All the lights were out. Jody had retired to her room hours earlier. Key, as usual, was out.

Bowie was semireclined on the corner cushions with Janellen sprawled across his lap. She was using his shoulder as a pillow for her head while she mindlessly strummed his bare chest through his unbuttoned shirt.

"It was so sad," she whispered. "She was standing there surrounded by all those boxes, looking like she was at a complete loss about what to do next."

"Maybe you read her wrong."

"I don't think so, Bowie. She looked like she didn't have a friend in the world."

"Doesn't make sense. She just found out her dead husband is alive."

"It doesn't make sense to me, either. Why isn't she with

him? If I had believed you were dead, and discovered you weren't, I never would let you out of my sight again. I love you so much that— " She raised her head. "Well, I'll be. That's it. Dr. Mallory doesn't love her husband anymore. Maybe she's fallen in love with somebody else."

"Calm down now. You're cooking up something in your mind that ain't necessarily so."

"Like what?"

"Like there's something brewing between the doctor and your brother."

"You think so too?" she asked excitedly.

"I don't think anything. I think that's what you think. Flying off to Central America alone together and getting captured by guerrilla fighters is pretty romantic stuff. Sounds like a movie. But don't go reading anything into it that's not there."

She looked chagrined and admitted that a romance between Key and Lara had crossed her mind. "Both of them seem so wretchedly unhappy since they got back. Key's itching to leave."

"He's always been a drifter. You told me so yourself."

"It's more than wanderlust this time. He's not rushing toward a new adventure, he's running away from something. And that describes Dr. Mallory, too. She didn't act like a woman whose beloved has suddenly returned from the dead." She made a face. "From what I saw of him on TV, I can't say I blame her. He sounded like a real jerk. Besides, he's not nearly as handsome as Key."

Bowie chuckled. "You've got a romantic streak a mile wide, you know that?"

"Key said that I'm in love and want everybody else to be as happy as I am. He was right."

"About you wanting everybody to be happy?"

"About my being in love." She gazed into his soulful eyes, her love exposed. Cupping his face, she asked earnestly, "When, Bowie?"

This subject often came up. Each time it did, it

either fanned their passions or squelched them. Tonight it caused a physical breach. Frowning, he disengaged himself from her embrace, stood, and began rebuttoning his shirt.

"We have to talk, Janellen."

"I don't want to talk anymore. I want to be with you. I don't care where it has to be as long as we can be together."

He averted his eyes self-consciously. "I found a place I think might do."

"Bowie!" She had a hard time keeping her voice to an excited stage whisper. "Where is it? When can we go? Why didn't you tell me?"

Choosing to answer her last question first, he said, "Because it isn't right, Janellen."

"You don't like the room?"

"No, the room is all right. It's . . ." He paused and shook his head with exasperation. "I hate sneaking in here every night like a damn kid, fumbling around in the dark, copping feels, having to whisper like we're in the goddamn library, then leaving by the back door. It's no damn good."

"But if you've found a place where we can go— "

"It would only be worse. You're too fine a woman to be snuck through the back doors of motels for a quick toss." He held up his hands to stave off her protests. "And another thing, you might think we could carry on without anyone finding out, but you're fooling yourself. We couldn't. I've lived in Eden Pass long enough to know how fast and accurate the grapevine is. It's too risky to take a chance.

"Sooner or later word would get back to your mama. She'd probably come after me with a shotgun or sic the law on me. Hell, I've been in scrapes before. If she didn't flat-out kill me, I'd survive. But not you. You haven't had a troubled day in your life. You wouldn't know how to handle it."

"I've had lots of trouble."

"Not the kind I'm talking about."

She'd learned from her brothers that men hated when women cried, so she tried her best to keep from bursting into tears. "Are you trying to get out of it, Bowie? Are you making up excuses when actually you just don't want me? Is it my age that's turned you off?"

"Come again?"

A small sob escaped. "That's it, isn't it? You're trying to worm out of it because I'm older than you."

He was equally vexed and incredulous. "You're older than me?"

"Three years."

"Who's counting?"

"Apparently you. That's why you're trying to back out. You could have a woman much younger than I."

"Shit!" He paced in a small circle, swearing under his breath. Finally he came back around and looked down at her with annoyance. "How long did it take you to dream up that crap? For chrissake, I didn't even know how old you were, and even if I had known, it wouldn't have made any difference. Don't you know me better than that? Shit."

"Then why?"

His aggravation dissolved, and he knelt in front of her, clasping her hands. "Janellen, as far as I'm concerned, you're way up there above any other human who's ever drawn breath. I'd rather lose my right arm than hurt you. That's why I never should have let this get started. The first time I felt that yearning for you, I should have packed up and left town. I knew better, only I couldn't help myself."

He paused, searching her face with such intensity that he seemed to be memorizing it. He ran his thumb across her trembling lips. "I love you better'n I love my own self. That's why I won't sneak you in and out of rented bedrooms, hide you like you were a floozie, and have you gossiped about like you're white trash."

He came to his feet and reached for his hat. "I won't do that to you. No way in hell. No, ma'am." He placed his hat on his head and gave the brim a firm tug. "That's the end of it."

Lara weakly leaned her head against the doorjamb. "This isn't a good idea, Key."

"Since when has anything involving you been a good idea?"

He forced his way past her. She closed the back door behind him after checking to make sure no one was around to see his arrival. It was a futile precaution. Having the distinctive yellow Lincoln parked in her driveway was as good as announcing it on local radio.

When she turned back into the room, he was leaning against a supply cabinet. His shirttail was hanging loose outside his jeans. He was an untidy, disturbing, sexy reminder of the first time she'd seen him in this same room.

That night he'd asked her for whiskey. This time he'd brought his own. The liquor sloshed inside the bottle when he raised it to his mouth and took a drink. The gash on his temple had closed, but the skin around it was still bruised. So were his ribs. His expression was insolent, his complexion flushed.

"You're drunk."

"You're right."

She folded her arms across her middle. "Why'd you come here?"

"Can Ambassador Porter come out and play?" he asked mockingly.

"He's still in Washington."

"But he'll be here tomorrow. They printed a story

about it in the evening edition. 'Hero Statesman Visits Eden Pass.' Big fuckin' deal."

"If you knew he wasn't here, why'd you ask?"

He grinned. "Just to get a rise out of you. To see if your heart would go pitter-pat at the mention of his name."

"I think you'd better go." Coldly turning her back to him, she opened the door.

His hand shot forward from behind her and slammed it shut; then he kept his palm flattened against the wood, trapping her between himself and the door. In the small wedge of space, she turned to face him.

"You never did answer my question."

"What question?"

"About your daughter. Since we made it back alive, I want to know. Was she Clark's kid?"

What did he want to hear? she wondered. What did she want to tell him?

The unvarnished truth.

Oh, God, what a liberating luxury that would be. She could fully explain the situation, fill in all the unknown details, and, by doing so, perhaps make Key feel more charitable toward her.

The mitigating circumstances were the critical ones. Ironically, because they were so very critical, they must remain a secret.

Especially from Key. Especially now that she knew she loved him.

"Randall was Ashley's father."

Regret flickered in his eyes. "You sure?"

"Yes."

She could see that it made a difference to him, but he tried not to show it. "So you suckered me into risking my life for nothing."

"I didn't persuade you to go to Montesangre, you persuaded yourself. I never even suggested that Clark was Ashley's father."

"You never denied it, either." He leaned in closer. His

whiskey-scented breath felt hot on her face. "You're a real piece of work, aren't you? A clever manipulator. A tricky chick.

"At first I couldn't understand how my rational brother could have such a careless affair with his best friend's wife. You did a real seduction number on him, didn't you? Pussy-whipped him till he didn't know which end was up. Then dopey ol' Randall stayed with you. What a sap. He's a prick, probably a liar, but even he doesn't deserve your royal treatment."

His hands clasped her waist and with one swift motion yanked her against him. He nuzzled her neck beneath her ear. "You're good at getting what you want from a man, aren't you, Doc? You mind-fuck him real good before he even gets his cock out."

Lara squeezed her eyes shut. The accusations were ugly. They hurt, especially coming from Key. Key, who more than once had risked his life to save hers, who had been tender and passionate, ardent and loving, whose touch she still craved and whose voice haunted her dreams.

Based on the facts, *as he knew them*, he had cause to insult her. His scorn was founded on what he believed was truth. It was a miscalculation she couldn't rectify—far more for Key's sake than her own.

She wanted him desperately. But not this way. She'd conditioned herself to tolerate the world's contempt, but she refused to nurture his.

"I want you to leave."

"Like hell." He dropped the liquor bottle, slipped his hand beneath her skirt, and tugged on her panties. "You're all I can smell. All I can taste. All I think about." His mouth covered hers and ground an angry kiss into it. "Jesus, I gotta get you out of my system."

"No, Key!" She pressed her thighs together.

"How come? It's not like you haven't been unfaithful before."

She swatted away the hand groping at her breasts. "Stop this!"

"You owe me, remember? Either the ninety thousand balance of my hundred grand. Or this." He forced his hand between her thighs and fondled her intimately. "I choose this."

"No!"

"Don't worry, I'll leave before sun-up. Your husband won't catch you in the act this time. I'm smarter than my brother. I'm also better. *Aren't I?*"

"No, you're not," she cried. "Clark never had to resort to rape!"

That sobered him as instantly as the cold water she'd once thrown in his face. He released her and staggered backward, his breath coming harsh and loud.

Knowing the root of his aggression, Lara felt more sorrow than anger. She longed to touch his face, run her fingers through the damp strands of hair clinging to his forehead, placate him, tell him she regretted having to hurt him in the worst possible way—by unfavorably comparing him to Clark.

Instead, she had to let her statement stand and watch his lip curl with repugnance for his brother's cast-off, adulterous whore.

He looked her over and made a scornful sound. "No, I'm sure he didn't. Relax, Doc. You're safe from me."

He reached around her and pulled open the door. The liquor bottle almost tripped him. He kicked it out of his way. It crashed against the wall and shattered.

He stormed through the door, leaped over the steps, and climbed into the Lincoln. He gunned it; the tires spun in the gravel before gaining traction. He sped away.

Lara closed the door and, with her back to it, slid to the floor. Folding her arms across her lap, she bent at the waist and released a keening cry.

Chapter Twenty-Seven

So this is it? This is what you're so reluctant to leave?"

Randall had strolled through the rooms of the clinic and wound up in Lara's private office, where she'd been packing books and files. He'd flown from National Airport to Dallas/Fort Worth and leased a car for the two-hour drive to Eden Pass.

For hours before his arrival, media vans had been cruising the street in front of the clinic on the lookout for him. When he arrived, reporters and cameramen flocked to him in impressive numbers.

His ordeal in Montesangre had atoned for the scandal involving his wife and Senator Tackett. Like a wayward child who'd taken his punishment and turned over a new leaf, he'd been warmly received by the president and the Department of State. Having experienced the Montesangren culture from the inside out, he was its reigning expert on Capitol Hill. He was newsworthy.

Lara remained indoors while Randall conducted an impromptu press conference. After fielding questions for several minutes, he begged to be excused.

"My wife and I have had very little time alone since our return. I'm sure you can understand."

After some good-natured snickering, they reloaded their Betacams and microphones into their vans and left. Many honked and waved as though bidding goodbye to a chum.

Now dusk was gathering outside, but Lara hadn't

turned on the lamps in her office. The semidarkness was more in keeping with her mood. It also hid the dark circles beneath her eyes.

Knowing she would never see Key again, she had cried herself into a stupor following his angry departure the night before. He'd left hating her. Her sense of loss was wrenchingly painful and came close to how she'd felt when she regained consciousness in Miami and realized that the terrible nightmare she'd had was indeed real.

Finally, sometime around 2:00 A.M., she garnered the wherewithal to make her way to bed, where she'd lain awake until dawn. She'd spent the day packing her belongings, working feverishly between lapses of immobilizing depression in which her hands were rendered useless and she stared vacantly into space through dry, gritty eyes.

The gloaming made the office feel cozier, warmer, safer, a refuge for her abject despair. She had come to like Dr. Patton's paneled walls and masculine furniture and wished she could look forward to years of enjoying this office.

"It's so provincial," Randall observed as he dropped onto the leather love seat.

"The equipment is modern."

"I'm talking about the whole setup. It's not like you at all."

He didn't have a clue as to what she was like. "Sick people aren't confined to cities, Randall. I could have had a good practice here." She folded down the flaps of a cardboard box and sealed it with duct tape. "That is, if I'd been given a decent chance to cultivate one."

"Tackett territory."

"Indisputably."

"I'm curious about something." He crossed his legs with the negligent elegance of Fred Astaire. "Why in God's name, when you had the whole continent to choose from, did you elect to practice here? In Texas of all places," he said with obvious distaste. "Why pick the town where you'd be most despised? Do you have a bent toward masochism?"

She had no intention of recounting for Randall the last three years of her life. In fact, she had no intention of letting him stay beneath her roof. Before sending him away, however, there was one thing she wanted him to know.

"It wasn't easy for me to pick up my career where it left off," she began. "Even though I had been badly injured and had lost my child and my husband to a bloody revolution, people were slow to forgive. I was still considered Clark's bimbo.

"I applied for staff positions at hospitals all over the country. Some even hired me on my credentials alone before linking Dr. Lara Mallory with Mrs. Randall Porter, whereupon I was sanctimoniously asked to resign in the best interests of the institution. This happened a dozen times at least."

"So you finally decided to hang out your shingle. I suppose you used my life insurance money for financing. But that still doesn't explain why you chose to practice here."

"I didn't buy the practice, Randall. It was deeded to me free and clear. By Clark." She paused for emphasis. "It was one of the last official things he did before his death."

It took him a moment to assimilate the information. When he did, he sucked in a quick breath. "Well, I daresay. He was buying absolution for his sins. How touchingly moral."

"I can only guess at his motivations, but yes, I think he felt he owed me this."

"Now I suppose you're going to present me with a bill. What do I owe you for accompanying me to Montesangre?"

"A divorce."

"Denied."

"You can't deny me anything," she said vehemently. "Key and I saved you from imprisonment in that miserable place! Or have you already forgotten? Has your instant fame wiped your memory clean?"

Gradually a smile spread across his face. It was as patronizing as his tone of voice. "Lara, Lara. So naïve. After all you've been through, you still fail to see beneath the surface, don't you? Hasn't experience taught you anything? Where there's smoke . . . and so on." His hand made a lazy circular gesture. "Haven't you learned to look beyond appearances and see things as they really are?"

"You've made your point, Randall. What the hell does it mean?"

"Do you honestly think that you and that hotheaded pilot precipitated my release?"

His voice had become soft, sibilant, and smug. It caused the hair on the back of her neck to rise. She had a premonition of dread. "What are you saying?"

"Put on your thinking cap, Lara. You passed medical school with flying colors. Surely you can figure this out."

"In Montesangre . . ."

"Yes," he said encouragingly. "Go on."

"Emilio . . ."

"Very good. What else? Stretch your clever little mind."

The mental barriers were opaque, but once she broke through them, everything was crystal clear. "You weren't his prisoner at all."

He laughed. "Good girl! I hate to sound unappreciative, but don't credit yourself with saving my life. My 'five-year plan,' as I like to think of it, was about to be realized in any event. Your comical misadventure with Key Tackett was merely a fortuitous development that Emilio and I used as our catalyst. It made the denouement so much more convincing."

Lara stared at the man to whom she was legally married and knew she was looking into the eyes of a madman. He was perfectly composed, exceedingly articulate, and dangerously sly, the most frightening portrait of a villain.

"It was all a hoax?" she whispered.

Randall left the leather love seat and came to stand close to her. "Following that morning in Virginia, I was despised in Washington. Clark had powerful allies, including the president. He was no doubt embarrassed over Clark's conduct, but he stood by his protégé. To a point, anyway.

"At Clark's request, he appointed me ambassador and called in favors in the Senate to have my approval rushed. On the surface, I accepted graciously, humbly, like they had done me a bloody favor. Actually, I despised it as much as you, knowing that it was a legal form of banishment.

"No sooner had I arrived at my post than I began to devise ways of returning to Washington a hero. Emilio was a bright boy who had his own ambitions, which were fulfilled with Pérez's death."

"Murder."

"Whatever. Together, we contrived a plot that would give each of us what he wanted. My 'escape' had to be carefully timed and fully capitalized upon. Once I returned to the U.S., rather than harboring a grudge toward my captors, I would insist on being reassigned to Montesangre, reopening the embassy, and reestablishing diplomatic relations with the new regime."

Imperceptibly, Lara was edging toward the telephone. "Emilio's regime."

"Precisely. Upon my advice to the president, Emilio's government would soon be acknowledged. With the endorsement of the United States, he'd have absolute control of his republic. I'd be credited with restoring peace to a hostile nation which could be strategic in fighting the drug wars. After a suitable time, my endeavors surely would be rewarded either with a plum appointment abroad or in Washington. A far cry from the cuckold, hey?"

"You're crazy."

"Like a fox, Lara. It's been well thought out, I assure you. After years, the realization is unfolding even better than anticipated. What I need now is a loving wife to round out my image as a exemplary diplomat.

"So, darling, you will remain faithfully and meekly by my side, smiling at the press, waving to the crowds, until I say otherwise. Don't even think of doing anything to jeopardize this."

She began to laugh. "You're a traitor with delusions of grandeur, Randall. Do you honestly think I'm going to participate in this traitorous 'five-year plan' of yours?"

"Yes, I think you will," he replied calmly. "What choice do you have?"

"I'll blow the whistle. I'll tell them about Emilio's brutality. I'll call— "

"Who would believe *you?*" He shook his head sadly over her delusions. "Who would trust anything said by the woman caught in adultery with Senator Tackett? You have no more credibility now than you did that morning we left his cottage."

He indicated the telephone she'd been inching toward. "I can see you're itching to call for help. Go ahead. You'll only make a laughingstock of yourself. Who's going to believe that a U.S. ambassador started a revolution which was contrary to the interests of the country he served?"

"'Started a revolution'? What do you mean? The revolution started when . . . when our car was . . . No, wait." She held up her hand as though to ward off a barrage of confusing thoughts. They were crowding her mind so quickly she couldn't arrange them.

"You're slipping, my dear," he said silkily. "The mental sluggishness must come from living on the frontier. Think, now. I said *five*-year plan. It took root when we reached Montesangre, not when I was kid-napped."

Her heart began to beat faster; she clutched her throat, which had suddenly gone dry. Something was just beyond her grasp. Something she should remember. Something—

The truth struck her with the impact of a bullet. The fog lifted from her memory and those forgotten instants immediately preceding the ambush were replayed in slow motion in her mind.

She was playing patty-cake with Ashley in the backseat. The car approached the intersection. As it slowed down, armed men rushed forward, surrounding it. The driver was shot and slumped forward over the steering wheel.

She cried out. Randall turned to look at her. "Goodbye, Lara." Unafraid, he smiled.

Her breath rushed out in a gust. "You knew!" she screamed. "You and Emilio arranged the ambush on our car! You had our daughter killed!"

"Shut up! Do you want the whole neighborhood to hear you?"

"I want the whole world to hear me."

He struck her across the mouth. Talking rapidly, quietly, he said, "You fool! I didn't intend for the child to be killed. The bullets weren't meant for her."

Lara didn't even stop to consider what that statement implied. She lunged for the camera bag. It was on her desk, where she had left it, undisturbed, since the day she returned from Montesangre.

Under the concealment of darkness, she plunged her hand into the bag. Her fingers closed around the butt of the revolver. She withdrew it and swung around, aiming the barrel at the center of Randall's chest.

"This is your last chance to change your mind."

Janellen smiled at Bowie. "I'm not going to change my mind. I'm absolutely, positively, one hundred percent sure of my decision. Besides, you were the one with cold feet, the one dead set against it. I finally wore you down, so I'm not about to back out or let you, either." She linked her arm with his and nestled her head on his shoulder. "Just drive, Mr. Cato. I'm anxious to get there."

"If anybody sees me driving your car— "

"It's dark. Nobody's going to see us. If someone does, they'll probably think that Key asked you to protect me from reporters again."

"Yeah, I saw them all over town today."

"They were hoping to catch a glimpse of Mr. Porter." The reminder intruded on Janellen's happiness and caused her to frown. "Mama watched him on the news. Seeing him really upset her."

"Why should it?"

"Because it calls to mind the scandal, Clark, all that. She skipped supper and went upstairs to her room."

"You waited until Maydale got there before you left?"

As prearranged, he and Janellen had met at the Tackett Oil office. "Yes. She came to spend the night. I told her I was going to Longview to attend a self-improvement seminar."

"What about Key?"

"Key never gets home before noon, sometimes not even then. He claims he's playing poker till dawn with Balky out at the landing strip. It's easier to sleep out there than to drive home, he says. Anyway, he'll never know I'm gone."

Bowie glanced nervously at every car that passed. "This sneaking around doesn't feel right. Something terrible is bound to happen."

"Honestly, Bowie." She sighed with affectionate exasperation. "You're the most pessimistic, fatalistic person I've ever met. A few months ago you were the one with the record, but I was living in a kind of prison. Both our fortunes have changed."

"Yours will if you stick with me long enough," he said glumly. "You'll lose your fortune."

"I've told you a million times that I don't care if I do. My family had lots of money, but we weren't happy. There was no love between my parents. That antagonism affected my brothers and me. We felt it even before we were old enough to understand it.

"It made Clark an overachiever who couldn't forgive himself even the most insignificant mistake. Key went too far the other way and lives like he doesn't give a damn about anything, although I believe that's a defense mechanism. He doesn't want anyone to guess how deeply he was hurt by our father's death and Mama's rejection.

"And I became a shy, introverted dullard, afraid to voice an opposing opinion on anything. Believe me, Bowie—money doesn't buy happiness and love. I'd rather have your love than all the riches in the world."

"That's 'cause you've never had to do without the riches."

They'd been over this ground so many times they'd trampled it to death. She was determined not to let an argument cast a pall over the happiest night of her life.

"I know exactly what I'm doing, Bowie. I'm beyond the age of consent. I love you to distraction, and I think you love me the same."

He glanced at her and answered with deadpan seriousness. "You know I do."

"That gives us the strength to face anything. What can possibly happen to us that we can't combat?"

"Oh, damn," he groaned. "You've just tempted Fate to show us."

"Bowie," she said, laughing and nuzzling his neck, "you're a sight."

Darcy spotted Key the moment she entered The Palm.

He sat alone at the end of the bar, hunched over his drink like a stingy dog with a bone.

She was in a buoyant mood. Fergus was at a school board meeting, which traditionally dragged on for hours. She loved school board meetings. They liberated her for an evening out.

Heather was on desk duty at the motel. Odds were highly in favor of her taking home the crown of homecoming queen this coming Friday night.

Darcy had spent over seven hundred dollars to outfit Heather for the occasion. Fergus would have a fit if he knew, but she considered the expenditure a good investment. If Heather won homecoming queen, it would boost her chances of getting into the best sorority when she went to college. Fergus might not appreciate the subtle way these things worked, but Darcy did.

Although she drove a new car every other year, belonged to the country club, wore expensive clothes, and lived in the largest house in Eden Pass, she still was excluded from the inner social circles.

She was determined that Heather would reverse that. Heather would be her ticket into every tight clique even if she would have to enter through the back door.

Key's posture smacked of potential danger, but she decided to approach him anyway. So what if the last time she'd seen him she'd spat in his face and he'd threatened to murder her? Things weren't going so well for him these days. Having been brought to heel, he might be in a more receptive mood.

She slid onto the barstool next to his. "Hi, Hap. White wine, please. Put some ice cubes in it." The bartender turned to get her drink. She glanced at Key. "Still mad at me?"

"No."

"Oh? You've learned how to forgive and forget?"

"No. In order to be mad, you have to give a shit. I don't."

She quelled her anger, smiled at Hap as he served her wine, and took a sip. "I'm not surprised that you're in such a bear of a mood." As she turned toward him, she brushed his knee with hers. "Must've been quite a shock to discover the dead husband was alive."

"I don't want to talk about it."

"I guess not. It's a touchy subject. Did you at least get to screw her before Ambassador Porter got dumped in her bathtub?"

Key's muscles tensed, telling Darcy he had. She was treading on thin ice, but the one thing she couldn't tolerate from a man was indifference. She'd rather be verbally or physically abused than ignored. Besides, she was curious.

"Was she as good as you expected? Not as good? Better?"

Better, she would guess by the way he tossed back the remainder of his drink and signaled for Hap to pour him another. Gossip around town was that you'd have to be real stupid to cross Key Tackett these days. He was truculent. Testy. Spoiling for a fight.

Just yesterday, at noon, right in the middle of Texas Street, he'd threatened to shove a journalist's camera up the guy's ass if he didn't get it out of his face. Later, he'd gotten into a fight at Barbecue Bobby's with a redneck from out of town who'd parked his pickup too close to the Lincoln to suit Key. Witnesses said it'd be a while before the redneck ventured into Eden Pass again.

Reputedly, he was on the brink of drunkenness at any time of the day or night, and he spent hours at the county airstrip with that dimwit Balky Willis. Someone said he was taking target practice at 4:00 A.M. on the lights at the football stadium, but that was unsubstantiated.

If Lara Mallory's performance in bed had disappointed him, he wouldn't care that her husband had turned up alive and well. On the contrary, the better he liked her, the angrier he'd be over the turn of events.

From what Darcy had heard and could now see for herself, Key was good and pissed.

Jealousy made her reckless. She dared to probe another tender spot. "Guess you know now why your brother was willing to risk his career for her." His jaw flexed. "Wonder how she compared the two of you and which one earned the most points. Did y'all discuss your merits?"

"Shut the fuck up, Darcy."

She laughed. "You did, then. Hmm. Interesting. Three people in one bed can get awfully crowded."

Key turned his head and fixed a heavy-lidded, blood-shot stare on her. "From what I hear, you've been one of a trio more than a few times."

Darcy's temper flared, then instantly subsided. Her laugh was low, seductive. She leaned closer, mashing her breast against his arm. "Damn straight. Had quite a time for myself, too. You ought to try it sometime. Or have you?"

"Not on this continent."

Again she laughed. "Sounds fascinating." She trailed her finger up his arm. "I'm dying to hear all the slippery details."

He didn't dismiss the suggestion out of hand. Encouraged, Darcy reached for her handbag and took out a latchkey. She dangled it inches beyond his nose.

"There are distinct advantages to being a motel proprietor's wife. Like having a skeleton key that'll open the door to every room." She ran her tongue along her lower lip. "What do you say?"

She leaned back a fraction so he'd be certain to see that contact with his biceps had aggravated her nipples to stiff points. "Come on, Key. It was good between us, wasn't it? What else have you got going?"

He finished his drink in a single draft. After tossing enough money on the bar to cover his drinks and Darcy's wine, he pushed her toward the door.

He said nothing until they were outside. "Your car or mine?"

"Mine. You can spot that yellow submarine of yours a mile away. Besides, if my car's seen at the motel, nobody thinks twice about it."

As soon as they were seated in the El Dorado, she leaned across the console and brushed a light kiss across his lips. It was an appetizer, a teaser for good things yet to come. "You've missed me. I know you have."

He remained slumped in his seat, staring balefully through the windshield.

Darcy smiled with feline complacency. He was sulking, but she'd have him revved up in no time. If it was the last thing she did, she'd prove that Lara Mallory was forgettable.

The Cadillac sped in the direction of The Green Pine Motel.

Jody knew Janellen well. The girl wasn't nearly as clever as she thought she was. Ordinarily, any alteration in her routine sent Janellen into a tailspin. She would cajole her to eat, beg her not to smoke, insist that she go to bed, implore her to get up. She hovered like a mother hen.

But tonight when she declined supper, Janellen's nagging had lacked its customary fretfulness. Even before tonight, Jody had detected remarkable changes in Janellen. She fussed over her appearance like never before. She'd begun wearing makeup and had had her hair screwed into that curly, bobbed hairdo. She dressed differently. Her skirts were shorter and the colors brighter.

She laughed more. In fact her disposition was cheerful to the point of giddiness. She went out of her way to be friendly to people she had shied away from before.

Her eyes twinkled with something akin to mischief, which disconcertingly reminded Jody of Key. And of her late husband. Janellen was keeping a secret from her mother for the first time in her life.

Jody guessed it was a man.

She'd overheard Janellen tell Maydale that cock-and-bull story about a seminar in Longview, when it was obvious she was keeping a rendezvous with her fellow, probably at the same motel where her father had entertained some of his tarts. The sordidness of it left a bad taste in Jody's mouth. Hadn't the girl learned anything she'd tried to teach her? Before some fortune-hunting Casanova ruined Janellen's life, she'd have to attend to it.

All the important family issues were her responsibility and had been since she said "I do" to Clark Junior. Where would the Tacketts be today if she hadn't helped maneuver their destiny? Never content to let events evolve on their own capricious course, she handled all the crises herself.

Like the one she was scheduled to take care of tonight.

Of course, first she had to sneak past Maydale.

Fergus Winston's mind was pleasantly drifting.

The school board treasurer was a soprano soloist in the Baptist church choir. She so enjoyed the sound of her own voice that she detailed each entry on the budget report instead of distributing copies and letting the other board members read it.

As she itemized the entries in her wavering falsetto, Fergus hid a private smile, reflecting on his own healthy financial report. Thanks to a relatively temperate summer that had attracted fishermen and campers to the lakes and forests of East Texas, the motel had enjoyed its best season yet.

He was seriously considering Darcy's suggestion of using some of the profits to build a recreation room with workout equipment and video games. Darcy hadn't steered him wrong yet, not since he'd hired her to coordinate his coffeeshop. She had a knack for money-making ideas.

She also had a knack for spending every cent he made. Like most folks, she didn't think he was too astute. Because he loved her, he let her live under the illusion that he didn't know about her extramarital affairs. It hurt that she sought the company of other men, but it wasn't as painful as living without her would be.

He'd heard a radio psychologist spouting off about deep-seated psychological reasons for aberrant human behavior that had roots in childhood. No doubt Darcy was such a case. It made him sad for her, made him love her even more. As long as she continued to come home to him, he would continue to turn a blind eye to her infidelities and a deaf ear to the ridicule of his friends and associates.

She thought he didn't know about the lavish amounts of money she spent on herself and Heather, but he did. His wife had a creative mind, but he was a bean counter. He knew down to the penny what the motel was worth. Over the years he had learned where to hide profits from the IRS, where to be extravagant, where to cut corners.

He smothered a chuckle behind a cough. Thanks to Jody Tackett, he saved thousands of dollars each year. He'd always hoped he would live to see his old enemy die. Before her health got any worse and she became insentient, he must decide whether to let her in on his little secret.

Timing would be critical. After all, he would be confessing a crime. He wanted her lucid enough to grasp the full impact of his admission, but incapable of doing anything about it.

Maybe he should put it in the form of a thank-you note. *Dear Jody, Before you take up residence in eternal Hell, I want to thank you. Remember how you screwed me out of the oil lease? Well, I'm pleased to inform you that—*

"Fergus? What do you think?"

The soprano roused Fergus from his woolgathering.

"I think you've been comprehensive. If there are no corrections or questions, I suggest we move on."

As the vice president introduced the first item of business on that evening's agenda, Fergus returned to his satisfying fantasies of vengeance.

"Your treachery killed my daughter." Lara's voice remained as steady as her extended hands cupping the Magnum .357. "You bastard. You killed my baby. Now I'm going to kill you."

Having the gun leveled at him gave Randall pause, but only momentarily. He recovered admirably. "You tried this dramatic posturing in Montesangre and it didn't play. Emilio saw through it just as I do. You're a healer, Lara, not a killer. You value human life too highly to ever take one.

"However, not everyone shares your elevated regard for his fellow man. Such lofty ideals prohibit you from seizing what you want. The final step is the only one that really counts, Lara. Whether or not you take it determines success or failure. One must be willing to take the final step or he might as well not put forth the effort. In this particular scenario, pulling the trigger is the final step, and you'll never do it."

"I'm going to kill you."

His composure slipped a fraction, but he continued with equanimity. "With what? An empty revolver? The bullets were removed, remember?"

"Yes, I remember. But they were replaced. Key had hidden extra ammunition in a secret pouch of the camera bag. The soldiers missed it during their search. He reloaded the gun before we left the hotel to catch the plane to Colombia." She pulled back the hammer. "I'm going to kill you."

"You're bluffing."

"That's the last judgment call you'll ever make, Randall. And it's wrong."

The racket was deafening. The darkness was splintered by a brilliant orange light as Lara was flung backward against the wall. The heavy revolver fell from her hand.

He inserted the latchkey into the lock. Unseen, they entered the honeymoon suite and closed the door behind them. He reached for the light switch, but when he flipped it up, nothing happened.

"Bulb must be burned out," he said.

"There's a lamp on the end table."

She crossed the sitting room, feeling her way in the darkness. His curiosity about mechanical things compelled him to try the light switch once again.

The light bulb wasn't at fault, but rather an electrical short in the switch. When he flipped it up again, it sparked.

The room exploded.

Chapter Twenty-Eight

*L*ara had the breath knocked out of her when she hit the wall. Collecting herself, she stumbled to the window. It seemed the whole north side of Eden Pass was ablaze.

Grabbing her medical bag, she raced from the house and ignored traffic laws in her haste to reach the roiling column of black smoke. She quickly determined that the site of the explosion was The Green Pine Motel.

She arrived within seconds of the fire truck and the sheriff's patrol car. One wing of the building was engulfed in flames. Periodic explosions within the conflagration sent plumes of fire into the night sky. Damage to the property would be extensive. The casualty rate would depend on the number of rooms occupied. Lara mentally prepared herself for the worst.

"Any signs of survivors?"

Sheriff Baxter had to strain to hear her over the roar of the flames. "Not yet. Jesus Christ. What a mess."

For all their valiant efforts, Lara knew that Eden Pass's fire department, which depended largely on community volunteers, didn't have a prayer of bringing this blaze under control. The fire chief was smart enough to realize that. He didn't send his willing but ill-equipped men into the fire, but gave them orders to try to keep it from spreading. He put in calls for assistance to the larger fire departments within driving distance.

"And call somebody at Tackett Oil," Sheriff Baxter shouted. "That well is too damn close for comfort." The deputy, Gus, got on his police radio.

"Sheriff, can I use the cellular phone in your car to call the county hospital?" The sheriff bobbed his head.

She slid into the driver's seat of the patrol car and placed her call. Luckily she was put through to an efficient emergency room nurse. She explained the situation.

"Dispatch your ambulances at once. Send extra emergency supplies, painkillers and syringes, bandages, portable oxygen canisters." They only had two ambulances, so she suggested that reinforcements be called from surrounding counties. "Also, alert Medical Center and Mother Frances Hospital in Tyler. We'll probably need their helicopters to take the most seriously injured to their trauma centers.

"Tell them to put their disaster teams on standby. Notify all regional blood banks that extra units of blood might be needed, and get an inventory of what types are immediately available. They'll also need extra staff. It's going to be a messy night."

"Over there!" Sheriff Baxter was wildly gesturing to the firemen when she rejoined him.

Shouts could be heard coming from the wing of the motel that hadn't been demolished by the original blast. Lara watched fearfully as a group of volunteer firemen entered the burning building. At any second, another explosion might take their lives.

After several tormenting moments, they began leading out survivors. Two of the firemen were carrying victims on their shoulders. Others were walking under their own power, but Lara could see that they were dazed, burned, and choking from smoke inhalation.

She instructed the firemen to line them up on the ground, then she moved among them, assessing their injuries, mentally noting the ones who were the most critically injured, dispensing the only medicine she had at the moment—encouragement.

The wail of sirens had never been so welcome. The first of the ambulances arrived and disgorged three paramedics. Working quickly with them, she started IVs, began giving oxygen, and indicated which of the injured should be taken immediately to the hospital. Paramedics unloaded several boxes of emergency supplies for her use, then sped away with their injured passengers.

The others looked at her through pain-glazed eyes. She hoped they understood how difficult it was to play God, to decide who would go and who would stay.

The firemen made other forays into the blaze. The number of survivors increased, but that made it more difficult for Lara to deal with everyone. Two were in shock. Several were crying, one was screaming in agony. Some were unconscious. She did what she could to administer essential first aid.

She was kneeling beside a man, applying a tourniquet to a compound fracture of his ulna, when car tires screeched dangerously close. She turned her head, hoping to see another ambulance.

Darcy Winston stumbled from the driver's side of her El Dorado. "*Heather!*" she screamed. "Oh my God! Heather! Has anybody seen my daughter?"

She charged toward the building and would have rushed headlong into the inferno if one of the firemen hadn't caught her and pulled her back. She fought him. "My daughter's in there!"

"Oh, no," Lara groaned. "No." Had the girl with whom she'd developed an instant rapport been a casualty? She looked for Heather Winston among the rescued, but she wasn't there.

"Sweet Jesus."

At the sound of Key's voice, Lara turned and realized with lightning clarity that he had arrived with Darcy. Shoving personal considerations aside, she said, "Help me, Key. I can't handle this alone."

"I'll get a chopper. On the way I'll call my sister and get her over here to help you." He glanced in the distance. "Christ, that well— "

"They've already notified someone at Tackett Oil."

"That's number seven. It's on Bowie's route, I believe. He should be along shortly. Once he caps off the well, he'll pitch in and help, too."

He had remained in motion since alighting, rounding the hood of Darcy's car and moving toward the driver's side. "You okay?"

"I'm fine. Just please help me get these people to the hospital."

"Be right back." He jumped behind the wheel and sped away even before closing the car door. Moments following his departure, three more ambulances arrived.

The volunteer firemen carried five more victims from the building, replacing the ones Lara had dispatched to the hospital. An elderly woman succumbed to smoke inhalation a few minutes after her rescue. Her daughter held her lifeless hand and sobbed.

A toddler, who appeared unharmed, was crying for his mother. Lara didn't know to whom he belonged, or if his mother had even been rescued.

"I'll take care of him."

The offer came from Marion Leonard. Lara's lips parted in surprise, but she didn't waste time on questions. "That would be very helpful. Thank you." She passed the crying child to Marion, who carried him away, speaking soothingly.

Jack Leonard was there too. "Tell me what to do, Dr. Mallory."

"I'm sure the firemen could use some help dispensing oxygen." He nodded and went to do as she suggested.

Fergus Winston had arrived, Lara noticed. He was holding his wife in his arms. Darcy was gripping the lapels of his coat and crying copiously. "You're sure, Fergus? You swear to God?"

"I swear. Heather called to tell me that they were having an extra cheerleading practice tonight. I gave her permission to leave her shift early."

"Oh, Jesus, thank you. Thank you." Darcy collapsed against him.

He held her close, smoothing back her hair, stroking her tear-ravaged cheeks, assuring her that their daughter was safe. But his long, sad face and woebegone eyes reflected the light from the fire that was rapidly consuming his business.

When the clap and clatter of helicopter blades reached her ears, Lara looked skyward. A Flight for Life helicopter had arrived. Minutes later it lifted off with two patients aboard. Shortly after that, Key landed the private helicopter he'd borrowed before to transport Letty Leonard. Lara directed two women who had sustained severe cuts and bruises from a blown-out window to the chopper.

"Have you seen Janellen?" he shouted over the racket. Lara shook her head. "Our housekeeper said she went to Longview." He shrugged. "No one at Tackett Oil can locate Bowie either."

"If she shows up, I'll tell her you're looking for her."

He gave her a thumbs-up sign. "I'll be back when I can." The chopper lifted off.

Lara returned to her task, which she worked at unceasingly until time had no relevance. She measured it only by the number of survivors she could keep alive or make more comfortable until they could be transferred to a hospital. She tried not to think about those whom she could not save.

She wasn't without volunteer help. Jimmy Bradley and his wife of two weeks, Helen Berry, arrived and offered her their assistance. So did Ollie Hoskins. Her former nurse, Nancy Baker, was a most welcome sight. She was able, quick, and experienced enough to handle even the most gruesome injuries. Other townsfolk who had previously shunned her volunteered their services. She didn't refuse anyone's help.

That night the motel had been staffed by six employees.

The total number of guests occupying rooms was eighty-nine—and two that no one knew about.

Bowie Cato carried his bride over the threshold of the honeymoon suite in the downtown Shreveport hotel.

"Oh, Bowie, it's beautiful." Janellen admired the sky-line view as he set her down in the center of the room.

"I shopped around. When I heard about this place, I had to get written permission from my parole officer to come over here on account of it being in Louisiana."

"You went to a lot of trouble."

"It was worth it if you like it."

"I love it."

"For what it's costing, we might not eat for the first month of our married life."

She laughed and placed her arms around his waist. "If you ask your boss nicely, I bet you'll get a raise."

"There's not going to be any favoritism to me just 'cause I'm the boss lady's husband," he said sternly. "I'm no gold-digger. I made that plain the night I talked myself right out of an affair and into an elopement." He shook his head in bafflement. "Still can't quite figure how that happened."

"You refused to let me be gossiped about like I was trash. And I said the solution to that was for us to get married."

He worriedly gnawed the inside of his cheek. "Your mama might have it annulled."

"She can't. I'm a grown-up."

"Key might shoot me."

"I'll shoot him back."

"Don't joke about it. I hate like hell to come between you and your family."

"I love them, but nothing is as important to me as you are, Bowie. For better or worse, you're my husband now." She coyly ducked her head. "Or you will be as soon as you stop talking and take me to bed."

In high heels, she was as tall as he. Leaning forward, she kissed him lightly on the lips. He made a grunt of acquiescence and took her into his arms, drawing her close for a deep kiss. He became fully aroused almost immediately and stepped back self-consciously. "Want me to leave you alone for a while?"

"What for?"

Nervously, he rubbed his palms up and down his thighs. "So you can . . . Hell, I don't know. Do what brides do, I guess. I figured you wanted some privacy."

"Oh." She was crestfallen and it showed in her expression. "I thought you might want to undress me yourself."

"I do," he said in a rush. "I mean, if you want me to."

She seemed to think it over carefully before nodding.

He flexed his fingers like a safecracker about to attempt his personal best and reached for the buttons on her blouse—small pearl buttons very much like the ones that had engendered his first fantasies about her.

Their restraint diminished with each article that was removed. They undressed each other leisurely, allowing time to celebrate each discovery. Even though she'd grown up with two brothers in the house, she had a childlike curiosity about his body. Whispering in wonderment, she told him he was handsome, and he said he hadn't realized her eyesight was so bad. When he told her she was beautiful, she believed it, because his caresses were strongly convincing. He made her feel like a goddess of beauty and romance.

"I don't want to hurt you. Janellen," he whispered as he poised above her.

"You won't."

He didn't, even when he was deep inside her. She was awkward and perhaps too eager to please, so he told her to relax and let him do all the work. She did as he suggested, and to their mutual delight and surprise, her climax was as tumultuous as his.

Afterward, they drank the complimentary bottle of champagne that came with the room. She selected names for their first four children. He swore that by Valentine's Day he'd have enough money saved to buy her a wedding ring like a proper groom, but she argued that she didn't need anything tangible to symbolize his love. She felt it with every breath she drew.

Drowsy with love and champagne, he murmured, "Want to try out the whirlpool bath, or watch HBO, or something?"

"Or something." She flashed him a gamine smile that would have amazed the matrons of Eden Pass who had considered her a hopeless old maid, then slid her hand beneath the sheet and boldly fondled him.

"Good Lord have mercy on us all," he said, gasping. "Miss Janellen's done turned into a regular sex fiend."

Had Bowie and Janellen turned on the television set in their honeymoon suite, they would have seen the news bulletins on the catastrophic fire in Eden Pass that had already claimed ten lives. All the victims had been identified and the authorities were notifying next of kin.

It was hours before the firefighters from six counties finally brought the flames under control. By dawn, the preliminary investigation into the cause of the explosion was under way. Inspectors began sifting through the smoldering ruin.

Early speculation was that Tackett Oil's well number seven might have been a contributing factor. Since Bowie couldn't be located, his supervisor had capped off the oil and gas lines.

Following that precaution, there had been no other explosions, indicating that the well had indeed been feeding the flame.

*   *   *

Key, the only Tackett readily available, was being questioned by federal agents from the Department of Tobacco, Alcohol, and Firearms.

"Y'all ever have any problem with that well leaking oil or gas, Mr. Tackett?"

"Not to my knowledge, but I'm not involved in my family's business."

"Who is?"

"My sister. She's out of town."

"I understood that your mother was the ramrod of the outfit."

"Not for the last several years."

"I'd still like to talk to her."

"I'm sorry, but that's out of the question. She had a mild stroke a few weeks back and is virtually bedridden."

Lara, who was standing by listening, said nothing to contradict him. Neither did anyone else.

"All I can tell you," he said to the agents, "is that Tackett Oil has always been stringent about safety. Our record is unblemished."

The agents huddled together for another conference.

Scores of curious bystanders milled about, eager to survey the damage now that the threat of danger had passed. They consoled Darcy and Fergus Winston over their enormous loss.

Darcy, who still looked spectacular while everyone else was covered with grime, continually scanned the gathering crowd for sight of Heather. She'd asked Lara several times if she had seen her. She wept softly and daintily and kept repeating to those who offered words of encouragement, "I just can't believe that all our hard work went up in smoke. But of course we'll rebuild."

Fergus, however, seemed more nervous than disconsolate. Lara found his behavior puzzling. Perhaps he hadn't kept up his insurance premiums.

"She ought to be here," Lara overheard Darcy say to

Fergus, her exasperation plain. Apparently she felt that Heather should be on the scene to round out the family image for the media.

Two shouts were uttered almost simultaneously.

Both came from the west side of the complex where the first explosion had occurred.

"Give me some help here!"

"Sir! Maybe you ought to look at this."

Lara and Key were among those who broke into a run. They and several others clustered around the man who'd shouted first. "There's a body underneath here."

Key helped him lift an iron support beam off the charred remains of a human being.

Before anyone had time to absorb that shock, one of the other agents said, "Christ. Here's another one." He'd made another grisly discovery several yards away.

"Sir!" The second agent who had shouted ran up to his superior. He was winded from his twenty-yard sprint. "I found something." He pointed toward an open field. "I think it's a gas line, but it isn't on the motel schematic. It's coming up vertically. My guess is that it's linked to an underground line that leads straight to that well."

Key shouldered his way up to the agent. "What are you saying?"

The senior agent frowned. "Mr. Tackett, it looks to me like somebody's been siphoning natural gas off your well."

Just then a scream rent the morning air. It came from the crowd behind the sheriff's cordon. Darcy was clutching a teenage girl by the shoulders and shaking her until her head wobbled back and forth.

"What are you saying? You're a liar!" She slapped the girl hard. "Heather was at cheerleading practice. She told Fergus she was leaving early to go to cheerleading practice. I ought to kill you, you lying little shit!"

The girl blubbered, "I'm not lying, Mrs. Winston. Heather told me to cover for her if you called my house.

We didn't have cheerleading practice. She said . . ." She hiccupped; the words came out choppily. "Heather said Tanner was going to meet her here and they were going to spend the night in one of the motel rooms." Misery contorted the girl's tear-bloated face. "She said it was going to be so romantic because they were going to sneak into the honeymoon suite."

Ollie Hoskins had worked tirelessly throughout the entire night doing whatever he could to help. He panicked upon hearing his son's name. "Tanner? Tanner? Tanner was here? No. It can't be. My boy, he . . . No!"

Darcy pushed aside Heather's sobbing friend and watched the grim firemen as they carried two stretchers from the smoking debris of what had been the honeymoon suite. On each stretcher lay a sealed black plastic bag.

"No. No. Heather? *NO!*"

Then Fergus stunned everyone by dropping to his knees and folding his arms over his head. With an anguished cry, he fell face first onto the ground.

"I could use a cup of coffee." Key approached her as she moved toward her car. "Besides, I don't have a car here." He had arrived with Darcy, and that hadn't been coincidental. However, mentioning that now would have been petty, so neither did. "I'll call for a ride at your place if that's all right."

He was as grimy as she, his clothes sweat- and soot-stained. She'd lost count of how many times he'd taken off in the helicopter only to return as quickly as possible to transport another casualty.

When all the injured had been taken to area hospitals, he began helping the volunteer firemen. Lara too stayed at the site to administer first aid for their minor cuts and burns. Subconsciously she had found herself listening for Key's distinguishable voice. Even in the predawn gloom she could easily pick him out among the others.

She motioned with her head for him to get into her

car. Once they were under way, she asked, "What do you think they'll do to Fergus?" He'd been taken away in handcuffs.

"He'll spend the rest of his life behind bars. Besides stealing from us, he's got twelve deaths to account for."

Lara shivered. "Including his own daughter."

"He'd better hope they never let him out. Darcy threatened to kill him if she got the chance. She would, too." After a moment, he said, "I only slept with her that once. The night she shot me."

Apparently the look she gave him was inadvertently accusatory, because he added, "Last night, I'd just told her to take me back to my car, and we were arguing about it, when the explosion occurred."

"I did her a disservice," Lara admitted in a quiet voice. "I didn't credit her with loving anyone except herself. She loved her daughter very much. I know how it feels to lose a child. I can also relate to her wanting to kill Fergus for the role he played in Heather's death. It was accidental, but he was ultimately responsible."

She pulled into the rear driveway of the clinic, reluctant to go in and face what she'd left. "Randall is in there."

"One of my favorite people." He expelled a deep breath as he opened the car door. Together they went inside. "Unlocked," he remarked.

"I left in such a hurry, I didn't bother."

They moved through the silent, dim rooms. The ugly facts that had been revealed to her moments before the explosion came back now, enclosing her in rage.

"I don't think he's here," Key said.

"He wouldn't leave."

"Hey, Porter, where are you?" he called. He approached the doorway to Lara's private office. The door was only halfway open. He gave it a slight push.

Apprehension crawled up her spine. "Key, before— "

"Porter?" He stepped into the room. "Holy shit!"

His expletive galvanized her. She bolted into the

room but drew up short on the threshold. "Oh my God!"

Key knelt beside Randall's prone body. There was no question as to whether he was dead. A congealing pool of blood had formed beneath his head. His face was a frozen mask of surprise.

"I didn't do it!" Lara gasped. "I didn't. I didn't pull the trigger."

Key raised his head and looked at her. "What the hell are you talking about? Of course you didn't do it."

"I pulled a gun on him, but— "

"*What?*"

"The Magnum." He followed her pointing finger to the revolver lying where she'd dropped it. "But I never pulled the trigger." She covered her mouth with her hand, for once made sick at the sight of so much blood. "The concussion from the explosion knocked me against the wall . . . But I didn't shoot him. Did I?" Near panic, she stretched forth her hand. "Key! Did I?"

He stood and nudged the Magnum with the toe of his boot. His expression was incredulous and bleak.

"I didn't," she said, vigorously shaking her head. "I swear to God! I couldn't. I only wanted to frighten him. I wanted him to experience some of the fear he'd inflicted on me at Emilio's camp."

"Lara, you're not making sense."

"Randall was responsible for Ashley's death," she cried, desperate for him to understand.

"How?"

"He was allied with Emilio from the beginning." In disjointed sentences and broken phrases, she related to him what Randall had told her.

"I know it sounds inconceivable. But it's the truth! I swear it. Oh no," she cried, pressing the heels of her hands against her temples when she saw his skepticism. "Not again! I can't go through this again. I can't be blamed for something I didn't do!"

"I believe you, Calm down."

"Oh God, Key! I did not shoot him. I couldn't. I *didn't!*"

"No, I did."

The husky confession came from behind the wedge of space between the partially open door and the paneled wall. Key reached past Lara and closed the door in order to see who was hiding behind it.

Chapter Twenty-Nine

*J*ody!"

Jody Tackett was sitting on the floor in the corner, her legs folded beneath her hip. A pistol, the obvious murder weapon, lay nearby. She was conscious, but had lost muscle control on the left side of her face. She had drooled on her blouse.

"She's had a stroke." Lara moved Key aside and knelt beside his mother. "Call 911."

"Don't bother. I'm dying. I want to. I can now." Jody's words were slurred, the consonants only partially formed, the sounds left open, like her lips. The vowels were guttural. But Jody was forcing herself to be understood. "Couldn't let him."

"Couldn't let him what, Jody?" Key knelt beside her. "Couldn't let him what?"

Lara called 911. For the second time in twelve hours she requested two ambulances—one for Jody, one for Randall. Then she returned to her place beside Jody and wrapped a blood pressure cuff around her upper arm. "She must have come in right behind me," she told Key. "He fell exactly where he was standing when I left."

"Couldn't let him tell about Clark." Jody struggled with the words.

"Don't talk, Mrs. Tackett," Lara said gently. She released the cuff and firmly pressed her fingers into Jody's wrist to take her pulse. "Help is on the way."

"What about Clark?" Key supported the back of Jody's

head in his palm. "What did Randall Porter know about Clark that you didn't want him to tell?"

"Key, this isn't the time. She's critically ill."

"She blew your husband's brains out!" he shouted at Lara. "Why, goddamn it? I want to know what drove my mother to murder. Do you know?"

"You're upsetting my patient," she replied tightly.

"Christ. You do know. What was it?"

She remained silent.

He looked down at Jody, realizing, as Lara did, that she was frantically trying to impart something before it was too late. "Jody, what was it? Did Porter know something about Clark's drowning? Was it a political assassination staged to look like an accident? Did Clark know that Porter was still alive?"

"No." Imploringly, Jody rolled her eyes toward Lara. "Tell him."

Lara shook her head slowly, then emphatically. "No. No."

"Lara, for God's sake. He was my brother." Key reached across Jody and took Lara's chin, forcibly turning her face toward him. "What do you know that I don't? What did Porter know that was such a threat to Clark, even dead? Whatever it is, it's why Jody didn't want you in Eden Pass, right? She was afraid you'd leak a secret."

"Porter . . ." Jody wheezed. "Porter was . . ."

"No, Mrs. Tackett," Lara pleaded. "Don't tell him. It won't solve anything and will only hurt him." She looked at Key. "Don't ask her. It crushed her. She committed murder over it. Leave it alone. I beg you, Key, leave it alone."

Her pleas fell on deaf ears. He bent low over Jody, until his face was inches from hers. "Porter was what? Plotting something with Clark? Was Clark caught up in a political intrigue he couldn't get out of? An illegal arms deal? Drugs maybe?"

"No."

"Tell me, Jody," he urged her softly. "Try, please. Tell me. I've got to know."

"Randall Porter was— "

"Yes, Jody? What?"

"No, Key. Please. *Please*."

"Shut up, Lara. Randall Porter was what, Jody?"

"Clark's lover."

For several seconds Key remained motionless. Then his head snapped erect and his eyes drilled into Lara's. "My brother and Porter . . .?"

Lara sank against the wall, defeated. The secret she had wanted desperately to reveal for five years, she now wished could have died with Jody Tackett, so that she wouldn't have to watch the disillusionment spread over Key's face like a dark ink spill.

"They were lovers?" His voice was as brittle and dry as ancient parchment. It crackled on each word.

She nodded forlornly.

"That morning in Virginia, my brother was in bed with Porter, not you. *You* caught *them*."

Tears ran down her cheeks. She rubbed them off with her fist. "Yes."

"Jesus," he swore, bearing his teeth. "Ah, Jesus." He propped his elbow on his raised knee and shoved his fingers through his hair, cupping his forehead in his palm. He held that anguished posture for ponderous moments.

Eventually he lowered his hand and looked down at his mother. "Clark confessed to you, didn't he?"

"When he gave . . ."

"When he bought this place for Lara," Key prompted. Jody nodded imperceptibly. Her eyes were swimming in tears. "You demanded to know why he'd do such a crazy thing for the woman who'd ruined his career. He broke down and told you the truth. You denounced him, probably disowned him. So he killed himself."

A terrible sound issued from Jody's chest.

"Key, don't do this to her," Lara whispered.

But it wasn't his intention to torment her. He slipped his arms beneath Jody and lifted her against his chest. She looked small and helpless in his brawny embrace, this woman who, using brains instead of beauty, had bagged the notorious playboy of Eden Pass, had driven Fergus Winston to commit a criminal act to exact revenge, and had for decades instilled in her employees a fearful respect and in an entire town fierce loyalty.

Key wiped the saliva off her chin with his thumb, then rested his cheek on the top of her head. "It's all right, Mother. Clark died knowing you loved him. He knew."

"Key." She spoke his name, not reproachfully, but penitently. She managed to lift her hand and place it on his arm. "Key."

He squeezed his eyes so tightly shut, tears were wrung from them. When the ambulance arrived, he was still cradling her in his arms, cooing to her like a baby, rocking her gently.

But by then Jody Tackett was dead.

"Thank you, Mr. Hoskins." Ollie had personally carried her groceries out to her car and stowed them in the trunk.

"You're welcome, Dr. Mallory."

"How is Mrs. Hoskins?"

He pulled a handkerchief from his hip pocket and unabashedly dabbed at his eyes. "Not much good. She sits in Tanner's room a lot. Dusts it. Runs the vacuum over the rug so much, she's worn down the pile. Doesn't eat, doesn't sleep."

"Why don't you bring her to see me? I could prescribe a mild sedative."

"Thanks, Dr. Mallory, but her problem isn't physical."

"Grief can be physically debilitating. I know. Encourage her to come see me."

He nodded, thanked her again, and returned to his duties inside the Sak'n'Save. This was one of the supermarket's busiest days of the year, the Wednesday before Thanksgiving. Texas Street was jammed.

A crew of volunteers was hanging Christmas decorations, stretching strings of multicolored lights across the street and mounting a Santa wearing a cowboy hat and boots on the roof of the bank building. Passersby offered unsolicited advice.

Despite the recent catastrophe, life went on in Eden Pass.

Lara was about to back her car out of the metered parking slot when Key's Lincoln loomed up directly behind her and blocked her exit. He got out and moved between her car and the pickup truck parked next to her.

Noisy honking and a shout drew his attention back to the street. "Hey, Tackett, you gonna move this piece of yellow shit, or what? It's blocking the whole damn street."

Key called back, "Go around it, you ugly son of a bitch." Wearing a good-natured smile, he flicked his middle finger at his friend, Possum. He was still laughing when he reached the driver's door of Lara's car. He knocked on the window and peeled off his aviator sunglasses. "Hey, Doc, how've you been?"

They hadn't been alone together since the day Jody died. If he could be cavalier, so could she, although her heart was racing. "I thought you'd gone to Alaska."

"Next week. I promised Janellen I'd stick around till after Thanksgiving. She and Bowie will be celebrating their first one together. It's important to her that I be here to carve the turkey."

"She brought him to meet me."

"The turkey?"

She rolled her eyes, letting him know her estimation of his joke. "I like your brother-in-law very much."

"Yeah, so do I. I particularly like him because he's touchy about folks thinking he married Janellen for her money. He works like a Trojan to prove he didn't. He's inspecting every Tackett well for safety violations. He'd blame himself for the disaster caused by well number seven, only Janellen won't let him. He knew something was out of kilter. Time ran out before he located the problem, is all.

"Anyhow, they're gaga over each other. I feel like a fifth wheel. Once I'm gone, they'll have the house to themselves. I've deeded over my half of it to her."

"That was generous."

"That house didn't hold any good memories for me. Nary a one. Maybe they'll make it a happy place for their kids." Shaking his head, he chuckled. "Who'd've ever thought Janellen would elope?" In a quieter voice, he added, "Her timing was off a bit. She'll go to her grave blaming herself for not being here when Jody had her stroke."

He was back to calling his mother Jody, but Lara remembered the tenderness with which he'd held her, calling her Mother as she died. "Did you tell Janellen about Clark?"

"No. What would be the point? It was hard enough on her to learn that Jody had murdered your husband."

There'd been an inquest. Key had cited Jody's dementia as the cause of her violent act. In her confusion, he told the judge, she'd linked Randall Porter's sudden reappearance with Clark's death. She killed him, thinking she was protecting her child. The court bought it. In any event, the killer was dead. Case dismissed. Sometimes the good ol' boy system was the fairest.

He turned his blue stare full force onto Lara. "You could have told the truth at the inquest."

"As you said, what would be the point? No one would have believed me five years ago. I couldn't prove anything then or now, and besides, it would only have dragged things out indefinitely. I was glad to finally see an end to it. The important thing to me was that Ashley's death was avenged."

She'd had Randall's body cremated. Since there had been a formal funeral for him years earlier, she didn't feel she owed the public another spectacle. She'd held a private memorial in Maryland for him. Only a handful of former colleagues had been invited to attend.

"What about the scheme Porter cooked up with Sánchez?" Key asked.

"When the president called to extend his condolences, I told him that I didn't agree with my late husband's assessment of the situation in Montesangre. I said that you and I had witnessed firsthand El Corazón's brutality to his own troops as well as his enemies. Speaking strictly as a citizen, I told him I wouldn't want my tax dollars to support his regime."

"He called me, too. I told him the same thing, in language a little more blunt."

"I can imagine."

He leaned against the rugged pickup parked beside her and raised one knee, flattening the sole of his boot against the dented door. He looked like he belonged there, comfortable in his Texas uniform—denim jeans and jacket. The brisk autumn wind tossed his dark hair around his head. His eyes were a few shades deeper than the sky.

She yearned for him.

"I thought you were leaving Eden Pass, Doc."

"I changed my mind and reopened the clinic. The people here have accepted me now. Business is so good, I've rehired Nancy. She's asking for an assistant."

"Congratulations."

"Thank you."

During a noticeable lapse in the conversation, neither knew quite where to look.

"Marion Leonard is pregnant," she told him. "She

wouldn't mind your knowing. They announced it immediately. She was among my first patients after I reopened."

"Ah, that's good." He nodded sagely. "Then there was never anything to that rumor of a malpractice suit?"

"I guess not."

They didn't go into the role Jody had played in starting the rumor.

"Did you read the TAF's report when they published it in the newspaper?" he asked.

After weeks of investigation, the federal agency had released their findings. The explosion at The Green Pine Motel had been caused by an illegal gas line running from Tackett Oil's well number seven to the motel. The gas was being used to heat and cool the motel. A leak in the line had filled the infrequently used honeymoon suite with odorless natural gas. It had compressed to a highly combustible level. The spark from the electrical short was enough to cause the blast.

Fergus Winston, against the advice of his attorney, pleaded guilty to all charges and was now weeks into his life sentence.

Darcy had closed their house and left town. Gossip was rampant. Some said she held vigil over Heather's grave by night and the prison by day, hoping for a chance to kill Fergus. Others said she had gone completely 'round the bend and had been committed to a psychiatric hospital. Still another rumor was that she'd latched on to a minor league baseball player and was shacked up with him somewhere in Oklahoma.

"As I understand it," Lara said, "Fergus tapped into the old flare line."

"Right. They were common. They burned off the gas from a well. Then Granddaddy decided to market the gas in addition to the oil. He tapped off that line. Anyway, flare lines became illegal. Fergus knew about the one on that well, reopened it, and extended it to his motel. He had free gas for years and probably laughed up his sleeve about it."

Again they ran out of conversation. When the silence became uncomfortable, Lara reached for her ignition key. "Well, I'd better run. I've got frozen things in the trunk."

"Before that morning, did you know that Clark and your husband were lovers?"

She didn't expect the question. Her hand fell away from the ignition.

He squatted down beside her car door so that their faces were on the same level. Loosely clasping his hands, he rested his wrists on the open window. "Did you?"

"I had no idea," she answered softly. "When I saw them, I went numb. But only for a moment. Then I went a little crazy. Became hysterical."

"Who called the press?"

She didn't even consider avoiding his questions or glazing her answers with euphemisms. "The phone on the nightstand beside my bed rang. I woke up and answered it. The caller identified himself only as one of Clark's close friends. He called him a few ugly names." A spasm of pain flashed across Key's face, but Lara went on doggedly.

"He asked if I knew that Clark had dumped him in favor of my husband. Then he hung up. I took it for a crank call and turned to tell Randall about it. But he wasn't in the other twin bed. I got up and went looking for him."

She bowed her head and rubbed her forehead with her thumb and index finger. "I found them in Clark's bedroom. Later, I figured that same caller must also have notified the media and told them that an explosive news story was about to break at the cottage. Anyway, reporters arrived within minutes of my discovery. Clark became almost as hysterical as I. It was Randall's idea to make it look like . . ." She raised her shoulders and sighed. "You know the rest."

Key muttered epithets to Ambassador Porter. "Why didn't the guy on the phone come forward to contradict the tabloid stories about you?"

"I suppose he lost his courage," she replied. "Anyway, he accomplished what he wanted. He brought down Senator Tackett."

"You could have exposed them, Lara. Why didn't you?"

She laughed mirthlessly. "Who would have believed me? Randall had had affairs with women. Many of them. They would have sworn that he was wholly heterosexual, and he was."

His brows furrowed with perplexity.

"He knew about Clark's sexual preference, and used it," she said. "One favor in exchange for another, I suppose. Randall wasn't above that sort of cruel manipulation. He used Clark. He used me. He'd do anything to get what he wanted."

"Like pretending to be dead for years."

"Yes. And it didn't bother him at all that our daughter was killed in a cross fire." She hesitated to broach the next subject because it was sensitive for several reasons. "Key . . ." She averted her eyes from his. "I didn't trust Randall to tell me the truth about his bisexuality. In fact, I suspect that he was also Emilio's lover. Anyway, I ran extensive blood tests on Randall and me while I was still in the first trimester of my pregnancy. I didn't want to transmit the AIDS virus to my child.

"Both of us tested negative, but I never took another chance. The night I conceived Ashley—which was only a few weeks before the incident—was the last time I slept with Randall." She met his direct gaze. "The very last."

"I didn't ask."

"But you have a right to know."

His unwavering gaze was disquieting. They were surrounded by noise and confusion, yet a ponderous silence

stretched between them. She found comfort in the sound
of her own voice.

"Back to my credibility—the concept of 'innocent until
proven guilty' is a myth. Before I fully recovered from
the shock of finding my husband in bed with another
man, I was branded an adulteress who'd been caught
in the act. If I'd come forward with the truth, it would
have been regarded as nothing more than a vicious
counterattack."

Sadly she shook her head. "Once I was photographed
in my nightgown, being hustled from Clark's cottage by
my husband, I was labeled."

"I thought my brother had more integrity than to let
someone else take the rap for him."

"He got swept up into Randall's lie, just as I did. The
consequences of it were so extreme that he really couldn't
consider telling the truth.

"But, unlike Randall, it ate on his conscience. Giving
me the medical practice here in Eden Pass was his way
of making restitution, of telling me he was sorry." She
smiled wanly. "Don't be too hard on him, Key. He'd
lived as a closet homosexual for years. That must have
been a terribly lonely and unhappy existence."

"I'm still wrestling with it, trying to reconcile the
brother I knew with the man in bed with Randall Porter.
I keep thinking about one summer when we went to camp
together. Naturally, we did what adolescent boys do when
they sneak off into the woods. We jacked off until we were
sore. We had come-comparing contests, for chrissake. If
we were that close, why couldn't he tell me?"

"Maybe he didn't know then."

"Maybe. But by the time he was elected senator, he
did. On election night, after his opponent had conceded,
and all the hoopla died down, we got stinking drunk to
celebrate." He smiled at the fond memory. "The next
morning, he had to meet the press with the worst
hangover in history. He threatened to kill me for doing

that to him. The last time I saw him alive, we still had a laugh over it."

Gradually his smile faded. He stared into near space. "I wish he'd had enough confidence in me to tell me."

"Would you have accepted it?"

"I'd like to think so." He pinched his eyes shut for a moment. "Jody's opinion of homosexuals was no secret," he said bitterly. "I think Hitler had more tolerance. It must have been quite a scene when Clark told her."

"I'm sure it was devastating to them both."

"Whatever she said to him pushed him over the edge." He stood up and slid his hands into the rear pockets of his jeans, palms out. He looked down at his feet, rolled back on the heels of his boots, then let them fall forward to slap the pavement.

"She was good at that, you know, pushing people to the edge. Good, hell." He scoffed at his understatement. "She wrote the book on it. She knew exactly which screw to turn, and when, and how tight to turn it. She just couldn't leave people in peace to be what they were. Not Clark, or Janellen, or me, or my daddy." He glanced up suddenly. "She left me a letter."

Lara cleared her throat. "Yes, Janellen mentioned it."

"Did she tell you what she wrote?"

"No. Only that each of you found a letter to be opened on the occasion of Jody's death."

"Yeah, well the date on mine indicated that she wrote it while we were in Montesangre." His mouth turned down at the corners, and he raised his shoulders in a half-shrug. "She said that everybody was under the impression that she hated Daddy for chasing other women and leaving her for extended periods of time. But the truth of it, according to her letter, was that she loved him. To distraction, she said. Beyond reason. Those are quotes."

He kept his head down, his eyes on his boots. "She loved him, and he hurt her. Badly. The letter said that every time he, uh, took another woman, it was like a knife in her heart because she knew she wasn't pretty and vivacious. Not the sort of woman who could hold his interest. She knew that the only reason he married her was to get out of a scrape. But he never knew, or if he knew he didn't care, that she truly loved him.

"To his way of thinking it was a marriage of convenience. Jody got to run Tackett Oil like she wanted; he used his marriage as a safety net if his philandering got him into a fix. Not a bad bargain except that Jody loved him, so his infidelities hurt her."

He removed his hands from his back pockets and rubbed them together, then turned up one palm and studied it as though trying to make sense of the crisscrossing lines. "And," he said around a deep breath, "her letter said that the reason she was always so hard on me was because I was exactly like my daddy. Looked like him, had his temperament, liked nothing better than to have a good time. Later I even raised hell and womanized like him.

"She . . . she, uh, said she had loved me all along, but that it hurt her to even look at me. The day I was born, he was with another woman. I was a living reminder of that, so it was impossible for her to show me any love. Mostly, in an odd sort of way, she was afraid I'd reject her love, just like my daddy did. So she didn't chance it."

He rolled his shoulders, a brave attempt to appear indifferent. "That's what she wrote me. Crap like that."

"I don't think it's crap and neither do you." He raised his head and looked at her. "Jody loved both her sons, Key. She fought to the bitter end of her life to protect Clark from scandal."

"Then why'd she struggle with her last few breaths to tell me about him?"

"Because she wanted you to know that Clark had disappointed her. He'd always been her fair-haired child and you knew it. She refused to die until she'd balanced things out. That was a tremendous personal sacrifice for her, which should prove to you how much she loved you."

He squinted, but she couldn't tell if it was from the sun's glare or because he'd been struck by an enlightening thought. "This personal sacrifice stuff is a big thing with you."

She tilted her head, looking at him with misapprehension. He launched into an explanation. "You didn't keep Clark's secret because you were afraid no one would believe you. You kept quiet because you loved Clark. You told me so yourself on the way to Montesangre.

"It was friendship, never a sexual thing. Even though Randall Porter was a roach on pig shit, you wouldn't have cheated on him while you were legally married. I learned that for myself. But you respected Clark as a statesman and loved him as a friend. That's why you didn't squeal on him even though he'd betrayed you.

"Then you banished yourself to Montesangre with Porter for the sake of your baby. Another personal sacrifice. You have a habit of making sacrifices for the people you love, Lara."

He leaned forward and placed his hands on the open window, bracing himself against it. "When Jody wanted to tell me that Porter, not you, was Clark's lover, you begged her not to. You were given a chance to prove wrong all the ugly things I'd said to and about you. But you didn't take it. Because you wanted to protect me from knowing the truth about my brother, you refused to say a word." His eyes went straight through her. "And ever since then, I've wondered why that was."

Lara's throat ached with emotion. "Have you reached any conclusions?"

"I think I'm close to a breakthrough." Suddenly he opened her car door. "Get out."

"Pardon?"

"Get out." He reached inside and pulled her out. Backing her against the car, he slid his hands under her hair and trapped her head in place for his solid, searching kiss.

"I don't want to go to Alaska," he announced abruptly when he pulled back. "It's colder than a witch's tit up there, and they won't know a chicken-fried steak from an armadillo. I have more charter business here than I can handle. And there's a pretty piece of property out near the lake that I've had a hankering to buy for years. Just seemed wasteful to build a house only for myself, without a wife and kids."

She pressed her face into the open wedge of his jacket and breathed in his warm scent as the fabric of his shirt absorbed her glad tears. Then, angling her head back, she asked, "Will you ever tell me that you love me?"

"I already did. You just weren't listening."

"I was listening," she said huskily.

He lowered his voice to an urgent whisper. "Then talk me out of leaving, Doc."

Her fingertips feathered over his eyebrows, his nose; they traced the shape of his beautiful mouth. "What could I say that would make you stay?"

"Say yes."

"To what?"

"To everything. We'll fill in the questions later."

THE WITNESS

Sandra Brown

At first the car crash seems to be just another calamity in
the troubled recent past of Kendall Burnwood.

But despite the fact that the accident has left one dead and
one seriously wounded, Kendall still has good reason to be
thankful. Firstly, she and her baby son Kevin are alive and
unharmed. Secondly, the man she dragged from the
wreckage woke up in hospital with a severe case of
amnesia, oblivious to the deadly chain of events that
brought them together. Who he was, who she was and
where he was taking her. Now these secrets are known only
to Kendall herself – and she isn't telling. Not until her
son is safe.

For she is still the witness – the only person who can bring
down the edifice of bigotry that destroyed all she held dear,
the only person who can expose a secretive cult of
prejudice and hate. But in doing so she will also expose
herself – and her son . . .

A TREASURE WORTH SEEKING

Sandra Brown

After years of searching for the brother she'd never known, Erin O'Shea had at last found his San Francisco address and made her way to his door – not knowing that she was about to walk into a heart-wrenching drama of shocking family ties and lies . . . and an intriguing, infuriating man who spoke to her innermost desire.

Sinewy, handsome and a consummate professional, Lance Barrett was a man for the toughest cases – like the big-money scam involving Erin O'Shea's brother and maybe the sassy Erin as well. Her ways and secrets arouse his suspicions as much as his passion, but he didn't yet know that his desire for her would drive him to break every rule in the book . . . and put his career, and her heart, on the line.

Other bestselling Warner titles available by mail: